EVIDENCE OF SIN

A SLAYING LOVE NOVEL
BOOK 4

AMANDA SIEGRIST

McCord Family Novel

Protecting You

Trust in Love

Deserving You

Always Kind of Love

Finding You

Dare You to Love

Mona & Mason

The Paranormal Chronicles, Volume 1

Perfect For You Novel

The Wrong Brother

The Right Time

The Easy Part

The Hard Choice

Psychic Love Novel

Exploding Love

Captured Love

Slaying Love Novel

Won't Let You Go

Doomed Love

Deadly Crazy

Evidence of Sin

Finding Redemption

Obsessed Hope

Short Stories

Paint By Murder

Follow Me, Sweet Darling

Sleighville Novel

Dashing Through the Fear

Here Comes Chaos

Standalone Novel

The Danger with Love

Conquering Fear Novel

CO-WRITTEN WITH JANE BLYTHE

Drowning in You

Out of the Darkness

Closing In

A TATTOOED BAD BOY WITH A RECORD. A POLICE DEPARTMENT ANALYST WHO SHOULD KNOW BETTER. A KILLER WHO'S MAKING IT PERSONAL.

1

HE SET his machine down and stretched his arms, then stood up with a sweet-ass grin. Damn, he was good. "Take a look."

The burly guy in the chair, Richard, stood up and turned his back to the mirror as he peered behind his shoulder. His nod said it all. He agreed. He just tattooed the most kick-ass tattoo.

A black-and-white dragon filled Richard's entire back. It took several sittings, but it was worth every second. The dragon's mouth was wide open, baring its frightening teeth, with his claws ready to attack. The lines were all perfect and precision straight, as always. He had a steady hand. Most days.

Shit. He didn't want to think about the pain he'd been experiencing lately.

"Looks amazing, dude." Richard turned in his direction and smiled wide. "Totally rad, Stitch. Thanks for doing this."

"Anytime. You were thinking something on your leg next, right?"

"Yeah. My girl's working on a sketch. I love the creative shit she does."

Stitch couldn't disagree with that. She drew the original sketch for the dragon piece. He tweaked a few things more to his liking, but overall, she had talent.

"Can't wait to see it."

Stitch motioned him to come closer so he could clean the tattoo before placing a thin wrap over it to protect it, then gave him aftercare instructions. Richard knew everything he needed to do, but Stitch always—and he meant always—followed his routine. When he didn't, shit always went sideways. Richard was used to the spiel, but he still listened and nodded as if he didn't. Most people listened when he spoke. The ones who didn't usually paid the price, coming back in because they screwed up their tattoo.

As soon as Richard walked out of his room, he pulled off his gloves and threw them into the trash can near his drawing table. Ignoring the slight pain in his wrist, he sat down to work on a drawing for another regular who wanted his tattoo done next week. He had plenty of time to finish it, but he always preferred to get things out of the way instead of procrastinating. Biding one's time never got a person very far. Getting shit done right away proved very beneficial for him.

Look at his life now.

He had a successful tattoo business, doing something he loved every single day. He had a wait list two months out, proving how high in demand he was. Because he rocked at what he did, and he wasn't afraid to admit it. To anyone.

How many people could say that? How many people could say they were happy with their life, their job?

Well, he knew one person.

Throwing his pencil across the desk, he backed away

and stood up, irritated at himself for letting his thoughts drift to *her*. The one woman he told himself repeatedly to stop thinking about since the night he walked out on her.

Susan.

Just thinking her name sent a chill down his spine, a tingling sensation of anticipation of what he would do if she stood in front of him.

Devour her from head to toe and never let her go.

Shit, so all aspects in his life weren't exactly fine. He couldn't complain about his professional life. His personal life, well, he didn't know what to say. It lacked something. He didn't realize it lacked anything until he met her.

At one time, he was happy. Dating here and there, scratching his itch when he felt the need. It wasn't too difficult to find a beautiful woman willing to share his bed until he got bored. Yeah, that sounded arrogant, but the women he took to bed knew the score. They knew he wasn't into long-term.

He was fine with that. He didn't need the whole white picket fence sort of life. He knew at a young age he wasn't destined for that kind of life.

Then he met her.

Everything he thought he believed sounded like total bullshit. Yet, as tough and dangerous as he liked to make himself appear—something he needed to do at times to make people see reason—he knew he wasn't strong enough to attempt a future with her. Not even something as simple as a sexual relationship.

Well, except that one night.

To distract himself from his wandering thoughts, he started to pick up the mess from his latest client, something he should've done right away. The ringtone from his phone broke his disastrous thoughts.

Swiping his phone from his pocket, the number staring back at him put a smile on his face.

"Hey, doll. How's it going?"

"Like shit. I need a favor."

Deena, his best friend from childhood, could always manage to brighten his mood. They lost touch for quite a few years, but a few months ago, she walked back into his life. Now she called him every so often, or him vice versa, and they talked. Her husband, Sauer, seemed like a decent guy, but he didn't hang around her if he was there. Her husband was a cop and he wasn't a big fan of cops. Deena knew. She understood. Just one of the many reasons they were best friends.

She sounded stressed, though. Not a normal thing he heard from her often, and it worried him.

"Anything for you, doll. What's the matter?"

She sighed heavily, then started talking like a racecar driver going two hundred miles an hour. "Rina's surprise baby shower is tonight, and I'm stuck at work, which is not where I need to be right now. I have so much I need to bring to the party, and I can't leave work yet. I need to leave now or the entire party will be ruined. Ruined!"

Well...okay.

This was awkward.

He had never heard Deena sound melodramatic. Right now she sounded like a drama queen hyped up on speed.

"What do you need from me?"

"Aren't you listening, Stitch? Why do men never listen?"

What was going on? She sounded almost...hysterical. Was she having problems with Sauer? He hoped not. Because then he'd have to do the best friend duties of beating the shit out of him.

His mind raced through everything she said, and then

made the only deduction he could, since she didn't actually say what she wanted him to do.

"I can bring the stuff to the party and..." Oh, shit, he didn't want to help set up a baby shower, but for Deena he'd do about anything. "...and help set up."

"I knew I could count on you. Everything you need is in the foyer of my house. There's a bunch of bags and a few cases of water and pop. There's a key under the flowerpot on the front porch, and the code to the alarm is 6969."

He snorted, figuring Deena had to have set the code. "Are you sure Sauer doesn't mind I know how to get into your house? How come he can't help right now?"

"Why would he care? He's busy interviewing some witnesses or something. I already tried him. Are you leaving yet? Are you in your car?"

Time to end the call. He couldn't stand to hear her hysterics when, generally, she wasn't a hysterical woman. Tough. Strong. In your face. But hysterical? Never.

He debated asking whether things were going okay between her and Sauer, but the words wouldn't come. "Where am I taking all this stuff?"

Good thing he didn't have any more clients for the day. Although, he would've figured out a way to help her. He always did. With a waiting list two months out, he had three other tattoo artists that worked for him, and he was extremely picky about who he took on as a client. Most clients went to his other artists. He only picked the tattoos he could make into a masterpiece. He saw every tattoo he did as that—a masterpiece. A work of art. A piece of his soul etched on another's skin. Tattooing a random butterfly or a flower or something simple wasn't something he enjoyed. He liked the challenge of creating something magnificent. If someone wanted a badass tattoo of a butterfly that had some meaning behind it, then he'd tattoo that shit without an issue. If it was some idiot doing it on a dare, or just because, they never stepped foot in his office.

"Susan's house. I'll text you her address."

His knees almost buckled. Her words were like a sucker punch to the gut.

Susan's house.

Holy. Shit.

"Stitch? Did you hear me?"

"On my way."

He said a quick good-bye and hung up, sliding his phone back into his pocket before he blurted out he couldn't help. He'd never gone back on his words before, especially to Deena, and he wasn't about to start now.

But Susan's house...

Thinking her sweet name once again caused his gut to churn like a rough current.

His phone buzzed in his pocket, but he didn't bother taking it out. He knew it was a text from Deena of Susan's address—something he didn't need. He knew it by heart. He'd been there once, a few months ago, and since then, he'd echoed her address over and over in his head, thinking, debating, aching to go there. But he never did.

He had to stay far away from her. From temptation.

Now he had no damn choice but to see her.

Making good time, considering he sped the entire way to Deena's house, he quickly made entry into her home, feeling odd doing so even with her permission, and grabbed everything. He reset the alarm before leaving and locked up the house tightly before replacing the key back under the flowerpot. What a terrible place to hide it. Anybody smart enough would look there first. Did Sauer know about this? He had an inkling Sauer had no clue his wife hid a key there, because it didn't seem like something a detective would approve of.

Not his problem.

He took a deep breath before starting up his 1969 Chevelle SS that was his pride and joy. It took over a year for him to save up enough money to start his business, tattooing on the side until he could finally purchase his own shop, then another few years of searching and buying this baby. Probably the only thing in his life that he loved more than anything.

Sure, he loved Deena like a sister. But this baby. This beautiful, red baby that always gave his heart a little jolt when he turned the key, well, he loved her like he hadn't loved anything in his life. She was his everything.

Cool leather seats, all original. Crimson red. A 396 V8 engine that purred like a newborn kitten.

He loved his car. With a passion.

The same could not be said about a woman. He had never loved a woman like he loved his car.

And Susan...well, he couldn't say he loved her, but she was something else.

What did it matter? She probably hated him.

Twenty minutes later, he pulled into her driveway, his nerves jangling forth like never before.

What the hell?

He never got nervous over a woman. He wasn't about to start now. Smoothing his hair back, he blew out a breath and got out of the car.

Grabbing a few bags from the trunk, he tried to appear nonchalant as he headed for her door. He would not let his nerves show. What was there to be nervous about? She was just a woman. Just another woman he slept with. No big deal.

Taking a moment, because he knew he needed it, even as pansy as that sounded, he hit the doorbell.

When the door swung open to the most beautiful woman he had ever seen, he couldn't stop the little dance his heart played out. Her light-blonde hair was pulled back into a ponytail, little wisps of hair framing her face. Her hazel eyes, so sweet and innocent, looked at him with shock. He could still picture how gorgeous she looked lying on her bed, her hair fanned out across the pillow after he helped take out all the pins she used to secure it into an elegant updo she wore to the ball. He loved her hair flowing freely around her. Temptation pulled at him to yank the ponytail out.

"Hi, Susan."

She opened her mouth, then closed it, clearly surprised to see him, which surprised him. He figured Deena would've called her. Why didn't she? He could see by the strain between her eyes and the stiffness of her posture she wasn't happy to see him.

"Deena asked me to drop some things off for the party because she's stuck at work." He lifted the bags in his hands to show the evidence.

He figured Susan could appreciate that, eyeing the evidence to back up his words, considering that was her line of work. She worked at the police department in the forensics lab. One of the reasons he walked away from her that night.

"I had no idea. She didn't tell me, but please bring it in. What's in those bags?" She stepped back a good distance, obviously not wanting to get too close to him as he walked inside.

"Some food and napkins and whatnot. There's more in my car." He took a small breath, holding in the urge to drop the bags to the ground and pull her into his arms. Of course, she didn't look too receptive to the gesture, but it didn't stop him from aching to do it. "Where should I put these? Go do whatever you were doing and I'll bring it all in."

She nodded, clearly loving that idea, too. Anything to get away from him.

Damn. He did that. He created the huge distance between them.

"On the kitchen table is fine. It's—"

"Down the hallway and to the right. I know."

Her jaw clenched, then her features smoothed out as if nothing bothered her. "Well, then. I'll let you get to it."

She headed to his left into the living room. He couldn't be sure where she had been working in the house to set up the party before he arrived, but he didn't think it was the living room by the way she glanced around the room figuring out what to do. When he stepped into the kitchen and saw the vegetables on the counter, a knife resting on a cutting board by some carrots, he figured she had been working in the kitchen. Obviously, she didn't want to be in the same room as him.

He could only blame himself for making her feel that way. It didn't make it hurt any less. Regardless of the tension between them, he couldn't change it. He wouldn't. It was for the best. She had to accept it.

Shit. So did he.

He worked as fast as he could, carrying in everything from Deena's house, trying his damndest not to peek into the living room every time he walked by. He failed every single time. One time he almost stopped to help her hang a banner that she was struggling with. She barely made it to his shoulders, considering he was much taller than her, and she was trying to hang a banner to the entry of the living room that almost touched his head.

When he walked out of the kitchen after unloading his last load of supplies, he couldn't leave without helping. She was still struggling to hang the banner, reaching on her tippy-toes. When she jumped, attempting to connect the piece of tape strapped across the corner of the banner to the wall, he couldn't hold back a chuckle. Then a full burst of laughter let loose as he watched the tape slide easily off the wall and the banner fell to the floor.

"So glad you find this humorous."

"I can help."

Her head snapped to him. "I don't want your help. But thank you."

He enjoyed how, even though she hated him, she couldn't help but be polite by adding in a thank you. As if her parents had ingrained in her the importance of always being respectful. And his Susan was the sweetest woman he ever met. She treated everyone with respect, at least from what he remembered from that night.

One night with her and he thought he knew her. His Susan—

Wait...No. Not his Susan. Just Susan. He couldn't call her his, even if he wanted to.

"Why not? What's so wrong with me helping? I helped bring all that shit in the house."

Her eyes blazed with fire. His body responded in the wrong way—a way he needed to suppress—but damn he loved seeing the fire in her eyes. Perhaps that's why he did it.

Plus, he honestly wanted to know why. So they had sex once. So he left the next morning...really, really early in the morning. Without saying good-bye. And never called her once as he said he would. It still didn't mean he couldn't help hang a dumbass banner.

"Like I said, Stitch, I don't want your help."

His jaw tightened, a muscle ticking in his cheek at the way she said his name. With disgust. "At least grab a chair, then. It'll help, shorty."

Her mouth dropped open at the way he said shorty. The anger in her eyes intensified. It ignited his desire even more. Damn, she was sexy as hell all flustered and angry.

"I'm not that short. I'll get it without a chair or your help."

Leaning against the wall, he crossed his arms and legs and flashed a brilliant smile. "I can't wait to see this."

"Leave."

"Now, sweetheart, we both know you don't really want that." He winked for extra measure.

He knew he was playing with fire—a hellish fire that was bound to burn him to the ground into nothing but ashes—but he couldn't help himself. This woman. This beautiful, amazing woman was always on his mind. To have her standing in front of him was torturous and painful and heartbreaking. He needed to soak up her beauty a few more minutes before he left, never to see her again. As it should be.

She tilted her head to the side as her eyes sparkled with a little bit of desire, and if he wasn't mistaken, a little bit more rage than he anticipated. Both things turned him on. His pants were getting tighter and tighter by the second.

"Oh, Stitch, you think you're funny. You're not."

"You sure? I had you laughing a lot that night."

Her eyes flickered, pain touching them, before it disappeared. He couldn't tell if he imagined it or not. Anger he could handle from her. Pain was a different story.

"Yeah, you did. Still do."

"See." He graced her with the cockiest grin he owned with a wink to go with it.

She took a few steps toward him and stopped about a foot away. Close enough for him to reach out and pull her into his arms like he wanted to do since the moment he saw her. "It's sad. You have no idea why I want to laugh *at* you."

"Enlighten me, sweetheart."

A wicked grin touched her gorgeous face. "You think I want you again, which is so damn hilarious. That night, while fun, wasn't, like, the best night of my life or anything. Sorry you thought so."

"I know you're not a liar, so why pretend to be one now."

"Poor Stitch, he can't handle the truth." She reached out and patted his cheek mockingly. "It was just sex. And honestly, it was only...meh." Her hand fell away. "So don't think for one second I'm dying to be in your arms again." She turned and started walking away to the kitchen.

Did she just say the sex was meh between them? That he wasn't even that good.

What. The. Hell.

What a crock of shit! There was no way she could think that. Yet, as he watched her walk away, her stance was steady, her stride purposeful, almost enticing, as if she knew how badly he wanted her. But, apparently, she didn't want him.

Meh.

No way.

"That was the best sex you've ever had, and you know it, shorty!"

For some reason, those words felt hollow as he hollered down the hallway, losing view of her as she turned the corner.

2

SUSAN'S HAND shook like a mini earthquake as she picked up the knife. She couldn't believe what she said to him. *It was only...meh.* That was so damn hilarious it wasn't funny. It was heartbreakingly sad.

But she couldn't let him get away with acting all cocky, like he was God's gift to women, as if she should be falling at his feet that he decided to grace her doorstep...finally! And why?

Because Dee asked him to. Definitely not because he wanted to.

She should've known better than to fall for his charm. Honestly, when they asked her to go to the King and Queen's ball, she didn't want to. But Dee, Rina, and Zoe insisted she come with them. Of course, they had a date with their husbands. Who was she supposed to go with?

Sauer tried to get Newman, his partner and friend, to go with her. As friends, of course. Newman shot that idea down. *I don't want to go to a ball...and I don't want to go with Susan.*

She wished she had never heard him say that, or the way

he said it. Like a dolt, she had a huge crush on him, even when he had a girlfriend, and he ruined that with little effort.

After that, the ladies decided she needed to go to the ball, and Dee said she had the perfect guy to take her.

Stitch.

From the moment she laid eyes on him, she didn't even understand why she had such a silly crush on Newman. One piercing gaze from him had her melting on the spot. He stared at her with such intensity, with such desire, she had almost been afraid to shake his hand when he offered it.

A bad boy all wrapped up in a nice fancy suit. Black hair, on the longish side, that he swept back with a simple style. Every so often, he would run a hand through it, making her wish she could do the same. Golden-brown eyes that gazed at her all night with need from the moment they made eye contact. A hint of a five o'clock shadow. Just enough, that every time his cheek grazed hers as they danced, it sent little bolts of lightning straight to her core. The sensation had driven her mad with lust. And his tattoos... Each time she saw a small patch of ink on his wrist when his shirt and jacket moved a certain way, or a small peek from his neck, considering he didn't bother to wear a bow tie and left the top button loose, she had ached to see more. Each and every tattoo that covered his body.

And she did.

He had been hers all night. They laughed. They danced. They drank. At the end of the night, he drove her home and they had sex. Mind-blowing sex.

He whispered such sweet and dirty things in her ear. No man had ever talked dirty and wanton with her. More like boring and unoriginal. Every word ignited her body on fire. She had wanted more and more and more until she couldn't walk. He gave her multiple orgasms that she never knew she could even produce.

He said he'd call her right before they drifted off to sleep because he already missed her. One of the sweetest things ever said to her. She fell into a peaceful sleep after that.

And nothing.

For the last six months, she heard absolutely nothing from him. Until today.

Yeah, the sex had been spectacular—nothing at all what she said—but she wouldn't let him see how much it affected her. She refused to let him see how much he truly hurt her. It wasn't the first time a guy let her down. Honestly, she didn't think it'd be the last.

Swiping a lone tear away, she started to chop the carrots. She didn't hear the front door close, but she figured he left.

She laughed.

Oh, yeah, he left. Thinking he was lame in bed. He wouldn't be sticking around now.

Well, it served him right for acting all cocky and like he hadn't ripped her heart out when he ditched her before the morning and then never called.

Her motions started to get faster, harder and rigid, as the anger started to consume her once more. How dare he act as if nothing happened between them. Like they didn't share an amazing night of sex together.

"Susan, I'm—"

She screamed, jumped, and slammed her hand down, the one holding the knife, all in one smooth motion. Instant tears started to form as the pain radiated from her finger and down to the very tips of her toes.

"Oh, shit." She clutched her hand to her chest. The blood trailed across the floor as she rushed to the sink behind her.

"Are you okay?"

Before she could answer his question, he was by her side and wrapping her hand with her good towels her grandma embroidered. His grip turned hard as he tried to stop the bleeding. She could feel his hot breath hit the top of her head. His warmth cocooned her, soothing her. Yet, he made her cut herself. He had scared the living daylights out of her.

"I'm sorry, Susan." His voice lowered an octave. "For everything. I never meant to hurt you. Not in the past...not right now."

She lifted her gaze, her eyes still swimming with tears. Her finger hurt like the dickens. The knife felt like it sliced right through.

He glanced away, his eyes lowering to the floor. She followed his gaze, eyeing the thick blood drops that made a pathway to where she stood. She knew blood inside and out. She had seen it splattered against walls in horrifying ways. Spread out across a bed like a pristine sheet covering it. Sprinkled around a room as if someone had tossed it for good measure. Pooled in a puddle on the cold, hard concrete. Blood didn't faze her. It couldn't. Not in her line of work.

But seeing the trail from the island counter to the sink, *her* blood trail, made her almost gag at the sight.

A warm hand cupped her chin, pulling until her eyes connected with his. "I should look at it quickly. We have to see if you need stitches."

Stitches. She felt like laughing. But she didn't. Not when the man who went by the nickname Stitch held her hand tightly, as if he never wanted to let go.

She nodded, too afraid to say anything.

With a swiftness that surprised her, he unwrapped the

towel, looked at her wounded finger, then wrapped it back up.

"Doesn't look too deep. But it does look nasty. A band-aid isn't going to cover it. I should take you to the hospital."

Her wits finally came back. She grabbed the towel right above his hand and pushed his hand away. Or at least tried to. He wouldn't budge.

"I'm fine. You're right. It didn't look deep, so there's no need to go to the hospital."

His eyes narrowed, as if he wanted to argue with her. She assumed most people would cower from that look. Not her. Working in the forensics department didn't put her in the path of too many criminals, considering she always arrived at the scene after everything occurred, but she had dealt with a few scary people in her life. Stitch wasn't one of them.

"Don't argue with me."

"Don't tell me what to do."

His eyes flared with intense heat as his grip tightened even more. Shockingly, it didn't hurt. The passion in his golden-brown depths did, however. A thin lock of black hair fell to his forehead. Suddenly, she ached to brush it back, as he always did.

No. What she needed to do was get away.

"Please, let me go to the bathroom. I have everything I need here."

"I'll help you."

She shook her head. Her gaze hit the cutting board and her bloodied carrots. She couldn't control the shiver that consumed her.

His warm hand covered hers as he leaned closer. "Fine. Go fix your hand and I'll clean up the mess."

The moment he released her from his death grip, she

fled the kitchen. She wasn't about to argue with him. Thinking about cleaning up the mess made her stomach curl, and she couldn't even decipher why. Damn Stitch for realizing it immediately, offering to do it for her.

Pulling her first-aid kit from underneath the bathroom sink, she started to bandage her pointer finger. The knife sliced it near the edge of her finger. She was lucky she didn't chop it right off.

The bleeding had slowed down, probably from Stitch's tight grip. She wrapped it with gauze, making her finger look like a tiny mummy, then taped it together.

She cleaned up the mess and took her time putting everything away. Rotating her hand around, she couldn't help but wonder if maybe she should get stitches. The way she had it wrapped, it looked like she should. But then Stitch would insist on going with her, and the last thing she wanted was for him to stay. He needed to leave. Seeing his handsome, yet annoying face was too much. Especially after she was finally starting to forget all about him.

She nearly tripped when she walked back into the kitchen and found Stitch at the island counter cutting the broccoli apart. The sight was...right. As strange as he looked, his forearms flexing from cutting, his tattoos sticking out in her girly kitchen decked out in shades of light green with flower decorations everywhere, from the doorknobs on the cabinets to the curtains hanging above the sink, he looked like he fit right in. The bad boy looked oddly domestic, and she liked the image a little too much.

A question she asked herself many times the past six months crossed her mind once again. *Was* he a bad boy?

His image said he was. His cockiness today suggested it. Even a few words spoken by Dee said he was. But was he?

He had been sweet, kind, and so attentive the night of

the ball. Not the picture of a bad boy, besides his tattoos, if she wanted to be judgmental, which she didn't.

She pushed all her trembling emotions away to be sorted out later, by herself, and cleared her throat. "You don't have to do that."

"Nope, I don't." His eyes caught hers. "But I'm going to. Go find something else to do. I'll finish the cutting around here. You can't be trusted with a knife." His lips curled into a devilish grin, one she found too enticing for her battered heart.

"Fine. I'll go finish hanging the sign." With a haughty tilt to her head, she started to walk away.

"Good luck with that...shorty."

His laughter followed her down the hallway.

Shorty.

Yeah, she was much shorter than him. It didn't mean he had to point it out and make fun of her.

As she picked up the banner from the floor, she chastised herself. She meant to make him leave, and here she was allowing him to stay.

A slow smile grew into one she shouldn't have. He wanted to help her. That damn sweet side of him again.

Oh, no.

Was he playing a game with her? Reel her in with sweetness once more and take her body to extreme pleasures. He had something to prove, especially since she essentially issued a challenge by claiming he was horrible in bed.

She wanted to hate herself for doing such a thing. She also wanted him to walk out of the kitchen and take her against the wall. A little hard and rough. Because she needed to release her pent-up emotions. Because she wanted it fast and dirty. Because she wanted...him.

As long as Stitch was in her house, she was screwed either way.

Newman ran a tired hand through his hair as he took his time walking up the porch steps to the front door. He nodded once at Officer Spencer and entered the house, preparing himself as best as he could for the scene about to hit his eyes.

Sometimes he hated getting up so early for a crime scene. He didn't even have enough time to make a cup of coffee. He could use a hot steaming cup of Joe right now to wake him up, to calm his nerves some.

That probably wouldn't even work right now. Nothing could. Not a damn thing could make his life better.

He swallowed hard, then took a step into the bedroom. His eyes made a quick sweep of the room, barely glancing at the dead woman on the floor, who had glaring red marks on her neck. The scene smelled like death, looked like a horror scene with a broken lamp, clothes scattered around the room, the bedsheets tangled in a mess, and all he wanted to do was flee. Run fast, and run hard. He didn't want to stop until he felt his world center back into equilibrium. Would he ever feel balanced and carefree again?

The room might look horrifying, yet he couldn't see any blood. He blew out a tiny sigh of relief, grateful for that small thing. He didn't think he could handle any blood right now.

"Dude, you okay?"

Newman averted his attention from the hallway, trying not to plan his escape like he wanted, and gave Sauer a weak smile. "Just tired. What do we have so far?"

"This is Tonya Moretta. Her sister found her. I guess she's been staying with her recently and got home late from a party. She saw her sister's bedroom light was on, which was unusual, and found her like this." Sauer stepped closer to him, walking carefully around the body, and Susan, who was collecting evidence. "She's recently divorced. Her sister, Jeanine, said she's been having problems with her ex-husband lately. He'll be a good place to start." He lowered his voice. "Are you sure you're okay?"

Newman nodded, even though he was far from okay. He wanted to spill his guts. He wanted to tell Sauer every sordid detail of his messed-up life, but he couldn't. His life would turn even worse if he did.

"Yep." Newman glanced around the room again, his eyes hitting the dead body a little longer than last time. "Looks like she might've been...raped."

"Yeah. Susan's waiting for Dr. Everly to get here so she can process the body for evidence, but she did find some fingerprints on the nightstand. Let's hope it's not the victim's. I say we start by interviewing the ex-husband."

His heart started to beat erratically. What he wanted to do was disappear. He wanted to slink away into the dead of night, erase every aspect of his life, and re-emerge as a whole new person. A different one. A respectful one.

"Why don't you interview the ex-husband and I'll start canvassing the neighborhood to see if anyone saw anything. We'll get more done if we split up."

Sauer cocked a brow, surprised by his suggestion. They never split up. They always interviewed, canvassed, and worked a case side-by-side. Why had he suggested that?

If Sauer would ask, he'd be tempted to say he needed to be alone right now. He wouldn't be fit for company. Of course, Sauer would never ask, and he'd never actually say that.

"Sure. We can do that."

Like Sauer could be, he let it go. He didn't question him. He didn't mess with the status quo. One of these times, Newman wished Sauer would. He wished he'd get into his face and demand some answers.

Today wasn't the day he'd do it, obviously.

"Let's get to work." He smiled for Sauer's benefit. Without another word, he walked out of the room without glancing at the dead body, or even a simple hello or good-bye to Susan, who looked overtired and oddly quiet herself. He knew that feeling well.

———

THE FILING CABINET drawer slammed so hard it shut and opened back up a little. The ringing in her ears that started at a dull tingle when she walked into work this morning flared to a full-blown roar as her mind tried to recall where she put the Moretta file.

Meticulous. Orderly. Put together. Organization kept her sane in a job that would put quite a few people in the bathroom puking their guts out.

But today...

Today went from one bad scenario to the next. It all started with waking up before the birds sang to a crime scene that still made her stomach roil with disgust. She hated rape cases. She hated thinking how much the victim must've suffered before she died. Of course, she wasn't positive the victim was raped, since Dr. Everly hadn't completed the autopsy yet, but there had been enough indication at the crime scene to suggest that's what happened.

She was tired and worn out, her finger throbbed, and she wanted to go home and crawl under her covers and not come out for a week.

"Where are you?" She shoved the drawer closed once again, feeling triumph it finally shut properly but the throbbing in her finger intensified as she had pushed harder than she anticipated.

"Susan, are you okay?"

She whipped around to the doorway of her office and produced a smile she didn't want to as Detective Ben Stoyer walked in. No matter how horrible she was feeling, no matter how bad of a day it was, she could always manage a smile for him and Detective Zeke Chance, two of her favorite detectives, and also the husbands of two of her good friends, Rina and Zoe.

"I'm fine. I'm having a little difficulty finding a folder."

Ben's eyes narrowed in concern. "Can I help somehow?"

"Nope. I'll find it. It's here." *It has to be.* She took a seat at her desk, a smile still on her face. "What's up?"

His eyes hit her finger that was still wrapped tightly with gauze. "How's the hand? Rina told me you cut it yesterday getting ready for the party."

She tried not to sigh heavily at the reminder of her mishap. And of Stitch. "It's fine."

The concern slowly dissipated as joy took its place. "I wanted to say thanks for putting on such a great baby shower for Rina. She was in tears at home, showing me everything she got." He looked panicked. "Happy tears, I mean. The littlest thing gets her so emotional, but they were definitely happy tears. She never expected such a wonderful party."

A genuine smile finally touched her features. "I'm so

glad to hear that. It was a great party." *Stitch helped set it all up.*

Of course, that wasn't something she wanted to talk about. Or even think about. She had to stop thinking about Stitch.

"You sure you're okay?"

"I'm fine." She leaned forward. "Was there something else you needed?"

"Well..."

She laughed as she grabbed the basket near the corner of her desk filled with the files she still needed to file. While nobody could call her unorganized, there were times she was so exhausted from working out in the field that she had no energy to put everything away. She had a simple basket on her desk to keep the clutter away. It gave her the sense of organization until it was done properly.

"The Turner case, am I right?" Her fingers fiddled with the folders until she came across the latest case Ben and Zeke were working on. "Dr. Everly pulled a .22 caliber bullet out. Close range shot to the head. I haven't had a chance to run it through the system for a ballistics match. I also found a few fingerprints. I'll try to get to it today."

His sweet smile inched up a notch. "You're the best, Susan. I'm liking the husband for this, even though he has an alibi. His daughter didn't seem to believe his alibi. I'm worried about her. I'd like to close this case for her."

"Well, it could be hard to prove it's the husband based on the fingerprints. They weren't divorced or separated, and his prints can easily be explained why they would be found anywhere in the house."

"He doesn't own a firearm. I'm hoping the ballistics come back helpful. Maybe it's stolen and he bought it off someone. I'm hoping I find that someone and they flip on him."

"That's a lot of maybes and hoping. I promise to try to get to it soon."

"Thanks again, Susan." Ben started to walk out, turning toward her at the last second. "If you ever need to talk, I'm here for you. You know that, right?"

"I do. Thanks, Ben."

He walked out.

Susan slouched in her chair, tired and exhausted. Not because she had a late night with the party. Thankfully, that ended at a decent hour and she was alone with her thoughts by ten. She didn't have a drop of alcohol to drown her sorrows. She couldn't even say she was tired from getting up at four in the morning to head to a crime scene.

Seeing Stitch again after months of silence took more of a toll on her than she would've ever imagined. The irritating man stuck around cutting vegetables, preparing food, and helping her set up the house to look as beautiful as it possibly could for Rina. By the time Dee made it, there wasn't anything left to do. Stitch made a quick good-bye and left. Surprisingly, Dee made no comment about why he was still there, or the awkward good-bye they had.

Maybe only she found it odd. They had stared at each other for the longest time. He had leaned toward her a little as if he wanted to kiss her. She drifted his way as well, wanting him to kiss her. Then they jumped apart as if they had been electrocuted.

Dee didn't make one little peep about it. Strangely, Dee seemed more frazzled than Susan was used to. While they had started to become closer in the last few months, she didn't feel comfortable enough to ask her what the problem was. She was never good at being the whole tell-me-your-problems kind of friend. Because then Dee would want to know hers, and she didn't want to talk about it.

Having to come into work on a Saturday should feel lame, especially as exhausted as she felt without even having a hangover. Instead, she was grateful for a distraction from her wandering mind. She'd only daydream and analyze the entire encounter with Stitch if she was at home.

"Slacking off, I see. Not really the way to earn your way to the supervisor position."

Her head snapped to the doorway to see Rachel standing there with her typical haughty look. She sat up slowly, refusing to let Rachel make her feel worthless, which was something she unfortunately excelled at.

"Can I help you, Rachel?"

She cocked a brow. "I wanted to say good morning." She paused as her brow rose even higher. "And to say I also put in for the supervisor position. It's nice you want to try, but I've been here longer, so..."

So Rachel obviously assumed she had no chance of getting the position. She agonized over a week whether she should put her application in, not entirely sure she wanted the responsibility. Then Scott, the current supervisor and her mentor, hinted how he wanted her to apply, as if he knew whom he wanted to hand the reins over to. The smile on his face when she handed in her application was magnetic. It filled her with hope and giddiness. Like she was making the right decision.

In one fell swoop, Rachel was dashing those hopes. She *had* been working here longer—by two years only. She also had a great working relationship with Scott. Susan almost thought they were sleeping together. Only a funny feeling she got, not any concrete evidence, of course.

Maybe she read Scott's words wrong. Maybe he didn't

hint she should apply. Maybe she was too young and too inexperienced.

Rachel's smirk widened, as if she knew how she was feeling and that she would never win. Which was exactly what this felt like now. A race needed to be won. Susan had no idea what to say. Anything she wanted to say wouldn't be pleasant, or the actions of someone who wanted to be in management. She offered a smirk of her own and nothing else.

Rachel's smile slipped a little. "Well, I have things I need to do."

She looked away, not interested in watching her leave, and stared at the folder in front of her. Working would help her. It would distract her from everything, especially Stitch. Yet, she couldn't seem to find the motivation.

A knock sounded on the doorframe.

Suppressing a groan from another interruption—she hadn't even been in the office for a full hour yet, considering she went straight to the lab after she processed the crime scene this morning—she looked up and almost produced a smile, then stopped herself. Newman didn't deserve a smile, not after what he said about the dance and making it sound like the worst thing ever to take her.

"Hey, Susan."

"Good morning." The professional in her had her offering a small smile. "What can I do for you?"

"I wanted to see if you processed those prints on the Moretta case yet." He walked into the office and stood in front of the chairs but made no move to sit down.

Her smile almost wavered at the reminder she couldn't find the Moretta case. That had never happened to her in her career. Losing a file could...well, she didn't want to think about it. It was crazy to think she lost it already, since she just got back from the crime scene this morning. She didn't have time to lose it. Her thoughts had been everywhere this morning, not just on the case, and that was her fault. She needed to leave her personal issues at home. Otherwise, dire things like this occurred.

"Not yet, but it's on my to-do list." No way would she admit she couldn't find the file. She managed to lift a few prints from the bedroom. While she liked to keep hard copies of everything, as well as digital copies, she hadn't quite entered the prints into the system, but they were locked safely in the evidence room. She could at least breathe a sigh of relief about that.

"Let me know when you do. Sauer and I are itching to close this one."

"Of course."

His eyes sparkled for a moment, with what, she couldn't decipher. Maybe anger. Maybe impatience. Maybe irritation. It was difficult to decide when he still had a smile on his face.

"Thanks, Susan." He patted the back of the chair and started to turn around, then shifted his gaze toward her. "Hey, do you want to get a drink tonight?"

She flinched in surprise, taken off guard. Newman wanted to have a drink with her? He didn't even want to take her to the ball, making it sound like a hardship of great proportions. When she thought about it, he didn't even say good morning to her at the crime scene earlier.

"If the gang wants to go out, I'm always game."

His eyes narrowed, then he tipped his lips into a grin. "Right. You know, maybe this weekend doesn't work for me. Another time?"

"Sounds good."

She slouched once again after he walked out. What was that? Did Newman just ask her out?

Why now? What game was he playing?

Because as far as she was concerned, men only liked to play games with her.

Look at how Stitch played her good, getting her in bed, and then never called as he said he would.

3

THE PAIN in his hand stretched from the tips of his fingers, past his wrist, and made a slow trail up his arm. Dropping the pencil down onto the table, he backed away as he rubbed his wrist fiercely. It wouldn't make the pain go away, of course, but subconsciously it made him feel better. It made him think the pain would disappear. He was careful not to do it in front of anybody. It wouldn't do well for anyone to know how badly his hand and wrist were starting to become a problem.

Hell, maybe Jensen, Stewart, and Todd, his other three artists that worked in the shop, knew there was a problem. He had to reschedule his client this morning, which was a rarity for him, and now Jensen and Stewart were the only artists working today as he sulked like a little baby in his office. He never canceled or rescheduled a client unless it was an emergency. The ache in his wrist was definitely an emergency. He couldn't even keep his hand steady as he attempted to sketch a tattoo he was set to do later this week, let alone apply an actual tattoo to someone's body today.

"Shit!"

Pencils, papers, and his cold cup of coffee went flying through the air, hitting the wall and the floor with a loud *thunk* after he swiped his arm across the desk. His mug sat in pieces on the floor, black liquid streaming down the wall. The sketch he had been working hard on all week lay scrunched and stained among the broken pieces and scattered pencils.

Control your temper, young man.

Yeah, that was one phrase he could never manage to do whenever his mother berated him for getting into trouble, usually at school, wagging her finger in his face.

He excelled at throwing things, punching walls— punching people on occasion—destroying things that meant something to him. Even knowing he shouldn't, he couldn't control the impulse to do it.

A knock sounded on the door. Everybody knew not to enter unless he instructed them to do so. Before he contemplated opening a shop, he knew he wanted his own office. His own space to tattoo. He knew some shops where the artists tattooed out in the open, one big space, usually where you could see everything as you stepped into the shop, but not him. He wanted to be alone when he created his work of art.

Now, someone wanted to bother him in his sanctuary. He wished he could ignore it. In all likelihood, it was Stacey, the college dropout he hired three months ago to run the front counter. He'd been trying to talk her dumbass into going back to school. She had brains. She also had skills where she could eventually start tattooing, but before he would even show her a thing or two about tattooing, he wanted her to go back to college, something he never managed to do. They were still arguing about it. They liked to argue about a lot of things, especially her annoying way of always getting into his business.

The door swung open.

"Did I say you could come in?"

"Uh-oh, Stitchy has PMS today, does he?" Stacey laughed as her eyes glanced around the room and zoomed in on the mess he created. "You have a visitor."

"I told you earlier, I'm not in."

"Yeah, I told the dude that and he wasn't believing me."

He wasn't in the mood for this shit. Dealing with a client, particularly at a time where his mood was ramping up to dangerous levels, was never a good thing.

"I'm not in."

"Stitchy, pull the tampon out and get your shit together and listen. He's not leaving until he talks to you." She laughed again as his eyes narrowed. She knew he didn't like it when she called him Stitchy, yet continued to do so. She snapped her fingers. "Oh, yeah, he's got a badge."

Great. That was worse than dealing with a client.

"Does the dude with a badge have a name?"

"Detective Sauer."

Wow. That surprised him. He wouldn't say they were friends, but they were friendly. Because of Deena.

Shit.

Did something happen to Deena?

Why else would Sauer come see him?

"You okay, Stitch?"

And there went Stacey's fun-loving tone to motherly. She was like a damn ping-pong ball with the way she switched her personality so easily.

"Send him back."

"Don't get that tone with me."

Young man. She forgot to add that part. Now he wanted to punch something, throw something, hurt something.

"Get out, Stacey."

This time her eyes narrowed before she walked out and slammed the door for good measure. Yeah, he acted like a jackass. He never pretended not to be one, especially with her. Nothing new in their relationship. New day, same old shit.

Another knock sounded on the door. He could ignore this knock like he had the previous one, but like Stacey, he didn't think that would stop Sauer from entering.

"Come in."

The door opened and Sauer stepped in looking tired and worn out. The look, an uncommon one for him, scared the living daylights out of him. Something had to be wrong with Deena. Of all the friends he had, and he'd say he had quite a few, none of them was his best friend until the end like Deena. He couldn't lose her. She understood him like nobody else.

Yeah, so why had they stopped talking for almost ten years?

That answer wasn't too hard to decipher. Him, of course. It always came down to him and screwing shit up.

But he wouldn't screw up their friendship again. He needed her in his life.

"You look like shit."

"And you look like you're having a bad day," Sauer replied as his eyes took stock of the room, not missing the mess.

"Deena okay?"

Sauer nodded as he walked farther into the room and shut the door. "She's fine. Mostly. Thanks for helping her yesterday. She was really stressed out about the party."

"Not a problem." Except the part where he had to help Susan, be surrounded by her heavenly scent, her sweet disposition, the reminder of what he shouldn't claim as his own. Oh, and the knowledge she thought what occurred between them was only meh.

"Have you ever had a woman tell you that you were lacking in bed?" The words popped out before he could stop them. It shocked the hell out of him, and Sauer looked just as surprised as his cheeks turned a bright red. Either because he had, or because the conversation was odd. Which it clearly was.

"No. Have you?"

"Hell, no." Stitch laughed to hide the lie.

"Right. Umm...so..." Sauer paused and cleared his throat.

Stitch figured he embarrassed the hell out of him, or he was nervous as shit to talk. He didn't care what the reason was; he just wanted to move the conversation along and forget he ever blurted out that stupid question.

"Spit it out, Sauer."

"Yeah, of course." He cleared his throat again. "You have to promise not to say a word to Dee. She'll...well, she won't be very happy with me."

As much as he could tell Sauer needed him to agree, he couldn't. He knew, oddly enough, they were a good match and didn't want to see any problems between them, but he couldn't promise to keep a secret from Deena. Not his style.

"I can't do that."

Sauer's jaw clenched. "Then maybe this was a bad idea."

"You think I won't mention this visit to Deena?"

"You're clearly going to do whatever the hell you want, Stitch." Sauer fisted his hands as he took a step closer. "It's not anything bad. I just don't know what to do anymore and

I thought...I thought maybe you'd be able to help. Feel free to tell Dee about this if you'd like. I happen to like makeup sex."

That garnered a small chuckle from him. He figured Sauer was trying to make him uncomfortable, and it would take a lot more than talk about sex to make him feel that way. A lot more.

"Then why can't I tell Deena?"

Sauer's entire body relaxed as the exhaustion flooded his system and he sank down onto the chair near him. "She had a lot of fun last night at Rina's baby shower. She told me everything, right down to the last detail, describing every little gift Rina received. It went from sharing a fun time with me to complete tears that I couldn't manage to get her to stop. Do you know what that feels like, Stitch? Do you know how it feels to watch the woman you love cry and you can't do anything to stop it? It guts me. It makes me come talk to a man I don't want to and admit that I can't help my wife on my own. It's hard to admit that."

Well, shit. What did he say to that? Deena and crying didn't sound right in the same sentence. Hearing that gutted him, too, knowing his best friend was hurting.

"Look, tell me what the problem is and I'll see what I can do. I can't promise to keep it to myself. If I think Deena needs to know, I'm going to tell her."

They stared in silence, both weighing each other.

Finally, Sauer nodded.

"Dee's pregnant. About three months along."

The widest smile spread across his face. "That's great news. Congrats, man."

Sauer smiled. "Thank you. We're both excited."

"I don't see the problem."

"She's three months along." Sauer stood up, agitated. "She

still doesn't want to tell anyone. She kept crying last night she was going to be a terrible mother." He ran a ragged hand across his face. "She doesn't believe she's going to be a good mother. You know Dee and her craziness. It's one of the things I love about her, but it's been getting worse. I'm worried about her...and the baby. This stress can't be good. I...I don't know. Can you talk to her? Reassure her somehow she'll be a wonderful mother. I know she will be. She's not like..."

"Her mother." Stitch shook his head, agreeing with him. Deena was *nothing* like her mother. "Dude, that's a touchy subject. Not even I venture into that territory. It's something we both avoid. If I did bring it up, she'd suspect something. Why doesn't she want to tell anyone?"

"I don't know. For the longest time she held the argument we should wait until the three-month mark for safe measure. Now she just says, let's keep waiting. I want to shout to the rooftops and it's hard to keep it in, but I do. For her. I thought maybe you could...I don't know how else to tell her that everything will be fine. Even before we started trying, she was worried about becoming a mom. We even talked about it at the ball."

The ball. Yeah, not a memory he needed to revisit. It only made him think of Susan.

No matter what Deena thought, Stitch knew she'd be a hundred times better than her own mother. Coming right out and saying that wouldn't work.

And like that, a crazy thought popped into his head.

"Look, I have an idea. Don't rely on it working or anything. For now, I won't say a word to her. I'd do anything for Deena."

"I know. That's why I came to you. I just want my wife to be happy."

"Never doubt that. She is happy with you."

He couldn't quite say the same about another person being happy with him. But he'd find out soon enough.

———

Susan opened her door to see the last person she ever wanted to see standing there.

"What do you want?"

Stitch leisurely leaned against the doorframe as a silky smile adorned his cocky, arrogant face. She wanted to wipe that look off with a kiss. No! With a slap to his face.

Who was she kidding? She wanted the kiss more.

"Well?"

"You look adorable as hell when you scrunch your nose in irritation. Am I interrupting anything, shorty? How's the finger?"

"My finger is fine. I've had a shitty day, Stitch. I'm not in the mood."

He slowly stood to his full height—not to intimidate her, she knew this, yet it did somehow. Not in a scary oh-my-God-he's-going-to-hurt-me look, but more of an oh-my-God-he's-going-to-devour-me look.

"I had a real shitty day, too."

She could see the truth reflected in his eyes...and a little bit of pain. She wanted to soothe that pain. Just like she wanted to soothe her own.

Stitch was standing at her doorstep, not including yesterday, after months of ignoring her. She didn't have the strength to question why, or to interrogate him. She did the only thing on her mind since yesterday. She reached out and grabbed his hand, pulled him inside, and shut the door without thinking about the consequences. Oh, and there'd be plenty of that. She knew it for a fact.

"I meant to push you out and slam the door in your face."

His grip tightened. "And yet you pulled me inside instead." His other hand cupped her cheek. "Did you mean it?"

"Mean what?"

He let her cheek go at the same time he let her hand go and grabbed her around the waist, then twisted her around and pressed her against the door.

"You know what I'm asking."

Oh, there was no mistaking what he meant. She called him terrible in bed. Uttering those words effectively issued a challenge he wouldn't be able to resist. Maybe that's why she said it. Maybe she wanted to tempt him back into her arms. Sex with Stitch had been fun and dirty and sexy. She missed the hell out of it. Of course she did. She only had the one night. Because he ignored her, never coming back for more. And she had wanted lots more.

"What do you think?"

His hands tightened around her waist as he leaned closer. "I think you're a damn liar. I made you feel good that night."

"Did you now?"

He chuckled as his lips connected with her neck, little nibbles making their way to her ear. His rough stubble grazed her skin, making her want to beg for more. He bit down, not too hard, but hard enough that it hit her core immediately. She wanted him. So badly. Right now.

"Tell me you don't like that. Tell me to stop. Tell me to get the hell out."

Her soft moan was the only answer she could give him.

"That's my Susan, so damn responsive in all..." A soft kiss to her neck. "The right..." A tender hand slid up her rib cage as another kiss attacked her collarbone. "Places." His hand stopped just short of touching her breast.

"Stitch..." It wasn't quite a beg or a plea, the way she whispered his name, but it was enough for him to keep going.

His hand closed around her breast, kneading, playing, and torturing her into pleasure. This was all wrong, yet so right. They were completely mismatched in every possible way, and she didn't care one little bit. She wanted to feel good and forget every horrible thing that happened today. Just as she wanted to make him feel good and forget his troubles for a while.

Her hands finally found the ability to move and went straight for the button to his jeans, undoing them quickly, as his hands made a pathway to her back and undid her bra. She made sure to be careful as she slid his zipper down slowly, not wanting to jar her injured finger in any way. She was about to slide her good hand inside when he yanked up on her shirt, making her raise her arms. Two seconds later, she was devoid of any shirt or bra and his lips were sucking hard on a nipple.

She let him have a few seconds of fun before she made him move his lips to somewhere else so she could touch him, since she couldn't reach him well enough when he was bent down devouring her breast. Sometimes, the height difference put a damper on things. She could suggest they move to the bedroom. But then his lips were back on her neck, his tongue swirling and doing the blissful things it excelled at.

She shoved his pants and boxers down and grabbed him. He was hard as a rock and throbbing within her hands.

Stroking him up and down, his kisses turned more frenzied. Exactly as she remembered. Nothing from that night had been slow and sweet. That's not what she wanted right now either. She wanted it hard and rough, right here against her front door.

"More, Stitch. I need you." She stroked him harder, moaning at the tender bite to her shoulder. "Now."

"Say no more, sweetheart. Take off your pants."

She quickly took off her sweats, refusing to feel embarrassed that she had on the worst, rattiest pair she owned as he dug around in his pants pocket, producing a condom. Within seconds, he had it on. He didn't hesitate as he lifted her off the ground and down onto him, then slammed her gently against the door.

"I can't do slow."

Placing kisses along his jawline and down his neck as her fingers combed through his thick, black hair, she whispered, "I never said I wanted it slow."

And then he started.

Thrusting in and out of her with complete abandon, he held her tightly against him, with her arms wrapped around him, her mouth wanting to be near his neck to kiss and torture him as he liked to do to her, but he was rocking her so hard she couldn't manage to kiss him like she wanted. It didn't matter. The sensations flying through every cell in her body took precedence. He felt wonderful and strong and everything she needed after the day she had today.

"Damn, Suzy baby, you feel..." His breathing became ragged and heavy as his thrusts turned rougher.

He didn't even need to finish his sentence. She knew. She understood what he was trying to say. She also knew he knew she lied about what she said. This, right here, was nowhere near meh. It was never that way. She could never lie to him again. He would never believe her.

His fingers dug into her hips as he continued the sweet, brutal pleasure. She wanted him to keep going on and on and on, but it hit her. The strongest orgasm that ever touched her body. Holding in her scream, something she never did while having sex, was impossible.

A few more thrusts and he came with her, his body tightening all around her. His fingers clenched her hips so hard, she wouldn't be surprised if he left a mark.

Slow, heavy breaths surrounded them as he rested his head against the door near hers.

"Shit. I needed that."

Chuckling, she couldn't deny she needed—wanted—it, too.

"I might need a little more."

He lifted his head, his eyes sparkling with the same desire she was experiencing. "Let's finish this in the bedroom."

"If you insist." She smiled wide at the cocky grin on his face.

"I do."

4

HE BRUSHED a hand up her side, circling her nipple before taking a taste. Lying in bed with Susan talking was just as fun as the sex they had. He couldn't say that about any other woman he had slept with.

Once against the door. Once in bed. Then an entertaining time going down on each other. Damn, Susan knew how to make him feel good.

"What are you going to do?" He popped her other nipple into his mouth as he waited for her answer.

Since the moment she pulled him inside her house, they took turns having amazing sex and talking. Well, mostly her talking as he played with the deliciousness before him. She told him about applying for the supervisor position. Another co-worker was applying as well and not being friendly about it. She sounded like a jealous bitch to him. Something he said a few times, hoping to make her feel worthy of the position, which he figured she was.

"Not much I can do. I'm going to keep doing my job and ace the interview."

He leaned away and propped his hand to his head, his elbow sinking into the soft bed. "When's the interview?"

"Next Wednesday." She fiddled with the edge of the bedsheet. "I want the position. But part of me doesn't want it because I know Rachel's disposition will get worse."

"Yeah, and if she gets it, your life sounds like it'll still be miserable. You can do this. I know you can."

"You barely know me."

His eyes grazed her body from top to bottom. "I know all I need to know, sweetheart."

She laughed as she lightly pushed against his shoulder. The movement made him lose his balance on his elbow. He shifted slightly, unable to hide the wince from the sudden pain in his wrist.

"Are you okay? I didn't mean—"

"I'm fine." He sat up.

"But—"

"I said I was fine." He shouldn't have been resting on his elbow like that. Just because the pain in his hand and wrist had disappeared for a while didn't mean it couldn't flare up without notice.

"You don't have to get snippy with me."

He tilted his lips into a shit-eating grin, because he wanted—no, needed—to forget about his pain. "Are we about to argue? Because I am down for some kinky makeup sex. A little fast and dirty."

Susan chuckled. "You're impossible."

"Irresistible, too. Don't deny it."

Another sweet, delectable laugh slipped from her lips. Each time he heard that beautiful sound, he wanted to hear more. He was riding a very dangerous slope with her. While he had fun with her in the bedroom—tons of fun—this thing between them couldn't go much further than that.

"You think you're so charming."

"I have my moments, sweetheart." The grin on his face slowly vanished, yet he tried to keep his tone playful. "Maybe one more round and then we call it a night."

A slight moment of panic entered her eyes as she sat up, scooting next to him against the headboard.

"Why did that sound like an end to...everything?" She inhaled and exhaled loudly, and then deeply. "Is that all I am, a quick, dirty go-round for you?"

He still hadn't decided what she was to him. A distraction. Because he thought about her all the time. A beautiful woman. Because whether dolled up in a gorgeous gown, or wearing sweats and a shirt, she was breathtakingly beautiful. A nuisance. Because she made him question what he wanted in life, something he rarely did, always confident in what he wanted. A hidden gem. Because on the surface, Susan was a goal-oriented, focused woman. But inside, she was soft and sweet and something else...He couldn't even find the right word to describe it. Well, he sucked in English class back in high school.

What was he?

A tattoo artist. A successful businessman.

Someone who never saw himself as a family man. Yet, the picture looked pretty damn good when he imagined Susan by his side.

A criminal. Someone who would ruin the life Susan had painstakingly built.

"You know it'd never work between us. The sex is great —" He turned his eyes to hers that simmered with irritation and sorrow intertwined into an ocean of agony he almost couldn't handle. "You're applying for a serious position at work. Dating me isn't going to help you get there."

"What? You're kidding me, right?"

"I'm serious."

"Because...why? You have tattoos. I didn't know that was such a crime these days. Or because you never called when you said you would. Yeah, that won't help me get the job. Or how about—"

"I have a record." He watched as her anger morphed into surprise. "I did a year in the slammer. I'm a criminal, Susan, and dating someone like me isn't going to look good for your job. A job at the police department. Think about it."

"It doesn't matter. You have nothing to do with my job and—"

"Trust me. That shit matters to people like that. They'll interview you, ask you questions, and eventually it'll come out who I am and what kind of record I have. I won't ruin your chances."

She cocked her head to the side as she stared at him for the longest time. He didn't say a word. There wasn't much more he could say. He did his time, something he was happy to do. Because even if he wanted to change what happened, he wouldn't. He would've done the same damn thing, no matter how he looked at the situation. So yeah, he happily served his time, then got out and focused on tattooing. Created a successful business and made it look like he was something when he was simply a guy trying to live his life any way he could. Having a record sure made getting his business up and running difficult, but he didn't back down from anything. Now look at him.

"You're being ridiculous."

"I'm being ridiculous?" He laughed at the lunacy of her words. "Don't you want to know what I did?"

"It couldn't have been bad because you're not a bad person. You made a mistake and—"

"Nope. I know what I did and I made no mistake. I went

into a situation fully understanding what would happen and I don't regret it. I'd do it again." He cocked a challenging brow, waiting for her to ask.

Her eyes narrowed as he could see the questions swirling around her mind. Oh, she wanted to know. The thing he couldn't figure out was why she didn't just say so. Well, hell, why didn't he tell her and get it over with?

Probably because the second she knew, she'd kick his ass out of her bed, and he couldn't bear to think of the loss. He didn't want to get tossed out of her life yet. The sex was phenomenal.

His feelings for her were muddled and riddled with questions and indecisions, but he also knew he didn't want to leave, or get kicked out.

"If you feel like telling me, go ahead, but it doesn't matter to me." He could see the honesty in her eyes.

She was leaving the decision in his court, and the thought scared the shit out of him. He didn't want to tell her. Not yet. He needed to love her body one more time, and then maybe he'd have the balls to admit what he had done.

"Where does this leave us?" She trailed a finger down his chest, her eyes roaming across his body, making him tingle with anticipation. Oh, she wanted him as badly as he wanted her.

"We aren't dating."

Her finger circled his nipple, the light touch making his dick throb for more. More touches. More caresses. More stroking.

"Of course not. You don't date." She leaned closer, her tongue grazing his nipple before backing away with a silky smile on her lips. "But the sex is nice."

Moving like a panther, he had her underneath him within seconds, his body pressed intimately against her, with the notion all he needed was one little push and he'd be deep inside her and in heaven. "The sex is not *nice*. It's amazing. Don't give me more of this meh shit."

She giggled as he rubbed against her. "Never. So no dating...just sex?"

"Take it or leave it, shorty. That's all I'm willing to give. You'll thank me when you get the position."

Her eyes turned cold and hard for a brief moment and then softened as a slow smile appeared. "Do that thing with your tongue. My body needs reminding...because it might've been so-so. I can't quite..."

Her words died as he slid down her body and his tongue started suckling and tasting and devouring her. Because if his Susan wanted him to do the thing with his tongue, then she got what she wanted.

And she tasted so sweet, he wanted it as well.

He was doing the right thing. Sex only.

She would thank him eventually. Because as soon as the bitch Rachel found out about him, and she would, he had no doubt Susan's chances for the position would lessen significantly.

Now that she was in his arms again, he refused to leave. Sex with Susan was everything...and more.

Susan set her phone on the nightstand and rolled back toward the sexy man sleeping next to her. Surprise, and a little disappointment that she had to leave, warred within her. He hadn't left this time. But now she had to.

"Who was that?"

Snuggling closer, she let him wrap an arm around her

waist and pull her even closer. "I have to go to work. A crime scene."

His mouth found her neck, little tender kisses followed. "Or you can stay right here."

Inhaling his warm, musky scent with a hint of spiciness, perhaps his cologne that still lingered, made her wish she could stay. But when work called, she went.

And she never delayed either.

Stitch's hand slid past her rib cage and down her hip and across her thigh. She almost cried out in pain because she had no choice but to leave.

"I need to get up."

His hand wove closer to the spot she craved for him to touch, but at the same time, she knew he couldn't. She stalled his movement a few inches away.

"Don't ever deny this man what he wants."

Chuckling, she kissed his chest and then tried to extract herself from his embrace. "You need to let me go, Stitch."

"And if I don't..."

Considering she didn't turn on the light yet, she couldn't see the cocky smirk on his face that matched his words, but she knew it was there.

"Then I won't visit you later."

He growled low, then slowly loosened his hold, but not before smacking her ass hard. "Come to the shop. I have to work later today."

A little demanding, more so than she was used to when it came to men, but she honestly didn't want to argue with him. She wanted to see him again. She'd been dying to see his tattoo shop, but she was always afraid to go see him, wondering how he'd react. Now was her chance. She didn't know if her semi-threat of not visiting him would even work. He said he wanted sex only, no relationship.

She didn't know what she thought about that, but for now, she'd take what she could get. She wasn't ready to cut him out of her life. Who was she kidding? The sex was amazing. She wasn't ready to cut *that* out of her life.

She crawled out of bed before he could tighten his hold once again, or worse, she tightened hers. Leaving to go to a crime scene was the last thing she wanted to do. But she had a job to do. This crime scene happened to be related to one of her other cases. The Moretta case. The same case where she lost the folder for over three hours.

Of course, lost was the wrong word. Stolen fit better.

Because she searched her office from top to bottom, coming up empty everywhere she looked. She left her office for twenty minutes tops, returning to find the folder miraculously in the basket on her desk in the corner. Which meant someone came into her office and put it back.

The question she couldn't figure out was who did it? Why take it and return it?

When she flipped through the contents, she found nothing missing or out of place. She debated for about ten minutes with herself whether to notify her supervisor, Scott, finally caving to the fact it was her professional duty to report what happened.

Scott was surprised, yet unconcerned about the whole matter. He dismissed her misgivings with a wave of his hand and said a coworker must've borrowed it and then returned it when they were finished.

She disagreed—not vocally—that it wasn't that simple. Someone stole her file for a reason. Nobody messed with her things. If a coworker needed something, they asked. Nobody had ever walked into her office and taken anything. She would find the culprit and make sure the appropriate actions were taken.

Dressing quickly, with also a quick brush of her teeth, she leaned over to where Stitch lay sprawled across her bed before leaving. Talk about a bed hog. Oh, how she wished to jump back in bed and push him over to his side, then slide her hands around his glorious body until they were both sated with pleasure once again.

She had to leave now. Before temptation took control.

"I'm leaving. Feel free to sleep, and flip the bottom lock before you leave."

He slapped her ass in response and in a low growl said, "Be quick and maybe I'll still be here when you get back."

She sincerely hoped so, but she didn't think it would happen. When it came to a crime scene, she was meticulous. She took her time to search, catalog, and bag all the evidence she could find. It wasn't easy or a quick thing. Of course, she didn't explain any of that. Instead, she kissed his cheek, brushed a hand through his hair, and left.

As soon as she walked into the house of the thirty-something woman who was murdered, she could feel death swirling within the walls, within each step she took. Death cloaked everything within its space with gloominess and despair. At times, she could almost feel the screams of the victims calling for justice.

That's why she did what she did.

Justice for the victims. A voice for them.

She was impartial. She didn't make assumptions about any aspect of the case. Her job was to collect the evidence to assist the detectives in their job. She felt empowered and invigorated to be a part of such a process. But she still wanted justice—any sort of justice—for each victim.

Stepping into the bedroom, she said hello to detectives Sauer and Newman, then glanced at the woman lying on the floor, handprints clearly marring the delicate, pale skin around her neck. Just like the first victim, Tonya.

Like Tonya, she had a bad feeling this woman had also been raped before she was killed. These cases always hit her the hardest, imagining the torture and pain the victim suffered before succumbing to a cruel death. Dr. Everly confirmed before she left the office yesterday that Tonya, indeed, had been raped.

"Did you get to those prints yet, Susan?"

Bending closer to the victim, she didn't even glance at Newman, especially with the way he delivered the question. So condescendingly.

Guess he was still in a mood. Not surprising, since he normally had an attitude with her lately. Maybe she imagined him asking her out for a drink, because his behavior didn't display a man who wanted to share an evening out with her.

"Not yet."

"Busy getting Zeke and Ben's shit done first, huh?"

Standing abruptly, she jerked a sharp gaze at him. "Excuse me?"

He shrugged, as if he didn't just insult her and her professionalism. She might have a weak spot for Ben and Zeke, but she didn't always bump their stuff up. If she did, it was for a damn good reason. Not to mention, she processed Tonya's crime scene yesterday morning. It wasn't her only case.

"Do you have anything to tell me about the case? Because if not, I'd like you to leave." She wasn't about to put up with his attitude. Not anymore. Not like she usually did because she didn't want to create tension. Well, he was creating it, and enlarging it, perfectly fine on his own.

"We don't have much information yet. According to the

responding officer, her roommate found her. We haven't interviewed her yet," Sauer said quietly, glancing between them, more so at Newman. "So far, the only difference I see in the two cases, there doesn't appear to have been a struggle here. Not a thing out of place. It's odd."

She nodded at Sauer and bent down again near the victim to start her work. Sauer made a good point about the state of the bedroom, but she didn't want to hash out the scene with him. She wanted them both to leave. Now.

Dr. Everly, the coroner, should be here soon. As soon as he arrived and looked over the victim as well, she could start collecting any evidence off the body, like swabbing her neck for DNA. Unless the perp wore gloves, which might've been the case with the first victim because no DNA had been found anywhere in the crime scene.

But her professionalism and respect for Sauer wouldn't let her ignore him and his comments.

"Sounds like the first victim, a roommate coming home late in the morning, almost as if the killer knew they wouldn't be interrupted. I don't know what to say about the lack of a struggle. Maybe he surprised her and subdued her rather quickly. In frank words, he had practice. He knew what not to repeat. Learned from his mistakes, so to speak. Or, maybe he cleaned up after himself, if there happened to be a struggle."

Sauer grimaced, but nodded. "I'm thinking the victims might've been stalked beforehand. Tonya's sister had been staying with her for the past three weeks. This victim, Bethany, she's had a roommate for the past year," Sauer said quietly, then cleared his throat. "Well, we'll let you get to work. Bye, Susan."

She waved to Sauer, ignoring Newman altogether.

"Your favoritism is bullshit. You're always putting Zeke

and Ben's work above others. Maybe I need to have a word with your supervisor about it. I'm not sure that would go over well, especially since I hear you're applying for the position."

Susan slowly stood up and took her time turning around to face Newman. Sauer had already left the room. Not that she needed him, afraid Newman would hurt her, but having a witness to the conversation would've been beneficial.

Because that sounded a lot like he just threatened her if she didn't push his case ahead of everyone else's.

"You're out of line, Newman. You do what you have to do." She jerked her hand toward the doorway. "Now get the hell out of my crime scene."

His jaw clenched, as if he wanted to say more, but must've changed his mind because he walked out of the room without another word.

Susan wanted to slump to the floor and cry, and she wasn't much of a crier. After everything that happened yesterday, from someone snooping in her office and stealing a file to Rachel's nastiness to the shock of seeing Stitch again and sleeping with him, and now this. She needed a good cry.

Newman had never scared her before.

He did now.

The scary glint in his eyes before he walked out suggested this was far from over.

5

SETTING HIS PENCIL DOWN, something he was grateful to do, he swiped his phone from the desk and glanced at the text he received.

I'm here, but the door is locked. No sexy time, then?

Chuckling, he set his phone down without replying to Susan's text and stood up. No need to reply when he could surprise her at the door.

Her playfulness was refreshing. The first time he met her, she had been quiet and a little bit shy. It didn't take long, after a glass of champagne kicked in and a few dances, for her to loosen up around him.

Now...now she was a little sex vixen. He liked it. A lot.

His mouth turned up into a grin when he saw her standing by the door glaring at her phone. Did she think because he didn't respond he was ignoring her? Maybe he should've texted her. He waited a long time this morning for her to come back, and by ten in the morning, he gave up and came to his shop to work on his drawing. For him, that was strange behavior. He never waited for women. They waited for him.

Flipping the lock, he pulled open the door and let her step inside with that sexy glare still on her face, then shut the door and relocked it.

"You didn't answer your phone."

"I answered the door. Isn't that better?"

A smile brightened her face finally. "It is."

Examining her smile a little closer, he realized he might've been mistaken about the glare moments before. Because, even though she had a beautiful smile on her face, her eyes looked tired and sad.

He wrapped an arm around her shoulder and tugged her into his embrace. "Everything okay?"

"Yeah, it was a busy morning."

She tightened the hold around him with a small shiver that didn't go unnoticed. Something was bothering her, but she obviously didn't want to share it with him. For now, he'd let it slide. Especially since he was trying to keep this thing between them sex only. Sharing thoughts and feelings brought everything into a territory he wasn't ready to step into.

"Follow me. My office is this way."

She giggled as she let him keep his arm around her shoulders as they walked down the long hallway. "That sounded so official. You don't think I'm getting a tattoo, do you?"

Stopping in front of his door, he took a step back and grazed his eyes up and down her delectable body. Her hair, as usual, was up in a ponytail. She liked to wear her hair up. Perhaps a small tattoo on her neck, maybe behind her ear where he could admire it, then lay a trail of kisses as he made his way lower. Oh, yeah, he would die to get his hands on her exquisite skin and give her the most gorgeous tattoo there was. The look in her eyes said that would never happen.

"You don't want a tattoo?"

Her eyes bulged. "Is that why I'm here? You're nuts, Stitch. I'm not getting a tattoo."

With a short laugh, he gestured for her to enter his room. "That wasn't my intention today, actually, but damn, Suzy baby, I'd love to give you a tattoo."

She hesitated, but then stepped inside. Her eyes glided around the room at the sketches and pictures on the walls. Some were drawn in pencil, pieces of inspiration he used when he was stuck finding creativity. Some were his favorite tattoos he ever created. He handpicked each piece. Occasionally, he switched them out. But it was rare. These pictures were the best of the best of his talent.

Susan slowly walked around the room looking at each piece with care. That simple forethought meant a lot to him. Most people walked in, looked around, and then dismissed them. Not Susan. She inspected each picture as if she were at a prestigious art gallery trying to find the meaning in the painting. Things like a skull, all black and white, with a pop of red for the eyes. A snake, long and fierce, wrapped around in tight coils, almost appearing like a maze. A portrait of someone's grandfather, a pilot back in the day, wearing his full gear and looking every inch the hero that he was. A simple rose, red and pink, with petals falling gently around it. When she stopped in front of a sketch of a pin-up woman dressed in a bikini, she smiled, and then turned to him.

"Wow. You have a talent that...it leaves me speechless."

"I love what I do."

Walking closer to him, she glanced at the drawing on his

desk. "I can tell." She touched the paper on the edge, her eyes squinting in concentration, then relaxed. "When you said you had to work. I thought that meant the shop would be open."

"No. I never open on Sundays. I like to have at least one day off." He gestured at his desk. "I was working on this. Gotta tattoo this one later this week."

A large tree, the branches protruding in every direction, but instead of simple branches, words replaced them. A small tree house sat squarely in the middle. He was creating it from scratch with a few ideas given to him by the client. The man, a father who recently lost his six-year-old son in a car accident, nearly cried as he tried to tell him what he wanted. A way to honor his child. His heart hurt thinking about the man's pain. Each word held a meaning to the father, just as the tree house symbolized something special to him. The drawing was only taking him so long to finish because he wanted it to look perfect. He wanted the father to find some peace within it. Because like him, some people needed a bit of peace from a tattoo.

The damn thing was also taking him so long because of his hand and wrist. He started to reach for his wrist to rub it, but stopped himself. He couldn't let Susan know it was bothering him. He couldn't let anyone know.

"It's beautiful, Stitch."

He grabbed her hand and pulled her closer, brushing a few stray strands of hair back from her face. "You're beautiful. You look tired. I'd love to take you hard and fast against my desk, but maybe I should take you home to a bed."

Her eyes glittered with desire. "I like that idea. I am tired. And hungry. I didn't eat lunch yet."

"We'll grab something on the way." He grabbed his

phone from his desk and slid it into his pocket. "And we need to talk about something."

AND WE NEED to talk about something.

Well, didn't that put her at ease.

She knew what he wanted to talk about. Obviously. He was done with her. With the sex. With everything.

Why else would he suggest going back to his house when they could've had perfectly good sex right there? Of course, that wasn't normal behavior for her. In fact, she wasn't adventurous when it came to bedroom activities. But with Stitch, she found herself wanting to be. Wanting to branch out and try new things.

Damn it. She wanted hard and fast sex against his desk.

He made her feel daring and bold and like a woman who was sexy. Not just plain old Susan.

She followed him to his house after they decided to order pizza. By the time they arrived, the pizza guy was pulling into the driveway as well. Perfect timing. Stitch paid the guy and they settled into the living room after he grabbed some plates and napkins from the kitchen.

After taking a few bites, eating in a semi-awkward silence, maybe only on her part, she couldn't take it anymore.

"So...what do we need to talk about?"

He took a bite of pizza, slowly chewed it, then decided to put the rest back on his plate. "Well, I actually had a reason to see you yesterday. Having sex was an added bonus."

Okay. She wasn't sure whether she was relieved or more terrified by what he had to say.

"And?"

"And it's a delicate situation and I'd like to know you'll keep it to yourself."

The conversation just took an interesting turn. He trusted her with something he considered important and obviously a secret. It touched her heart more than she cared to admit. But he only wanted sex with her. A man full of mystery and confusion. She didn't like feeling that way.

"Of course. I know how to keep my mouth shut."

His eyes narrowed, as if he were assessing her, weighing his decision to say something.

"Sauer came to see me yesterday."

She set her pizza on the plate, puzzled even more. She didn't know how close they were—clearly not as close as he was with Dee—but she didn't think Sauer visiting was normal.

"Is there a problem? Can I help somehow?"

The hesitation in his eyes finally melted away as a sweet grin punctured his face. "I think you can." He leaned forward. "He's worried about Deena."

"Is she okay?" Setting her plate on the couch near her thigh, she leaned forward as well. "Please say it. You're making me nervous."

Running a hand through his hair, he then set his pizza behind him on the couch. "She's pregnant, but she doesn't want to tell anyone, and she's stressing herself out with worry that she's going to be a horrible mother, which is absolutely not true. Sauer came to me to see if I could talk to her and calm her down some."

Joy and happiness touched her heart that Dee was pregnant. The four of them—her, Dee, Zoe, and Rina—had gotten in the habit of going out every Friday night for drinks and girl time. Since the ball, she had joined their group and outings. She looked forward to every week.

They talked about their respective works and their husbands and about everyday life. Dee had never given the impression they were trying to have a baby, or that she was pregnant.

Although, as she shuffled through her memories, she couldn't remember the last time Dee ordered an alcoholic drink.

"You okay, Susan?"

Realizing she must've zoned out, she jerked her attention from the floor to his gaze and smiled. "I'm so happy for them. That's wonderful news. Why doesn't she want people to know? I don't understand how you want me to help."

"Well, Deena and I, we're close, but we don't talk about... that kind of shit. So I was wondering if you'd say something to her. I mean, don't come out and say Sauer told Stitch who then told me, but...you know...do that woman thing."

She laughed, as a sinfully sexy smile touched his lips. "That woman thing? Like we have some sort of magical powers." He smiled with a hint of cockiness that she would know what to do. Which, oddly enough, gave her an idea. "We go out every Friday night for drinks. I don't think she's ordered a drink in a while. I can't believe none of us noticed it. I've noticed she's been on edge lately, but I hadn't realized she was so stressed."

"She has to be. Sauer and I don't have that kind of friendship. He's Deena's husband, that's about all he is to me. Just get her to confess and reassure her somehow."

Scooting closer, she laid a hand on his thigh. "Don't worry about it. I'll do my best. I know Dee is your best friend."

"She is. We've been through a lot. It's kind of why we don't talk about that shit." He placed a hand around her waist and pulled her closer. "Now, about that sex? You still tired and wanna go to the bedroom, or will right here do fine?"

Susan looked around the small living room that wasn't furnished with much. A TV sat across from the couch on a small stand with a stack of movies in one cabinet on the left side. There was no coffee table in front of the couch, so the pizza box sat on the floor. He had a few tattoo pictures on the walls, but nothing else filled up the room.

She reached beside her and set her plate to the floor, then she leaned closer, snaked her hand behind him, and tossed his plate to the floor. The piece of pizza slid half off the plate.

"I like it right here."

Desire spiked in his eyes. "That's my girl." Then he was devouring her body as if he were starving.

That's my girl.

If only she was.

SUSAN LET OUT a long sigh as she sat down at her desk. Yesterday had been a horrible day. Nothing too extreme occurred. She was bogged down with too much work, trying to process evidence for every case that existed. Detective after detective walked into her office as if she would magically have an answer for them. Each time she said no, she swore she saw a hint of disdain in their eyes. It gave her a nasty feeling that Newman was spreading lies and hatred around the precinct about her. She couldn't figure out his deal.

Today wasn't faring much better. Still busy and stressed with her caseload, which wouldn't be dying down any time soon, she wanted to go home, take a hot bath, and go to bed.

Why couldn't Friday be here yet? She could go out with the ladies and have a drink. She didn't like to drink during the week, even though a glass of wine or one beer wouldn't hurt her. She liked to reserve that for the weekends.

It was only Tuesday.

She sucked in a deep breath and let it out slowly to hold back the tears that suddenly threatened to flow.

She could handle being overworked. She could handle cops rotating through her door asking questions. She could handle a messy crime scene that would take her all day to process.

What she couldn't handle was being reprimanded and warned by her boss for something she didn't do.

A soft knock sounded on her door.

Steeling her features, unwilling to let any tears fall or even pool in her eyes, she waved her hand. Zeke smiled through the door window, then opened the door and closed it quickly. His sympathetic smile as he sat down in the chair in front of her desk didn't soothe her nerves as she figured he was trying to achieve.

"How are you? I heard."

"I'm fine."

He cocked a brow. "Really? Newman puts in an official complaint against you, and you're just fine about that."

She shrugged. "There's not much I can do. If that's the way he feels, it's his right to lodge a complaint."

"It's bullshit. Ben and I come to you all the time about pushing evidence up, like every other cop in this place. Sometimes, you do, and sometimes you don't. You're just doing your job, and I'll tell—"

"Please don't, Zeke." Susan cut him off. "Don't go to Scott."

"I don't know what his problem is lately. He's been tense

and edgy." He shifted in his seat as he rubbed a hand across his jaw. "I'm not going to let him do this to you. Maybe it's petty, but I talked to Captain Ganderson today about him."

Susan couldn't hold back her groan, a sinking feeling in the pit of her stomach. "About what?"

"About his behavior. About his attitude. If he's going to try to get you in trouble for no reason, then he's going to pay the price for his own actions."

"I appreciate what you're trying to do, Zeke, but don't do anything else. Word travels fast around here. I'm already feeling some backlash from other officers and detectives. Heck, if anyone sees you in my office right now, they'll probably agree with Newman that I'm playing favoritism."

Zeke leaned forward. "And we both know it's bullshit."

Susan couldn't hold back her smile, and she almost couldn't hold back the tears that wanted to flow once again. She didn't think she played favoritism. Did she move Ben and Zeke's cases a little faster on occasion? Yes, she wouldn't deny that. She also did it for a lot of other detectives. Sauer and Newman were one example. So for Newman to go to her supervisor and say she purposely put their cases at the bottom of her pile, that her professionalism at crime scenes bordered on rude, that she ignored him when calling for work-related questions, didn't make any sense. She couldn't understand why Newman was out to get her suddenly. It had been two days since she last saw him at the latest crime scene, and today he decided to lodge a formal complaint. Why? Why the delay? Why now?

Just...why?

Listening to Scott berate her like a small child for taking the word of one person without asking her any questions hurt. It hurt so much she almost quit on the spot. And she loved her job. She never once thought about quitting. The unfairness of the situation almost had her blurting out she quit.

"Are you going to be okay? That's all I want to know. If there's anything I can do to help, please let me know, Susan."

"I'm fine, and I appreciate your concern. It'll be okay, Zeke."

He nodded and stood up. "I want you to know Ben and I are here for you."

She said good-bye and wanted to crawl into a corner and cry her eyes out until all the pain from the last few days disappeared. When did crying ever solve anything? It didn't. So she blinked a few times to resist the temptation of shedding some tears and got to work.

Twenty minutes later, when her phone rang and she heard the familiar voice on the other end, she should've known she'd get a call like this.

"So, we were thinking we needed a ladies night out tonight."

She chuckled at Zoe. "Because Zeke's worried about me and couldn't help himself. We never go out for drinks on a Tuesday."

"Yeah, and sometimes you need to vent to your friends about how some men are complete douches. You know how much Dee loves to say that about Newman. She's never liked him."

Susan wasn't up for a night out with her friends. A quiet night alone with her troubles, soaking it up in the bath, sounded more like her style at the moment. But Stitch's request to help concerning Dee popped into her head. She could make tonight more about Dee rather than about herself. Even though she hadn't seen or talked to Stitch since Sunday, she wanted to do this for him, and for Dee, if she was struggling with her pregnancy.

"Okay, I give in. I'll meet you guys at Rockster's at seven. Sound good?"

"Well, considering I wasn't going to take no for an answer, yep, it sounds good."

Susan hung up with Zoe feeling a little better, a little lighter inside. She wanted to cry once more. Because it was so wonderful to have great friends. Those three ladies were always there if she needed them. To help pick her up when she was feeling down.

She would be okay. She wouldn't allow Newman to hurt her and bring her down, which he was clearly trying to do. So instead of tonight being about her, she'd make it about helping Dee see what kind of wonderful mother she was going to make.

Then she could call Stitch and share the good news. Right now, she needed any excuse to see him.

This sex only stuff sucked.

6

Taking a long swig of beer, she tried not to roll her eyes as the concern in her friends' eyes made her uncomfortable.

"Honestly, ladies, I'm fine. Thank you for coming out tonight with me, but I'm fine."

Dee scoffed. "Newman's acting like an asshat, potentially ruining your chances at making the supervisor position, and you say you're fine. Don't bullshit us, Susan."

Susan knew Dee never held back what she thought, and she had said some pretty blunt statements before, but for some reason, her words sounded harsh. Too harsh.

"What Dee meant is we're here for you." Rina smiled gently with a side-glance to Dee. The small warning in her eyes to Dee had her grinning.

"I know that. I appreciate it. There's nothing I can do, so there's no need for me to worry. All worrying is going to do is make me go out of my mind."

"So you're going to ignore the problem? You're just going to let that asshole get away with ruining your reputation?"

Zoe placed a hand on Dee's arm. "She's not ignoring the

problem. Zeke made a formal complaint against Newman today with Captain Ganderson."

Susan wasn't sure when she should steer the conversation away from her problem, since she didn't want to keep talking about it, and to the fact Dee was pregnant. When Dee shook off Zoe's hand a little too roughly, Susan figured now was a good time.

"Zeke should've made that complaint a long time ago. I don't know how many times I've told Sauer to say something about him. His attitude has been terrible, and I hate some of the things Sauer tells me. He's such a softy about him, saying he's his partner and friend and he's going through a rough patch. He's a douchebag. Plain and simple." Dee scrunched her hair and pressed her lips together into a tight line.

"Why don't we all take a shot? I think that might make me feel a little better." Susan threw them a smile to ease the sudden tension swirling around the table.

Zoe nodded enthusiastically at the idea, Rina shifted uncomfortably, which Susan knew she couldn't have one being seven months pregnant, and Dee's face turned an ashy-white before glancing away from everyone.

"I don't feel like a shot," Dee said a lot quieter than her words from moments before.

Susan hated to push her to her limits, but she had to. Stitch was counting on her, and Sauer was counting on Stitch. She didn't want Dee to worry either.

"You're drinking water right now. Are you feeling okay? You always have a drink with us." Susan scrunched her face into contemplation, as if she was actually thinking it through, when she already knew the answer to what she was about to imply. "In fact, when's the last time you had a drink with us?"

Dee's eyes narrowed. "I'm here every Friday."

"Right, but I can't recall when you last had a drink." She feigned a surprised look. "Are you…" Her words died, as she suddenly felt horrible for playing Dee like this. She knew Dee was pregnant, but it felt wrong and deceitful, and that's not the kind of person she was.

"Holy shit! Susan has a point. Are you pregnant?" Zoe piped in, her eyes round with shock. "You are, aren't you? I keep trying to think back, and Susan is so right. I can't remember when you last had a drink with us."

The pressure in her chest for being so devious started to lessen. Not by much, but enough that she didn't suddenly spill her guts about what Stitch had told her. She couldn't hold back the smile as she watched Rina's face glow with happiness and tears start to form in the corner of her eyes.

"Don't be ridiculous, Zoe. Quiet down." Dee shifted in her chair as she refused to make eye contact with anyone.

"Don't bullshit us, Dee."

Susan almost burst out laughing at Zoe's loud comment that she clearly didn't try to keep down. She always loved how Dee could voice her opinion without thinking about it. And she especially loved when the tables were turned and Zoe gave as good as she got.

"I'm not…It's…" Dee's voice started to crack.

Rina, who sat on the other side of Dee, placed a calm hand on her shoulder. "What's the matter? You know you can tell us anything and we'll understand."

Dee looked around the table, pausing a little too long on her, before taking a deep breath. "Okay, I'm three months pregnant."

Zoe let out the loudest squeal, several patrons glanced in their direction, and then she grabbed Dee into a big hug. Rina was next, offering her congrats and a small hug.

Susan didn't know whether she should stand up and hug her or say the words of congratulations because every time their eyes met, it's as if Dee knew what Susan was up to. It hurt to think she hurt her friend, even if it was in her best interest.

In the end, she stood up, grabbed a hug, and whispered her words of congrats.

"Why didn't you tell us sooner? Why don't you seem excited?" Zoe's voice fell to a whisper. "Is everything okay with the baby?"

Dee cracked a smile and laughed a little. "The baby's fine. Everything's fine."

"Then what's the matter?" Rina asked in her sweet, soft voice.

Just like that, Dee spilled it all. Her concerns about becoming a mother, whether she'd be good enough or turn out like her own mother, who had more concern for herself than she ever had for Dee. Like the good friends they were, they tried to beat it into her head that she'd be a terrific mother. They also gave her hell for keeping her pregnancy a secret for as long as she had. Well, mostly Zoe gave her hell for it. Rina was her quiet, soft-spoken self. And *she* felt terrible for outing her secret the way she had to say much else.

By the time they left Rockster's, it was eleven o'clock and Dee's eyes looked a little brighter, as if a small weight had lifted off her shoulders. For that reason alone, Susan couldn't feel terrible for doing what she had done because it helped Dee. That's all she wanted to do.

She had parked close to Dee. Before she could open her door, Dee stopped her.

"I don't know how you knew, but...I really want to be mad at you right now, and at the same time I want to hug you. And now I kinda wanna cry." Dee's eyes filled with tears. "These damn hormones are killing me."

Susan burst into laughter, as did Dee. As they hugged each other, one lonesome tear slipped out. She wiped the evidence before she let go of Dee and looked her in the eyes.

"You're going to be a beautiful mother. Never doubt that. I mean, look at you already. You're stressing how horrible you'll be, when to me, that's a sign of a great mother. So concerned about your little one. You have all of us to help you through these tough times. Call me if you ever need to."

Dee smiled as she wiped her eyes. "Ditto, Susan. This shit with Newman is wrong, and you keep saying you're fine, but I'm not so sure you are. Don't ever hesitate to call me."

They hugged one more time, which was very unusual for them, but Susan just chalked it up to pregnancy hormones. If Dee needed a dozen hugs, she'd do it. Anything to help her friend.

As she got in her car and started it, she hesitated with what way to turn. Left to home? Or right to Stitch's?

It was late. Dropping by unannounced might not be the brightest idea.

But hey, she accomplished her goal, and it had been two days since she last saw him. She needed a Stitch fix.

Honestly, any excuse would do.

Susan had to control the impulse not to slam on her brakes and jump out of her car in a high-speed run.

The flashes of red and blue in front of Stitch's house made her heart beat double-time, putting more caution rather than urgency in her movements. She was honestly afraid to turn the car off and step out.

What happened?

Why were the cops here?

She couldn't see him outside or in any of the patrol vehicles in front of his yard. There were three vehicles and an ambulance. The ambulance had her heart rate skyrocketing to dangerous levels.

After a shitty day at work and putting Dee's emotions through the ringer, she wanted to snuggle with Stitch, even if he wasn't the snuggling kind of guy, and tell him the good news. That she helped him like he asked.

Now she had to deal with this. Finding out what *this* was scared her right down to her very core. It looked like she was arriving to a crime scene, and nothing ever good happened at a crime scene. She would know. She dealt with them day in and day out.

Sucking in a deep breath and then letting it out slowly, she finally found a small ounce of courage and opened her car door. What felt like minutes later, she stepped out of her vehicle and made her way down the sidewalk and to his front door.

Officer Spencer stood there jotting something down in his little notepad that most officers carried.

"Hey, Susan. I didn't know we called you guys."

Swallowing hard first, she offered a tiny smile, shocked she even managed to produce one. "Nobody called me. I was..." Well, she didn't want to admit Stitch's house was her destination. "I was driving by and saw the commotion. Stitch lives here. He's best friends with Dee. Is everything okay?"

She swore her heart was ready to fly out of her chest as she waited for him to answer. It had to be a good sign they didn't need to call in any crime scene techs. But why three cop cars? Why were they here?

"Yeah. It's just a domestic call. I didn't know he knew Dee."

Domestic call? What did that mean? She needed answers. Ones that would ease her panic and calm her racing heart.

"So he's okay? I need some details, Spencer." She laughed to make it appear like it was no big deal when deep inside she was terrified to hear it.

He glanced down at his notebook, then back at her. "Looks like a verbal argument with his girlfriend that almost turned physical. When we got here, she locked herself in his bathroom. Officer Brockman got her to open the door. Looks like she broke his mirror and tried to cut herself. Hence, the ambulance. The paramedics are still in the house. He's fine. As far as I know, he didn't call the cops. The neighbors did. He's not being very cooperative."

Susan nodded at everything Spencer said, but only one word stood out.

Girlfriend.

Stitch had a girlfriend.

And the bastard had the nerve to sleep with her. Multiple times. Wow. She sure knew how to pick some real winners. She'd been on the receiving end of a cheater once. She'd dated a workaholic who wasn't even sad when they broke up. She'd dated a single dad whose kids hated her simply because she was the new woman, and he honestly never stopped them when they said horrible words to her face. She'd dated a nice, boring man who never wanted to venture out of the house for a quiet date night. A big, boring homebody.

Now, she could tack on lying, cheating bastard where *she* was the other woman.

Honestly, how much worse could this week get? It was only Tuesday.

"Everything okay, Susan?"

She nodded with a smile. "I wanted to make sure everything was good. I'll just…" The word 'leave' was on the tip of her tongue. She wanted to run as fast as she could and pretend this didn't happen. But Stitch needed to know who he was dealing with. She wasn't some meek and mild woman that would let a man run over her heart and play games with her. "…say a quick hi to Stitch."

Spencer smiled and stepped to the side so she could enter the house. She waved at Officer Brockman, who stood in the living room where the paramedics were dealing with a woman who looked to have seen better days. Her dark-brown hair was a tangled mess. Her clothes hung on her gaunt body. Her eyes were deep pits surrounded by shallow black circles. She didn't look like a woman Stitch would date. But what the hell did she know? She honestly couldn't say she knew Stitch all that well. Obviously. Because he played her for a big stupid fool.

She found Stitch in the kitchen by himself.

The minute she stepped into the room, his eyes darted to hers. He looked surprised with a hint of panic, then masked it all with his cocky smirk he probably perfected as a rowdy teenager.

Dragging a hand through his hair, his smooth voice asked, "What are you doing here, shorty? Did they call you?"

She didn't admit outside to Spencer his house had been her destination, and she wasn't about to admit that to Stitch either. His dumb nickname for her was obviously his way of distancing himself from her, to hide what an asshole he was. Well, news flash. She knew how big of an asshole he was.

"I was driving by and saw the commotion. I wanted to make sure you were okay."

The slow way his eyebrow rose said he didn't believe her. Yeah, okay, it was a ridiculous lie. She had no reason to be driving by in his neighborhood.

"I'm fine."

A small, lame chuckle left her mouth. "I see that. Your girlfriend doesn't appear to be fine, though."

"Who told you she's my girlfriend?"

"So you're not denying it?"

He hung his head down, effectively averting his eyes. Not that she needed to read his expression to know the truth. "You should've never come."

"No, Stitch, you should've never turned out to be such a bastard."

With those parting words, she left. He didn't try to stop her once. She wanted to hate him for that as well. He could've at least given her the courtesy of the truth. Tell her why he'd sleep with her when he was dating someone else.

Well, now she understood why he wanted only sex with her. Because he had the relationship part with someone else. She apparently was only good for sex.

She barely said a word to anyone as she walked out of the house, or even glanced at the woman as they walked her to the ambulance.

She didn't look in the rearview mirror once as she drove away.

Stitch could go screw himself.

7

STITCH LOCKED the door after the last officer left and then grabbed the bottle of whiskey from the kitchen and poured himself a full glass. He downed the entire glass with one long swallow. The smooth liquid burned his throat but soothed his nerves.

He poured another full glass.

He couldn't erase the look on Susan's face. The look of shock. Of shame. Of disgust. He had no one to blame but himself.

A simple explanation would've cleared up the whole misunderstanding. A stupid misunderstanding.

He assumed one of the officers had to have told her Clarissa was his girlfriend. Maybe once upon a time she was. Now, she was turning into a big headache. A slow, smoldering one that gradually grew until you couldn't take it anymore.

He was reaching his boiling point with her, which was probably why he didn't try to stop them from arresting her. He didn't make excuses for her, although, he barely told the cops what occurred between them. He didn't even say good-bye before they hauled her out of his house.

He hoped like hell Clarissa got clean before she came back knocking on his door again. This shit had to stop. Her stopping by, high as a kite, looking for money for more drugs, although, claiming in her sweet, innocent voice it was money for rent and food. He wasn't an idiot. Something he told her tonight, then the word no. After that, it all unraveled into a big cluster. She slapped him hard across the face, then started to scream at the top of her lungs. He didn't do anything but stand there and wait for her to calm down, which would've happened if his dumbass neighbor hadn't called the cops, who then knocked on the door, frightening her into locking herself in the bathroom and hurting herself.

Yeah, he felt guilty all of that went down, but he wasn't sorry to see her go.

The only woman he wanted to say good-bye to, hell, not even let her leave, he told to get out.

Susan called him a bastard. He couldn't deny it.

It was for the best she left. She would've figured out soon enough how much of a bastard he could be. Today worked fine.

Pouring one more shot, he downed it with haste then chucked the glass at the wall. The glass shattered, raining down over the floor. Before he could control himself, he threw the bottle of whiskey in the same spot and watched, with a hollowed, empty feeling, as the golden liquid splattered against the wall and slid down in streaks.

He wasted an expensive bottle of whiskey, only half consumed, and he didn't feel an ounce of remorse. The only guilt he felt was his behavior toward Susan.

What a dick. A complete and absolute dick.

It just showed how unworthy he was of someone as sweet and pure as her.

He went to bed, barely sleeping a wink, and walked into work the next morning with the foulest mood he had had in a long time. Even Stacey didn't try to speak to him to find out the problem, and she normally didn't shy away from him.

By mid-morning, he still hadn't wiped clear the bad mood and figured he should've rescheduled his next client for another day. He didn't.

When John walked in to get the tattoo he worked hard on in remembrance of his son he lost, he attempted to clear his mind of any negative thoughts. About the only thing he could be thankful for as he started to apply the stencil to John's back was his wrist felt good today. Strong and healthy, as if it never gave him problems.

The tattoo was big, covering the majority of John's back. It would take several sittings. Today they would tackle the outline. Despite his sour mood, he was looking forward to working. Tattooing, creating art, always pulled him into a Zen-like status. Everything in his life always disappeared. The only thing that mattered was the work of art before him.

He figured out drawing was his escape at an early age. Sketching little scenes as his mother hollered and yelled, sometimes at no one in particular. Drawing pictures in school, drowning out the insensitive and cruel words flung at him.

Then meeting a man on his way home from school one day.

A tattoo artist.

Tattooing saved his life.

Drawing calmed him down. Tattooing centered his entire world into peace.

Several hours later, a small twinge in his wrist said it was time to quit for the day. He sadly had two more clients in the afternoon. He hated to do it, but he'd move them to Jensen's schedule. There were certain perks to being the boss.

Those few hours gave him some peace he had been lacking since last night. It gave him some clarity into the situation he created.

He needed to apologize to Susan. She deserved an explanation instead of a big ol' screw you.

A loud knock sounded on his door as he was clearing up the mess from John's session. Before he could deny the person entry, the door swung open.

"Is there still a bug up your ass?" Stacey asked as she chomped her gum, then blew a bubble and popped it with a loud snap.

Dangerous, spiteful words sat on the tip of his tongue, especially since she knew he hated when she chewed and snapped her gum like that. It was one of his worst pet peeves. Like nails on a damn chalkboard.

She snapped her gum again. "You got a visitor, Mr. Crabby Pants. I'll send him back."

Before he could disagree, she stepped back and slammed his door shut. He flinched, suddenly exhausted from the day, from the harrowing emotions swarming his system and invading his veins like a needle filled with drugs.

He wanted to go home and think about the right words to say to Susan, not deal with whoever had the misfortune to walk through that door, because he wasn't sure he'd be pleasant with the person.

When a soft knock sounded on the door, he grumbled for them to enter and went back to clearing up his mess. He couldn't hide his surprise when Sauer opened the door.

"Deena okay?"

Sauer nodded with a huge smile. "She's much better." Sauer ran a hand through his hair as he stepped farther into the room. "She told the ladies last night that we're expecting our first child, and I can already see a small weight has lifted off her shoulders. I mean, the worry is still there that she'll be a terrible mother, but she seemed less stressed. Thank you, Stitch. I don't know what you did, but thank you."

"I didn't do anything." Susan did all the hard work. He figured right then, that's why she must've stopped by his house last night to tell him the news. Instead, he acted like a dick.

"Well, you must've done something. I didn't think she'd ever tell them."

Stitch laughed. "I'm pretty sure a large belly would've been clue enough of what she was trying to hide."

Sauer laughed with him. "True enough. I didn't mean to bother you again. I wanted to tell you in person thank you. Whatever you did, or may not have done, thank you." He glanced at his watch and groaned. "I better go. I had to make this quick. I don't want to leave Newman alone at a crime scene without me, especially when I know Susan will be there. Thanks again."

Sauer turned around to walk out. Stitch rounded the chair standing between them with a speed he wasn't accustomed to using and stopped him from leaving with a firm hand to the shoulder. Sauer flinched and jumped as he looked at him.

He dropped his hand. "What the hell are you talking about? Is Susan okay?"

Confusion sprinkled Sauer's face, which didn't concern him. The shock that lit up his eyes should've, but it didn't. He needed to know Susan was okay, and by that semi-cryptic statement, it didn't sound promising.

"Uh...she's fine. They...it's been tense at work lately."

Why didn't he know this? Why didn't she tell him?

Well, that didn't take a genius to figure out. Because he didn't want anything more from her than sex.

"Have you..." Sauer hesitated, his cheeks turning a slight shade of red. "Have you seen Susan since the ball?"

A fair question. One he deserved to be asked, especially with the way he reacted to hearing her name. He almost knocked Sauer down when he tried to stop him from leaving.

"I've seen her here and there. If she's having a problem, I'd like to know."

Sauer nodded but didn't say anything.

"Well?"

He averted his eyes, his cheeks turning a darker shade of red. "It's...it's a work thing."

"Tell me, Sauer."

Maybe it was the tone of his voice, sharp and foreboding, but Sauer's head snapped in his direction. They stared hard at each other.

"Do you like Susan?"

"None of your damn business."

"If you want me to talk about her, then it's my business."

He wasn't in the mood to tell Sauer shit about his relationship, or lack thereof, with Susan. Sauer might be Deena's husband, but he'd hit the guy if he had to. If Susan had a problem, especially with a guy, he wanted to know.

"You don't scare me, Stitch."

"Why, because you think I won't take a swing because you're married to Deena?"

"She'd be upset if you did that, but no. I can hold my own in a fight, if that's what you're gearing for. Susan is my friend." He hesitated, then his eyes narrowed. "I'm not about to add more issues on her plate by telling you anything if you're going to add to her problems."

He already added to her problems last night, but Sauer didn't need to know that. He still owed her an apology.

"Forget it. I'll ask her myself."

"Just know one thing, Stitch. Susan's my friend, and *nobody* hurts my friends."

Well, if he didn't know any better, Sauer just threatened him. It was almost laughable, because Sauer didn't scare him one bit. But he didn't laugh. Because he needed someone to say shit like that to him.

He might end up hurting her even more than he already had. Someone needed to beat the shit out of him when he did.

Sauer could be the guy to do it.

THIS GUY WAS ESCALATING, and quickly. This was the third death in less than a week. Three women. No connections. No evidence at any scene...that she knew about yet. She was still currently processing the third scene.

All strangled. All raped.

For once in her life, she didn't have any motivation to do her job. She felt tired and weary. Everything happening in her life was starting to bring her down and hold her there with no room to breathe. She could feel herself drowning and she didn't know how to rise back to the surface to take a breath.

It didn't help walking into work this morning and having her boss breathe down her neck once again for something so petty and ridiculous, she stood there and took it. She always voiced her opinion in a respectful and thoughtful manner. But today, she was so thrown and confused, she stood there as Scott berated her for going into the evidence room and logging out evidence for one of Rachel's cases without asking her first. So laughable.

One, because she never touched any of Rachel's cases.

Two, because someone came into her office last week and took one of her files and Scott brushed it off as a co-worker borrowing a file.

Now he was yelling at her for supposedly doing the same thing. How dare him.

Except, so stunned, she walked out without defending herself. Without telling him she never touched any evidence in Rachel's case. It had to be Rachel creating this mess. Which meant she forged her signature on the evidence log. It shouldn't be too hard to solve that little problem. She could have Gus look at the surveillance tapes to see who signed her name. Then she could shove the evidence in Scott's face and watch as Rachel was taken down a peg or two.

Well, if it turned out Rachel did it.

It had to be her. Who else would do something so cruel and vicious?

She didn't even ask if the evidence logged out was opened and contaminated in any way. It would've been a good question to ask. Speaking one little word would've been good.

She figured nothing too terrible occurred since he only reamed her out for logging the evidence out, not screwing with it somehow.

She never touched other cases that weren't hers, unless someone asked her to. He should know that. He should know her. Trust her.

That's what hurt. He obviously had no faith in her.

"Hey, Susan. How's it going?"

She blinked a few times, unaware she had zoned out in the kitchen of the third victim's home and turned around to Sauer, who stood a few feet away.

For his benefit, she produced a smile. "I'm fine. I found a few prints on these wine glasses. I'm sure some are from the victim. I'm hoping the other prints are from the killer. Which means..."

He nodded. She obviously didn't need to finish the sentence. If the victim was sharing a glass of wine with her killer, it meant she let the person in. She knew the killer. The other two victims' homes didn't have any indication their homes were broken into. Perhaps this killer knew all the women. The only problem was, so far, Sauer and Newman hadn't found a connection between the women. If they all knew the killer, then did they know each other as well?

"Umm...so...no problems, then?"

She smiled, hoping to ease the stress written all over Sauer's face and in his posture. It was sweet of him to worry, but she didn't want any of her friends to do that. She was fine. She could handle this. She could handle Newman and his attitude problem. She could handle anything thrown her way. At least, that's what she kept telling herself.

"No problems, but thanks for asking."

She made sure there were no problems. As soon as she walked into the house, she beelined it to the farthest room from Newman. Talking to him, even breathing the same air next to him, was too much to handle after the latest incident with Scott. The kitchen appeared to be the safest place. Newman, as far as she knew, was still in the victim's bedroom. She'd tackle that room as soon as he left, which he should be doing soon since Sauer finally made it.

"Umm...so..."

She eyed Sauer quizzically as he stuttered over his words once again. He clearly wanted to ask her something but was afraid to. She always found his nervousness and shyness so endearing. He was one of the sweetest men she knew.

"Honestly, Sauer, I'm fine. You guys have to stop worrying about me."

He cleared his throat, his cheeks turning a slight shade of pink, and smiled crookedly. "I know. I wasn't going to say anything about Newman again. I was going to..."

Her brows dipped farther, even more confused now about what he wanted to say.

Then his eyes glossed to her finger that she had wrapped with a band-aid instead of the bulky gauze. It was slowly starting to heal. Today was the first morning where she was able to let the wound breathe and it didn't hurt to touch.

"I wanted to ask how your finger is."

"It's fine. I'm fine. Everything is fine."

Maybe if she repeated the word *fine* enough, she'd actually believe it. Because everything wasn't fine. Everything was a complete cluster. She had no idea how to fix any of it.

"Well, if you need me, you know I'll be there in a heartbeat."

"I know that. Thank you, Sauer."

She knew she'd never bring any of her problems to his doorstep. Especially the one concerning Stitch. Talk about awkward when his wife was Stitch's best friend.

Stitch.

Now, that was a man she didn't even want to think about. But like a glutton for punishment, she couldn't stop thinking about him since she left his house last night.

Damn him for playing her as he had.

And damn her for falling into his sexy, dirty charm.

Thankfully, Sauer and Newman left not too long after her slightly awkward conversation with Sauer to interview the neighbors. Hopefully, someone saw something because, so far, all three cases were lacking in any clues that pointed to a killer.

According to Sauer, when they talked about the case yesterday, Tonya, the first victim, her ex-husband, Chris, had no alibi, claiming he was home by himself sleeping and couldn't provide any clues for who would want to hurt Tonya. He said they had been having issues lately because they shared custody of their dog, which had created a lot of tension during the divorce. He claimed it wasn't something he'd kill her over. Sauer wasn't sure what he thought about the guy, and without any evidence to put him at the crime scene, he couldn't arrest him even without an alibi.

The second victim's family and friends couldn't provide any additional information to aid in the case, and most of them had a solid alibi.

So far, Chris was their only suspect because he had no alibi, but they couldn't find any evidence he knew the second victim, and she figured Sauer would start right away finding a link to the third if he could.

Stress emanated from the guys at having to find this killer, using pure skill with no evidence to help their case. She didn't envy them one bit. Her job was to find a tiny scrap of evidence to help lead them in a certain direction. So far, she'd been failing miserably.

After dusting for prints over almost every available surface, training her eyes to pick up any anomalies in the house, tagging and bagging evidence in the bedroom where the victim died, she was ready to go home and crash. With all that meticulous hard work, taking her time in each room, checking windowsills for tampering or prints, dusting door-knobs, taking swabs of blood samples from a few smears in the bedroom, she couldn't believe she had been at the crime scene for over five hours. She usually took her time, but it generally didn't take her that long unless the crime scene was a disaster. This one wasn't terrible. Although, it did appear as pristine as the second crime scene, as if the killer cleaned up and replaced anything that might've been displaced during a struggle.

She was optimistic about the blood she found. The first two crime scenes didn't have a speck of blood, considering all the women had been strangled. The latest victim didn't have any wounds or bruises that she could see to indicate the blood was hers. Perhaps Dr. Everly would find a wound during the autopsy that she hadn't seen. Or, maybe the blood came from the killer when the victim tried to fight back. That's what she was hoping.

By the time she made it home, her body was so exhausted and tired, she didn't know if she'd make it from the garage to the house. The entire day, everything that happened, wore her out.

She closed the garage door with a touch of a button and disarmed her alarm as she walked inside the house.

She needed a shower. She felt dirty and disgusting. A normal feeling after working a crime scene. Her shower was longer than normal as she let the hot stream of water soothe her weary bones. Her mind wandered over everything.

Should she rescind her application for the supervisor position?

Should she take a vacation to get her mind back to a restful place?

Should she accuse Rachel of trying to frame her for something she didn't do? Well, she would as soon as she had the evidence to prove it. She'd talk to Gus tomorrow to look at the surveillance video for the evidence room.

When the water started to chill her to the bone, she knew it was time to get out. After drying off, she wrapped herself in her thin blue robe and couldn't decide if she should go to bed right away or watch some television or a movie. Or even grab a bite to eat. She hadn't eaten supper yet.

At that moment, her stomach grumbled loudly. Chuckling, she knew then what her decision would be. Food.

Scrounging through her pantry and fridge, she couldn't decide what to eat. Nothing looked appetizing. She should eat. Her stomach was telling her to eat, yet she couldn't make up her mind.

Her eyes glossed over some salad, the leftover chicken dinner from two days ago, and the fixings for a sandwich. Not one thing appealed to her.

Maybe she could order Chinese food. That sounded yummy. And easy. She wouldn't have to make anything or heat anything up, just a simple phone call.

She started to dig through her purse that rested on the kitchen counter near the garage door when her doorbell rang. Glancing at the microwave, she wondered who was visiting, although, it wasn't horribly late.

8:06 PM.

The doorbell rang again before she could reach the door. As soon as she looked through the peephole, she figured she should change first. Being completely naked underneath her robe, a robe that was thin and almost see-through, didn't seem like the smartest idea when she had to open the door to Stitch. Even though she was as mad as a hornet at the man, her body instantly responded to seeing him.

The doorbell rang once again.

Clearly, he wasn't planning to leave until she opened the door.

Should she open it?

During her shower, she thought of everything that happened recently, her mind jumping in circles, going round and round and round until she felt dizzy trying to come up with a solution to all of her problems.

Except the only thing she didn't think about was Stitch. She didn't want to think about how he took her heart and crumbled it so easily.

But one thing she knew: she never backed away from a challenge. She never ignored her problems. Right now, Stitch was a problem she needed to deal with.

She unlocked the door and slowly opened it. She refused to let the sadness that cloaked his eyes weaken her defenses she had erected the moment she found out he had a girlfriend.

"What do you want, Stitch?"

His eyes grazed up and down. The fire in his eyes instantly made her heart hammer in her chest, made her ache for his touch, for his sweet, dirty words.

"Are you naked underneath that flimsy-ass robe?" His breath hitched. "Damn, Suzy baby, you have no idea what you do to me."

8

HE COULDN'T STOP his eyes from grazing her delectable body one more time. By the look on her face, she wasn't appreciating his predatory gaze. What could he say? She got him hot and bothered with one simple look. He couldn't help how he reacted to her.

"If you came looking for sex, you can think again."

He figured that out on his own, but he was hoping this conversation turned in his favor and he'd be getting some before he left. He had to play his cards right, though.

"Can I come in so we can talk?"

Her eyes narrowed. "And how does your girlfriend feel about you coming here to speak to me?"

He tried not to sound exasperated. "She's not my girlfriend." He had no idea how Clarissa was feeling right now. He hadn't spoken to her since last night, and he honestly had no intention of speaking to her anytime soon. Her behavior was out of line last night. He was done trying to help. Perhaps some jail time would clear her head. At this point, he wasn't sure how to help her anymore. Maybe staying away would be the best solution. For both of them.

"So Officer Spencer lied to me? Not likely."

"Look, I don't know what Clarissa might've said to the police, but we haven't dated in a long time."

"So she was once your girlfriend?"

"You gonna hold my past against me, Susan? I didn't think you were that kind of person."

"And I didn't think you were a sniveling dirty snake."

He took a deep breath before responding, his anger slowly building that she wasn't taking his word for what it was—the truth. "We dated when we were nineteen. She's a friend now. Nothing more."

"What was she doing at your house, then? I have to say, Stitch, I'm not friends with any of my ex-boyfriends. I have this feeling if I was, you wouldn't appreciate it much."

His blood started to boil. Hell, no, he wouldn't like that shit. He hated the point she was making, but the fact was, Clarissa was a friend. A friend he couldn't turn his back on. He wouldn't. Not even for Susan. Not even if Clarissa was starting to become a pain in his ass.

He might not be prepared to go see her, but if she showed up on his doorstep again, he knew he'd never shove her away, even if he wanted to with every breath in his body. It was messed up, but he couldn't change the way he felt.

"Can you please let me in so we can talk about this without your neighbors gawking at us?"

She made a point to look behind him, her eyes widening with mock horror. "Oh, my. I see no one paying attention to my front door. So, no, I don't think I want you to come in so you can try to weasel your way into my bed, because that's ultimately your end game, isn't it?"

His jaw clenched at how well she read him. Of course he wanted back into her bed. Every time they had sex, it got better and better. Usually, sex was sex. But with Susan, the crazy things they did together was something he couldn't express properly with words. Each time they came together, it stepped up a notch in those nameless words.

"I'm sorry how I acted last night, but she's not my girl-friend. She's a friend who needed some help. Before I could stop her, it got out of hand."

"What does that even mean?"

His hands clenched and unclenched. Explaining would take more time than she was obviously willing to give him. He didn't want to have this kind of conversation on her doorstep. Hell, he didn't want to have the conversation at all. But he would. He'd force himself if she let him inside.

"Can I come inside...please?"

The anger slowly drifted out of her features. Now she looked sad and tired. "Not tonight, Stitch. I'm exhausted. I can't do this with you." She swallowed hard before whispering with her voice cracking a bit, "I thought I could do a casual fling with you. But that's not who I am. I want more from a guy. I want commitment. If you can't give me that, then we're done here."

His heart had never been broken by a woman before. He never let a woman in that far to let it happen. For the first time, he felt a small tear in his heart. A tiny seepage of pain that made it difficult to breathe.

He wasn't ready to lose Susan, even though he knew it'd never work out. Commitment? He wasn't that kind of guy, especially for a woman like her. Someone pure and sweet and as fresh as a drop of rain.

"Your silence is answer enough." The door started to slowly close. "Take care of yourself, Stitch."

The door shut with a quiet click.

He stood there for a brief moment wondering whether he should knock on the door again. Beg forgiveness some more. Weasel his way back into her bed with empty promises. That's how badly he didn't want to walk away. But that's all those promises would be. Empty. Irrevocably empty.

Well, he could say it was fun while it lasted.

He turned around and walked away.

Susan rubbed her hands over her pants, trying to wipe away the nerves that had suddenly flooded her system.

She had to admit, she was still reeling from Stitch's visit last night. She gave him an ultimatum, and he made the choice she dreaded as soon as the words slipped out.

Sure, she could've let him inside to talk about his friend that was supposedly not his girlfriend. She sensed there was a big story behind their friendship and that he was willing to tell her, but only if she let him inside. But where did that leave them? She'd have more knowledge of who he was, what kind of man he was, and her heart would soak it all up. He couldn't—wouldn't—offer more than sex, so why should she continue to open her heart to him? She'd only end up hurt after it was all said and done. Feeling the pain now, only a tiny bit, rather than struggling to mend her heart down the road, sounded like the better option.

She made the right decision, even if it didn't feel like the right one. Casual sex wasn't her thing. She didn't sleep with men just for the pleasure of sex. She had meaningful relationships before they all fell apart. That's what she wanted from him. That's what she should've insisted from him before they slept together.

Lesson learned.

She wouldn't fall into that mistake again.

One problem solved in her life.

Now she had to fix another, but she found it difficult to move her feet forward and enter the evidence room. She wanted vindication, the proof she didn't do what she was accused of. She also wanted to ignore it. Because she felt so tired. Exhausted from everything.

Swiping her hands across her pants one more time, she took a deep breath and pushed open the door that would lead her to the evidence room at the end of the hallway.

She produced a friendly smile as she greeted Gus, who sat at a desk behind a caged window. "How's your morning going, Gus?"

"Oh, same ol', same ol', Susan. And yours?"

"You know me, busy bee." Her smile got brighter, more intense, as did her nerves. "So, hey, I was wondering if you could do me a favor."

"Yeah, sure thing. What can I do for you?"

This might get a little tricky. Because she didn't want to insinuate he wasn't doing his job by not paying attention who signed in and when. When she thought about it, he didn't usually glance at the signature when she signed in and out of the evidence room; he always looked at her face. She didn't blame him. He didn't need to look at the sheet when he knew who it was. Which was what Rachel probably relied on when she forged her signature. Saying all of that would indicate he didn't do his job correctly. Unfortunately, as much as she didn't want to point it out, it was the truth.

"Well, you know, Scott mentioned to me that I signed out some of Rachel's evidence the other day, and I didn't. I was wondering if we could look over the forms and the videos to see why he'd think that." She blew out a tiny breath that she hoped he didn't see, and waited with her entire body coiled with tension that he wouldn't take offense.

Gus's eyes narrowed, a frown marring his features. The friendliness they exchanged moments before suddenly gone.

"I don't recall you signing out someone else's evidence. You don't do things like that."

Thank you, Gus. Why couldn't her boss have that same faith in her? That trust? Not to mention, it sounded like Scott didn't even talk to Gus about the incident, he only took Rachel's word for it.

"Right, I don't. Except Scott thinks I did, and he didn't seem too happy about it. Can we take a quick peek?"

The frown on his face wouldn't disappear. Her heart started to pound that he would dismiss her and perhaps cause more waves with Scott. Definitely not something she needed.

"Yeah, let's do that. It doesn't make any sense." A gradual smile appeared.

With that, her heart rate slowed, the nerves slowly disappeared, and relief took its place.

Finally, something going in her favor.

Problem two almost solved.

That left problem number three to take care of.

Newman and his attitude problem.

9

NEWMAN TRIED to keep his cool as Sauer went down the list of all the victims' known friends and family. So far, nobody stuck out to them knowing all three victims. They were assuming they had to have known the killer. Otherwise, how did the killer get inside their homes? The last victim even appeared to have shared a glass of wine with her killer. Did Susan get any good evidence from that?

Shit...Susan.

He didn't want to think about her, or think about the complete asshole he had been to her lately. Why? Because his own life was complete hell.

He knew what he had done was wrong. When he made the formal complaint to her boss, he hadn't been in his right mind. The anger and fear had taken control, forcing him to act out. Stopping that erratic behavior was starting to become harder and harder to ignore.

Glancing at a photo of the first victim, Tonya Moretta, he knew what his erratic behavior cost him. He didn't know how long he'd be able to hide his dirty secret from Sauer.

From everybody. Eventually, everyone would know. Where would that leave him?

Jobless, perhaps. Friendless, even. Up shit creek without a paddle. Hell, he was already there.

"So, victim number one, Tonya, was divorced, a school teacher, loved by her students and faculty. We can't place the ex-husband knowing the other two victims, but he has no alibi for any of the murders, claiming he was home alone asleep. Victim number two, Bethany, was single, living with a friend from her high school days, and a dental hygienist who wasn't always gentle while working. There could be some irritable people looking for revenge."

Newman cocked an exaggerated brow at the last statement.

Sauer chuckled. "Okay. Yeah, that's reaching a bit. Victim number three, Amber, was a recent college grad, who doesn't appear to have any problems in her life that we found yet." Sauer sighed heavily. "So the million dollar question, how did they know the same person, if they even knew the killer?"

"There's gotta be a connection somewhere." He didn't want to think about what the connection was. In fact, he wanted to pretend these murders never happened, because then it would seem like his life wasn't spiraling out of control.

"Why don't we go interview Amber's boss at the clothing store she worked at. We should also head to the university and speak to her professors. We'll find this killer."

Newman offered a lame smile and stood up to toss his jacket on. Yeah, they'd find the killer. In the process, Sauer would probably learn the truth about him.

He wasn't looking forward to that day.

He had lost so much already. When Sauer found out the truth, he'd lose everything else.

Susan knocked confidently on Scott's door and waited patiently while he finished a phone call and then gestured her inside his office. She didn't want to be nervous, especially with the proof she went searching for, but she couldn't deny the nerves were there.

"What's up?"

She smiled casually as she sat down in front of his desk, even though there wasn't an ounce of friendliness behind the smile. While she should tread carefully, considering he was her boss and she was applying for a position she wasn't even sure she wanted anymore, she couldn't hold back the satisfaction that she was about to decimate Rachel and her precious reputation with Scott.

"First, I wanted to say how much I did not appreciate being reprimanded for something I didn't do. For not having faith in me that I wouldn't do something like that. It hurt, Scott."

She almost couldn't suppress the pleasure at the way his jaw dropped at her candid words. He should know she wasn't one to hold back. She normally said what she felt, but in a professional, kind manner. Not today. Not when he popped her bubble of trust she had for him.

"Look, Susan. You can't—"

"I wasn't finished."

His eyes narrowed as she interrupted him.

"Rachel and I have always had a strained working relationship. She clearly doesn't want me to get the supervisor position because she had to resort to some underhanded behavior, which I take offense to."

"Rachel would never do something like that."

Those words, for some strange reason, confirmed to her that he was, indeed, sleeping with Rachel. Her stomach started to churn with disgust, bile rising to her throat at the thought.

She set the evidence log and video Gus graciously made a copy of in front of Scott.

"Since evidence is our forte, I figured you'd appreciate some to prove I didn't go into the evidence room and log any of her evidence out. In fact," she tapped the top of the CD case that held the video hard, "you'll find evidence that Rachel forged my name and logged it out herself. And if you still don't believe me, or your own eyes, you can speak to Gus about it."

Scott glanced between her and the things lying on his desk, his eyes distrustful, yet wary, almost a hint of guilt as well.

She stood up. "I might not be the right person for the job, but neither is Rachel. And you shouldn't be making the ultimate decision about who gets the job," she paused for effect, "especially when you're sleeping with her."

His jaw dropped. No words came out.

She held his gaze for a few beats, waiting for him to deny the truth, which he couldn't do since he *was* sleeping with her, then turned around and walked out, satisfied with the way that went. She'd take him speechless any day over his berating words and tone of voice.

That problem was officially completed.

How did she solve the problem with Newman?

Maybe if she ignored him and did her job as best as she could it would disappear on its own.

Yep. That would be her plan. Because she was fresh out of energy to deal with any more problems. At least, for the day.

Tomorrow was a new story.

"Hey, Susan."

She smiled wide—extra wide since she was feeling mighty proud of herself—at Zeke, as he met her by her office door.

"How's it going?"

"Just fine." The worry that had been lining his face slowly disappeared as a smile took its place. "I was about to ask you how you're doing, but you look like you're in a good mood."

Oddly enough, even though part of her life was swaying towards pitiful, she was in a good mood. Not much would be able to bring it down.

"I'm great. You guys have to stop checking in on me and seeing how I am doing. I'm fine."

Today, saying she was fine, she meant it, felt more fortified saying it.

"I know, I know. We can't help it. You're our friend." His smile grew. "So, Zoe asked me to pass a message along. Instead of girls' night out Friday, she thought a small get-together at our house to celebrate Dee and Sauer having a baby would be fun. What do you think?"

Her eyes lit up with pleasure as a giddy feeling washed over her. "That's a fabulous idea. Dee needs as much support as we can give her right now. We need to help keep her stress level down."

Zeke nodded. "Yeah, that's what Zoe was saying. So, about seven work for you?"

"Works perfect. Who's going to be there?"

She figured Newman would be invited since he was

Sauer's partner, but she needed confirmation so she could mentally prepare herself. Dealing with him lately was a testament to her restraint.

"Ben and Rina. Sauer and Dee, of course. Newman." He rolled his eyes. "Unfortunately, we have to invite him."

"It's fine, Zeke. He's Sauer's friend."

"Doesn't mean I like how he's been acting lately."

"Do you need me to bring anything?"

"No, we have it all covered. I'll let Zoe know you'll be able to make it." Zeke grinned as he started to turn to leave.

"Sounds great."

Susan pulled out her office key, unwilling to trust her coworkers to leave her office unlocked while she wasn't around. As she unlocked the door and turned the handle, Zeke turned back toward her and snapped his fingers.

The sound startled her, making her twitch a bit, but not a full-blown jump to embarrass herself that such a simple gesture would scare her.

"I forgot to mention that Stitch will be there, too. That's it. Small, like I said."

A tiny smile graced her face, but she found it difficult to hold. "Oh...that's great."

"Yeah, it'll be nice to get everyone together." He sighed heavily. "Well, besides Newman. I haven't seen Stitch since the ball. It'll be nice to catch up with him. He seemed like a decent guy."

She knew her smile would crumble at any moment, even the possibility of tears streaming down her face. As much as she didn't want to appear rude, she couldn't stand to break down in front of Zeke. Then she'd have to explain why she was having a meltdown.

"I'll see you Friday. I have tons of work to get done." She

pushed open her door and closed it quickly, not even waiting for a reply.

Flipping the lock, not necessarily worried that Zeke would question her about her behavior, but more so to keep out any other coworkers that decided they needed her for something.

Right now, she needed to be alone. She needed to process the fact she'd have to see Stitch. Be in the same house, even the same room as him.

She gave him an ultimatum last night, one she knew he wouldn't take in her favor. It still hurt to think about, to know she wasn't good enough for him, or whatever lame excuses he wanted to use with her. He actually thought he wasn't good enough for her. That he would ruin her chances for the supervisor position.

Well, big news flash, especially for him, it wasn't looking good to begin with, and it had nothing to do with him. Now she wasn't even sure she wanted the dumb position.

Honestly, she wasn't sure what she wanted.

She told him she wanted commitment and she wouldn't settle for anything less. At the time, she meant it.

Right now, especially last night when she longed for him in her bed, she regretted her words.

She missed him. His laughter and wry sense of humor. His sultry talk and sexy words that ignited her body instantly. His glowing golden-brown eyes that, when he looked at her, felt as if he were undressing each article of her clothing with slow and delicious precision. His company when, most nights, she was alone with her own thoughts.

She just missed him.

Despite that melancholy feeling, she knew she wouldn't accept anything less from him but what she deserved. She deserved to be more than just a bedroom toy, a means to an end, a way to scratch his itch.

Here she thought she wouldn't have to deal with him again. Well, she had a long, lonely night and a full day ahead of her tomorrow before she had to put her defenses in place and pretend like he didn't have any power over her.

She could do it.

She could pretend he didn't sneak into her heart and completely steal it away with little effort.

She could act nice and feign indifference.

She could totally do that.

A lone tear slid down her cheek as she took a seat at her desk.

If she kept repeating it, maybe it would ring true.

She could do it.

STITCH GLANCED up from the tiny sketch he was working on as the stupid bell Stacey wanted to hang above the door rang with merry. What was so merry about the day?

A client canceled his appointment, and instead of tattooing to occupy his time, he was hanging out in the front of the shop holding down the fort for Stacey.

He sure in the hell didn't want to deal with this guy either. Absolutely nothing was merry about the conversation they were about to have, even if he didn't know the reason for his visit. He knew he wouldn't like it.

"What do you want, Sauer? This is becoming a little too regular, these visits from you. I don't like it."

Sauer's brows puckered low. "Sometimes, I wonder how you and Dee became friends."

"Is that why you're here? To break up our friendship."

"No, you asshole, I'm here to invite you to a party."

Stitch laughed, especially when Sauer's assertiveness came out of nowhere. Not many people could get away with calling him an asshole, even if he was acting like one. When it came out of Sauer, the same guy who could blush like a red tomato at his wife for saying something outrageous, it was hilarious. He couldn't hold back the laughter.

"I'm not sure what you find funny."

Leaning forward over the counter, resting his elbows down and his forearms stretched out, he smirked. "You're just a funny guy sometimes, Sauer. What kind of *fun* party are you inviting me to?"

"A...I don't know...congratulations of sorts because we're expecting our first child." Sauer's features softened. "It was Zoe's idea. I think it'll help calm down Dee some. I think that's why Zoe decided to do it. I'm thankful she has such wonderful friends." He started to frown. "And you're her friend. She'd like to see you there."

Standing tall, he tried not to let any expression show as he contemplated going. Would Susan be there? Should he ask? If she would be, should he go? Would she want him there?

"Zoe wants a head count. Will you be there tomorrow night around seven?"

Stitch had no idea. He wanted to be there for Deena. Yet, he didn't want to be around Susan. Around the reminder of how dumb he could be. He let a good woman get away. Why? What damn reason did he have to let her get away?

None. He had no good reason.

Well, that was a lie.

Maybe two good reasons.

One, because he wasn't lying when he said he could

honestly ruin her chances at snagging the supervisor position she applied for.

And two...a reason he didn't even want to admit.

He was scared to let her in completely.

Problem was she had already penetrated his defenses. That small crack in his heart from last night was simmering and smoldering and slowly growing into a deep sinkhole.

"Stitch? I need an answer, not silence." Sauer's eyes narrowed. "Susan will be there."

A lame chuckle escaped. "Is that another warning, or an incentive to come?"

Laughter finally found its way into Sauer's demeanor. His face lit up with amusement. "I have no idea, actually. Maybe a bit of both. I don't know what's going on with you and Susan, but...Susan deserves a good man. Are you that kind of guy? Do I need to issue another warning?"

Swallowing hard, unsure of how he wanted to answer, if he even wanted to answer that, he shrugged, figuring Sauer could interpret that any way he wanted. *He* didn't even know how to interpret it. "I'll be there. Where's it at?"

"Zeke and Zoe's." Sauer started for the front door. The stupid bell rang merrily once again. Before Sauer stepped outside, he turned toward him. "Thank you, Stitch. Dee will be happy to see you."

The door shut. He was left alone in his shop to his wandering thoughts. Stacey left to grab lunch, so not even her annoying voice could fill the space. Right now, he needed something, anything, to distract him. Because all he could think about was Susan.

Sweet, sexy Susan.

His Susan.

Damn right his.

She wanted commitment. Well, he wasn't a commitment

kind of guy. Never tried it before. But for her, he'd give it a shot.

This aching hole forming in his heart was too much. He didn't like it. He didn't know how to handle it. If letting Susan have her way with commitment got him back into her life, her bed, he'd give her what she wanted. Because, no matter which angle he looked at it, eventually everything would fall apart. It always did in his life. They could enjoy each other, with the word commitment thrown in there if it made her feel better, but ultimately, they weren't headed for forever. He wanted to enjoy every second with her that he could.

Yeah, Susan was *his*.

She'd damn well know it tomorrow night.

10

THE WINE GLASS slammed down hard on the dining room table. "I can't take it. What's up with the scowl, Dee? This is supposed to be a fun party, not angry and depressing," Zoe said as she pierced Dee with a hard glare.

Susan took a sip of her drink, glancing back and forth between Zoe and Dee as they had a stare down of sorts. Rina sat next to her doing the same exact thing. Susan was glad Zoe finally said something, because since the moment she arrived about an hour ago, Dee had been sullen and moody. The guys had ventured to the living room to chat guy stuff, while they decided to hang out in the dining room sipping their alcoholic and non-alcoholic drinks and talk girl talk.

Right now, she was happy to be separated from the guys. She didn't have to force herself not to stare at Stitch or make weird eye contact with him, as they had when he walked into the house shortly after her. To stop herself from trying to peer into the living room, which she could see slightly from the dining room, she sat with her back to it. She didn't want to fall into the temptation to keep seeking him out. She needed to accept the fact there would never be anything between them and move on.

"Well? I can sit here all night staring at you, waiting for you to spill the beans." Zoe reached out a hand toward Dee and whispered, "Are you still worrying about what kind of mother you'll be? Because you'll be fantastic. This stress isn't good for the baby."

Dee's eyes turned down, which was an unusual gesture for her. "It's not." She glanced back up and smiled at Zoe. "But thank you for the reassurance."

"So what's wrong? You know you can tell us anything," Rina replied softly.

A heavy sigh released as Dee's scowl deepened. "I happen to like makeup sex, but I don't like the fighting part that happens beforehand."

"What are you and Sauer fighting about?" The worry on Zoe's face increased. "Is everything okay?"

Dee's eyes swiveled to the living room, her eyes narrow and foreboding. Susan almost chuckled as she imagined laser beams shooting from her eyes. She had never seen her so angry before. And at Sauer, she couldn't imagine what they were arguing about to make her so upset.

"I told Sauer I didn't want Newman here. He still had to invite that jackass." Dee looked at her, her expression softening some. "You shouldn't have to deal with him here, Susan."

"Thanks for looking out for me, but I don't want you and Sauer arguing for that reason. I don't want you guys to argue at all. Newman is his partner and friend. I get it." She smiled, more for Dee's benefit rather than wanting to smile.

"It doesn't mean he should treat you the way he is," Dee snapped.

"Well, since Zeke made a formal complaint against him

with Captain Ganderson, a few other guys have stepped up as well. Apparently, Captain Ganderson talked to him today, but Zeke doesn't know what happened or what he said. He's still working, so maybe it was a slap on the wrist." Zoe took a large swallow of wine. "I agree with Susan, though. You and Sauer shouldn't argue about that. Just ignore him."

"I can't," Dee said with a pout. "I told Sauer I think he's hiding something. I don't trust him. He's shady as hell, and I never liked that douche."

Rina chuckled.

"What's so funny, Rina?" Dee asked as she cocked a brow, yet with laughter in her eyes.

"The way you say douche. That's the Dee I know and love. This party is to celebrate you guys expecting your first child, not being upset that Newman had to be invited. Let's have fun."

Dee leaned over and gave Rina an awkward hug, since neither stood up to give a proper one. "You're right, of course. Always my voice of reason."

"Ooo, I know what we can talk about that sounds like fun," Zoe said a little bit too cheery as she gave her a side-glance.

Susan had to admit, she didn't like the little teasing glimmer in her eyes.

"You're obviously dying with anticipation. Spill it already, Zoe," Dee said with a laugh.

The tension in the room immediately evaporated as soon as they heard Dee's laughter. A beautiful sound.

"Yeah, spill, Susan," Zoe said mischievously, as she looked her directly in the eye.

Her face turned beet red as three sets of eyes looked her way. She didn't want the attention on her. Although she was happy Dee was back in a good mood, she'd rather have the attention on her.

"About...what?" Her brows dipped into a frown. "I don't want to talk about work drama. It's been a stressful week. I want to forget about it for the weekend."

Zoe still had a wicked smile as she took a sip of wine and shook her head. "That's not what I'm talking about. You know."

Zoe couldn't possibly be talking about Stitch. There's no way she could know. Nobody knew that they hooked up and broke up within days. They weren't exactly cloak-and-dagger about seeing each other, but they also didn't announce to their friends what was going on. Could she really know?

Well, she wasn't about to go there, if that wasn't what she was talking about.

"I have no idea what you're talking about."

They broke their gaze with her to look behind her. She turned slightly to see what caught their attention, only to connect eyes with Stitch, whose expression lit up with desire immediately. She could see the fire in his eyes, the delicious intent in his smile. He winked as he disappeared down the hallway where she assumed he was going to use the bathroom.

When she turned back to the table, all three of them stared at her in shock and a little bit of giddiness.

"Do you and Stitch have a thing going on?" Dee leaned forward toward her as she whispered the question she *so* did not want to answer.

"What makes you think that?" Susan wasn't prepared to answer that, if ever.

"Because he sure in the hell didn't wink at any of us," Dee said with a laugh.

"He's your best friend. I'm sure he was winking at you." Why in the world would he be winking at her? She demanded commitment and he threw it back in her face. If he thought he could keep jerking her around, he was mistaken.

Dee shook her head no adamantly. "Nope. He doesn't wink at me. Ever." Her jaw dropped as true happiness lit up her face. "Did you sleep with him?"

"Geez, Dee, talk a little louder. I'm not sure all the guys heard you," she said a little too snippily.

"Damn, ladies, do you hear the denial in her tone? She has a thing for Stitch." Dee chuckled with Zoe and Rina.

"He's hot as hell. And a total sweetheart. It'd be great if you guys got together. You make an adorable couple," Zoe said.

Adorable couple?

He was at least five or six inches taller than her. He had tattoos lining his body, whereas her skin was free and clear. He was arrogant and cocky and all too confident. She was firm, yet timid in ways that she hated to admit. He had the bad boy persona written all over him. She probably looked like the girl next door. Unfortunately, as he pointed out, he had a criminal record. She worked for the police department.

Adorable was not how she would describe them. Completely mismatched was more like it.

Rina smiled and nodded, but thankfully didn't add her two cents to the conversation. Susan didn't need any more words to shove the dagger that was centered in her heart in any further. They thought they were encouraging her, when they were just cementing in her head that he'd never be hers or willing to try a committed relationship. She didn't want to explain everything that happened between them.

"I know that look. Something happened between you two and I'm not getting the good kind of vibes." Dee's smile slowly withered away. "Do I need to kick my best friend's ass for hurting you?"

"No, Dee. I..." The words were there, but difficult to say. "I knew what I was getting myself into. We had fun, and now it's over."

Dee looked perplexed for a second. "So, you're admitting to sleeping with him, that it didn't work out, yet he's winking at you like you might get some tonight. I'm confused. You need to explain from the beginning."

Susan sighed in defeat. She wouldn't be walking away from this table without spilling her guts. Maybe that wasn't such a bad thing. She'd been dying to tell them since the beginning, but was afraid of what they would think. Afraid of what Dee would think. Right now, she didn't look like she had an issue with the thought of them together. Only an issue that it didn't work out.

"Okay, I'll tell you." She grinned. "Are you sure it won't be awkward, because that man...you might need to turn the heat off and turn the air on. It's going to get hot in here."

The entire table roared with laughter, especially Dee, which made Susan as happy as can be. Because in the end, keeping her friend happy and stress free was what she wanted. If she had to do that at her own expense, then so be it.

Talking about Stitch might turn out to be a good thing. Perhaps Dee could give her a little insight into the mind of Stitch. Who better to tell her the good stuff than his best friend growing up.

Two nights ago, she gave him an ultimatum, resigned to the fact it was over.

Now, she saw a little hope in the air she could try to

work things through with him. Maybe help change his mind somehow that they'd be good together. She wasn't ready to lose him from her life.

That smoldering look he gave her a few minutes ago told her exactly how horny she was. Her body reacted instantly, her heart starting the low pitter-patter of anticipation, her body aching and waiting for his touch.

She wanted him.

She decided she would fight for him.

GRIPPING the sides of the sink, he tried hard to keep his cool. Walking past Susan, displaying his intentions with such an obvious wink, might've been the wrong move.

What was Deena thinking? Did she approve? Hate the idea of him and Susan together?

He had no idea what she would think about him dating one of her friends. That wasn't something he had ever done before, and vice versa. They always avoided that territory.

He sincerely hoped Deena didn't disapprove of the idea because he wouldn't be walking away from Susan, not even for his best friend.

Wow. What did that mean? He couldn't believe he even felt that way toward a woman.

When he walked into the house tonight, his palms sweaty, an unusual occurrence for him, he felt like he had been punched in the gut by the sight of her. It didn't matter what she wore. Tonight, dressed in casual jeans and a T-shirt, she was breathtakingly exquisite. He had ached to pull her into his arms, shove her against the wall, tug lightly on that simple ponytail she always wore, and thrust deep inside her right against the wall, be damned that everyone stood in the room, and devour her from head to toe. That's how fired up Susan always got him.

For the last hour, torture like nothing else consumed him, knowing he was in one room and her in another.

His erratic thoughts, his distractions from the conversation going on around him, further cemented the idea that he needed to be with Susan. He needed to give them a chance, even though he knew it was doomed to fail.

He needed to get his shit together in this bathroom, his calm, cool demeanor back in place, and walk out there like everything was good when he wasn't positive if he could control himself. He still wanted to shove her against the wall and love her body like he'd never loved her before.

Three taps and one loud knock sounded on the door.

Shit was about to hit the fan. Only one person would knock on the door while he was in the bathroom.

Deena.

She hated the idea of him and Susan together. Why else would she be knocking on the door? He should've never winked at Susan.

Ignoring her wouldn't make the inevitable argument go away.

He opened the door. Deena stood in the hallway with the most evil smirk he had ever seen.

"So?"

Cocking a brow, he held onto the door for a tiny morsel of support. Which was strange to realize he needed. This was Deena. This was his best friend. His rock through his childhood.

"What? I'm trying to take a piss and you're bugging me, doll. Is this a hormonal thing because of the pregnancy?" He chuckled. "Oh, wait, no, that's you being you. Annoying me at every available opportunity."

She placed a hand to his chest and pushed him inside the bathroom, then shut the door and leaned against it, as if it would keep him inside. As if she could block his escape. Which was something he seriously wanted to do. Escape as fast and far away as possible.

He didn't want to hear what she had to say. He didn't want to tell his best friend to go to hell. Because he would if she said something he didn't like to hear.

What kind of friend did that make him? What kind of friend would act that way over a woman? Not him. But right now, he was all kinds of prepared to do that.

"Is there something you want to tell me?"

Figuring he didn't like how nonchalant she looked, that he needed to display the same kind of composure, even though he was as jittery as if a thousand ants were squirming around his body, he took two steps back and leaned against the sink as if he didn't have a care in the world.

"I don't think so." Lifting a brow, he smirked back. "Is there something you want to tell me?"

Probably a dumb question, but he wanted to end this conversation. Of course, without him being the one starting it.

What he wanted to do was shove her away from the door and run. He'd never do that, of course. Because, one, she was his best friend. Two, she was pregnant. Why did she have to corner him? He felt like a trapped animal, ready to fight for his life.

She pursed her lips, as if she were contemplating how to gut him from head to toe.

"What's the deal with you and Susan?"

Done.

She said it.

She brought it out in the open.

And he had no clue what to say.

He knew he wanted Susan in his life. He knew he would say the words Susan wanted to hear so he could keep her for a little bit longer. He knew they would never work out in the long run. He didn't know how to explain that to Deena, or if he even should. It wasn't any of her business. Did Susan know what Deena was doing? Maybe she did. Did she send her in here?

"You're honestly not going to tell me. Since when do we keep secrets from each other, Stitch?" Deena stepped away from the door and closer to him. "You must like her a lot to keep silent like you are."

"I do like her."

Deena shook her head as she laughed. "That's it? That's all you're going to say?"

He stepped closer and couldn't stop the sneer-like expression as he all but growled, "It's not really any of your damn business, doll."

He was as shocked as her by his words and tone of voice. She backed away to the side, moving away from the door, which gave him the opportunity he had been looking for since she walked into the bathroom. An escape route.

Grabbing the door handle and gripping it hard, he looked at Deena and paused. He knew he shouldn't walk out, but he didn't know what to say. An apology for snapping at her would be a good start. She could also say something to him. Stop him from leaving. Neither said a word.

The door whipped open, his anger skyrocketing. Angry for talking to Deena that way. Angry for not keeping his cool. Angry for letting a woman make him feel this way.

"Stitch, don't leave."

The pressure he was exerting on the handle made his

hand hurt as he stopped at the sound of Deena's soft, whispered words. It was probably a good thing he wasn't holding the handle with his dominant hand because that one already hurt like hell. Just as her words did. All he was doing was hurting his best friend. Hurting Susan. He had no idea how to stop hurting the people he cared about.

He let the handle go and walked away.

Walked away from a friend he had never walked away from. He had never in his life turned his back on Deena and left things hanging like that. Did he push her out of his life years ago? Yeah, but she's the one who walked away back then. Not him. He was better at convincing people to walk away rather than him doing the walking.

Even as much as he wanted to stop moving forward, he couldn't make himself halt. His feet kept going faster and faster until the front door appeared before him. He yanked it open and stepped outside, not looking back once as he fled to his car.

He just ran like a frightened animal. Like a wuss.

Deena didn't deserve that.

As he started his car, the beautiful engine purring like a contented cat, he knew he needed to shut the car off and walk back inside to apologize.

He backed out of the driveway instead.

What the hell happened?

He intended to get Susan back in his life tonight. In turn, he found himself losing his best friend.

What. The. Hell.

11

Susan set her work phone back on the cradle and sighed heavily, hating that she didn't have better news for Sauer. She came into work on her day off, on a Saturday, no less, to get ahead of some of her cases. Sauer and Newman's latest string of murders being one of them. She was starting to make this a bad habit, coming to work on a Saturday when she could be doing something fun on her day off. What was wrong with her?

It creeped her out they had a potential serial killer on their hands, but she also wanted to show Newman she didn't play favorites. She could bump their stuff up as much as she bumped other detectives' stuff up.

Except she had nothing good to inform Sauer. No viable prints came back from the latest victim's home. Not in the house. Not from the wine glass they assumed the killer used. Instead, she found the prints she lifted from both wine glasses were from the victim herself, which would make sense if she grabbed them from the cupboard and filled them up. Which meant the killer must've never touched them. But why would she grab two glasses? She must've been expecting someone to visit.

The blood she found in the bedroom also belonged to the victim. Maybe she was losing her focus, because Dr. Everly confirmed it probably came from the victim when the killer hit her in the nose. He found traces of blood on the inside of her nose, and a small bruise forming on the outside. She didn't notice that when she looked at the victim at the crime scene.

Although, when she thought back, did she really look closely at the victim? If she was losing focus, then she wasn't doing her job as well as she should be. That was unacceptable.

The prints she found in the first victim's home turned out to be prints from the victim herself. No good evidence popped up in the second victim's crime scene either.

So far, they had nothing. She had nothing to help Sauer and Newman find this killer.

Cases like this frustrated her. It made her think she was missing something. Or maybe the killer was just that good.

She had one theory that had been filtering through her mind recently. Since last night, actually, because she couldn't sleep. She couldn't shut her mind off. Thinking about the case had been better than thinking about Stitch and the reason he stormed out of the house without a good-bye to anyone. When Dee came back to the dining room, it was obvious she had talked to Stitch, but she wouldn't say why he left.

Susan wasn't dumb. Because of her. Because Dee didn't like the idea of them dating. But she could never get the question out—why don't you like the idea of us together? When they were talking about it, it didn't seem like she hated the idea. Then she disappeared from the table and

Stitch stormed out of the house. Only one conclusion could be drawn from that: Dee didn't like the idea of them together.

Perhaps that little wink from him meant nothing. He didn't call her last night, or visit. Still no call or visit this morning.

She had been prepared to fight for him. Now the doubts were creeping back in. Did she want to put herself out there like that just to be rejected by him again? Did she want to screw up her friendship with Dee over a guy? Did she want Dee and Stitch's relationship to be ruined because of her?

The answer for each question was a big fat no.

Trying to forget about Stitch brought the case front and center in her mind. That's when her theory popped into her head and she couldn't get it to disappear.

She wasn't a detective. Solving cases wasn't her forte. Collecting evidence and processing it was. Which was why she didn't voice her theory to Sauer. She didn't want to appear stupid and silly.

Because it was. Stupid and silly.

There's no way the killer could be a cop.

"So Susan found no good prints on the wine glasses?" Newman ran a hand through his hair with frustration.

"Nope. We got nothing. Captain Ganderson is up our ass to solve this before another victim pops up. We don't want the FBI to come in and take over." Sauer leaned closer, or as close as he could sitting across from him at his own desk, and whispered, "We have a serial killer on our hands. Three victims, no good evidence, no clues. This asshole knows what he's doing."

Newman couldn't do anything but nod in agreement. What could he say? He agreed with every single word. The one thing he could say would start the downfall of his career, his friendship with Sauer, and basically, his entire life.

But his lie was starting to fester, to burn a hole in the center of his chest. He didn't know how much longer he could keep it to himself before he succumbed to something far worse.

"We went over Tonya's life with a fine-tooth comb and her ex-husband is the only one who sticks out like a sore thumb, and he has no solid alibi. Nobody can corroborate his whereabouts since he claims he was home alone." Sauer swiped an agitated hand through his hair.

Newman's hands started to sweat, his heart started to race, his world as he knew it flashed before his eyes.

He was never going to survive this case.

He could feel Sauer's eyes on him, yet Sauer said nothing. Again, straying away from confrontation. It annoyed the hell out of him when Sauer never spoke up when he thought he should. Sauer knew something was bothering him, yet he wouldn't ask him about it. *Just do it already.* Make him speak. Maybe he would feel better.

"Victim number two, Bethany, her roommate, said she wasn't dating anyone, but she was on one of those dating websites. Tons of possibilities for suspects."

Newman nodded to indicate he was listening, but still added nothing. It was like a panic attack was teetering on the edge of his sanity, something he never experienced before in his life. He never lost control. Yet, he could feel himself slipping into a deep chaos. He was afraid he wouldn't be able to pull himself out.

"None of her clients stood out like they were murderers.

The few complaints she had lodged against her for being a little too rough on their teeth had solid alibis. Dead end there." Sauer paused again, perhaps waiting for him to jump in. When he didn't, Sauer continued, "Victim number three, Amber, her college professors and boss all had good things to say about her. None of her friends could report anyone strange following her, or any recent problems she had been having in her life. She also wasn't dating anyone."

"I don't know what the point is of hashing everything out that we already know, Sauer. We got shit. Just say that."

Sauer's eyes narrowed. He finally decided to speak and nothing good came out of his mouth. Was he surprised? Was Sauer really surprised?

That's who he was lately. An asshole. No matter how much he wanted to stop himself, he had no control.

His life was spinning into a madness he couldn't stop.

"Sometimes it helps to re-examine everything. We might've missed something the first time. How many times have we done this before and saw something that changed the case? Tons." A dangerous glint entered Sauer's eyes. "I've almost had enough of your attitude. I don't know what's going on with you, but you have to start talking. Tell me what's going on."

Finally.

Sauer finally took the initiative to confront him. To help him solve his problems.

But he couldn't help. Nobody could. He couldn't even help himself.

He jerked to his feet. "Nothing's wrong. I'm sick of everyone treating me the way they are."

Sauer stood up as well, his hands pressed firmly to his desk as he leaned forward. "You've been starting most of the problems around here, and you damn well know it."

"You got a problem with me, Sauer?"

"I have a problem with the way you've been treating Susan. I have a problem with the way you've been acting. I have a problem that you won't tell me, your partner and friend, what the hell is going on with you. You haven't been yourself since you broke up with Chrissy. You need—"

"Go to hell, Sauer."

He turned around and walked away. He couldn't stick around to hear any more, to let Sauer dig any deeper. The funny thing was, he had wanted Sauer to confront him, and when he did, he lashed out. Guess Sauer didn't push hard enough sooner.

He was letting the fear and anger take complete control. He honestly didn't know how much longer he'd survive.

Sauer wasn't going to hell.

He was.

"I CAN ALMOST recall moment to moment the first time Rina, Zoe, and I went shopping when we found out Zoe was pregnant. I didn't say it to Zoe, but that shit was overwhelming. I mean, the prices for a crib was ridiculous. Geesh, they still are," Dee said with disgust as she dropped the price tag that was attached to a mocha-colored crib.

"Yeah, but you're a pro now shopping for everything. You went with Zoe and Rina. You got this." Susan believed that wholeheartedly. She wanted Dee to believe that, to understand that.

What she didn't understand was why Rina and Zoe weren't shopping with them. She couldn't have been more surprised when Dee called her and asked her to go shopping. She said Sauer was working and she needed to get out of the house or she'd go insane. Right now, she didn't seem too enthused to be baby shopping. It had been her idea. Susan was tagging along trying to figure out the real reason for the outing.

Well, that was a lie. She knew the reason. She was simply trying not to think about it. Dee wanted her to stay away from Stitch. This was her chance to warn her away.

"So..." Dee's eyes darted around the store, then landed on her. Dee's piercing glare said she was about to be decimated. "What crib do you like?"

All the pent-up fear evaporated, as she let out a tiny breath of relief. If Dee was going to say anything about Stitch, why didn't she already? She hated waiting for it to come. Get it over with.

Maybe that was Dee's plan. Make her sweat until she couldn't take it anymore. Dee could be devious. Was she that cruel?

Susan made a real effort to look around until her eyes landed on a tan crib that had a sleigh-like back that reminded her of Santa and Christmas and happiness. Of course, it had to be the most expensive crib in the store, which Dee would hate.

"I don't know. They all look nice."

Dee rolled her eyes, not even trying to hide it. "Yeah, but you totally eyed the sleigh crib, which I hate to admit is super cute. I hate it because that's the one I want."

Susan couldn't help but laugh. "Don't sound so happy about it."

"It's so damn expensive."

"Yeah, but think of how beautiful it will look in the baby's room. It's very durable and safe. And..." she smiled brightly, "it'll last you through all the babies you have."

Laughter, strong and clear, bellowed out of Dee. "Oh,

what a good point. Oh my God, Susan, I can't have more than one. I'm freaking out over this one."

Although Susan could hear the panic in her voice, she was still laughing, which was a good sign.

"But you're shopping and thinking of the baby, and that's a good thing. You're going to be a wonderful mother, Dee. You already are."

Dee's laughter slowed down as she started to breathe heavily, almost borderline panic attack. "Thank you. I need to hear that to believe it. I..." She blew out a breath. "I can't stop the worry. I've tried and tried and tried. Sauer's been so patient with me, and I don't know how to stop it."

"It'll get better every day. You're strong, Dee. You can do this. I believe in you. Zoe and Rina do, too. And you know Sauer does."

A slow smile crept onto Dee's face. "You're strong, too, Susan. You'll need to be with Stitch."

She finally brought the issue out in the open.

But wait, what?

She'll need to be strong? With Stitch?

Did that mean she liked the idea of them together? Why did it seem like she hated the idea last night after Stitch left?

"There's nothing—"

"Stop." Dee arched a brow. "There is something between you two. I know there is. And..." She hesitated, then looked away as a slight blush flushed her cheeks. "I might've been the reason Stitch ditched out so early last night."

"Yeah, I kinda figured you guys had a chat. It's okay if you don't like—"

"No, I love the idea of you two together." Dee smiled. A real, authentic smile that held no malice behind the depths. "I might've pushed Stitch too hard on how he felt about you. I apologize if I screwed anything up between you two. Honestly, sometimes that man needs to be pushed a little. You think I worry and analyze and hide shit, he's just as bad. He's been through a lot, like me, in a different way, of course. Be patient with him, and don't back down. You gotta get in his face."

Susan chuckled. "Oh, we've gone toe-to-toe before. I have no problem getting in his face."

"Good. I knew you wouldn't. Because you're strong."

Her laughter and smile died. "But a girl can only put her heart on the line so many times."

Dee stepped closer and laid a hand to her shoulder. "Try it one more time. For me. Don't give up on him."

Susan's heart thumped like a racehorse as she contemplated it. Could she put herself out there one more time? Could she handle hearing again that she was good for only sex? Even if the sex was amazing, she wanted more. She deserved more.

"One more time."

She hated the plea in Dee's tone. It made her think she was missing something vital from Stitch. Some secret that made him keep taking two steps back, avoiding a relationship. But if he wouldn't share with her, how could they move on? How could they make anything work?

"Okay. One more time."

Dee squealed like a little girl, something that sounded so foreign, but it made Susan's heart swell with joy. She loved when Dee was happy, especially lately when she'd been so stressed about the baby, and stress was the last thing she needed.

"Awesome. I want two of my favorite people together and happy. This is just awesome."

Susan giggled, especially at the way she said awesome

both times. Her hormones must really be messing with her, because she couldn't recall Dee saying that before.

Dee wrapped an arm around her shoulder and started to walk. "I hate to admit it, I like that dumb crib that costs an arm and a leg, but I can't make any decisions until Sauer sees it. Let's grab a bite to eat and then hit up some other stores. I'm all for buying tons of baby clothes."

"I love that idea." Anything to keep Dee in a good mood.

Dee loved shopping for clothes, no matter who it was for. She had been on the receiving end of her shopping madness when they prepared for the ball. Finding a dress had been a trial, considering Dee made all of them try on dozens and dozens of dresses before she felt satisfied. Not them, but her. Dee had to be completely satisfied before they moved on to shoes, then makeup, then hairstyles. It had been a fun time. None of them complained. Dee had a great sense of style. Her baby would probably be the best dressed baby on the block.

They chatted as they made their way through the mall to the other end where the food court was located. Dee's earlier mood, borderline annoyed and angry, was back to upbeat and excited. Susan couldn't have been happier. She had no idea why the sudden change. Maybe because she found a crib she liked, even though it was expensive. Maybe because she planned to talk to Stitch. Maybe a combination of both.

Susan felt better about the situation with Stitch. She had Dee's blessing, which was so important. She would never mess with their friendship simply to have a guy. There's no way she would've been able to live with herself if they were mad at each other. She felt guilty already because they argued last night because of her. If nothing else, she had to fix that, even if Stitch still rejected her. Which was a high possibility. The only outcome she foresaw. He already said multiple times he only wanted sex. She didn't have high hopes he'd suddenly change his mind. But she said she'd try one more time, and she would.

"What do you feel like? You pick."

Dee scrunched her lips as she thought about it. "Pizza, maybe? I honestly don't know."

"Well, it's a food court, so we have lots of choices. Pizza sounds good."

"It does. I think that's what I want."

Decision made, they headed for the line in front of the pizza place and stared hard at the menu. They moved forward as the line did as well. She wasn't sure what she wanted as she glanced at all the items on the menu. Everything sounded so good. She knew she wanted breadsticks. That was a no-brainer. She always got breadsticks when she came here, and they were to-die-for.

As they moved forward once again, the line extremely long, the woman in front of them suddenly jerked around with her phone in her hand, her eyes glued to the screen.

"Chrissy?" Dee said with surprise.

The woman looked up. Susan hadn't crossed paths with her often, but often enough to recognize her as Newman's ex-girlfriend. She still didn't know the reason they broke up, only that it had gutted Newman to the core. Obviously, with the way his behavior had been.

"Oh, hey. How are you, Dee...and...and..."

"Susan," she supplied for her. She wasn't too surprised Chrissy didn't recognize her. They rarely interacted. The few times they had, it had been short.

"Right, Susan. Please, go ahead of me. I have to go."

"Everything okay?" Dee asked. Although it sounded like a friendly question, Susan heard the disdain in her tone.

"No, but it's not any of your business."

"It's not, but I was trying to be polite."

Chrissy gave a lame laugh. "Yeah, it sounded so nice."

"Well, excuse me if I'm not a fan of you. Honestly, I'm not a fan of Newman either, but what you did was disgusting and wrong." Dee moved to the side and gestured with her hand as she smiled sickeningly sweet. "Please, get out of my face."

Susan stood quietly as a mouse as Chrissy glared at her, probably deciding whether to say something back. Not many people could withstand Dee when she got a certain way, especially when she was extremely candid with her words. Thankfully, Susan hadn't been on the receiving end of such words. She honestly didn't know how she'd react.

"What *I* did?" Chrissy finally responded, sounding surprised. "And what exactly is it you think I did?"

Susan was curious to know as well. She wasn't a full-blown gossip junky, but she did like it from time to time, especially if it would explain part of Newman's nasty behavior lately, not that it gave him a reprieve to act the way he was.

"You know," Dee insisted.

"I don't, actually. I know what he did to me."

Susan glanced behind Chrissy to see the line had moved forward. It was their turn. They were holding up the line. "Maybe we should—"

"Newman's a douche, I don't deny that. I can't stand the guy, but what did he do to you? I know you cheated on him." The smile on Dee's face disappeared as she replaced it with a nasty smirk.

Although Dee interrupted her, she was now speechless. That's why Newman had been acting the way he had since he broke up with her. Because Chrissy had cheated on him. That would gut any person. It gutted her when she got cheated on. Wondering what she did wrong. Wondering where things went haywire. Wondering what she could've done to prevent it. It took her a long time to realize it hadn't been her fault, but his. Her ex-boyfriend had been a douche, treating her as if she meant absolutely nothing.

Chrissy's mouth dropped in shock. "I never...is that the lies he's been telling? Because that's all they are. Lies. That asshole cheated on me. For the longest time he wouldn't stop contacting me. I almost thought I'd have to get a restraining order against him. I even thought about talking to Sauer about it."

Dee's demeanor sagged, as if she believed Chrissy. Susan was very inclined to believe her, especially since Newman hadn't been that nice to her lately.

"That's not what he told Sauer. He said you cheated. That you kicked him out of the house."

Chrissy nodded. "Yeah, I kicked him out. It's my name on the lease. Not his. I want him to leave me alone. Thankfully, he hasn't bothered me for the last two months. His calls weren't every day, but they were often. He...kind of scared me. I was a little shocked when I saw...I should go."

Dee grabbed her arm to stop her. "When you saw what? I believe you, Chrissy. I should've known better than to believe any word that came out of his mouth. I can't wait to tell Sauer the truth. Tell me what you were going to say."

Torture was written on Chrissy's face. Her shoulders slumped as Dee let go of her arm. "I never thought he'd hurt me, or get violent. He never was with me. When I saw the murder in the papers about that woman...I thought maybe...he did it. But then, I didn't see anything about him being arrested. Now, I'm creeped out there's been two more murders. I feel terrible for even thinking he could murder one person, but he definitely wouldn't murder three."

Time for her to say something. Because now she was curious about quite a few things. Why would she think Newman would kill someone?

"What woman are you talking about?"

Chrissy looked at her, her eyes round as saucers. "Tonya Moretta."

"What about her?" Susan asked, her heart suddenly pounding.

"She's the other woman. The woman he slept with."

Susan couldn't believe her ears. "Are you sure?"

"Oh, I'm positive. I found them in my bed together. Her face and breasts are ingrained in my mind. He'd been sleeping with her for a while before I found out. He didn't think I'd be coming home early, but I did."

Susan almost couldn't breathe as the implications Chrissy just dropped at her feet flashed before her. "Are you saying that Newman had an affair with Tonya Moretta, the first woman who was murdered recently?"

"Yeah, I am." Chrissy looked perplexed. "Don't you work for the police department? You didn't know that? Newman didn't share that news? Wow. Somehow, that doesn't surprise me."

Susan's heart rate sped up as she shifted through all the evidence in her head, her theory that she couldn't shake all morning, Newman's lies, and his recent behavior.

She thought a cop could've killed all three women.

Now it looked like she might actually be right.

12

_____

HE RAN the pencil back and forth over the paper he had been working on for over an hour with way more strength than was necessary. Nothing but garbage. The long gray marks scribbled over the design made his heart ache. The sketch had been decent. But that was the problem. Decent, not awesome. Not awe-inspiring, something he tried to achieve in every piece of artwork.

Stitch pushed away from his desk and stood up. He glanced around his office, at the artwork adorning his walls, around the livelihood he created. He was proud of everything he had accomplished. He was proud of his work.

But he wasn't proud of his behavior last night. How he walked away from Deena. How he walked away from Susan without declaring some sort of feelings for her.

Mid-afternoon already and he still hadn't found the nerve to call either one of them to apologize. Better yet, speak to them in person.

He had a few clients today, and he could've rescheduled them and did it right away this morning. He'd been making a nasty habit of that, though, and he didn't feel right rescheduling again.

Of course, he knew that was a lie. A handy excuse for his fear.

Fear of losing his best friend altogether.

Fear of rejection from Susan.

Fear of speaking the truth.

He could do the crime and time, but spilling his guts was something else. Would Susan still want anything to do with him when she heard the truth?

A knock sounded on his door. Short and to the point, which signaled Jensen wanted to talk to him. Him, he could handle. Stacey would only drive his already forming headache to deeper proportions.

"Yeah, come in."

The door swung open. Jensen swaggered in as he normally did anywhere he went and plopped down into his chair. He didn't hesitate to roll up his sleeve and tilt his arm to show a small patch of skin that looked funny, devoid of any tattoos, considering most of his arm was covered in some sort of ink.

But like some, Jensen only wanted a tattoo when it had a specific meaning behind it. If he had nothing to fill the space, he'd keep it blank no matter how dumb it looked.

"You think I have time for that shit right now?"

"Yep."

A man of few words. Jensen never spoke unless he had something to say, which wasn't very often. Some of his clients even made comments about it at times that Jensen was bizarre. He sympathized to a point. Jensen could act strange, but he was also one of the best damn tattooers in the city. Suck it up, or get the hell out—the only thing he always said. He had yet to lose a client over his candid words. Because, ultimately, they all walked out of his shop happy campers. As they always would.

He nodded once and prepared to do a tattoo he hadn't been set to do today. The only consolation at this point was his wrist hadn't been bothering him today. Besides, he still wasn't ready to speak to Deena or Susan. This gave him another excuse to delay the inevitable.

Nobody could ever call him a chickenshit. Today, they could. It bothered him to no end, yet it didn't get his ass in gear to do the right thing. Apologize.

"What do you want?"

"A robin."

Since the moment he met Jensen five years ago, nobody else tattooed him. Jensen preferred it that way. Jensen always had the utmost ability in his craft. So when he started to apply ink to Jensen's skin without a stencil, he didn't flinch. He knew that shit would come out looking just as he planned it. Although, he did pull his phone out and skim the internet a bit to find some pictures of robins to get a base of what he wanted to do.

A robin was an odd choice. It would be a tiny robin, since he didn't have a ton of room to work with. He had questions for Jensen on why he wanted this particular tattoo, this particular animal. Robins symbolized a new beginning. What did that mean? He sure hoped it didn't mean he was leaving. He couldn't afford to lose one of his best tattooers, especially when his wrist was starting to become a problem.

But he didn't say a word. He got to work and let the buzzing noise from his machine calm him into a sense of peace. His mind drifted away from his problems, from all the issues that had been plaguing him lately.

His creativity came out front and center, his attention

solely focused on the robin he detailed down to the feathers and to the bird's beady little eyes that spoke of such wisdom. He made that tiny-as-shit bird come to life, as if it would fly right off Jensen's arm and into the big wide world, into a new beginning.

A few hours later, his arm ached with a dull throb forming in his wrist. He scooted back and shut off his machine.

"Done."

Jensen smiled, stood up, and turned around to the mirror. His smile grew. "Thanks."

Stitch cleaned up the tattoo, applied the cream, and sealed the tattoo as he always did. The entire time Jensen stood quietly and with the same damn smile on his face. It wasn't the smile that bothered him; it was the way Jensen kept staring at him. As if he knew something he didn't.

"You got any more clients today?" He didn't know what else to say as he ripped off his gloves, but he needed to say something to get that look out of Jensen's eyes.

"Nope." Jensen started for the door. He paused as his hand touched the handle. "Hope that helped." With those parting words, he walked out.

Hoped what helped?

That dude *was* weird as shit.

As Stitch continued to clean up his area, he tried to figure out what Jensen meant. He said the strangest things at the strangest times.

As he started to crumble his drawing from earlier in his hand, he stopped squeezing, as it hit him.

A robin. A new beginning.

Not for Jensen.

For him.

They didn't talk once as he tattooed, but Jensen still

managed to make that tattoo session into a therapy session of sorts. That was his way of calming him down, centering his focus on what was important. Tattooing always did that.

It was time to talk to Deena and Susan.

He'd have to thank Jensen later.

And now he had a badass tattoo of a robin. They both came out winners.

"DEE, you have to stop pacing. I'm getting dizzy watching you."

Dee rolled her eyes and continued back and forth in the living room as they waited for Sauer to come home. "Where is he? Why isn't he home yet?"

Susan tried to sound calm, even though she was just as anxious for Sauer to get here. "He should be home any minute. We called him on our way home from the mall. He said he'd come right away."

"I should've told him the reason why. He would've driven faster."

Susan stood up and stopped Dee with a hand to the shoulder and a smile that she hoped would calm her down. The stress couldn't be good for the baby. "It's better we talk to him about this in person. And we don't know if Newman was with him."

She still couldn't wrap her mind around the idea that Newman could be a killer. Not any killer, but a serial killer. Murdering three women. It didn't sound like him.

Yet, the evidence she had, which was nothing but enough to give her a bad feeling, said it was a possibility. The killer could definitely be a cop. Why wasn't there any good evidence at the crime scenes? Why couldn't they find out how the killer got in? Now it could easily be explained. Most people would open their door to a cop and let them in. Tonya would've opened her door to a former lover.

"I need a drink."

Susan chuckled. "In six more months you can."

Dee smiled and slumped down on the couch. "Do you think it's possible he killed those women?"

She took a seat next to her. "I don't want to think it's possible."

"He did it. I know he did."

"Just because he's a douche doesn't mean he's a killer."

"It's good enough for me."

Dee stood up again and resumed pacing. Susan didn't want to argue with her. She didn't want to think that Newman killed anyone, and she wouldn't. She would do like she did on every other case: find the evidence to prove it. Not assume guilt because she held a grudge against the man. Dee might not agree with that, but she didn't care. She wouldn't change her mind either, or break her professionalism because she knew him.

The front door finally opened and Dee didn't hesitate to rush to Sauer and wrap her arms around him without giving him a chance to remove his jacket. He smiled and chuckled as he embraced his wife back. The look was sweet and endearing. It made her wish for things she might not ever experience. At least, not with the man she wanted it with.

Thinking about Stitch right now wouldn't help her. She'd wallow in that pity later at home when she was by herself.

"What's going on? Are you okay?" Sauer suddenly looked panicked. "Is the baby okay?"

"The baby's fine. We're fine. Newman's a serial killer,"

Dee said, deadpan, as she let go of him and started to pace once more.

Sauer's mouth dropped open, then shut, then opened again. Dee had that effect, rendering people speechless. Susan honestly had no clue what to say, but she didn't think Dee had to drop the bomb like that and not provide any further information. Of course, she wasn't surprised. Dee loved her suspense and intrigue.

"Umm...okay. Why do you think that?" Sauer finally asked as he stopped Dee from walking and cupped her chin. "What's going on?" He kissed her lips softly, then pulled her in for a hug. "I love you."

Susan suddenly felt like she was intruding on a personal moment. Or maybe she could call it jealousy at seeing the tender moment, Sauer trying to calm down his wife and kiss her so lovingly.

Damn Stitch for making her fall so easily for him. She should've known better than to let her heart open. Now, she was aching so much for his touch, his cocky words, it hurt to see her friends happy and in love when she never felt jealous before.

"I love you, too. I said Newman's a serial killer."

"We don't know that, Dee." Susan couldn't keep hearing her say that. No matter how it looked right now, they needed evidence to corroborate that statement before they accused an innocent man of anything.

Dee pushed out of Sauer's arms, pointing a finger at her. "We do. Don't be dumb, Susan."

"Don't convict a man before you have all the evidence. Innocent until proven guilty, Dee."

"He's a killer."

"You don't know that."

"He's—"

"Enough." Sauer stepped between them. "How about someone tell me why we're having this kind of conversation?"

Dee smirked. "Yeah, Susan, how about we tell him."

She didn't know why Dee was acting this way toward her. Maybe it was fear or worry for her husband because they were about to tell him what kind of person his friend was. She tried not to let it bother her, but she couldn't help but feel a little hurt at the attitude.

"You know what? I can't do this right now. I can't think about that asshole." Dee kissed him on the lips and left the room.

"What's going on, Susan?"

She hated the worry in his eyes. She hated what she was about to say, especially since Dee left the room and put it all on her shoulders.

"We ran into Chrissy at the mall today. Have you talked to her since she broke up with Newman?"

"No."

"I had no idea why they broke up. According to Chrissy, the version Newman told you is a lie. He cheated on her."

Sauer ran a hand through his hair. "We don't...we don't talk much about that, but I can't see him lying to me. Why would he lie about that?"

"Why would Chrissy? She said he wouldn't stop calling her for a while after they broke up. That his behavior almost scared her."

"He moved out because of what she did."

"No, Sauer, she kicked him out because of what he did. It's her name on the lease."

He sighed heavily. "Okay, I don't want to argue the point on whether my friend is a liar. What does him possibly cheating have to do with him being a serial killer?"

This would be the hard part. She didn't want to tell him. She hated how broken he already looked.

"Well, Chrissy saw the reports in the paper about the recent murders. Apparently, Tonya Moretta is the woman she found in bed with Newman. I'm guessing he never told you he knew the victim, did he?"

Sauer's face fell ashen as his hands started to tremble. She wished Dee hadn't walked out of the room. She didn't know how to comfort Sauer hearing that his friend lied to him. Multiple times. A huge lie that could possibly implicate him as a killer.

"He wouldn't...he'd never..." Sauer ran a hand through his hair. "He hasn't been himself lately. I can see why he lied about the cheating, but why would he not say he knew the victim?"

"Do you think he's capable of murder?"

His eyes met hers. "No. He's a lot of things, but I don't think he's a murderer. Do you?"

"I...people can surprise you sometimes."

"He wouldn't do that."

"Sauer..." she sighed heavily, "we have to be objective and look at the evidence, not what we think about him."

"He's my friend. He's my partner. He wouldn't do something like this, Susan."

"Yet, he's been lying and withholding information about the case from you. That says something. Maybe not that he's a killer, but it's not good."

Sauer fell silent. They stared at each other, neither saying a word.

He ran a hand down his face as he grimaced. "He's been acting weird about this case. Obviously, I know why now. I wonder if he ever met her ex-husband."

"Why?"

"He wanted to split up the day we found her body. He didn't come with me to interview him. We never split up. I thought it was odd."

"Do you know where he is right now?"

Sauer started to pace, almost imitating Dee's movements from earlier. "No. We had an argument today. I have to talk to him before I tell Captain Ganderson."

"Are you sure about that, Sauer?"

"Yes. I want to know why he would lie to me." He stopped pacing and glanced toward the hallway. "I should go check on Dee. Tell her I have to go find Newman. Will you stay with her?"

Susan wanted to say no. Was this his way to keep her from saying something to Captain Ganderson? In all fairness, she should've reported this new evidence immediately before talking to Sauer. The way Newman had been acting toward her, he didn't deserve her silence. She should report him for withholding information in an investigation, and she should do it now.

"Please, Susan. Let me talk to him first."

The plea in his voice was her undoing. "Okay. I'll stay with Dee."

"Thank you." Sauer headed down the hallway when the doorbell went off. "Do you mind getting that?"

Sauer didn't leave her a choice as he kept walking away. Susan sighed and made her way to the front door.

What a day, and it was only half over.

She opened the door and tried not to faint from surprise.

Standing tall and a little tired looking, and oh so remorseful, was Stitch.

"Can I come in, shorty?"

Her heart ached even more as she realized he hadn't

come to see her. He came to see Dee. He probably never wanted to see her again. His use of that dumb nickname was evidence enough. She didn't see it as a term of endearment as she did when he called her sweetheart, or better yet, when he called her Suzy baby.

She stepped back and opened the door wider. "Sure. I'll go get Dee for you."

She turned to go find Dee, to get away from him, now determined to leave whether Sauer liked it or not. She wouldn't go to Captain Ganderson yet, but she wouldn't stay here while Stitch was here.

A hand grasped her arm, making her jerk to a stop. Warmth instantly soothed her as Stitch twirled her around and into his embrace.

"I'm sorry, Suzy baby. Don't be mad at me. I'm a dumb-ass...about everything. Forgive me?"

Forgive him? And then what? What was he saying?

Because she would forgive him, but she wouldn't let him back in her life unless he gave her one thing.

Commitment.

13

HE TIGHTENED HIS HOLD. She hadn't responded to his apology, something he obviously wanted to do, just not so abruptly. When she started to walk away from him, he saw her walking away for good, and it scared him. He honestly didn't like how much it scared him.

Damn Jensen and his dumb robin. He got it now. He understood the point of the tattoo. It wasn't a meaning for Jensen, or a healing process he needed. Jensen did it all for him. To get his head out of his ass.

Now, if someone asked Jensen what the robin meant, he'd probably mutter 'new beginning' and leave it at that. He'd know the meaning. Jensen would know. That's it. Nobody else needed to know.

He thought starting his tattoo business had been a new beginning.

But shit, it didn't mean he couldn't start another one again. Life took turns unexpectedly all the time. He always rolled with it. He could this time, too.

Opening up, actually talking about shit he didn't want to because he cared what Susan thought of him, would take a lot of strength. Something he didn't think he had until Jensen stepped in and showed him he did. The crazy bastard did it with as few words as possible.

"Stitch...I can't breathe."

Realizing he was squeezing Susan harder than he intended, he loosened his hold but didn't fully let her go. He wanted her. He wanted to try...commitment. Thinking the word had him itching to flee. No matter how hard it would be to take that leap, he'd try. For her. Only her.

"Sorry. Again." He cracked a smile. "Am I forgiven yet?"

A slow smile emerged on her beautiful face. "I forgive you."

His grin grew, as did his desire. "In that case—"

"Oh, did you get your head out of your ass finally and declare your intentions?"

Stitch jerked at the sound of Dee's voice. His arms fell away from Susan. She took that opportunity to take a few steps away from him. He hated that. What did it mean? She said she forgave him, but in what way? Did stepping away mean she wouldn't let him back in her life?

Shit. This was why he hated dating. Simple sex with ground rules was easier. Less messy. This emotional crap took too much thinking and analyzing. He hated it all.

"Hey, doll."

"Don't 'hey doll' me. Are you two an item yet? Take her home and make sweet love to her. Show her how much you care." Dee cocked an eyebrow as she placed a hand to her hip.

Sauer chuckled behind Dee, a stupid grin on his face.

"I like that idea, but we haven't gotten to the item part yet." He then smiled, hoping to convey his apology to Deena without having to say the words.

Saying sorry wasn't something they did. This wasn't the

first time they had words with each other. Probably wouldn't be the last. One of them usually made the move to talk first, and that was that. Issue over. Friends again.

The smirk on her face said as much. He was forgiven. Well, he figured as long as he didn't break Susan's heart, which was something he'd try his damndest not to do, but he couldn't promise it. Relationships weren't his thing and he was bound to screw up repeatedly. He was a realist. He knew his limitations. His strengths. His weaknesses. Relationships were definitely a weakness.

Hell, he didn't even have a relationship with his parents. He hadn't talked to his mother since the day he left home at seventeen. She could be dead right now. He had no idea. And his father died in prison years ago. Before he was locked up, he hadn't spoken to his old man in months. Then he died after another prisoner stabbed him. Just a deadbeat asshole that he didn't even miss.

His father went to prison for beating his mom, yet his mother was no better. She didn't use fists to tear him down. Her words were always enough.

You're weak. Just like your father. You'll never amount to anything.

Yeah, those words echoed in his head from time to time. Odd how they decided to pop up now. Probably to remind himself he wasn't weak. Her words had no control over him. He wanted Susan, and he'd have her. Simple as that. No weakness here.

"Mind if I steal Susan from you? We have things we need to talk about."

He heard Susan scoff, as if she couldn't believe he was asking Deena instead of her, which he figured he probably should've. He was relying on her coming with him willingly.

He wanted Deena's approval, though, especially since Susan was visiting her.

"Steal away."

"Thanks, doll."

"Do I have a say in this?" Susan piped in. "I'm actually busy."

He took his time turning toward her, almost afraid to see a bit of hatred in her eyes. Thankfully, he only saw anger. Anger he could handle. Hatred was a whole other ball game. She was sexy as hell when she got angry. He liked it when she got irritated with him. It was wrong and evil and treacherous, but he couldn't stop himself from provoking her sometimes.

"Busy with what?"

"Work."

"Susan, you promised," Sauer said quietly.

Stitch glanced at Sauer, noting the panic in his eyes. What was that about?

"I didn't promise anything."

"You said you'd let me find him first. What do you plan to work on, if not to talk to Captain Ganderson?"

"Maybe I should go to work. Maybe I should revisit the crime scenes. I might've missed something."

Sauer stepped around Deena, his features turning fierce. Stitch wasn't sure he liked the look on his face. Deena's husband or not, if he said shit he didn't like to Susan, he'd pay the price.

"To what? Find evidence that isn't to be found to convict a man for something he didn't do?"

"How dare you! Are you insinuating I'd plant evidence?" She took two steps and pointed an accusing finger at Sauer. "Is that what you're saying?"

"That isn't what I said, but Newman didn't do this." He

frowned, sadness coating his eyes. "You don't miss evidence. Ever. You're meticulous and thorough. What do you think revisiting the crime scenes will do? What do you think you'll find?"

"I'm not perfect, Sauer. I've been distracted lately. Maybe I did miss something. Maybe I would find something to help Newman's case. Did you ever think about that?"

"The douche is guilty," Deena scoffed.

"Don't say that," Sauer said quietly to his wife.

"Open your eyes. He lied. He's an asshole. He's been treating Susan like shit. He's—"

"None of that makes him a killer," Sauer insisted, interrupting Deena.

"Someone want to tell me what's going on?" he finally decided to ask, confused about what they were talking about.

At that, the room fell silent.

"It's about work stuff," Sauer said without looking at him, his eyes trained on Susan.

"Yet, Deena knows," Stitch said, then took a step closer to him, "and if you don't stop shooting daggers at Susan, you and I are going to have issues."

"You don't scare me, Stitch."

"Whoa. Back up." Deena stepped between them. Looking at him, she said, "Go home. Take Susan with you." She then looked at Susan. "Go with Stitch. Work things out with him." Her eyes trained on Sauer. "And you. Go find that asshole. Don't start fights with my friend. I'd hate to see you two fight."

"I'd win that fight," Stitch muttered.

She gave him a side-eyed glare. "Don't be so sure, Stitch. Sauer fights well. Quit threatening my husband."

He nodded. He didn't want to argue with her anymore. Tension between them never felt good.

"Tell him to quit talking to Susan that way and looking at her like that." He hated tension with her, but he also wouldn't allow Sauer to treat Susan like that. She was his. Nobody treated his woman like that.

"Done. Now, macho man, go away. With Susan." Deena pointed at the door.

He didn't argue with her. He gave Sauer one long, menacing glare, then grabbed Susan's hand and headed for the door. She resisted a bit with her footsteps, but gave in when he opened the door.

"I need my purse and jacket."

He nodded, hating to let go, but did. She grabbed her things from the living room and then met him by the door. He grabbed her hand again to make sure she followed him outside. Her grip tightened as she looked at Sauer and Deena, then stepped outside.

"I don't see your car here."

"Dee picked me up. We went shopping." She eyed him funny, then laughed. "Where's your jacket? I rarely see you wearing one. It's cold out."

"The cold doesn't bother me. I hate wearing jackets." Jackets always felt confining to him. He liked to feel comfortable. Something big and bulky always made him feel claustrophobic in a way. It could get extremely cold in Minnesota, but unless it hit single digits, he never wore a jacket.

He stopped at the passenger side of his car and opened the door for her. "Hop in."

She hesitated, then extracted her hand from his and slid inside.

He rounded the car quickly and slammed his door

harder than he intended. But shit, he was still ramped up from everything that happened inside.

"You didn't have to do that. With Sauer. He was fine. He didn't hurt my feelings or anything."

Turning toward her, he cupped her chin lightly. "Nobody will treat you that way. Not when you're with me." His grip tightened, not to hurt, but to show his possession. "Nobody."

"With you? What does that mean?"

His hand fell away. He started the car, the beautiful purr of the engine bringing his anger level down a notch. "Means what it means. You're mine, sweetheart. Commitment and all that shit."

A laugh echoed between them. "Wow. You have such a way with words. What makes you think I still want you?"

His lips turned into a wily grin. "Oh, you know you want me, sweetheart. Don't deny it. I could take you right here and now and we both know you'd love every minute of it."

"You're too cocky for your own good." A cheeky grin of her own appeared. "Maybe I want you to take me right here and now."

Damn, this was why he wanted her. She was his perfect match, giving as good as she got.

Would she still want him after he told her everything? Because if he wanted to try to make a relationship work with her, she needed to know it all.

His past and everything.

He revved the engine and backed out of the driveway before he changed his mind and took her in the front seat of his car.

"Suzy baby, I'm gonna love you so hard when we get home. You just wait."

He would. After he told her the truth.

NEWMAN STARED AT HIS HANDS, knowing the power that teetered on the edge. He could do this. He could take control.

Or he could walk away.

Walking away would be easier. It would be the smart thing to do.

But when had he done anything smart lately?

All he was doing the past few weeks was alienating his friends, pushing them away, making waves in every department. Acting like a jackass to a woman who didn't deserve that kind of behavior.

Where did it all fall apart?

How did his life suddenly go down the drain?

One moment, on top of the world, reunited with the woman he fell in love with in high school, the next, he was getting kicked out of her house for being a world-class jerk. He couldn't deny it, or any part of his behavior the last few months.

Every time he wanted to get on his hands and knees and grovel for forgiveness, he felt the beast, the monster break free instead. It's as if his guilt morphed into rage, masking his wrongdoing into making believe he was the injured party. He knew it was wrong. But it didn't stop him.

Nothing seemed to stop him anymore.

He kept digging further and further down the hole. Soon, he'd probably be able to see the gates to hell. That's how far he dug himself in.

His hands held all the power right now. So much power in his hands. So much rage and remorse and sadness.

A gentle ring sounded. He pulled his phone out of his pocket and grimaced.

Sauer.

Third time now he had called within the last twenty minutes. Each time, he slid his phone back into his pocket. Each time, he ignored his friend. Each time, he felt the power in his hands get stronger and stronger.

It was time.

Time to find some peace.

There had to be peace with what he was about to do. Because if there wasn't, he was exchanging one hell for a new one.

He put his phone back into his pocket, looked around the room, and then at his hands once again as he wrapped them around the woman's shoulder and pulled her against him.

SAUER PACED in front of the fridge, wanting to grab a beer and down it in one long swallow. He knew he couldn't do that, of course. He needed all of his wits. He had to find Newman before...

Well, he didn't want to finish that thought. Nothing good would come from finishing that thought.

Dee seemed to believe he was a vicious killer. Susan as well. At least, that was the impression he got, even though she wasn't as vocal as his wife.

But he knew Newman. He worked day in and day out with the man. He was no killer. Did he have issues? Yes. Could he be an asshole? Of course. Would he kill three women? Absolutely not.

So why the doubt in his head now?

Probably because he had been everywhere around town

where he thought he'd find Newman, and nothing. He couldn't find him anywhere. With at least twenty phone calls and a dozen texts, Newman still hadn't responded or called him back.

He knew why the doubt was there, but he wanted to pretend it didn't exist. Why was Newman ignoring him? Sure, they got into it before. Disagreements on a case. Arguments about dumb shit going on in their lives. But they never ignored each other like this.

He couldn't doubt his friend. He couldn't. Someone needed to be on his side. Especially since he caved in and called Ben and Zeke, and it didn't look promising. The suspicion swirled in the depths of their eyes. They were siding with Dee.

It tore through his heart like a swift, sharp blade.

"Sauer, we need to talk to Captain Ganderson. You know we do," Zeke said quietly, as he stood on the other side of the kitchen.

"Not yet. We can find him. We can talk to him."

"And how do you think that talk is going to go? He hasn't been himself lately, Sauer. You can't deny this. He's a loose cannon. We don't know how he's going to react when we tell him we know he lied," Ben said, using the soft voice that Rina did better than him.

It irked him that Ben was using that tone of voice with him right now. Like he needed to be coddled like a small child waking up from a terrible nightmare, the dark frightening them.

"He didn't kill three women. He didn't." He stopped his pacing and stared hard at both of them, willing them to take his side. Piercing a stare so fierce, they wouldn't be able to deny the truth.

Newman was not a killer.

"Evidence could suggest otherwise. We honestly don't know that." Zeke held his gaze, unafraid.

"No. I know Newman, and I know he's not a killer."

"Then why isn't he answering? Why can't you find him? What do you think he's doing right now?" Zeke demanded harshly. "I'm not saying he's guilty, but you should prepare yourself a little bit that he could be."

"And you should prepare yourself that he's not!"

Ben and Zeke both took a step back at the way he shouted. He felt remorse immediately for raising his voice, but he couldn't find the words to apologize. He wouldn't. Not when they couldn't show a hint of trust for Newman. It's as if nobody trusted Newman but him.

Sure, he had been acting strange lately. Acting harsher toward coworkers. Being a big fat dick, basically. But Sauer knew his friend, and he wasn't going to doubt him at a time where he needed someone to believe in his innocence.

"Whoa, the testosterone levels in here are off the charts. Don't make me slap you silly for putting my husband in a bad mood," Dee said sharply to Zeke, as she wrapped an arm around him, squeezing tightly. He appreciated the support, but only to an extent. She also believed Newman was guilty.

His own wife wasn't even on his side. That hurt. That hurt deeply, as if she took a tiny knife and nicked him, then stuck the knife in again a little deeper. Then again. And again. Every time she voiced her displeasure with Newman or called him a killer, the knife jabbed him a little more.

Right now, her arm was around him, but he felt no support.

But he loved his wife no matter what, even when she hurt him. He kissed the top of her head and stepped out of her arms. The look of pain that flashed across her face hurt. Everything hurt.

"I'll find him on my own. If you have to tell Captain Ganderson, then I can't stop you. I'm going to find my friend and ask him what's going on. He didn't do this. He lied, yes. But he's not a killer."

He headed out of the kitchen. Ben's soft words stopped him.

"We'll find him together."

He turned toward him. He could keep walking out, or he could wait. The way Ben said it, he meant what he said in a kind gesture, not in a way to throw Newman under the bus. He nodded, then glanced at Zeke, who almost rolled his eyes but stopped himself. "Yeah, we'll find him together. And I'll let you do all the talking when we do because I'm sure nothing nice will come out of my mouth."

Sauer finally offered a small smile. "Deal."

"Hey, buster, you don't think you're leaving this house with just a kiss on my head, do you?" Dee snapped as she threw a hand to her hip.

Ben and Zeke chuckled and dismissed themselves from the kitchen. He was grateful to have a moment alone with his wife. His beautiful, pregnant wife. The stress lately had been something he never experienced before. Worrying whether he could calm her down, make her feel better. Worrying whether he should ask Stitch for help, thankful he did, yet irritated every time he spoke to him. He didn't know what to think about Stitch, or the fact he had a thing going on with Susan. A sweet woman who deserved the best. Was Stitch the best for her?

Now, more worry for his partner. The whole situation was creating unwanted tension between him and Dee, and he hated it. He hated it so much he almost wanted to say screw Newman and the mess he found himself in. He shouldn't care so much, but he did. He wouldn't turn his back on his friend.

It didn't mean he wouldn't give him a piece of his mind for what he did. For putting the tension between him and his wife. His gorgeous wife, who was smirking and pinning him with eyes that said he was in trouble. Of course, when didn't she pin him with that sort of gaze. Life was never dull with Dee by his side.

He walked closer and drew her into his arms, pulling her in for a kiss. One that spoke of sweet promises for later. "I love you. So much. But I...I need you to stop...voicing your opinion on Newman...just...I..."

A soft hand grazed his cheek as her smirk died and a tender smile replaced it. "I love when you blush that sweet shade of red. I know I've been terrible lately, and not just with this Newman crap. With everything. These hormones are killing me. It's like the craziness inside me increases a hundred times over."

"I'm not blushing." Which he knew was a lie. But he really needed her to stop talking about Newman, and he didn't know how to say it. He hated being blunt, especially with her. She thrived on confrontation and chaos. He liked it nice and easygoing.

She cupped his cheeks and pulled him in for another kiss. "You are, but it's so adorable and one of the things I love most about you. Go find your friend. I'll tone down my aversion to him...for you."

He chuckled and snatched one more kiss. "I love you. I'll be home as soon as I can."

"I love you, too."

He reluctantly stepped out of her arms and headed for the front door. Her whispered words made him pause.

"Be safe."

Glancing at her, he smiled. "Always."

As he walked out with Ben and Zeke, he couldn't help but wonder why she said those two words. Yeah, he worked a dangerous job, dealing with criminals and violent people on occasion, the knowledge that anything could happen on any given day for any given reason. Life just happened sometimes.

But she never said those words.

Why now? What did she think would happen?

Newman wouldn't hurt him.

14

A WARM, comforting arm pulled her closer. She didn't resist the urge to snuggle with him, even though she knew this had been a terrible idea.

Instead of taking her home like she thought Stitch would, he brought her to his house. He had said they needed to talk. She could handle that. They did need to talk.

Except when they made it to his house, the second he unlocked the front door, he was on her. She was on him. They couldn't control the desire and the passion that had been building since the last time they spoke.

He took her hard and fast against the front door. It had been delicious and dirty and everything she never knew she wanted—needed.

Then afterwards, after coming down from the sensual high, he swung her into his arms, something he had never done before and felt a little like a romantic gesture coming from him, he walked her to his bedroom where he loved her one more time. Slow and sweet. A huge contrast from the way they normally had sex.

It scared her. It made the frightening emotions she had

been feeling all week surface, skimming the top, floating, just waiting for the huge wave to take her back under and sink to the bottom. Because the love she suddenly felt for Stitch would break her when he wouldn't reciprocate.

She loved him.

The damn aggravating man got her to fall in love and she wasn't sure she'd ever be loved back.

His sweet, soft lovemaking from moments before made her hope and wonder whether he felt the same. Yet, she knew he probably didn't. If he did, he wouldn't voice it. Well, she wouldn't voice it first either. She already put herself out there declaring her intentions, wanting commitment from him, and he broke her heart the first time.

Now he wanted to talk.

They needed to. They should've never slept together without talking first.

Oh, but she couldn't deny how wonderful it felt to be in his arms once again. Feeling his slow, steady heartbeat. The delicate way his hand brushed up and down her back as they lay there. His quiet breathing in a room filling with tension.

He knew they needed to talk. She could sense it in him.

Except neither said a word.

Her eyes glided across his chest and to the tattoos that covered him everywhere. Her finger started lightly tracing the outline of a skull that looked menacing and fierce. Then it trailed to an eagle, as if soaring through the bright blue sky.

She wondered what they signified. She knew they had to have some sort of meaning. He had a reason for everything he did, including the tattoos on his body. She could ask.

She could also start the conversation that might make her leave his house.

And that's why she was afraid to voice the first word. She didn't want to leave. She didn't want to leave his arms.

"You feel tense. I know damn well I did my job making you feel good."

The soft rumble of his voice sent a shiver up her spine. The promise in what he didn't say made her anticipate his hands roaming farther down her body and where she always craved his touch. He did make her feel good. He could make her feel good once again.

Or she could start the conversation they needed to talk about instead of letting him distract them from it.

His hand started to drift lower down her back and caress her ass. Another ripple shifted over her body at the soft touch.

"What's going on here, Stitch?"

There. Done. She brought it out in the open as he obviously wanted since he pointed out how tense she was. They just had amazing sex, but she was so wound up with worry that she couldn't fully relax yet.

"We're...doing that thing. You know." He chuckled. "Commitment or whatever."

A tiny giggle escaped at how ridiculous he sounded. She lifted her head to look him in the eyes.

"Commitment or whatever? You don't think you can give me words I want to hear so I don't kick you out of my bed, do you?"

A wily glint entered his eyes. "First, sweetheart, you're in *my* bed. Second, what makes you think you're that good I need to give you words to keep you in my bed?"

"Are you saying I'm just meh?" she asked as she cocked a brow.

The smirk on his face grew. "I would never say that."

"Then what are you really saying?"

He sighed. "That I want you in my life." His expression turned fierce. "You're mine, and only mine. I don't share. Hell, I don't like it when men look at you."

"Are you going to be one of those possessive, jealous types?"

"Maybe. You got a problem with that, shorty?"

Susan stared at him, weighing the question. *Did* she have a problem with that? She never dated a man like that. She had seen some serious cases where jealousy went too far in a relationship. Although, she didn't think Stitch would ever physically hurt her.

"I guess this is where we should talk." He started to shift, making her move away. He sat up and put his back to the wall, his arms almost crossing. His entire posture looked like he was saying, "Stay away." He started to absently rub his right wrist.

She meant her original question jokingly. In a sense, she thought he answered back in the same manner. Perhaps neither of them were really joking.

"What do we need to talk about?" She joined him in a sitting position, but made sure not to touch any part of him. She couldn't even explain to herself why she did that. Perhaps she knew she needed space as much as he did. "Do you actually want commitment? You can say the word as if you mean it, can't you?"

"For such a tiny woman, you pack a hard ball. I can say the word."

An eyebrow lifted. "And mean it?"

"What part of you're mine and only mine didn't you understand?"

The cold, menacing way he said it made a slight shiver coat her body. She had no idea why it suddenly felt like they were arguing. And about what? A simple word.

Commitment. Why did she have to make a big deal about it?

"I understand that fine. Just as you better understand I don't share either."

His eyes narrowed. "I would never touch another woman while I'm with you."

She wanted to believe that. She really did. But what happened the other night popped into her head.

Girlfriend.

That woman said she was his girlfriend. He said they used to date. What was the complete story? Why did she feel threatened by this woman?

"I don't like jealousy either. It shouldn't be a big deal when a guy looks at me."

"It's never okay when a man looks at *my* woman in a way I don't like."

She could see the rage in his eyes at the thought. "And if they do…"

"I can control my temper." He looked away. "But they'll know not to do it ever again."

HE *COULD* CONTROL HIS TEMPER.

He wasn't like his father, who loved to hit his mother at the slightest provocation. In and out of jail like a revolving door.

And his mother, beating him down with words. Making a small child feel useless and unloved.

His anger and rage at both of his parents always simmered and bubbled to the surface. But did he ever lash back? Did he ever throw a punch when his father stopped hitting his mother and moved on to him? No. The rage had always floated to the top, wanting to hit him back, but he never did. He took the beating like a man, just like his father spat at him as the punches rolled out.

Did he ever shout angry, vile words back at his mother after she stomped on his heart with cruel, evil words? No. He sat there and took it, his anger rising after each word left her mouth.

He could control his temper when it came to his parents. A cool, even composure. His temper never let loose in front of them. Of course, when he finally managed to break free to his room, his temper let out like a fierce roar of a lion. Holes in the wall. Clothes scattered around the room. If he could throw it, he broke it.

Sometimes, his temper broke free outside of the house.

Fights at school with kids who couldn't mind their own business. A bunch of bullies thinking they were better than everyone else, including him.

A punk-ass gang that thought they controlled the neighborhood, picking on people because they figured they could. His fists had something to say to make them understand that's not how it worked in his neighborhood. He tried not to use his fists, but sometimes he needed to show he meant business.

The bastard that dared to touch Clarissa and broke her to pieces. He pummeled that asshole so hard he served his time for it.

The sad, empty truth kicked him in the gut.

His parents never scared him. It was just a way of life. He knew he'd never be able to change it, so why even try?

But everyone else? He could change that. He could show them who was boss.

He could never control his temper with everyone else because he had been scared. Fear and anger drove him.

Could he control his temper like he claimed with Susan? He wasn't positive if that wasn't a big fat lie. Because fear and rage swarmed his veins like a deadly virus attacking the body simply thinking of another man looking at Susan and her walking away from him as if he were nothing.

A soft hand wrapped around his fingers. Linking his fingers with hers, he squeezed her hand and raised it to his mouth, planting a tender kiss upon it.

He didn't know how to voice his fears, his worries with her. He didn't even know if he should.

"I think—"

"I served a year in jail for beating a man. He's lucky I didn't kill him." His grip on her hand tightened as he turned slowly to look at her.

Her eyes looked round with shock. He hated the expression on her face. One of distrust and a little disgust. Instead of loosening his grip, it became even tighter, not even caring that he might be hurting her. He couldn't lose her, and what he was about to say could do that very thing.

"You mean...you're lucky he didn't die."

"No. I meant what I said."

"Why don't you feel...why doesn't it sound like you don't feel...remorseful?"

"Because I don't." Her face twisted with confusion. He hated making her feel that way, but he wasn't going to lie to her. "He deserved it, and much worse."

"Why?"

He relaxed his hand, feeling shameful that he might've hurt her as a tiny breath escaped from her. He placed another soft kiss against the back of her hand and then rested their hands on his lap.

"Clarissa and I only dated for a few months when I was nineteen and she was eighteen. It was just sex. We both knew going into it that's what it was. When we decided to move on, it was no big deal. We were still friends."

"Are you like that with all the women you date?"

He hated the way the question spilled out of her mouth. So disgusted with him.

"No. She's the only one. I wouldn't want to be friends with any other woman I slept with."

"Why? She was that good in bed?"

He met her eyes. "No. Because she was my best friend's little sister. He never knew we slept together. He probably would've kicked my ass if he had known. We were horny. We got it out of our system. We moved on. That was that."

"What does this have to do with beating a man?"

"Deena doesn't know half of this shit. We sort of drifted apart around this time. She wasn't a huge fan of Stu, Clarissa's brother. Thought he was a douche."

The sweet sound of Susan's laughter filled his heart with a tiny bit of hope. If she could still laugh right now, it had to be a good sign.

"In hindsight, we were a bad influence on each other. We did shit we probably shouldn't have done." He blew out a breath that didn't help. He wanted to run hard and fast and away from this conversation. "He was shot and killed by a local gang that thought we stole some drugs from them."

Susan's grip tightened as she inhaled sharply. "Did you?"

He turned to meet her stare. "I didn't, no. But I think Stu did. I'm no saint. I'll never be one. I did some drugs when I was younger. Stu was always...a little more different than me. He wanted something, he took it."

"Did they think you had something to do with it, too?"

He shrugged. "No clue. They kicked my ass until I almost couldn't breathe. A warning to stay away from them that I understood loud and clear. Clarissa took her brother's death hard. I did, too. But I had to be the strong one. I had to keep her together. He never told me to look out for his sister, but it was something I knew I had to do. The more I tried to help her, the more she shoved me away. She hooked up with this asshole that had no respect for her. He beat her so badly one day she was in the hospital for a week." His voice dropped to a whisper. "She lost her baby."

Susan's sweet, delectable body slid closer. "I'm so sorry, Stitch."

"It wasn't mine or anything," he said with a shrug, "but losing that baby broke her even more. She lost her brother, and then she lost a piece of herself. The cops arrested him, but he was out within a day. He thought his shit didn't stink. So I taught him a lesson about what happens when he touched a woman like that. I made sure I beat the importance into him what would happen if he ever did it again. I served my time...and I'd do it all over again."

He took solace in the fact her grip was still tight and her body close to his, almost wrapping around him. "That's the kind of man I am. Can I control my temper? Yeah...for the most part. Sometimes, shit needs to be done. Can you handle that? Because if you can't, then I guess we're done."

"Can I handle you beating a man? Is that what you're asking? I work for the police department. I believe in the law. That's not a fair question."

"And yet, I'm asking. I'm not going to pretend to be something I'm not. Clarissa is still a part of my life, even if she is a pain in my ass. She's my best friend's little sister, and I can't turn my back on her. You'll have to deal with that, too."

"Gee, you're making it all so easy on me. That's so sweet of you."

"I don't need your damn sarcasm."

Her face morphed into anger. "You're being an asshole and you know it. Do you want to be with me? Or is this your way of pushing me away? What are you scared of?"

Good question. One he didn't want to answer, or even analyze.

"Look, shorty—"

He scowled as an upbeat ring tore through the tension-filled room. He didn't stop her as she pulled her fingers out of his grip and left the bed to get her phone. Her face filled with horror as she listened to the person on the other end, then ended the phone call with a few brisk words he hated to hear.

Part of him was pissed. The other part was relieved.

"So, you're just going to leave? Where in the hell does that leave us?" He couldn't stop the harsh way he spoke.

"It's work. I have to go."

"Yeah, sure. Go."

"When you're done being an asshole, let me know."

She dressed quickly in silence.

Would he ever stop being an asshole? Probably not. He wouldn't change for anybody.

Well, maybe he could.

If he stopped letting his fear take control.

"Please take me home, Stitch."

He could see it in her eyes. She wanted to get as far away from him as she could. But she had no vehicle here. She needed him.

And he needed her.

If he only had the nerve to tell her how much he truly needed her in his life.

"This conversation ain't over, Suzy baby."

She leveled him with a piercing stare. "It is for now." Then she walked out of his room.

15

SUSAN PREPARED HERSELF. She tried to clear her mind and put herself into work mode. Something she usually never failed at.

Today, she felt like she was failing at everything. Why couldn't the day end already? How much more could she take?

Learning Newman was a liar.

Not being able to find him.

Sleeping with Stitch again.

Fighting again.

And now another murdered woman.

"Hey, Susan."

Whipping her head a little too fast, she ignored the sharp pain in her neck. The pain almost felt nice. A reminder that she could still feel something. Because fighting with Stitch again was starting to make her numb. She couldn't take the up and down battles. Why did it have to be so difficult dealing with him?

"Susan?"

Shaking her head from her wandering thoughts, she didn't even attempt a smile for Ben. "Hi."

"Are you okay?"

"I'm..." Saying fine wouldn't do anymore. She was far from fine. "I'm going to survive, but it hasn't been a good day. What are you doing here?"

"Zeke and I have been trying to help Sauer find Newman."

"And?"

"Nothing. Then this call came in. Sauer's tense and very edgy with the slightest word against Newman."

"Well, I don't want to offend him, but it's not looking good for Newman."

Ben nodded. "I agree." He held out a hand in front of him with a comforting smile. "After you."

She finally offered a tiny smile in return and walked into the house first. Death swarmed her immediately. The emptiness filled her senses and created a deep melancholy she wasn't sure she could erase.

This poor woman. Why did she deserve to die? Why did this madman pick her? Did Newman kill her?

She took her time walking down the hallway to the woman's bedroom where she found Sauer and Zeke. They stopped talking as soon as they saw her and Ben. Zeke smiled while Sauer barely managed a decent grin. She did neither.

Her eyes zoomed to the dead body, even as she wanted to turn away and walk out. She looked like the other women. Strangled, barely any evidence of a struggle.

This killer was strong. It didn't take much effort to kill these women.

"I spoke to the victim's sister, Wendy, and she said her

sister's husband is on a business trip right now. We won't be able to speak to him right away," Ben said quietly next to her.

She knew she should step forward and start doing her job, but she couldn't seem to move. She couldn't do anything but stand there and stare at the body.

"Well, we should split up. One start canvassing the neighborhood. One start digging into Julie's background," Zeke said as he glanced at the dead woman on the floor, "and one keep looking for Newman."

"He didn't do this," Sauer said softly, yet laced with barely controlled anger.

"Figure it out somewhere else. I have work to do." She took her time looking at each of them, conveying how much she didn't want to hear the argument about whether Newman was guilty or not. "Please."

"Call us if you need anything," Ben said, and headed out of the room without any arguments.

Zeke followed, offering a small smile on his way out.

Sauer trailed behind them, but stopped in the doorway. "Did something happen with Stitch? Did he hurt you?"

Hurt could be defined in so many different ways. Did Stitch hurt her? In some ways, yes. In other ways, no.

"I'm fine."

Sauer nodded gently. "You're my friend, Susan. I know he's Dee's good friend, but you're *my* friend. I don't want him to hurt you."

"Thank you, Sauer. It'll be fine."

He hesitated, then walked out. Would it be fine? How many times could they argue, make up, have sex, argue again, and everything turn out fine? She wasn't made for this kind of stress. She liked things nice and quiet. Orderly. Smooth relationships.

Yeah, and where did those kind of relationships get her?

Nowhere. Cheated on. Dumped. Boring. No zing in the relationship.

Maybe this chaotic relationship was what she needed. Liven her life up some. Put a little zing in it.

It didn't mean she liked the fighting.

She had no idea how she felt about his confession. He beat a man and didn't feel an ounce of remorse. Did the other man deserve it? She had to admit, maybe he did. Maybe he deserved to feel the kind of pain he had inflicted upon Clarissa. But did he *have* to beat him? Was Stitch right to take the law into his own hands? Absolutely not. That's where she didn't agree with him. Maybe the man did deserve to feel some pain, but it wasn't up to Stitch to decide.

Could she date and fall in love with a man like that?

Well, correction, she already fell in love with him. The question now was could she date him? Could she see a future with him? Sometimes, love just wasn't enough.

As her eyes grazed over the dead woman, a woman who now had no choice to live her life, she knew.

Stitch might not be the perfect choice. The right choice. But he was her choice. She refused to hold his past against him. He paid the price for his crime. She could respect that. She wanted to make things work between them, and she knew he wouldn't make a moment of it easy on her.

"Another terrible crime scene. I do believe I heard Captain Ganderson is on his way here."

Startled, Susan jumped as she twisted toward the bedroom doorway. Placing a hand over her heart, a low chuckle escaped. "Quiet as a mouse, Dr. Everly. You have to stop sneaking up on me."

Honestly, he did. She couldn't count on her hands how many times that man walked into a crime scene, popping up out of nowhere. His footsteps, quiet as a ghost. His movements, light as a feather.

"My apologies. Any leads yet?" he asked as he stepped near the victim.

Well, if she didn't count Newman, no. How did she want to answer a question that should be simple to answer?

"I believe Zeke and Ben are helping to find a good lead."

"That's good. This needs to stop." He sighed as his eyes perused the body from head to toe. "Probably won't find anything different from the last three victims."

"I'll let you do your thing and come back when you're ready for me."

She didn't give him a chance to say anything, walking out of the room as if she were running a marathon. She couldn't explain, even to herself, the need to be alone. To be free from others' prying, knowing eyes. She saw the concern, the worry in his gaze. He probably wanted to ask her if she was okay, as everyone else had been doing lately. He wouldn't. Dr. Everly usually stayed clear of all that mushy stuff, as he put it. If someone wanted to share their problems with him, he'd listen, but he never initiated the conversation. That was his philosophy. That it wasn't his business. It didn't mean he didn't hide his concern.

She wanted people to stop being so concerned about her. Maybe she wasn't fine. Maybe she couldn't hide the pain and hurt and confusion going on in her life recently, but she would be fine. She wouldn't allow anything, or anyone, to bring her down. Not her style.

Besides, she wanted a relationship to work with Stitch. She wouldn't allow his words to hurt, or his actions.

Boom!

The floor loomed before her. A strong hand grabbed her arm before she fell face first into the hardwood floor.

"I'm so sorry, Susan. Are you okay?"

Again.

Are you okay?

Such an innocent question. The more she heard it, the more she wanted to scream in frustration.

This time, everything had been her fault. Fleeing the room. Running as if that would solve her problems. Not watching where she was going.

She straightened, trying not to wince at the minor pain in her knee at the funny way she had twisted going down. Even though she didn't want to smile, she offered one anyway.

Captain Ganderson gently smiled back at her.

"I'm the one who is sorry. I wasn't paying attention. I'm okay."

He let her arm go, obviously satisfied with her answer.

"Dr. Everly is in the bedroom."

"I was actually looking for Detective Sauer and Newman. Are they still here?"

She couldn't stop the look of panic that entered her eyes. What did she say to that? Admit Newman didn't show up? That they couldn't even find him? That he could possibly be a suspect in these murders?

What would Sauer think of her? How upset would he be when he found out she told Captain Ganderson before he had a chance to find Newman?

"Susan?" His brows dipped low, confusion etched across his face.

Taking a deep breath, she let it all out. She did her job. Her duty to report the facts.

If Sauer hated her for that, well, then he did. She had no control over that.

She did her job.

THE DOOR SLAMMED HARDER than he intended, but he didn't care at this point. The anger, the rage, the disappointment consumed him more than caring whether he slammed doors or not.

He couldn't say he was angry or hurt or disappointed in Susan. He knew why she confessed everything to Captain Ganderson. He knew it wasn't in her to lie to his face. He respected that about her. Being mad at her for doing her job wasn't right. And he wasn't.

He was pissed at himself.

Newman was his partner. His friend. He should've seen what was going on. He should've been able to find him without much problem.

Instead, he couldn't locate his friend to find out the truth before the captain knew everything, and now that he did, nothing would help Newman.

He felt like a little boy as Captain Ganderson laid into him, Ben, and Zeke for keeping this information from him as long as they had. He tried to apologize to Ben and Zeke for getting them involved and in trouble. Of course, they blew him off, saying it was no big deal. But it was. This was his responsibility, and he should've never asked anyone else to step in and help.

He jerked at the sudden arms sliding around his waist and a soft head resting against his chest. So dazed, he didn't realize he had stopped in the middle of the foyer, staring into space. Even with Dee's warm embrace circling him, he felt miles away.

"What's the matter?"

Where did he start? Did he even want to tell her what was going on? She was the last person he wanted to argue with. If he told her everything, she'd go right back on her kick that Newman was guilty and a douche. He couldn't hear that right now. He loved his wife, but he couldn't hear any of that from her.

"I won't...I won't say anything harsh. I promise." She lifted her head and caressed his cheek. "I don't like seeing you like this. I know he's your friend. I'll try to be more supportive."

These moments. These rare, tender moments when she admitted she was wrong always took him by surprise. Because she never liked to admit she was wrong, considering she wasn't wrong often. He had no problem admitting that.

What scared him was she might not be wrong. Perhaps that's why he didn't want to keep hearing it. He didn't want her to be right.

Now he felt like an ass, hearing her apologize for something that maybe she shouldn't be apologizing for.

"I can't find him. Captain Ganderson knows. There's another victim." He sucked in a sharp breath. "And I can't find him."

"But you tried, and that counts for something. You're a good friend."

"Am I? I didn't even know how serious his problems were. What kind of friend is that?"

She slapped his chest as she cocked a brow. "Don't do that. Don't blame yourself for his idiocy. He should've been honest with you about his relationship with Chrissy. He's the liar. He's the one who ruined your friendship, not you."

"I feel like I should've seen this. I should've known something was wrong."

She grabbed his hand and pulled. "Come on. No more of this. It's not your fault."

He let her drag him down the hallway, trying to accept her words and failing miserably. "Where are we going? I should probably go back out and look for him. Look for the killer. The real killer."

Stopping in front of the doorway to their bedroom, she smiled softly. "First, I'm going to make my husband feel better." Her eyes glided to the bed. "No arguments, mister. Get naked."

He didn't have time for this. There weren't many times he denied sex. Well, actually, there never was a time he did that. But right now didn't seem like the best of times. He should be focusing on finding Newman. On finding the killer.

She snagged a hand in his waistband and pulled him into the room. "You are not denying this pregnant woman—this horny, pregnant woman—what she wants."

When she was naked two seconds later, she was right.

He couldn't deny her anything.

Maybe this would help him relax.

Maybe this would help clear his head.

Then he'd track down his friend and find out if he was a murderer and why he lied.

SUSAN TOOK A DEEP BREATH, then forced herself to walk. No big deal. She didn't know why she was making it into a big deal. She talked to these guys all the time. It shouldn't be so difficult to put one foot in front of the other to talk to them like she always did.

Except, she had never ratted them out before.

How upset were they? Did they hate her? She hoped not. If they hated her, then Zoe, Rina, and Dee would hate her, and she'd have no friends. Before them, she worked too much to keep up with the few friends she made in college. And her high school friends, she didn't know what any of those people were up to anymore.

"Hey, guys."

She waited with bated breath for Zeke or Ben to speak as she stood near their desks. Both stared at her. She didn't see anger, but they also weren't jumping to speak.

"Hey, Susan," Ben said softly, the corner of his eyes crinkling as a small smile appeared.

She could work with that. That had to mean he wasn't too upset with her. Did she talk about the case? Apologize? She shouldn't have to apologize for doing her job, but she didn't like knowing they may have gotten into trouble for withholding information from Captain Ganderson.

"Find anything useful for us?"

A smile broke free at Zeke's question. He didn't say it with an attitude. Perhaps neither of them hated her as she feared. What did Sauer think about her?

"No. It's the same as the other crime scenes. He—this killer knows what they're doing."

Saying *he* could imply Newman. Maybe it was a woman. Maybe a vengeful woman mad at other women.

As soon as that idiotic thought rolled through her mind, she wanted to slap herself silly. Of course it wasn't a woman. Each victim had been raped, and not with an object or anything. Only a man could've done this.

Unless there were two of them. A man who raped the women, and a woman who killed them.

What the hell was she thinking? Creating ridiculous scenarios to try to lessen the fact it could be Newman as the killer.

"You look like you're thinking hard there, Susan," Zeke said, cracking a grin.

She chuckled. "Yeah, just silly things floating around. I wish I had more for you guys. I searched that house from top to bottom. I..." She paused, unable to keep going without saying it. "I'm sorry."

"Hey, we know it's not your fault you can't find any evidence. If you couldn't find any, then there's none to be found," Ben said.

"No, that's not what I meant. I'm sorry about the thing with Captain Ganderson. I—"

"Don't." Zeke stood up. "Don't apologize. You were doing your job."

Relief flooded her, grateful they didn't hate her. "Any word on Newman yet?"

Zeke shook his head, then smiled warmly. "You know Sauer's not mad either, right?"

That one she had a harder time believing. "I hope not. But I couldn't lie to Captain Ganderson. Not to his face."

"He knows that." Ben also stood up, grabbing his jacket from behind his chair.

"We're heading out. Sauer left a little bit ago. There isn't much we can do right now. I think we all need a break. Ben and I already talked. We'll be coming in tomorrow to help on the case and to find Newman." Zeke sighed and rubbed a hand down his face. "I don't want to think he's guilty, but the longer he's missing, the worse it looks."

"Maybe he has a good reason. Maybe he had a family emergency or something." She knew that was a flimsy excuse, and she wasn't even sure why she was giving him an excuse. What had Newman done recently to earn that from her? Nothing. He'd been nothing but a jerk.

"Yeah, maybe. Are you done for the day?" Zeke asked as he slung his coat on.

She nodded. "I just wanted to check in with you guys. I'll see you tomorrow."

She didn't normally work on weekends, unless a particular case brought her into work. These recent murders were definitely a good reason to come into work on her day off.

They said their good-byes after Ben and Zeke graciously walked her to her car. She wasn't afraid of walking alone to her car at night, but it was nice of them to see her safely to her vehicle.

The drive home was slow. She took her time, dreading the silence and emptiness. She figured she could stop in to see Stitch, pick up their conversation where they left it. But she wasn't in the mood to fight again.

Would it ever stop between them?

Hitting the garage door button a few houses away, she didn't notice the sleek red car in her driveway until she started to turn.

Stitch.

He came to her.

Was she prepared to see him so soon? Would they fight? All of her energy was slowly dwindling to nothing. She wanted to change into her comfy pajamas and lie in bed and forget about everything. Even the issues between them.

This day had been forever long. So much happened, it felt like an entire week had passed.

She drove by him, barely making eye contact as he stood leisurely outside his car, and parked in the garage. Before he could meet her at her car door, she hit the garage door button.

Perhaps that was a childish move, closing him out.

Maybe it even made a statement. Would he still be in the driveway when she walked to her front door to check?

Why did she close the door on him?

She wasn't ready to face him. Face the inevitable fighting. They always managed to argue. Every single time. It was getting old.

She disarmed her alarm, then took her time walking to the front door. When she unlocked the door, she didn't have time to twist the knob herself. The door swung open, making her take a step back.

Stitch stepped inside without asking, which didn't surprise her, and slammed her door shut.

"Trying to hide from me, shorty?"

"No."

"You've been gone a long time."

"I was working." She wanted to ask how long he had been waiting, but the words wouldn't come.

"We got shit to talk about."

"Yes."

"I've been thinking about this all night and..." His words died on a whisper.

Maybe it was the way she looked at him. Maybe it was the tears gathering in the corner of her eyes. Maybe it was the way she started to shiver and shake.

Her reaction wasn't only from the thought he was officially done with her. But from everything. The entire day. The entire week. The stress of everything.

"Shit, Suzy baby. Don't cry." One step and she was in his arms. He swung her gently, cradling her close to his chest, and walked to the living room where he sat down. His arms tightened around her, as if he were unwilling to let her go for even a second. "Don't cry."

Even as he said those soft words, a tear slid out. She

couldn't have stopped it if she tried. She wasn't a crier. What did tears ever solve?

But she couldn't hold them in.

Tear after tear slid out. Silently, but strong.

Stitch held her tightly, his strong arms wrapping around her as if he could shield her from everything. Oh, how she wished that were true.

The silence circled them. Something that should've been uncomfortable, yet somehow she felt his comfort straight to the core of her heart. His head tucked over hers, his hands splayed across her back, stroking, soothing. His warm body relaxing her.

As her tears fell, he held her. No words exchanged. Nothing but calm, sweet peace filled the air.

That's all she needed. She didn't realize this was all she wanted until he gave it to her.

It was crazy scary how well he knew her already.

Minutes passed. Her tears lessened, yet she wasn't ready to face her problems. The reason why she cried.

Soon, they stopped. Her eyes were dry. He still held her tightly in his embrace, the room silent. The lights were off. The darkness should've been eerie and foreboding, but it helped the peace settle in a little easier.

"Talk to me, Suzy baby. What happened?"

Besides the part where they always argued, everything else happened. How could she explain? Did she even want to talk about it?

A soft kiss touched her forehead, reassuring and sweet. She enjoyed this tender side of him. Willing to console her when it probably wasn't something he did often, or liked to do.

Such a mysterious man. So strong and defiant at times. Controlling and domineering at other times. Sweet and tender. What part was the real Stitch?

All of it. That's what made him so special. That's why she didn't want to lose him. Yet, she didn't know how to keep him. She wouldn't be able to until he allowed her to. So far, he'd been keeping her at a distance, not willing to let her get close enough to latch on and keep a firm grip.

"Sweetheart?"

So many different endearments he loved to call her. Even when he called her shorty, one she didn't particularly like, she could almost imagine it as an endearment. Just one when he was annoyed with her. Right now, calling her sweetheart and Suzy baby, he was worried. Concerned.

Then it all came out. Everything about work. About Newman. About telling Captain Ganderson. Everything but the issues between them. She wasn't ready to touch that subject.

Hell, she shouldn't even be telling him half of this stuff. Not that she talked about the murder cases, but even grazing the surface about it felt borderline weird, as if she were betraying her professionalism. But she couldn't keep it in. She had to tell someone. She had to tell a neutral party.

Maybe telling Dee's best friend wasn't that neutral, but she felt like she could trust Stitch. She wanted to be able to trust him.

"I'll kick Sauer's ass if he says one mean word to you."

A real laugh fell out as she tilted her head to look at him. "And how would Dee take that if you beat up her husband?"

"Right now, I don't care."

Her heart skipped a beat. This felt monumental. As if he just admitted something he didn't want to admit. Her feelings were more important than his best friend's? Did he... love her?

Well, she wasn't going to ask. She wasn't even going to

admit she loved him. Unless, of course, he decided to say it first.

"He better not hurt you."

She sighed softly. "Sauer would never touch me."

"Maybe not physically. I don't give a shit who he is. Nobody will hurt you."

So possessive. Did she like it? Could she handle this? Something as simple as hurting her feelings and he wanted to beat a person.

"I wish you wouldn't say things like that."

"It's never going to change."

"I know," she whispered so softly, she wasn't sure he heard her. When he placed a gentle kiss to the top of her head, she knew he did. A simple gesture that he understood. It didn't mean he would change.

She didn't want him to change. Not really. But she didn't know if she could handle the possessive, jealous part of him.

"Do you think Newman is guilty?"

"I don't have enough evidence to say either way."

He shifted a little, his arms never loosening. "That's not what I'm asking."

She settled her head on his chest. "I honestly don't know. I want to say no. But then...he's been acting weird lately."

"If he comes near you, you call me." His arms tightened into a death grip. "Immediately."

"He's not—"

"Non-negotiable."

"What are you going to do? Punch him, even if he hasn't done anything? Violence isn't the answer to everything, Stitch."

"I don't have to lay a finger on that asshole to let him know to stay the hell away from you."

"I work with him. It's impossible not to have contact with him. I'm not afraid of him."

"Call me."

"Stitch..."

"You'll call me."

She twisted in his arms. "You need to stop this...this...possessive behavior."

He squeezed her fiercely, kissing her forehead. "And if I don't?"

Good question. Could she handle it? Did she want to handle it?

"You're mine, Suzy baby." His soft words slid down her spine in delicious tingles. "Whether you like it or not."

16

THE POUNDING on the door made him bolt upright in bed. It was like a shot of adrenaline straight into his veins. He shoved back the covers and started to scramble out of the bed when a soft hand on his arm stopped him.

"I got it," she whispered sleepily.

His eyes narrowed at the beautiful woman lying in bed, half-naked, the sheet covering her lower half, with her breasts on display. If there wasn't some asshole knocking on the door at four in the morning, he would show her how much he loved her breasts.

"Go back to bed. You're not answering the door. Especially looking like that."

She glanced down and grinned. Her eyes tilted back up mischievously. "I'll put some clothes on. It's my house, Stitch."

"Stay in bed."

He didn't give her a chance to argue. He swiped his pants and shirt from the floor and dressed somewhat awkwardly, then slid his shoes on and walked out of her bedroom and to the front door with determined footsteps. Halfway there, he realized he didn't zip his pants. He pulled the zipper up gently, considering he left his boxers on the floor, and tried to erase the erotic image of Susan waiting for him in bed. He needed his full wits to deal with whatever asshole decided to knock on her door so late, and then take his fill of her once he got back to bed.

As he was about to open the door, he heard some beeps from the kitchen. A second later, Susan's gorgeous face appeared around the corner. She was dressed in her flimsy robe, and he had to wonder if she was still naked underneath that, because it did not look like she put on a shirt before tightening the robe around her slender waist.

"You didn't want the alarm to go off, did you?"

He smirked instead of answering. Obviously, he hadn't been thinking about the alarm. Just the fact he wanted to ream into whoever was on the other side of the door. He didn't like being woken up like this. Or that someone felt the need to bother Susan so late. He especially didn't like her walking his way dressed the way she was.

His hand tightened its grip on the handle and then opened it. He didn't bother to hide the snarl on his face. "What the hell do you want?"

Sauer blinked in surprise, then tried to glance behind him. "I'm looking for Susan."

"At four o'clock in the morning? Go home to your wife." He leaned in closer. "Stay the hell away from Susan, especially if you have nothing nice to say to her."

Sauer looked confused with a mixture of shock. "I'm always nice to Susan. I should say the same to you. You hurt her, and you'll answer to me."

"Are you threatening me?"

"Maybe I am."

Before he could throw a punch in Sauer's face, even

though he knew it'd be a terrible idea, hurting Deena in the process, a soft hand pressed against his chest and made him step back.

"Is everything okay, Sauer? What's going on? You never show up like this."

He hated the fear he heard in her tone. Fear that Sauer would hurt her? Or something far worse? The unknown grated on his nerves, making him jumpy as hell.

A slow sigh escaped as Sauer ran a hand through his hair, his eyes darting from him to Susan and back to him.

"We found Newman. We had a cop car staked out at his house and he finally showed up around two. The officer called Captain Ganderson, who then called me, and we knocked on his door together. Needless to say, the conversation didn't go well and..." Sauer's face twisted in horror.

A shiver rippled across Susan's body. She obviously didn't want to hear what he was about to say. He wrapped an arm around her waist and pulled her closer. She didn't hesitate to grip his arms, as if she were sinking to the bottom of the ocean and he would keep her afloat. Keep her safe. He would. No matter the cost.

"Sauer? And what?"

"We had to take him in for questioning. He's refusing to talk. He hasn't admitted to anything, but his silence isn't..." Sauer's eyes squeezed closed as a dose of pain shot across his features. His eyes popped open. "I don't want to think he's guilty, but he's not giving me a choice right now. Why would he do this?"

"Some people are assholes."

Sauer's eyes whipped to his. Susan also twisted her head to gaze up at him. He shrugged. It was the truth. Sometimes, there was no rhyme or reason. People just did something because they were an asshole.

Susan leaned into him some more as she turned back to Sauer. "What do you need from me?"

Sauer lifted his hand, the tremors clear as day as he held out a piece of paper to her. "It's a warrant for his house. I need you to come with me and process...process any evidence we might find."

She nodded and took the paper from his hand. She tried to walk away, to get out of his embrace, but Stitch's hold on her didn't weaken. If anything, he tightened it. He didn't want her to leave. He knew he had no right to stop her. This was her job. But after last night and the things she shared about Newman, he didn't want her to have anything to do with this. How dare Sauer keep bringing her into the mix. How dare he think it was okay to come to her house at four in the morning, rip her out of his arms, and make her leave him.

She tried to twist around, but instead of letting her do that, he twisted instead, his back now to Sauer.

He lowered his mouth to her ear. "Don't leave."

"This is my job."

"You don't want to leave. Someone else can deal with this shit."

She trembled slightly. He was right. She didn't want to leave, and he wasn't going to let her.

"Stitch, I have to. It's my job."

"Screw that. You don't have to." He dropped his arms and turned around, shoving Sauer back. "Go home. She isn't leaving."

"Watch it, Stitch," Sauer warned as he righted himself before falling on his ass, something Stitch wished would've happened.

"What are you going to do about it, Sauer? Huh? Fight me? Take your best shot."

"I don't know what your problem is lately, but I'm not going to sit here and take it. How about you leave. I'm not sure I want you at Susan's house." Sauer took a step closer.

"It's not any of your damn business." His fists clenched.

"I'm making it my business."

"Stop it. Both of you." She shoved between them, putting a hand on both of their chests to make them step back. She turned to Sauer. "Let me get dressed. I'm coming with you." Then she turned toward Stitch. "Knock it off. This is my job."

"Even if you don't want to do this? Screw your job. That Newman asshole scares you. Someone else can take care of this."

"He doesn't scare me."

He cocked an eyebrow. "Yeah, keep telling yourself that, but that's not how I heard it last night."

"Do I have to ask you to leave, Stitch?"

"You kicking me out, shorty?"

Her eyes narrowed to little slits, something she liked to do when he called her that. He knew she didn't like it, which was probably why he did it. What an asshole. Why couldn't he control his temper with her?

She stepped closer, her hand on his chest heavy as she pushed him a little—not enough to make him move back, but enough to make a point. "I don't want you to leave, but you need to stop acting like this."

Lowering his head, his mouth brushed her ear. "I'll never stop acting like this. Not when I can see how much it's hurting you to do something you don't want to do."

"It's my job."

Every time she said that, this time in a gentle whisper, he wanted to pound something. The wall. A face. Anything to unleash the anger those words made him feel. She shouldn't have to do something she didn't want to do, job be damned.

She stood on her tippy-toes. A soft kiss landed on his neck. "You should know the feeling. Having to do your job when you don't want to sometimes."

"What the hell does that mean?"

"Your wrist."

He jerked back in surprise. No way. She couldn't know how much his wrist had been bothering him. He hid that. He didn't let anyone see how much it bothered him.

Pain shimmered within the depths of her eyes as she walked around him and into the house, presumably to change. He hated every step she took.

"What's your problem?"

His gaze slowly connected with Sauer's. "Right now, you're my problem."

If he didn't walk away, he was probably going to do something he would regret. Something that would have Deena—and Susan—pissed at him.

A flash of anger glittered in Sauer's eyes. "I don't think you're the right person for Susan. Do her and yourself a favor and leave her alone."

Just like when he was growing up, he felt useless. Like a nobody. Like he wasn't ever good enough. Deena's husband, a man he usually didn't have a problem with, a man he wanted to like because he was her husband, crossed the line. He hoped Deena forgave him. Because nobody talked to him that way.

A fist went flying right into Sauer's jaw. He went down hard, stumbling down the two porch steps and landing on his ass. Sauer was quick to get back up on his feet and dodge the next fist he tried to land on his face.

He surprised him some, even though Deena warned

him Sauer knew how to fight. When a punch hit him near his left eye, he tried not to cringe from the pain, instead, throwing one of his own punches back.

Back and forth they went. Dodging blows, taking punches, and grunting in earnest as they fought on Susan's front lawn. He didn't attempt to slow down his assault until he heard a voice screaming from behind.

The terror and aching pain in the scream had him stopping immediately, backing away from Sauer, even though he wanted to pound him into the ground until he couldn't walk. That's how high his anger was.

Sauer retreated from him as well, touching his cheek and swiping his hand down his side. Probably making sure his gun was still there. Stitch had never touched a gun in his life. He didn't need to. His fists were all he needed. He wasn't stupid enough to grab a cop's gun, no matter how pissed he was.

Susan didn't hesitate to walk right up to him and shove him hard. "What is wrong with you?"

"What? You think I started this?"

"Okay." Breathing heavily, she looked between them. "Who threw the first punch?"

Well, if that's what she wanted to count starting it, then he was guilty. But that's not how he saw it. His silence, apparently, was answer enough. Her brows dipped low, the anguish visible in her eyes.

"Violence isn't the answer, Stitch."

"It is when someone threatens me. You want me out of your life, Susan? That's what that jackass wants." His hand whipped toward Sauer. He had to ignore the pain as he did. "I guess I'm not good enough for you. Shit. Maybe he's right. When have I ever been good enough?"

Jamming his hand in his pocket, finally cringing from

the pain, he wretched his keys out and climbed into his vehicle without glancing at her once. If he did, he might cave and beg her to stay home. To work this shit out.

Maybe she didn't want to work it out. She didn't even try to stop him as he backed out of her driveway.

Maybe it was never going to work out.

Yet again, he wasn't good enough.

This was why he avoided relationships. Too messy. Too tangled up with emotions.

Never again.

17

Susan didn't say a word to Sauer after he apologized for what happened in her front yard. He said he would drive to Newman's house, she nodded, walked inside to set her alarm, and then slid into the passenger seat of his car.

Sure. He said he was sorry, but he didn't go into detail of what caused the fight. She knew Stitch had been brewing on the edge, waiting, perhaps hoping, for a fight.

As crazy as it seemed, he knew her so well.

She didn't want to go process Newman's house. She didn't want to talk to Newman—not that she had to. She was only going there to do her job collecting evidence. She didn't want to deal with this Newman business anymore.

But it was her job. She couldn't walk away from her responsibility. Even though she appreciated Stitch stepping up and voicing what she couldn't, she had to do her job. He should understand that.

Not good enough? Why did he think that? Who made him think that? She couldn't imagine Sauer being that heartless and cruel.

Perhaps he had been if Stitch felt threatened enough to

throw a punch. Who originally made him feel not worthy enough?

It would be impossible to make things work if he didn't give in a little. Talk to her.

Like his hand.

She wasn't dumb.

Evidence was her forte. A keen eye, looking for things was something she excelled at.

She didn't miss the way he would absently rub his wrist on occasion, thinking she didn't notice, and when he thought she might, he stopped.

She wanted to know how badly it hurt. Did it hinder his job? Did he need to see a doctor? She wanted to ask him a few times, each time she saw him rub it, but too afraid to voice one word. Would he ignore her? Walk out on her? Their relationship was tentative at best. She didn't want to do anything to rock the boat so soon.

But she couldn't keep it to herself. Not when he threw the words he had at her. So she threw some back.

"I apologize, Susan. I didn't..." Sauer paused, as if weighing his words. She preferred honesty over anything else.

"You didn't what?"

"I was going to say I didn't mean to cause problems between you two, and I didn't. Not really. But I'm not sure he's the right one for you."

Her eyes jerked to his. Perhaps he couldn't handle her glare because he immediately looked back to the road. "What makes you think you know what's right for me?"

"Oh, so he treats you right, huh? I find that hard to believe."

"Why? What did he do to make you think he doesn't?" Her voice dropped an octave, not wanting to say anything, but she refused to let Sauer get away with his actions as if he had done the right thing. "He's the first man to treat me with honesty. With a level of respect I didn't know I needed. He's real. He doesn't bullshit me like other men. He told me in the beginning he only wanted sex. I was okay with that. Then I wasn't. And he walked away."

"I don't get it. Why was he at your house at four in the morning? Just visiting for a chitchat."

"Wow, Sauer. I've never heard you speak this way."

"He's using you for more sex. What pretty words did he give you to get back in your bed, Susan?" He slammed the wheel hard. "I don't like people like that. I don't want someone like that to hurt my friend. Excuse me for trying to protect my friend."

"Stitch is the last person to use pretty words. He doesn't know the meaning of that." Her hands tightened into fists in her lap. "Did you goad him into hitting you? Is that what you wanted, Sauer? For him to walk away? Well, congratulations. He did. Again."

"I didn't want him to hurt you."

Her eyes met his once more. Briefly. "Well, he did. And so did you."

The conversation ended. A few minutes later, they pulled into Newman's driveway and she hastily exited the vehicle. She almost didn't stop outside the door to say hello to Ben and Zeke. Guess they called in all the troops.

"Hey, Susan," Ben said quietly.

"Geez, what the hell happened to you, Sauer? Did Newman do that?" Zeke exclaimed as he glanced behind her.

Susan turned toward him, a slight triumph coursing through her at the way his cheeks blossomed a bright red. A bruise was forming around his right eye, a busted lip, his hair a mess, his clothes disheveled. Even in the pale night, with the porch lights on, she could see the way he couldn't hold his blush in. Served him right. Did he see how his actions messed things up? What made him think she wanted him stepping into her business? Who did—

Her mind stopped throwing accusations around as her eyes beamed to his hand that was shaking like a leaf.

Of course.

Why didn't she see it right away?

Sauer was worried about her. He wanted to be the protective friend, something she appreciated. It felt nice to know he cared. But that wasn't his motivation. She didn't think so anymore.

He was worried about Newman. His gut was probably churning with agony at the thought his partner and friend was a killer. His nerves were high. His temper short. And he decided to lash out at the easiest target in front of him.

Stitch.

Right now, though, she wasn't willing to forgive his behavior, even if he had a lame excuse for it.

"Dude, your lip is still bleeding. What happened?" Ben asked when Sauer continued to ignore Zeke's question, his eyes darting from her to them.

She couldn't hold back a glare, his head dropping, maybe in shame, maybe in guilt, maybe in sorrow, but dropping, nonetheless.

"He got into a fight with Stitch. I'd appreciate it if all of you would stay out of my business. Stop asking if I'm okay. Now excuse me while I process this scene."

Susan walked into the house, finally feeling a little calmer since leaving her house.

She was done with people asking if she was okay. She

wasn't. Her life was a mess. There was absolutely nothing okay with it.

She probably took a good working relationship with three great detectives and shoved it down the toilet, and most likely, her great friendship with three wonderful ladies.

Oh, well. That was life. Shit happened to her, and she moved on.

Her parents got divorced. She ignored the tension and the fighting between the two and moved on.

College wasn't as exciting as she hoped. That's okay. She did what she had to do, got her degree, and moved on.

Couldn't seem to land a steady, reliable boyfriend. Nothing new there. She always moved on, hoping the next one would be a winner.

Her job was suddenly becoming a nightmare. Well, she could most definitely move on.

Or just move. Start fresh. A clean slate.

That was an idea she never contemplated before. She might have to think about it a lot harder when she got home.

But first. Work.

STITCH RUBBED HIS WRIST, then picked his pencil back up. He wouldn't quit. He'd work through the pain even if it killed him. The pain was all his fault for starting a fight with Sauer. The ache in his wrist and hand hadn't receded since he threw the first punch.

The sketch didn't need to be done until later next week, but he was going to take today to get tons of shit done he had been letting slide. Too much lately.

No more using his pain as an excuse. Yeah, his wrist hurt, but it wasn't an excuse to slack on the job. People relied on him. He was the owner of one of the best tattoo shops in the area. He couldn't reschedule clients all the time and expect to stay one of the best shops in the area. That was simply idiotic thinking.

After leaving Susan's house, pissed at himself for losing his cool with Sauer, he debated turning around and apologizing. Of course, it would've been useless. She wouldn't be home. She was going to process a scene she didn't want to do and he couldn't stop her.

He could've called her. He even dug in his pocket to pull his phone out and call her a few miles from her house, but realized in his haste to leave, he left his phone on her nightstand in the bedroom. Hell, he left his boxers there, too.

Now, no matter what he wanted, he had to go back to her house to retrieve his phone. And he *did* want to go back. He wanted her.

Throwing a few punches, getting a few good licks in felt good. He felt vindicated a little. He wished he could take back the words he said to Susan. *Maybe he's right. When have I ever been good enough?*

He never let shit like that take him down. Today, he let it get to him. He let Sauer win by walking away. By not yelling from the top of his lungs he was good enough.

Damn right, he was good enough.

Dropping the pencil again, he couldn't resist rubbing his wrist.

Would he be good enough if he lost his shop? Would she still want him, then?

She asked him to stop using violence. It wasn't his normal go-to on things. He rarely used violence, even back in the day. Did his temper get up and words fly out of his mouth? Hell, yeah, he wouldn't deny that. But his fists rarely came into play. Only when absolutely necessary, because using his fists reminded him of his old man, and he was nothing like that deadbeat asshole.

Today, he just couldn't let Sauer speak to him like that. Make him feel like he was worthless. He had already been feeling like that on his own this past week, especially with the way his wrist had been hurting.

Look at him now. He couldn't work on his sketch without stopping every other minute to take a break. If that wasn't pathetic, then what was?

He'd finish this sketch, and then conquer the other three sketches waiting to be done. He'd make good use of the day, and then go grovel to Susan. Again. He'd keep groveling until he won her heart for good.

He picked his pencil back up, pressing the tip lightly against the paper, and suddenly it snapped, broke off, as a loud banging from the front of the building jolted him in surprise.

Wanting to ignore the visitor, he grabbed a new pencil from the cup on the corner of his desk. He started to work on the sketch, the bangs and knocks drowning out of his mind. He needed to focus and center himself. He didn't give a shit who wanted to bother him right now. He wasn't answering the door.

Then a voice drifted with the knocks.

A voice he knew he couldn't keep hanging.

Setting the pencil down gently, he stood up and took a deep breath. He needed to prepare himself. Although, nothing could've prepared him for the wrath on her face as he unlocked the door to his shop.

The door swung closed quietly as they stared at each other.

He didn't know what to say. Sorry was on the tip of his tongue, but he wasn't *that* sorry. It'd be a lie. One thing he wasn't was a liar.

"Well, at least you look just as terrible as my husband. Serves you right." Deena's hands went to her hips as her eyes broke into tiny little slits. "Aren't you going to say anything? An explanation, maybe?"

"He said shit. I hit him. He hit me back. Done."

"Don't bullshit me. Sauer tried, and I let it go because I know he's stressed out right now with Newman. But you're not getting away with it. You tell me right now why you'd hit my husband." Her voice broke as she said, "I love him. I need you two to get along. I can't lose either of you."

"I'm not asking you to pick sides here. I'm also not going to play nice with him when I can't stand the asshole. I'll stay away from him."

Her bottom lip quivered. "Which means you'll stay away from me. That's not fair."

"What do you want me to say? There's nothing I can say to make it all better."

"Tell me what happened."

He turned his head away.

That's not something he wanted to do, sit here and explain to Deena how her husband didn't think he was good enough for one of her friends. He didn't want to potentially see the look in her eyes that maybe she might think the same thing. Maybe he really wasn't good enough for Susan.

She was an amazing woman with a good job, respectable friends, most likely a happy family life, and what was he? A guy who came from a broken family. Grew up with a terrible childhood. Yeah, he could claim he was a successful businessman. He also had a criminal record. That didn't mix well with someone who worked for the law. It didn't mix at all.

A soft hand touched his chin and forced him to look at her. Her hand grazed the bruise that formed near his left eye, then down to the crack in his bottom lip. He wanted to be embarrassed and ashamed Sauer got in so many good hits, but he couldn't be. Sauer could fight. That was a good thing. He was glad Sauer could protect his wife if need be.

"You and Susan?"

He took a step back. Her hand drifted away, which was exactly what he wanted. "What about us?"

"Is there an us? I saw her at the precinct as well, and she didn't have much to add about what happened. The entire precinct is in a big uproar with one of their own potentially being a murderer. I couldn't...I didn't press her either."

"Yay for me. So you think I have all the answers? Well, I don't, Deena. Go home and wait for your husband. Have a nice, happy life."

Her mouth dropped in shock. He had to admit he was a little shocked himself. He hadn't meant to say those last few words. He didn't want to lose her from his life. He enjoyed being able to call her up and talk about nothing, or send silly texts to make each other laugh when one of them was having a bad day. She was his best friend. It hurt to think about losing that.

He survived the first time he pushed her away, and he'd survive this time, too.

"With you in it. Don't push me away. Kind of like you pushed me away ten years ago. You started running with people I didn't like and you made me choose. Hell, you didn't even give me a choice. You shut the door on my face. And I let you." She shoved a hard finger into his chest. "I'm not letting you today."

"Maybe you should."

"Why? What's the matter with you? We used to be able to talk about anything. Now, you won't say shit. Stop acting like a dick." She shoved him again in the chest, this time with her entire hand.

"I can't stop what I am."

"You've changed. You were never like this with me. You could always tell me anything."

He wanted to agree with that. He did, in a sense. What she didn't know was he didn't always share everything. He didn't share how he always felt a little under her status. Like, why would she even want to be friends with a punk like him? A family that shouldn't even be called a family. He was no good. People used to say that all the time while she stood next to him. Each and every time, she defended him, sometimes even getting close to using her fists, and then she always turned to him with the sweetest smile. "You're the best. Don't let anyone tell you otherwise."

But was he really? He wasn't as good and nice as her. He wasn't as pure as her. He did shit he wasn't ashamed of. Things that if she knew, she'd whack him upside the head for his idiocy. He had yet to fess up that he served time for assaulting a man. Because he didn't want to see the disappointment in her eyes.

He was still shocked Susan didn't walk away after he confessed. But Deena. He wasn't sure how she'd react. Fear of seeing her turn her back to him, not glancing once as she flipped him off and walked away, held him back from saying anything.

They always said they'd have each other's back. They always said they'd be friends forever. Would she want to be friends if she knew what he was capable of?

"I think you should leave."

"Are you..." Her eyes welled up with tears. Something he rarely saw from her. He hated putting that look on her face, but he couldn't stop it. He would never ask her to choose between him and her husband. So it was better if he shoved her in Sauer's direction. He was the worthless one, anyway. Or so everyone thought.

"I don't want you to cry, Deena, but—"

"Well, I am, you bastard," she shrieked as she started to whack him in the chest with her tiny fists, barely hurting him, yet hurting him deep inside. "How dare you try to break up our friendship again! How dare you hit my husband without explaining it to me! How dare you act like a douche! How dare you!"

Her hits ceased the moment he wrapped his arms around her in a big hug. Her body weight sank against his as hot tears seared through his shirt. If that wasn't clue enough she was balling her eyes out, her loud sobs would've been.

He did this. He hurt his friend.

He wanted to apologize and make it all better, but he still couldn't. He couldn't force those words out because he couldn't be sorry. He was defending his own honor. His integrity. He *was* good enough for Susan. He didn't care who didn't believe that. He needed to believe that. Because if he started to let it sink in he wasn't good enough, he might start believing it and walk away from her for good.

Walking away from Susan would never happen. She was in his veins, like a drug attacking the system.

She was his everything.

She was his from the moment he met her. Which was why he ran as fast as he could after that small taste of her. It scared the living shit out of him. It still scared him.

Look what happened when he let people in. He always

let them down. Right now, he was letting his best friend down.

If he couldn't keep her happy, then what made him think he could keep Susan happy? That's why he kept letting the fear take control and push her away again and again.

Deena suddenly pushed away from him and out of his arms, wiping at her face and the tears that wouldn't stop streaming down.

"Asshole. You're a big fat asshole."

He nodded. What else could he say? He knew that. He'd never deny it. Not to anyone.

"Well, guess what, asshole? You can't just stop being my friend. I won't allow it. I'm going to bug you every day. So get used to it." She poked his chest. "If you ever touch my husband again, be prepared for more bruises. I might take my own swing at you. And I know you'd never hit a woman."

His arms went wide as he smiled. "Take a swing now, doll. You know I'd never hurt you. Or any other woman like that." His smile died as he let his arms drop to the side. "You can beat me up right now if it'll make you feel better. Please. Do it."

She wiped more tears from her cheeks, but didn't say anything. He could see it in her eyes she was tempted, though.

"I can't apologize for what I did. I won't. I...Susan means a lot to me. He told me...Sauer basically said I wasn't good enough. He deserved every last punch, and some more. I only stopped because Susan asked me to." He shrugged. "Maybe I'm not good enough for her. Maybe I'm not even good enough to be your friend. But it's not going to stop me from having her. Nobody is going to threaten me and get between us. Not even your husband."

She couldn't hide her surprise, but the understanding reflected in her determined eyes. "Sauer's stressed. He didn't mean it. You're plenty good enough for Susan, and for me. Don't ever think otherwise."

He stepped closer, swung an arm around her, and pulled her in for a hug. A tender hug that said his apology, because no words would ever leave his mouth.

"Oh, he meant it. But whatever. I know what I want. And it's Susan. I'll stay away from your husband. Then I can guarantee I'll never hit him again."

Her arms tightened around him. "I don't like that one bit. I want you two to be friends."

"Yeah, I don't think that's ever going to happen, doll."

She lifted her head. "But we're friends and it's not changing. Got it?"

It'd be easier if she left that alone. If she walked out of his shop and didn't contact him again. He didn't want to cause problems between her and Sauer, and he was no idiot. Staying friends would cause tons of problems. All he wanted was his best friend happy. Sauer made her happy. That's what mattered to him. Even if that meant they couldn't be friends.

"I said, got it?"

But the thing about Deena, she never did things the easy way. She always pushed and pulled and gutted a person right down to the core until she got her way. He loved that about her.

"Yeah, doll, I got it."

18

NEWMAN LEANED back in his chair, his hands clasped together tightly on the table. He wasn't sure how much longer he could sit here and not speak. Not spill the truth. One person after another had rotated through the door. Zeke. Ben. Captain Ganderson. Sauer.

No one could get him to talk.

How could they? He was one of them. A cop. He knew all the interrogation techniques. He wasn't about to let them use that shit on him.

Or he could man up and tell the truth. Spill his guts. It was the least Sauer deserved.

Because out of everyone, it hurt him to the very core that he hurt his friend the way he had—was.

His eyes darted to the door as it swung open. Not a peep sounded as Sauer took a seat across from him.

Sauer looked like shit. Like he had been in a bar brawl and perhaps came out the loser. Bruises covered his face. A busted lip that looked like it hurt. His eyes, besides the bruise circling the right one, looked worn out and tired. He ached to ask what the hell happened, but didn't. He went this long without speaking, he could last a little bit longer.

"We executed a search warrant on your house. You know that. If we find anything, you will be charged with four murders. I don—"

"Three."

They both looked shocked. Since the moment they dragged him into the precinct and shoved him into an interrogation room, he hadn't said a word. When asked if he wanted a lawyer, he didn't even say the word no; he shook his head to decline.

Sauer's jaw clenched. "Four, actually. While you've been...wherever you were, another woman was murdered. I'm surprised nobody else told you that yet. Why do you think we want to know where you were?"

He cut his eyes away from Sauer's, unable to endure the pain and torture written in the depths. Did they tell him and he chose to ignore it? He honestly couldn't say. He couldn't remember anyone telling him that information.

The moment he sat down, his life flashed before him, and all he could think about was he'd never get it back. He'd never go back to his carefree life where everything was good and happy and something to be proud of.

What was there to be proud of now? Nothing.

"Newman..." Sauer whispered his name so harshly, yet with such emotion, he couldn't help but turn back toward him. "I know you. I know you'd never kill anyone. I've believed in you from the beginning. Please...just talk to me."

The truth was in his eyes. He meant every word. What had he done to deserve such a great friend? One that stuck by his side when everyone else thought he was guilty.

This was why Sauer would always be one step above

him. A good reason why he resented him. He wanted to be a step above. He didn't like being under anyone.

He always had to be better.

The better son.

The better student.

The better football player.

The better cop.

The better partner in a relationship.

He would never be better. From day one, he was always a step below.

"I didn't kill those women."

"I know." Sauer said it with such conviction, he almost wanted to weep with joy that he still had one person believing in him.

"What happened to your face?"

Sauer flinched and glanced away. "It's nothing." He met his eyes once more. "Tell me where you were."

His hands dropped to his lap. His head swung down, his eyes grazing the floor as if trying to find the meaning of life. As if the answer could be found if he stared hard enough.

"Newman? Come on. I can't help you if you don't help me."

He couldn't look up. He couldn't confess by keeping eye contact. "Check my wallet. You'll see a...receipt."

The room suddenly became heavy with tension. Immediate and foreboding. Like someone had filled the room with smoke, his lungs clogging instantly, the ability to breathe nonexistent. He was suffocating and he didn't know how to drag in a deep breath.

"What will I find?"

His head snapped up. "The truth about me." A maniacal laugh came out. "I cheated on Chrissy. I loved her and I cheated anyway. I turned into a liar. I turned into an asshole with my co-workers. I turned into someone I hated. I can't seem to turn that asshole part of me off. I needed to release some of the turmoil going on." He looked down again. "I was at a motel with a...hooker. It's the only way I know how to cope." His head whipped up as he slammed his hands down hard on the table. "And no, I don't know how to find the woman I slept with. All I have is the damn receipt for the motel."

Sauer swallowed hard, his Adam's apple moving as if in slow motion. "Were things that bad with Chrissy?"

"Haven't you talked to Chrissy?"

Sauer nodded.

"Then you know what kind of asshole I was. I can't change anything I did. But I didn't kill anyone."

"You knew the first victim. You had an affair with her."

Sauer didn't phrase it as a question, but he nodded to confirm.

"Why'd you lie? Why wouldn't you tell me?"

"Gee, I don't know, Sauer. Maybe so you wouldn't look at me the way you are now." He slammed his hands down hard again. The sting from the hit radiated up through his hands and to the top of his shoulders. "I'm ashamed of myself. I hate seeing it from you."

Sauer's jaw clenched, a muscle ticking in his bruised cheek. "Did you know the other victims?" He pulled a folder from the side of the desk and flipped it open. After digging through the contents, he produced a picture of a woman, probably in her mid-thirties, smiling and happy, her arms around two kids. "Did you know the fourth victim, Carrie-Ann Jenkins?"

"I've never seen or heard of or spoken to any of the victims but Tonya. I did not kill them. I am a lot of things." He stared at him intensely. "But I am not a killer."

SUSAN STOOD in the background behind the two-way mirror on the other side of the interrogation room listening as Sauer talked to Newman. She had no idea the problems he'd been hiding. Clearly, by the expressions from Zeke, Ben, and Captain Ganderson, none of them had any idea either.

She felt uncomfortable being in the room. This wasn't normal protocol for her, and she still wasn't sure why Captain Ganderson asked her to listen and watch. Instead of asking questions, she stood in the corner of the room, behind everyone else, and listened.

She found it difficult to keep her focus, especially when some of it was so heartbreaking, she almost wanted to walk into the room and give Newman a hug. Yeah, he had been quite the jackass with her. But he looked devastated and hurt and...lonely. He looked like he needed a hug.

"Zeke, I need you to start verifying his alibis that he's giving Sauer for each murder," Captain Ganderson said quietly, yet the soft words rang in the small confines of the room.

"Sure thing, Cap."

Captain Ganderson then turned to Ben. "Why don't you and Susan head to the motel he claims he was at and find out if you can verify that alibi." His eyes zoomed to hers. "Is that okay with you?"

"Yes." Short and simple. She honestly had no idea what else to say. She glanced at Ben. "I'll go get my gear and meet you in the lobby of the building." She smiled gently, and then left the room.

She didn't want to be in there anymore. It felt claustrophobic, intense, and something she wasn't used to. She had no idea how those guys did that day in and day out. Although, she figured people probably said that about her job as well.

She took her time grabbing her evidence kit, and fifteen minutes later, she was off with Ben to a seedy motel on the edge of town. She felt dirty thinking about it.

"You ok—sorry." Ben cleared his throat.

She smiled sheepishly. "I'm sorry, too. I should've never been so harsh. It's been a long week. I have no excuse. I'm sorry, Ben."

"It's all good. It has been crazy. I just can't picture the Newman sitting in the room with the Newman I know."

"Yeah, me, too."

The drive remained silent after that. What more could they say?

By the time they arrived at the motel, exhaustion coated her body. She knew her day was far from over. She followed Ben silently to the main office of the motel where he questioned the guy behind the counter. He had a slightly creepy looking vibe, like one you'd see in a B flick horror movie. Dirty, greasy hair. Unkempt clothes. Teeth that probably hadn't seen a brush in months. He kept turning his eyes her way, smiling, or at least, he thought he was offering a smile, when all she saw was a creepy leer. She was glad to have Ben by her side.

The guy confirmed Newman checked in the day before around four in the afternoon. He didn't check out until one the next morning. The guy never gave any indication that was odd behavior of someone.

Then he shocked them both.

"Dude's a regular. He's been coming in every few weeks for the past two months or so."

Ben sighed. "Do you have any surveillance video of him checking in and out?"

"Yeah, sure."

Susan didn't want to be a part of that process, or in the presence of the weird guy, so she asked for permission to look at and collect any evidence from the room Newman used and decided to leave the video evidence to Ben while she processed the room. She needed to work, especially if this motel was used for *that* sort of activity quite a bit.

Ben met her thirty minutes later with confirmation of Newman signing in and out, but no video of the woman he was with.

"So, creepster says the woman never came into the lobby, which apparently they never do." Ben raised his brows in a gesture that said it didn't surprise him. Susan couldn't help but chuckle at the name he gave the guy. Creepster worked very well.

"Meaning we can't really verify Newman was here with someone."

A slow smile erupted on his face. "Not exactly true. Mr. Creepster is a chatty Cathy. Plus, a real douche, as said as well as I can in Dee's voice." Ben laughed with her. "He likes to look when men sign in. And I don't mean look at the men."

She rolled her eyes. "I get your meaning."

Ben cleared his throat and shoved his hand in her direction with a bunch of photos. "He also doesn't just look. He likes to take pictures of the women coming and going. He graciously handed it all over to me."

Susan couldn't hold back her laugh. "Graciously, huh?"

Ben grinned. "Well, I might have encouraged him to do so." His grin grew. "What can I say? I have a way with words. Anyway, now we have to put a name to a face. I'm sure this woman has been arrested before, sad to say, but true. Talk to her, get an alibi, and he's free and clear on murder number four."

"Which is a good thing."

A heavy sigh broke free. "It really is."

They drove back to the precinct, this time with conversation. They steered away from talking about Newman, more so talking about Rina and how her pregnancy was going. They even steered away from talking about Stitch, although she could see it in Ben's eyes he wanted to know. She appreciated his strength to hold back and leave the subject alone.

They went separate ways once they hit the precinct. He went to find the hooker Newman slept with, and she headed for the lab to process all the swabs she had taken. It looked like a daunting task ahead of her. But she needed to be prepared for the off chance another dead woman popped up. Maybe the same woman Newman took to that motel and slept with.

She couldn't hold back a groan when she walked into the lab and saw Rachel also working. Rachel pierced her with a haughty smirk, but said nothing. She was honestly grateful for that. Getting into a verbal spat with her wasn't high on her list. She was done getting into arguments with people. At least, that's what she kept telling herself. Stopping it would be a lot more difficult. Especially with Stitch.

A few hours later, running sample after sample, she decided it was time for a break. She thought it might even be time to go home. It was getting late. She skipped breakfast and lunch, and her stomach was telling her it was time to eat.

She'd been making that a bad habit. No more. She had to start taking better care of herself before she got sick.

She ran into Ben on her way to her office.

"Any luck?"

He looked exhausted, probably as tired as she felt. "My eyes feel ready to fall out. I think I found her. But the arrest photo I have looks a bit different from the one Mr. Creepster took yesterday. I'm headed out right now to track her down and question her."

"Good luck. I hope you can find her before she...you know...finds a friend tonight."

Ben chuckled. "Me, too. I'll see you later." He started to walk away.

"Hey, Ben?"

"Yeah?" He turned slightly, a friendly grin on his face.

"How's Sauer?"

The grin slipped. "Hanging in there. It's been a long day. For all of us."

She nodded and waved as he turned back around and walked away.

She didn't want any hard feelings between her and Sauer. All day it ran through her mind what happened this morning with him and Stitch. She was upset. He was. Stitch was. A lot of high emotions circled around them. Things were said and done and she was ready to move on. Get back to the way things were. Easy and friendly and carefree.

Unlocking her office door, she walked in with her head down, her heart aching, and a tumble of emotions out of whack, even as hard as she tried to keep them contained, and closed her door.

"Hey, shorty."

Jumping, she hit the back of the door as she stared into the eyes of Stitch, who looked entirely too comfortable in her chair.

"How did you get in here? My door was locked."

That sleek, sexy grin of his emerged. She missed that

grin all day. "I have many talents. Picking locks happens to be one of them. We need to talk."

Those dreaded words she was starting to hate hearing from him.

Well, maybe she didn't want to talk.

Maybe she wanted to forget everything. Forget the day. Forget the issues. Just forget.

Move on.

19

STITCH WATCHED as she moved away from the door, but didn't say anything. Maybe he already screwed up too much. She wasn't looking too receptive to an apology. Not that he wanted to apologize. He didn't regret hitting Sauer. He only regretted hurting Susan in the process.

Would she understand that explanation?

"That's my chair."

He loved this sassy side of her. Did it matter that he was sitting in her chair? Probably not, but she obviously needed to feel like she had some kind of control.

As soon as he stood up and walked around her desk, he figured he was kidding himself. She had all the control. His life, the way it could turn, either for the good or for worse, was in her hands. He couldn't stop a damn thing if it didn't go the way he wanted.

She chose to walk around the desk on the opposite side, which prevented him from pulling her into his arms. It was crazy. Illogical how much he needed to wrap her in his arms and show her his apology. He was much better at show rather than tell. Even in school when he had to bring in his favorite toy in his kindergarten class. He could remember standing in front of the class with a truck he loved playing with. He didn't say why it was his favorite, that it was the only toy his dad ever bought him, that it was the last toy he ever received from him. He just stood there silently with a smile on his face until the teacher called the next student to come up.

"What are you doing here? What...do you want to talk about?"

There. Right there. He hated how she hesitated. How she didn't sound sure of herself. What did she think he wanted to talk about? He honestly wanted to avoid the conversation about what happened with Sauer, but he knew he couldn't.

He glanced at her, then toward the door when he heard a noise. He watched as people passed by the window, and suddenly he hated that anyone could stop and look and watch what was going on. Not that they'd be able to hear what was going on, but he never liked people watching him. Judging him.

Stalking to the door, he didn't miss the sharp intake of breath from Susan, as if she thought he was walking out on her. Not this time.

He twisted the lock on the door and then slammed the blinds down, taking a few tries before the window on the door was covered properly.

"I hate having an audience." He turned back toward her.

"I'm pretty sure nobody would've stopped to stare."

"Maybe not. But I hate having an audience."

She looked confused. "We're not doing anything but talking."

"For now."

She backed away. The back of her legs hit her chair, which then hit the filing cabinet behind it. "What did you want to talk about?"

With quick, long strides, he made it to her side. He didn't hesitate to wrap an arm around her waist. The tension running through his veins settled instantly. He felt like he found his home. "Us."

"Us? What—"

"Don't finish that sentence if you're about to say what us. There is an us. There is something here."

"I was going to ask what happened today with Sauer. There's too much stuff hanging in the air. I can't think about any kind of us without it cleared."

His grip tightened around her waist. It's not as if he knew he could keep her there forever, but he suddenly dreaded the moment when she would push him away.

"You have to start talking to me. You have to stop using your fists."

"I rarely do."

"Yeah, except the first time you served a year in prison for it. And this time...you hit a cop, Stitch. I haven't talked to Sauer, but he could charge you, you know that, right?"

It never crossed his mind. Thinking back to the conversation with Deena earlier, she never brought it up either. Which made him think Sauer wasn't going to do that. But if he did, oh well. There was nothing he could do about it. Did he regret hitting him? No. The only thing he regretted was Susan hating him.

She shivered in his arms. He couldn't tell if that was a good sign or not. He didn't like that he couldn't decipher it. Bringing one hand up to brush across her cheek, the other still wrapped tightly around her waist, he could only stare at the beauty in his arms.

Her hair was in her usual simple ponytail. He ached to take it down, see her lying in his bed, her hair fanned out across his pillow. Later. Much later he would do just that.

"You know I'd never lay a finger on you. I might take a swing at some asshole, but I'd never hit you. Never."

"I do believe that. But why do you have to hit anybody?"

Good question. Sometimes, he couldn't control it. Especially when he felt threatened. Sauer had been a threat to him and his relationship with Susan.

"I'm..." The words clogged and stalled. So he tried clearing his throat. "I'm..."

A tiny grin appeared. "Yes? You're...what?"

He chuckled. "Sorry."

A full bout of laughter fell from her lips. "I'm so proud of you. Did the world crack open? Did you fall into the pits of hell? But what are you sorry for?"

"Damn, shorty, do you have to drag me through the mud here? I said the words."

"Maybe I need to hear why. A lot of whys from your life."

Walking forward, he pinned her between the desk and his body. "I'm sorry for hurting you when I hit Sauer."

"But not the actual hitting part."

He shrugged. "I'll never lie to you, Suzy baby. I can't be sorry about that. He deserved it. He made me...this talking shit is overrated."

"He made you what?"

Leaning his forehead against hers, he hated to voice it. He hated to lay out his feelings like a painter showing their love on canvas.

Her delicate hand reached up and brushed a lock of his hair back, then slid down his cheek and held its position.

Her soft touch, in such simple movements, gave him strength he didn't think he otherwise would've had.

His voice lowered to a whisper. "He made me feel like I wasn't worthy of you. And maybe I'm not. Maybe I'm not good enough for you. I haven't been good enough for anyone in my life. I feel like I've always failed people who should've been able to count on me. My best friend Stu. Dead and gone. I could've saved him if I could've talked him out of the lifestyle he was dragging us into. Clarissa. I still have yet to save her. She's a walking disaster. I'm a disaster. My life looks like it's screwed on tight, but it's far from perfect. I'm not perfect. I'll never be perfect. I am who I am, and all I have to offer you is me. Bullshit parts and all. You deserve better than that, and I'm selfish enough not to care. I want you, and only you."

Her hands grasped his cheeks, forcing him to lift his head and look her in the eyes. "That is the most honest and real thing a man has ever said to me. You can't save everyone. It's not your job. It's not something that has to define you. Do you think my life is perfect? My parents are divorced, and visiting either one of them is like walking on eggshells because they still can't stand each other. I have a bunch of superficial friends from college, and I haven't spoken to anyone from high school in ages. The only people that really matter are the ones I spend every Friday night with having drinks and talking girl talk. My job hasn't held the same appeal lately, and I feel like I might need a change. I'm lost in what direction to go, and the only thing that has been keeping me sane, as crazy as it may sound, is you. You're my perfect disaster."

His lips tipped up into a grin. A grin that said more than any words he could think to say. This was the first time they were both open and honest. Putting out all the shit he never wanted to talk about. He hated every second of it, but he also loved every part.

His eyes glided to her lips. Her sweet, delectable lips that turned him on with one simple look.

"You know, I've never kissed you."

She giggled, as her hands fell from his cheeks and down to his waist. "You kiss me all the time."

His grip intensified on her waist as he pulled her closer, his hard dick throbbing against her. She felt right and delicious and perfectly made for him.

Then his mouth touched her neck with a soft kiss. "I've kissed you there." He made a path to her ear. "And here." He pulled off her shirt with one swift move and clamped his mouth over her nipple covered by a black lacy bra. "This is one of my favorite areas to kiss." His eyes tilted down to where she was pressed firmly against him. "And, of course, I love to devour you down there. That's where I've kissed you." Then he met her eyes. "But I've never kissed you on the lips."

Her eyes look confused, as if she were tumbling around her memories for that one time he kissed her on the lips. Perhaps even just a small peck. A graze. A simple touch of mouth to mouth and then done.

She wouldn't be able to recall any because he never had. It wasn't something he did. He loved to kiss a woman. Anywhere but the lips. Kissing on the lips signified deep feelings. An intimacy he was never willing to share with a woman. He had never kissed Clarissa on the lips. Call him crazy or dumb or a guy who needed to lose his man card, but he didn't kiss a woman on the lips unless she meant something to him. He had yet to meet a woman who made him feel like she was more than a scratch to itch.

Until Susan.

"So...kis—"

His lips slammed down hard upon hers. He didn't ask permission to enter. He tangled tongues with her as if they were starting the tango. They danced, they twirled, they soared to the top of the sky. The kiss was everything and more. Just as she always felt perfect in his arms, limbs tangled together in a sweaty mess from lovemaking, her lips were made for his.

He never wanted to stop. Not even to rip her clothes off so he could feel her skin to skin. Because that's suddenly what he needed. He needed to feel her completely against him. To know that she was his. Only his. He needed to claim her. Possess her. To show her that he was all in to take this relationship to the next level, and he was never letting her go.

Her bra fell off with ease with a flick of his wrist. Her pants went just as quickly, although not as smoothly, because he had to lean away while she shimmied her pants down to the ground but not lose his attachment to her lips. Now that he had a taste, he never wanted to let go.

She made good work of unzipping his pants and freeing his hard dick, palming it into her hands, stroking the way she knew he liked. It made him want her even more.

Groaning in dismay, because it was unavoidable, he disengaged for a few seconds to toss his shirt off and grab a condom from his pocket.

With his pants halfway down his legs, circling his knees, otherwise naked, he sheathed on the condom and brought his body close to hers, pressing them skin to skin, lips to lips.

He took his time entering her, feeling the beautiful way they joined as one, the gorgeous way she moved against him as if she couldn't get enough.

Oh, he'd never get enough of her. Each time was always better than the last.

They moved slowly, up and down, their kiss slow and easy, as if they had all the time in the world. Why should he be in a rush when he had the most precious woman in his arms, loving her as she deserved to be loved?

"More," she mumbled against his lips.

Another reason he couldn't leave this woman. Ever. When she demanded something from him, he gave her what she wanted. She didn't want slow and tender anymore, then that was fine with him.

"Lay back, Suzy baby." He slowly moved things out of the way on the desk, his lips still attached to hers. The kiss turned hot and heavy as he started to thrust deeper and harder. Although, not as rough as he knew she wanted when he was lip-locked with her.

Sucking hard on her tongue, a tender kiss afterwards, he let go and stood upright, grabbing her hips tightly. "Hold on, sweetheart."

He was rewarded with the deadliest, sexiest grin yet from her. She grabbed his ass as he thrust hard and deep. Over and over. In and out. He didn't shout out his love for her, which he now saw clear as day, her lying spread out gorgeous as hell across her desk. He showed her with each dirty, rough thrust inside and out.

Her tiny moans, her hands grabbing and digging, were answer enough that she felt the same. He knew. He didn't have to hear the words to know.

"So close, Stitch. More."

He started to slam a little harder, although not so hard he hurt her, but hard enough the desk moved. Neither of them paid it much attention. The tension in his body started to climb, the desire swirling in his veins, ramping up for an orgasm that he knew would be hard to top.

Suddenly, she was squeezing around him so hard, a soft scream echoed in the room. He fell from heaven with her and held on tight as they came crashing down from the clouds together.

Leaning forward, he brushed light kisses across her cheeks, her lips, her neck, everywhere.

"You were kind of loud, Suzy baby. That's so damn sexy."

A bright-red hue covered her face as she realized they were still in her office and anyone who was walking by could've figured out quite easily what happened. Her eyes closed in embarrassment.

"Hey. No, you can't do that. You can't be ashamed. That was amazing." He kissed her thoroughly, yet tenderly, so she would know how truly amazing she was.

"I've never done anything like that before. If anyone heard—"

"They don't matter. I'd threatened to kick their ass for saying a word..." He chuckled at her expression. "But I don't think you'd like that." He grinned to make it appear like he was teasing when he was dead serious.

"Not funny."

"It's a little funny."

"Stitch..."

He wasn't sure what she wanted to say, but he didn't want to hear it. The way she said his name, almost as if she regretted what they had done, gutted him in a way. He never wanted her to regret things between them, especially sex.

Should he have waited until they were alone at home to attack her with such passion? Maybe. But he didn't, so he refused to regret the moment. He regretted not taking her hair out of its ponytail so he could've seen it all fanned out across her desk. Now, *that* would've been sexy as hell.

Reluctantly, he pulled away from her, plucked the condom off, and threw it in the trash next to her desk.

"Gross. I can't keep that in here."

His eyes twinkled with mischief. "It'd give the trash guy something to talk about."

"I'm so glad you find this amusing."

He zipped his pants and grabbed his shirt from the floor. "Hey, I'm not sorry for loving my woman on a desk in her office. I'd do it again if you weren't so red in the face."

She bit her bottom lip, almost as if she wanted to say something but couldn't seem to.

He couldn't tell if what she wanted to say was good or bad. He hated the self-doubt about their relationship seeping back in. He thought they settled things between them. There was an us. They were going to make a go of things. Did having sex on her desk ruin his chances after all?

"Let's go home. Finish this in a bed."

To his delight, she smiled, yet a bit of sadness entered her eyes. "I'm not quite finished here. But I shouldn't be too much longer."

He watched as she put her bra back on and then her shirt. Now fully clothed, but still looking sexy as hell and like she had been thoroughly loved, which she had, he wanted to do it all over again. And again. And again.

"Why don't I grab some food, because I haven't eaten yet. Have you?"

She shook her head.

"All right. I'll grab some food and meet you at your house in, let's say, an hour. Is that enough time to finish here?"

"Yeah. I like the sound of that plan."

"Good. Me, too."

He grabbed another kiss, now dying to kiss her anytime he could, and left.

Maybe he'd stop and pick up more than just food. Maybe he'd show her how serious he was about them.

Just maybe.

20

————

Susan hit the garage door button and opened the door. Disarming the alarm quickly, she almost shivered at how quiet the house sounded. Since Stitch appeared in her life, it had started to sound more lively and full and filled with... love, dare she say.

Hey, I'm not sorry for loving my woman on a desk in her office.

What did he mean? Making love? Actual love?

She couldn't believe what they had done in her office. In her place of employment.

Was she embarrassed a co-worker might have heard her in the throes of passion? Um, yeah. Totally.

Was it completely unprofessional of her, and should she be ashamed of herself? Yes and yes.

Did she regret doing it? Definitely not.

Stitch always managed to bring the fun, dirty side out of her that she didn't even realize she had. He always made her feel alive and free. How could she regret those moments? She couldn't.

But she didn't want to share those moments with others.

And his kisses.

Oh, boy. She had been missing out.

When he said he had never kissed her on the lips, she thought he had to be joking. When she shuffled through all of her memories, she realized he was right.

He had been worth the wait. That man knew how to use his tongue right. Deliciously. Deliriously. Decadently.

Tossing her keys on the counter, she checked the time on the microwave and sighed happily. She'd have time to take a shower and wash off the grime from the day before Stitch arrived.

Newman was still sitting in an interrogation room. Ben was out searching for a woman who could clear him in the fourth murder. Zeke was trying to verify alibis on the first three. And Sauer. Well, she didn't know what he was up to when she left.

Things with Stitch were better. She didn't want to get into an argument with Sauer. And she would've. She would've given him a piece of her mind for making Stitch feel the way he had.

Was Stitch right to hit him? No. She never thought violence was the answer. Did Sauer deserve some sort of reprimand? Yes. His words hurt Stitch, and unfortunately, Stitch reacted in the only way he knew how. To show a little pain back. Obviously, she needed to work with him on that. Because she didn't want to worry he would hit a guy anytime he felt threatened, or even threatened on her behalf.

She liked his protectiveness, but only so much. He would have to dial it down.

Jumping into the shower quickly, she let the hot water soothe her bones for a minute before scrubbing like crazy and then finishing her hair faster than she normally did.

She slipped on a pair of comfy pajama pants and a thin tank top, sans the bra. She wanted to be comfortable, yet sexy while they ate. Enticing him to eat a little faster would be fun. But she did need to eat. Her body had been deprived of food all day and she wasn't sure how much longer she could wait.

Leaving her bedroom, she headed for the living room as she tossed her wet hair into a messy bun. Reaching her destination, she realized she left her phone in her room. She needed that in case Stitch called or texted. He should be here any minute.

She froze.

The cold barrel of the gun against her back made her tremble.

"I suggest you turn around slowly."

Tiny shivers wracked her body as she took tiny steps to face her attacker. She didn't recognize his voice. More confusion touched her features when she met his gaze. Who was he? How did he get into her house?

The gun was easy enough to decipher. A .38 revolver. As close as he stood to her, it would do plenty of damage. Hell, he could've been standing at the end of the hallway and she'd be dead if he fired. A gun was a gun. She'd never been on the receiving end of a gun before.

"What do you want? I have money in my wallet. I even have some in my safe in the bedroom."

"I don't want your damn money. I want your evidence."

"Evidence?"

"Don't you know who I am?" He waved the gun at her as he yelled.

Right in that moment, she wished she knew, but she had no clue who he was. Obviously, someone in one of her cases. But she wouldn't know. She collected evidence and passed on the results. She didn't dig into cases, see faces, and interview people.

"Tonya Moretta. Does that name ring a bell? That bitch..." He stopped, clenched his jaw, and waved the gun again. "Where's the evidence?"

Evidence? Tonya Moretta?

It all suddenly made sense. Chris Moretta. Her exhusband.

A crazy sense of relief washed over her. Newman wasn't guilty. He didn't kill those women, although she started to believe in his innocence after watching him in the interrogation room.

Apparently, the killer had been the first victim's exhusband all along. How did he know the other three women? What evidence was he talking about? She didn't get any evidence, other than the prints in the room. Being her ex-husband, even if those prints would've been his, they could've easily been explained by the defense. But they weren't his. They had been Tonya's.

"There is none."

"You found prints. Where are they?"

Then it hit her.

"Did you break into my office?"

"Listen, bitch, I need those prints. If I have to break into another office, I will. Where are they?"

Well, she could cross off another mystery. He's the one who broke into her office, took her folder, and then replaced it in a different place. The brazenness of his actions. Walking into a precinct and breaking into her office. There weren't any cameras near her office, but there would be in other parts of the building to prove he was there.

Not that it did her any good right now when he had a gun pointed at her chest.

Could she talk him down? Could she get him to turn himself in?

"The prints are in the evidence room, which can only be signed out by an employee. There are cameras everywhere." She didn't add they were also in the database. She could easily sign in and pull them up, but she assumed he wanted the hard copies.

The sneaky grin that appeared on his face intensified the fear crashing through her veins. "I can just hack into the system and mess with the cameras. That doesn't scare me."

Clearly not. She had to agree, he broke into places well. He broke into four homes and murdered four separate women without announcing his presence. He managed to subdue them, rape them, and murder them without them putting up much of a fight.

He broke into her house without her hearing.

She couldn't think about those other women. She had to keep her head on straight and the fear at bay.

"Where's it located in the evidence room?"

"I can—"

"No! Do I look dumb to you? You're not going anywhere. I'll retrieve it myself."

She swallowed hard, her eyes settling on the gun. If he didn't need her to go with, then what would he do with her? She knew who he was. He wasn't going to let her live.

Which meant, she couldn't tell him that she already processed the prints. That they didn't come back as his. They had nothing to pin the murders on him, except what he was doing right now. If he had his way, she wouldn't live to tell anyone.

"Tell me now, or things are going to get worse for you. I can make this painless." His eyes glittered with delight. "Or painful."

"Why did you kill all of those women?"

He looked surprised by the question. She was a little surprised herself. What was the use of getting him to confess if he was going to kill her? Well, it would buy her time.

"Why not? Because I could. Because my ex-wife is a lying, cheating bitch. Because the other women thought they were better than me. Well, I showed them, didn't I?" His devious smile grew. "You look like you think you're better than me, too. Well, news flash, you whore. You're not."

She tried not to visibly shake, to show him any fear. Men like him, psychos, fed off that. She refused to feed him any more ammunition. Oh, but it was hard to stand still, the gun glaring in her face.

He suddenly looked sheepishly at her. "I honestly didn't mean to kill Tonya. That bitch took everything in the divorce. My house. My car. My dog. I bought that dog. She didn't even want it. One thing led to another and I found myself squeezing the life out of her. I have to admit, it felt good. Then it occurred to me how bad that looked. I'd be the first suspect, obviously. They always look at the spouse, or ex-husband in my case, first. So I had to add a few more women to the pile to make it look like someone else did it."

The man was certifiable. But, she had to admit, smart. Never left any evidence. Broke in the house without leaving any clues. He knew he'd look like a suspect. What better way to throw the police off. Provide more victims. Although, she had a feeling he didn't pick random women by the way he spoke about them. There had to be some small connection between him and each victim.

"When I was there being interrogated, finally able to be released, I overheard you. I heard you found some prints. I need those prints. You're going to tell me exactly where to find them."

No, she wasn't.

He could rot in hell before she told him how to get into the evidence room. She'd probably die tonight, but she wouldn't put any of her co-workers in danger.

A loud knock sounded on the door.

Stitch.

She forgot all about him coming over.

The knock was enough to surprise Chris. The gun lowered, his attention riveted to the door. She took the opportunity to kick him in the nuts, hitting her target with finesse.

He went down hard.

The gun went off.

Pounding started on the door. "Susan!"

Running for the front door, her hands shook like a leaf as she attempted to flip the deadbolt and unlock the other lock.

She swung open the door.

A shriek let loose as a rough arm went around her neck and slammed her against a thick body. The cold barrel of the gun pressed against her temple told her how terrible of a mistake she made.

"Back up." Chris's voice was strained, yet his hold on her was steady. She hit him good, just not good enough to keep him down on the ground.

"Easy, man. Don't hurt her." Stitch took a step back, almost tripping over the Chinese food he picked up for them to eat.

"Keep backing up." His voice sounded stronger, the gun pressing harder into her temple. She couldn't hold back a moan from the pain.

Stitch's face twisted with rage. "Stop hurting her." His eyes looked deadly. "Or I'll kill you."

"I'm the one with the gun, asshole. You have no say." She felt him jerk his head. "That your car, big guy?"

Stitch nodded.

"Toss the keys to her. I guess I gotta change my plans now."

She connected eyes with Stitch. She could see the wrath, the fear. He didn't want to hand over the keys. She didn't want to get into the car.

"Take me instead. She's not going anywhere with you."

Chris laughed. "Yeah, that's not happening. She's going to get what's coming to her, especially for hitting me in the balls."

"I'm going—"

"Stitch, give him the keys." She choked out each word, hating to say it, but having no choice. If he kept threatening him, Chris could turn the gun on him and shoot. She couldn't bear to see that.

Their eyes met once again. She watched as he reached slowly into his pants pocket and withdrew the keys. The pain in his eyes as he tossed them to her was too much for her to take. She had to look away.

"Come on. Back up some more."

Stitch complied, backing farther down the porch steps and onto the lawn. They walked down the steps carefully, with enough distance that would make it impossible for Stitch to reach out and grab her. Not that she thought he would.

They walked around to the passenger side of the car where he demanded she unlock the car and crawl into the driver's seat. With the gun away from her head, she found that task easier to handle than she thought. Soon, they were both seated in the car, her hands in her lap, gripping the keys hard, and the gun pointed at her head.

"Drive. Now. Before I shoot through the window and kill your boyfriend."

With trembling hands, almost dropping the keys to the floor with how badly they were shaking, she started the car. Without thinking, she buckled up. The smooth purr of the engine made her think of Stitch and how proud and happy he was when he relayed the story of when he bought this car. She couldn't help but glance out the window.

He looked ready to charge the car. He looked every inch the bad boy she knew he could be. His sleeves were halfway rolled up, his tattoos peeking out on his forearms. Why wasn't he wearing a jacket? It was chilly out.

Geez, why was she thinking such silly things?

Their eyes connected. The rage in his eyes actually managed to calm her down. He wanted to murder the man next to her, and she was more than happy to let him. If only he had the chance.

Pain radiated in her head as the gun slammed into her temple.

"I said drive!"

Ignoring the pain and the shouts outside the window, she shifted the car in gear and backed out of the driveway so fast, the tires squealed in anger. Then she shifted again and started driving away. Driving as fast as she possibly could.

Because she couldn't let him shoot Stitch.

She couldn't watch him die.

Her death would be the only one happening tonight.

STITCH WATCHED with fury as the woman he loved drove away.

The pain in his chest radiated into every vein, every pocket, every core of his being. The look of fear in her eyes. The way that asshole held a gun to her head. The way her head jerked as he hit her with the butt of the gun.

He'd kill him.

When he found out who he was, and where to find him, he'd kill him.

"Hey, man. I called the cops."

His head jerked to the right where a young kid, maybe college age, stared at him with fright in his eyes.

"I heard the shot, then I saw the dude come out with a gun to her head. I like Susan. I know she works for the police. I told them that."

He didn't know if her neighbor was nosy, or if she was friends with this kid. At the moment, he didn't care. He nodded to the car sitting in the kid's driveway.

"You just get home? Give me your keys and phone." He didn't phrase it as a question because he wouldn't be taking no for an answer.

"Yeah." The kid looked freaked out, but then tossed him the keys and started running for the passenger side. "Let's go, dude."

Not in the mood to argue, he climbed into the driver's side and peeled out of the driveway almost as fast as Susan had. He wasn't sure what way they turned but he hoped he made the right choices.

"I saw them turn right."

He glanced at the kid and nodded. "Your phone? Where is it?"

The kid produced it out of his pocket. "You want me to call someone?"

As he turned right, he thought he saw a flash of red down the street take a left. A matter of seconds had to have passed before this kid said he called the cops and they jumped into his car. Susan didn't have much of a head start, and she clearly slowed down once he was out of her viewing range.

Damn her.

She drove away like that for him. The asshole must've threatened to shoot him. He would've gladly taken a bullet. Except, relief washed over him he didn't. Because now he could chase after the son of a bitch.

"Yeah, I need you to call my friend for me. Put it on speaker."

He rattled off Deena's number and waited impatiently as it rang. Then his heart soared the second he saw another flash of red. He picked up speed. He had a clear view of his car, but they still had a good distance on them. They were heading out of the residential neighborhood and into the busy part of the city. Too much traffic to deal with. That would actually be to his advantage.

"Hello?"

His heart rate sped up as soon as he heard Deena's voice.

"Deena, it's Stitch. I can't explain right now, but I need Sauer's number and I need it now."

"Stitch, if you're about to—"

"Don't argue with me. Some asshole has taken Susan hostage in my car. I'm following them right now. I need his number." His voice broke. "I can't lose her. Not like this."

If not for the seriousness of the situation, he figured that would've left her speechless. She gave him Sauer's number, repeating it three times so he or the kid wouldn't forget and then they hung up. The kid didn't need any prompting to dial the number immediately.

As soon as Sauer answered, a tired hello echoed throughout the car.

"It's Stitch. Some asshole has Susan at gunpoint. Her neighbor called it in. It's gotta be all over the police channels. I'm following them. They're in my car."

His baby. The only thing he had always loved. Now, that beautiful piece of metal held the only other thing he loved more than life itself. The car could get tangled up into a big mess and he wouldn't care. He only wanted Susan back safe and sound.

"Sauer?"

"I'm here. I'm sending texts out to Ben and Zeke. Who is this guy? What is your license plate number? Where are you?"

Stitch started with the easiest of those three questions. He relayed his license plate number, what road they were on, and how traffic was picking up. He didn't think the asshole realized he was being followed. What was even better, he was only three cars away now.

He heard Sauer speaking, to what he assumed was a police radio, about the information he provided.

"What happened?" Sauer asked as soon as he finished.

"I don't know who he is. I visited Susan at work. She said she had another hour to finish, so I said I'd pick up food and meet her at her house. I knocked on the door. Then I heard a shot. I ..." He blew out a deep breath. "The door was locked. Then it swung open and before I could even touch her, this asshole wrapped an arm around her neck and put a gun to her head. I had..." He almost couldn't breathe, but managed to let out another deep breath. "I had to step back. He wanted the keys to my car and forced Susan into the driver's seat. The bastard hit her in the head with the gun.

She must be okay because she's still driving. I'm three cars behind them."

"Stay close, but don't let him know you're following him. When the cops catch up—"

"Don't even think about asking me to fall back. It's not happening."

"Do you want Susan to make it out of this alive? Leave it to us."

"What makes you think I trust you guys? This is Susan. *My* Susan. I'm not backing off. The minute he sees lights and sirens, he could do something stupid. A high-speed chase or something. I'm not risking her life."

"Then how about me? I'm in my car right now. Stitch, I won't let anything happen to her."

He saw her blinker light up to take a right at the next stoplight. "You know you can't say that and promise me nothing will happen."

"Maybe I shouldn't, but you can trust me. This shit between us...let's forget it. Trust me to do my job."

Yeah, maybe he did trust him to do his job. Maybe he could relinquish that control.

But the thing was...

He didn't want to.

21

HEART POUNDING. Hands sweating. Knees shaking. Susan attempted to focus on the road and not the gun beside her.

To her horror, he wouldn't stop talking. She preferred turn here, go straight, simple things like that, rather than the disgusting things he was saying right now. She figured he was only speaking like this because she wouldn't be making it out of this alive.

The hatred he had for his ex-wife was phenomenal. How had Sauer and Newman missed this? He had to be the best actor there was, because normally they read people very well. He wouldn't stop talking about Tonya, the horrible deeds she committed against him, or so he imagined, how much of a bitch she was, how she deserved to die. She didn't want to hear any more. She wanted blissful silence.

She had no idea where he was taking her, but the longer they drove, the more frightened she became. He was leading them out of the city. They were still on a heavily populated road, but soon he'd be able to turn and suddenly they'd be in the boonies. No houses. No other cars. No people. It would just be them.

Her eyes quickly glanced into the rearview mirror.

And Stitch.

She didn't notice him following her until there was one car between them. Her eyes had been darting to and fro trying to find a way out of this mess without her getting shot and nobody else getting hurt. That's when she recognized her neighbor's car. Brandon was twenty-one, one more year of college left, and he loved to shamelessly flirt with her. Oh, she knew it was something silly he liked to do. He had college girls in and out of the house he rented next to her all the time.

He was a sweet kid.

Harmless.

A little immature, too.

He had the most ridiculous bumper sticker on the front bumper of his car, instead of the back, that said, "Let's bump and grind."

The first time she saw it, she rolled her eyes at him. He laughed and said one day he planned to turn the car into a derby car and smash every other car to smithereens. It seemed like an appropriate bumper sticker for such an occasion.

She would've agreed, except the car wasn't that old and she couldn't see his parents, who owned the car, letting him use it in the demolition derby, especially since he had never competed in an event like that in his life. But she said she'd be there if he ever did, cheering him on and his crazy bumper sticker.

Now it was the one thing keeping her sane and in control, because she knew it was him and Stitch behind her, following them, making sure they didn't lose her and where this psycho was taking her.

The only problem was, they would be hitting an old

highway soon, with little traffic, and it wouldn't be hard to notice a car following them. She needed to do something. She had to end this. But, how? Without getting hurt in the process?

"Take the exit. Now."

Her eyes darted to him, almost freezing in terror at the sight of the gun pointed at her, and did as he directed.

Maybe she should keep him talking. Keep him distracted.

"I understand why you killed your ex-wife...because of the things she did." She didn't understand, and even saying that made her want to gag. "But why did you kill those other women? How...how did you know them?"

He sneered at her. "What makes you think I did?"

"They were random women?" Her heart broke even more for them. They lost their lives because it was their unlucky day.

"I didn't say that." He chuckled. "You wanna know who my favorite was to kill?"

She didn't dare look at him as that question swirled between them. Of course she didn't want to know. He knew she didn't want to know, yet he wanted to torture her with the knowledge. She'd let him, if only to buy herself time and to keep him distracted.

"Who?"

He snickered. The sound sent chills down her spine. "Amber. The beautiful college student who thought her shit didn't stink on campus. I broke into her house so easily. I watched her from the hallway, surrounded by the dark, waiting for my moment. It's always something watching people, knowing you're the one in control and they have no idea what's about to happen. She pulled a glass down from the cupboard and filled it with wine. She was so fluid in her movements, as if she did it nightly. I accidentally made a noise, which made her jump. It was so funny to watch her look around, wondering where it came from, but she never noticed me, and I didn't try to hide my presence. Then she walked to the cupboard, pulled out a glass and filled it with wine. When she turned away from the fridge, she noticed the first one she filled up and set them down together on the counter, staring at them. I scared her so much she forgot about the first glass. I couldn't hold in the laugh. At that, she ran. Oh, what a chase that was. As soon as she hit the bedroom and I grabbed her—"

"Stop! Please!"

Another terrifying snicker floated between them. "I thought you wanted to know." He lifted the gun, pressing it firmly against her temple. "Don't be dumb, Susan. I know what you're doing, trying to distract me for some reason. You can't escape what's going to happen. I'm going to kill you slowly and enjoy every minute of it. And don't worry, since you're dying to know how each woman died, I'll whisper everything in your ear as I do the same to you."

She couldn't control the trembles that coursed through her body as he shoved the gun harder into her temple and his cold words sunk in. If she didn't do something, she wouldn't live through the night.

"I suggest you shut the hell up now and just drive. Got it?"

Nodding, she didn't breathe until he lowered the gun. Of course, he didn't lower it completely. It was still trained firmly in her direction.

She found it difficult not to make it obvious as she looked in the rearview mirror once more. Stitch had managed to follow them and was still keeping a healthy distance. Not close enough to warn Chris they were being followed. But definitely not too far away to lose them.

The traffic on the road started to thin out. A few cars mingled with them, but the numbers kept dwindling down as they drove. The dark night cloaked the area in a menacing glow, almost as if waiting to swallow them whole and send them down to the pits of hell.

Now or never.

Time to make her move. Whatever it happened to be. She had no idea yet.

At any moment he could demand she turn on a side road. Then it'd be obvious as hell they were being followed. She couldn't let that happen.

"Take a right up here."

Her eyes had adjusted to the night, but not enough to see what turn he was talking about. Which didn't bode well for her. This road clearly wasn't used often. It didn't even have a street lamp lighting its path.

"It's close. Slow down. Let that car pass us."

Oh, shit.

The jig would be up.

She glanced at him, the gun glaring in her face, and then it hit her.

She had her seat belt on. A force of habit. Slide into the driver's seat, turn on the car, and then buckle her seat belt. Every single time she got into the car.

He forgot to put his on.

What were her odds if she crashed the car and a bullet didn't manage to hit her?

She honestly had no clue, but she was willing to test those odds. Because that alternative sounded better than his version of killing her.

Pressing her foot to the gas pedal, she suddenly swerved toward the ditch.

They hit the ditch hard.

She jerked in her seat.

Her head hit the steering wheel.

A loud shot rang out into the dark night.

Then nothing but blackness descended.

"SHIT!" Stitch swerved the car to the side of the road and slammed on the brakes. He just watched his car crash into the ditch and a gunshot echo into the darkness. "Stay in the car, kid."

He jerked out of his seat and made a mad dash for his car. Smoke rose from the engine, the entire front end scrunched up, almost like an accordion.

When he pulled on the handle to get Susan's door open, it wouldn't budge. He could see her through the window, slumped against the wheel.

"Susan!" He slammed his hand against the window as he shouted her name.

The door was jammed and slightly dented from the crash. He could yank and pull with all his strength, but he'd never get it open. He ran to the other side. His safety was the furthest thing from his mind, but it wouldn't have mattered if he had taken his time coming around the side, making sure the asshole didn't shoot him.

Because he wasn't in the car. A large hole framed the windshield, glass scattered around the outside of the car. Good. The asshole had been ejected out of the vehicle.

Pulling on the passenger's side door, he sighed in relief

when it opened without an issue. Crawling across the seat, he shifted Susan so her head lay against the headrest. A large gash cut across her forehead and blood dripped down her arm.

Tearing off his shirt, he hesitated which wound to staunch the bleeding first. Her arm won out when the blood looked to be flowing more steadily than her head. He wrapped his shirt as tightly as he could and then tied it into a knot.

She moaned at the contact.

He cradled her head, bending low to her ear. "Oh, I'm sorry, Suzy baby. I know it hurt. I had to."

"Stitch..." Her eyes opened slowly.

"Yeah, I'm here. Right here."

"I crashed your car."

"I don't care. You can crash it ten times over and I wouldn't give a shit. You are what matters." He pressed a tender kiss against the side of her head. "I have to pull you out of the car. We have to get you to the hospital."

"I'm sorry about your car."

Grasping her cheeks softly, he kissed her. "Stop talking about my car. It doesn't matter."

"But you love her."

"Yeah, but I love you more." He grinned at the sparkle in her eyes.

Then he panicked when she closed her eyes.

"Susan? Baby, wake up."

He shook her a little, but nothing happened. No moan. No opening of her eyes. Nothing but silence from her and the hissing of the engine outside.

"Shit. Hold on, Suzy baby." He unbuckled her belt, twisting the strap off her as best as he could without jostling her too much.

He couldn't help this next part, but he needed to get her

out of the vehicle and to the hospital. Sauer had said he would catch up with them, but surprisingly enough, even with all the information he had relayed, he never saw one cop car.

Figuring the easiest way to get her out was to pull her, he gently twisted her body, tucked his arms under her arms, and dragged her across the seat until he was able to step outside and pick her up and cradle her in his arms.

With quick, even steps, he climbed out of the ditch and headed for the kid's car. Not too far away he could see the first sign of red and blue flashing in the night.

"I called that Sauer dude. He said they were right behind us." The kid hesitated. "I told him we might need an ambulance."

"It has under thirty seconds to get here or I'm driving her myself. She passed out on me. She hit her head hard and I think she got shot in the arm."

"Where's the guy?"

"Somewhere in the field. The birds can have him for all I care."

To his relief, the entire area suddenly swarmed with cop cars and an ambulance.

The paramedics took her from him and immediately went to work. When they started to close the doors on him, he gave them one look that said that shit wouldn't fly.

He connected eyes with Sauer before the doors shut and they drove away. So much was communicated in one simple glance. Almost like he could communicate with Deena at times. A simple understanding that Sauer had stood down and given him the distance he demanded on the phone. Sauer had put his trust in Stitch.

In the end, Susan saved herself.

Because his Susan was one tough woman. She didn't

need anyone to save her. It didn't mean it would stop him from being protective and possessive of her in the future.

The drive to the hospital felt like forever. Like his entire life flashed before his eyes and he was old and gray and waiting to die.

This time, when they tried to wheel her out of his sight, a nurse, who had a scarier glint in her eyes than even he could produce, waylaid him. She also happened to threaten to call hospital security and have him banned from the premises if he didn't stand down and wait in the lobby like everyone else.

He conceded that small battle and took a chair in the corner away from all the other harrowing people waiting on news of their loved ones.

As he sat there, he realized his heart was pounding with dread that he might still lose her. But he wasn't freaking out over the fact he confessed he loved her. To her face, no less.

He was damn calm about that.

It felt good to say. Like he should've said it a few days ago. A strange kind of calm peace settled over him immediately as soon as the words came out.

The twinkle in her eyes could only mean one thing.

She loved him back.

Now he had to wait for her to wake up and hear her say it. Or demand it. He wouldn't settle for anything less. Of course, he wouldn't be a complete asshole about it. He'd give her a few days to heal before he pried those words out of her.

She had to love him. She just had to.

"Stitch, where is she? Is she okay? Are you okay?"

He didn't have time to react before Deena was flinging herself into his arms, not even waiting for him to stand up.

"Talk to me."

He managed a small chuckle before her arms started to

cut off his airflow as she squeezed his neck a little too tight. "If I could breathe, I would."

She backed away, a strained smile on her face. "You scared the shit out of me with your phone call."

"Yeah, I know the feeling. My heart was pounding right out of my chest the entire time. Still is." He stood up slowly, surprised to find Zoe and Rina behind Deena. "You guys didn't have to come. How did you know where to find us?"

"I've been on the phone with Sauer like a crazy woman. Like triple crazy than my normal crazy. Is she okay?" Deena all but shrieked.

A calm hand on her shoulder from Rina instantly had the panic in her eyes slowing down.

"How bad is it? Sauer didn't go into detail," Rina said softly.

He could deduce pretty quickly why Sauer wouldn't go into detail. Deena couldn't handle hearing it.

"She crashed the car. He wasn't wearing his seat belt, so I'm assuming she figured that was her only option to get out of the situation." While he commended her quick thinking, he hated himself for not saving her before she even left in his car. He should've done something. He should've tackled the guy to the ground and pounded the life right out of him.

Yeah, and then that asshole would've shot Susan right in the head. She'd be dead, and his life would feel meaningless.

"How badly was she hurt?" Rina asked again, this time a little more firmly.

"She hit her head on the steering wheel and...and I heard a shot when the car crashed. She was bleeding pretty steadily from the arm, so I'm thinking his gun when off and hit her before he flew through the window."

"Bastard better be dead or I'm gonna—"

"Gonna do nothing, doll," he said quietly, as he wrapped her into a hug and cut off any more words before she could go into another rant that could send her stress level up. "You gotta calm down. For the baby. For me. I need someone in control when all I feel like doing is pounding the walls until I break my hands."

"I can do that. I can totally do that." She hugged him tighter. He could feel the tension drain from her body, which, surprisingly, helped the tension in his as well.

"Susan's tough. She'll be fine," Zoe said as she took a seat next to Rina.

He and Deena joined the other two and they waited. And waited.

By the time the doctor met them in the waiting room, his nerves were wired to the extreme and he was ready to punch something. Unfortunately, if the doctor had bad news, he'd be the one on the receiving end of his fist.

"She's going to be fine. The bullet grazed her. We stitched up her arm and bandaged the gash on her head. I've spoken to her a few times. She's in and out of it right now. She has a concussion and will need to spend the night. Perhaps a day or two to make sure she's fully recovered. She can have one visitor. But a short one."

"Me." Stitch took a step forward, the anguish on his face clear, as well as his determination. "And I'll be staying with her until she leaves this hospital."

22

SHE GRINNED at the obstinate man pacing in front of her bed as the nurse walked out of the room with a scowl on her face.

"I'm okay, you know. You don't have to jump down everyone's throat."

"I didn't like her tone."

"It's sweet when you get like this." Her smile dimmed a little. "But you have to stop."

Stitch stopped and walked to the left side of the bed. Sitting down, he gently grabbed her hand. "Suzy baby, I can't help it. I'm trying as hard as I can, but every time a nurse walks in here, or the doctor, and they even hint at something remotely wrong, I go nuts. She said your blood pressure was a bit high."

Yeah, maybe because he spent all night with her since she arrived and not once said he loved her again. Perhaps she imagined it. Maybe she hit her head harder than she thought on the steering wheel.

She couldn't be sure that's why her blood pressure was a bit high, but her nerves were jangling like a jolly elf bouncing around, waiting and hoping he'd say it again. But nothing.

She was also praying the doctor gave her the all clear to leave today. One night in the hospital was enough. She needed to get him away from people and lower his stress level. She found it sweet, and a little bit crazy, how worked up he got when he thought she was hurt or in pain. He wanted to fix it immediately, and when he couldn't, he went nuts.

She honestly didn't think he'd ever stop this protective behavior. Somehow, she had to get him to tone it down. Just a notch.

"Don't be mad at me, shorty." A silky, sweet, and deadly grin punctured his face. "I am trying here. I've held back quite a few nasty words I wanted to say."

She didn't doubt that. She could see it in his eyes every time someone came in and said something he didn't like. How much more did she need him to tone it down? Maybe she didn't. She couldn't help but adore how loved and protected she felt by his behavior.

Ugh. But did he love her? Why didn't he say it again? She didn't want it to be a figment of her imagination.

"I know. You know how much I appreciate you staying here with me, right?"

"They would've never pried me from your side."

No doubt whatsoever about that. She smiled, then shifted, moaning in pain from the wound in her arm.

"Do you need more pain medication? How bad does it hurt, Suzy baby?"

"I just had some. I'll survive."

He lowered his head, resting it on the bed.

For some reason, he blamed himself. Like he could've stopped that madman with a gun from taking her. There was nothing they could've changed without someone getting shot and probably dying. No matter how many times she tried to tell him it wasn't his fault, he shook his head and ignored her. He wouldn't believe her.

Him and his crazy thoughts that he could save everyone. That he had to.

She didn't want saving.

She wanted his love.

"Knock, knock."

Stitch's head snapped up with wariness and a bit of anger as soon as he saw Sauer, who looked just as wary, walk farther in the room with Dee by his side.

"Hey, Susan. I'm so glad you're okay," Dee said as she walked to the opposite side of the bed from Stitch. "Zoe and Rina wanted to come, but we figured we'd bombard you with a bunch of visitors when they release you. Do you know when you get to leave?"

"I'm hoping later today. It's been a long night. My head hurts, but not as bad as last night. My arm's bothering me some."

"I'm glad it wasn't worse. We'll crash your house when you leave, which I hope is today. I hate the hospital." Dee rolled her eyes at Stitch. "Don't look at me like that."

He stood up. "Like what? Like you're nuts. She's going to rest. Without visitors."

Dee ignored him and laughed as she looked at her. "How long has he been acting like some macho man? Did you tell him to knock it off?"

"I've been trying. It's sorta cute."

Stitch groaned at the word cute as Dee laughed like that was the funniest thing in the world. "No wonder he won't stop. You're encouraging him." Her smile wouldn't die. "It's nice to see you two together." She nudged Sauer's shoulder. "Isn't it?"

Sauer, who had been very silent and the red slowly tinting his cheeks, went into a full-blown blush. "Yeah."

"Oh, that sounded convincing."

She squeezed Stitch's hand, warning him not to start anything. She couldn't handle it. Not right now. In fact, she didn't want to deal with that ever again. If they were going to be together, she couldn't let him act that way with her friends. Hell, Dee was his best friend. Didn't he know he shouldn't act that way with her husband?

"I mean it." Sauer sounded tired, but the truth was in his eyes. "It was a long night...for all of us. I don't want issues, Stitch. I apologize for the other night. Let's start over." He held his hand out toward him.

Stitch eyed it warily.

She wanted to encourage him to shake his hand and move on. It was the easiest route. The best route to make amends.

With a quick glance to Dee, she saw Dee wanted to compel Stitch to do it as well, but her lips were in a tight line as if forcing herself not to say a word.

Finally, after what felt like ages, Stitch reached out and shook his hand. "I ain't apologizing for hitting you. I'll do it again if you make me. But I'm sorry for hurting Susan and Deena."

Sauer nodded. "Fair enough. No hard feelings."

"Yep."

Dee clapped merrily. "Well, now, that wasn't so hard, gentlemen. So proud of you two."

Stitch nearly rolled his eyes and Sauer pulled her into his side and kissed the top of her head.

"How..." She glanced away and started to fiddle with her

blanket. Stitch's warm hand slid into hers once again, offering her the comfort she needed so badly.

She met his eyes and conveyed her thanks at how he always knew what she needed, then looked at Sauer. "How did it go last night? How's Newman?"

She had been dying to know. She even said something to Stitch once, who told her she shouldn't worry about any of that. At the time, she wanted to shout and cry and argue with him. Ultimately, he had been right. When she asked, she had been in and out, the pain raging a war in her head. It hadn't been a good time to talk. She was ready now. Sauer and Dee were the first to visit her. Well, besides Captain Ganderson, who took a quick statement from her about what happened. He never mentioned Newman, and she didn't ask.

"Well, Chris Moretta is alive. He was thrown from the vehicle. He's in the ICU. The doctors aren't too receptive that he'll wake up. We still have an officer standing by in case he does." Sauer finally displayed the first smile since walking into her room. "You did the right thing, Susan. You saved yourself, and that's what matters. We should've connected the dots sooner."

Her face must've displayed the horror at hearing how badly he was injured. Part of her felt guilty. Part of her was angry he didn't die on impact. Part of her hoped he woke up and paid for his crimes by spending the end of his life in prison.

"You can't blame yourself either, Sauer. He didn't leave any evidence. He was a master actor at hiding his true feelings for his ex-wife. He overheard at the precinct I pulled some prints. That's why he broke into my house. He wanted those prints. He wanted to know where he could get them."

"We've all been working hard this morning trying to find

a connection with him and the other women. So far, it's slow going."

"He did say he knew he'd be a suspect in his ex-wife's murder so he had to make it look like someone else by killing more women. It could be as simple as he picked them randomly." She hesitated, not wanting to talk about anything else. Eventually, she'd have to. She didn't even mention anything to Captain Ganderson. Her statement had been short and sweet, but she promised to make a complete statement once she was released from the hospital. "But...he said things...that suggested that might not be the case."

"Get better. We miss you already," Sauer said with a sweet smile, obviously understanding she couldn't talk about it right now.

At the moment, she didn't miss her job at all. She missed her friends. But the thought of going in and processing any kind of crime scene made her shiver with unease. What would she do if that feeling never went away?

"And Newman? How is he?" She still wasn't sure she was ready to forgive him for his actions against her, but she cared how he was doing. Deep down, she didn't believe he meant what he did. He was hurting, acting out in the only way he knew how.

"We released him. He had to turn in his gun and badge. He's on suspension until a full investigation is completed, but he probably won't be coming back. He withheld information in a murder investigation. He has issues that he has to deal with." Sauer sighed as he rubbed a hand through his hair.

"And you'll be there to help him," Dee replied quietly.

"Even if you hate that idea?" he asked with a sweet smirk.

"I won't call him a douche...all the time." She smiled

sweetly to show she was teasing, but also serious. Dee couldn't help herself. It made Susan laugh.

It felt good to laugh. To see her friends happy and the stress lessening and life finally going back to normal, or at least, starting to.

"Okay, chat's over. Susan needs to rest."

Stitch's voice boomed around the room and held no arguments.

Dee cut a dangerous gaze at him, but nodded. "Don't think you can boss me around all the time, Stitch."

"Only when I know it's the best thing for Susan." His eyes softened as he glanced at her, then back to Dee. "Plus, maybe you two need a break as well. Have you been home yet, Sauer?"

"No. Like I said, it's been a long night and day."

"Then maybe it's time you go home and take care of your wife."

To her delight, Sauer smiled at Stitch. "I think you're right." Sauer looked at her. "We'll see you soon. Dee won't stay away for long."

"Damn straight. Like I said, the rest of the gang will crash your house later when you get released."

She couldn't wait. When she caught Stitch's eyes, she didn't think anyone would be crashing her house anytime soon. Somehow, she was okay with that.

As soon as they walked out and the door to her room shut quietly, she realized Stitch had been right once again. She was tired. The visit wore her out.

She closed her eyes to rest. His hand still held hers tightly. Then a tender kiss touched her lips.

"Take it easy, Suzy baby. I'm right here."

HE WANTED to groan from the exhaustion, but instead, he pulled Susan closer and snuggled with her as best as he could without hurting her arm.

It was difficult to lay with her in bed without touching her more intimately. He knew it'd be a few days, maybe even a week, before he could love her body up and down without it hurting. He could survive that long. As long as she was okay, he could live with anything.

She sighed contentedly, relaxing in his arms as they lay there silently.

The doctors thankfully released her a few hours ago. He didn't want to spend another night in the hospital, the awful reminder of what put her there in the first place, but he would've. For her.

She already told him multiple times that what happened wasn't his fault. He knew this. He almost believed it. But he couldn't get past the fact he should've at least tried. He didn't do a damn thing. He stood there and let that asshole drive away with her.

What kind of man did that make him?

He loved her. His job was to protect her. To keep her safe. What did he do? He let some lunatic take her from him.

Well, at gunpoint.

That's what he kept circling back to.

He didn't have a choice. The guy had a gun. All he had were his fists. Not a fair fight.

Maybe over time the guilt would disappear. For now, it lingered like an infection slowly invading the body. Eating him alive.

"You're thinking too hard. Stop." A soft kiss landed on his forearm as a tender hand brushed back his hair. He always loved when she did that simple gesture. "You didn't do anything wrong. You did everything you could. If anything, I'm the terrible one."

He squeezed her tighter, the anguish sucking him dry at those words, but not hard enough to add to the pain she already felt in her arm. "Why would you say that? You're far from that."

"I crashed your car." Her whispered words broke his heart.

At one time, yeah, his car was his everything. His pride and joy. His one true love.

It hurt to think it was mangled into pieces. But not as much as it hurt to think he could've lost her.

"I already told you what I thought about that."

Her sharp intake of breath finally clued him into what she was gearing for.

Well, wasn't he the biggest dumbass?

Considering he never had a real relationship in his life, he shouldn't feel guilty at his idiocy, but he did. He'd rectify his mistake right now.

Pressing a light kiss to her shoulder, he savored the beautiful way she trembled in his arms. The sweet, delectable tremors that always told him how much she loved it when he touched her.

"I love you, Suzy baby. Unless you don't remember me saying that."

She tried to twist to look at him. He let go of her so she could without hurting herself. She lay on her back as he rested on his side to look at her.

"I heard. I wasn't sure if I imagined it or not."

"And..."

This was the part he didn't like. Should he say I love you again? Hell, he didn't mind saying it over and over and over until she told him to shut up. But only if she said it back. She hadn't yet.

Now he needed to hear it. He had to hear something from her. If it came out she didn't, he had some work ahead of him to convince her. Because he wasn't walking away. Not ever.

"And, shorty?"

Why wasn't she saying anything?

Her eyes narrowed at the nickname she never liked, then her lips tipped up into a delightful grin.

"And I love you, too, you big annoying man."

"Well, then. Glad that's settled."

He smiled right before he lowered his mouth to hers and kissed her as if he were drowning and he needed her to save him. To resurrect him from certain death. It took all of his control and restraint to pull away before he devoured her from head to toe. She wasn't ready for that yet.

He shifted her again without asking, making sure not to jostle her too much, and cuddled her against his body once more. Everything felt perfect and right. As it should be.

"Stitch?"

"Yeah?"

She clutched his arm with a fierce grip. "Thanks for not leaving my side. It really helped to have you in the hospital."

"Never, Suzy baby. I'm never leaving your side."

23

SUSAN BLEW out a breath before she had to step into Scott's office. What a long week. But a much-needed week.

Even Stitch took the week off, lying around the house with her while she recuperated from her injuries. She told him several times he didn't need to, but every single time he shook his head and said, "Not leaving you, Suzy baby. Stop arguing with me."

So she did.

Who wouldn't love a sweet, sexy, tattooed man caring for her, getting her comfortable on the couch, making her meals, picking up the house, doing everything he could to make sure life went smoothly for her.

Honestly, it had been a little too perfect. She was waiting for the quiet peace to erupt into chaos once again. Would it last?

Dee, Rina, and Zoe had visited as promised. After, of course, Stitch deemed it an appropriate time. He didn't allow anyone to visit her the first two days, insisting she needed her rest. She thought about arguing with him, but she kind of liked him acting all authoritative and protective.

She wouldn't let him do it all of the time, but it didn't hurt to let him have his way. She honestly thought it made him feel better and lessened the guilt he felt that he didn't do something to stop her from being taken.

They were both slowly coming to terms with what happened. Together. She didn't think she would've otherwise. It helped to have him by her side.

Sauer, Zeke, and Ben also showed up with the ladies, and for a brief time they talked about work. Newman didn't wait for them to finish the investigation. He quit and left. Sauer was taking it hard, wondering how he was doing. Newman told him he needed time away to think and process it all. He said he was going up to his cabin in northern Minnesota, and when he was ready, he'd call. Susan thought that was the best thing for him. He needed to come to terms with what happened before he could with anyone else. She knew Sauer understood that, but he struggled with it.

She had to admit, it was somewhat awkward talking about Newman. Zeke still held some strong resentment toward him but didn't voice it too much. Ben felt sorry for him but wished him well. Zoe and Rina didn't say much, and she figured Dee wanted to say a lot but held back only for Sauer's sake. He had smiled and squeezed her hand every time she did. She knew then, whatever Sauer was dealing with, he'd be okay. Dee would make sure of it.

Unfortunately, they also talked about Chris Moretta. Of course, she was the one who brought it up. He was still in a coma. Part of her felt guilty. The other part was relieved. She didn't think the guilt part would ever leave. He was a cruel, vicious man, but she didn't like knowing she was the one who hurt him. That wasn't in her job description. She didn't deal with criminals face-to-face, and she didn't like it one bit.

They were able to find a small, very loose connection with Bethany, the second victim. She had a profile on a dating website. So did he. His internet browsing history said he looked at her profile several times, although never reached out to her. After digging deep through his social media history with a fine-tooth comb, they found how much he resented and hated women. His ex-wife taking him to the cleaners in the divorce only started the downfall of his anger.

They found one reference where he might have seen Newman and her together, the time frame matching when he slept around with her, but they couldn't say whether that set off his fury, knowing his ex-wife had moved on with another man.

Susan told them how he confessed that he didn't plan to kill her. That it sort of happened. She wasn't sure she believed him. All of that rage and anger simmered below the surface for a while. He was a ticking time bomb waiting to blow. She figured deep in the back corner of his mind, he wanted to kill his ex-wife. He had done it for the simple fact he wanted her dead.

Every day, the hurt ebbed away a little more. But not enough. Not to where she felt peace and contentment. That's all she wanted. She wanted to go back when she enjoyed her job. Enjoyed picking through a crime scene and finding the clues. That's what she needed.

Blowing out one more deep breath, she knocked on Scott's door and waited somewhat impatiently for him to grant her entrance.

He stood up and smiled when she walked in, giving her a semi-awkward hug that she figured he felt compelled to do, but it wasn't necessary.

They both took a seat. It made her sad to think she didn't

see him as a mentor anymore. That she lost so much respect for him because of his actions with Rachel.

"How are you, Susan? You know you can take more time off work if you need it. I extended the interview process for the supervisor position. We don't need to do this now."

She smiled gently, touched that he would do that for her. Although, it was unnecessary. "Thank you, Scott. Please, make a decision. I'm not here for an interview. I actually want to retract my application. I'm not ready for the position."

Like that, the stress that had been building inside of her since she handed in her application suddenly let go. Washed away as if she had cleansed herself. She never wanted to apply in the first place. She only did it because she thought it was what she needed to do. What she thought Scott wanted her to do, and she still couldn't figure out why when he didn't appear to respect her anymore.

But no more. She was going to do what she wanted, not what was expected of her. Nobody would push her to do anything she didn't want to.

"I think you'd be great for it. I was going to hire you, regardless how this interview went."

She wanted to scoff at those words. "Really? Rachel wasn't in the running at all?"

He turned his eyes down, the shame clear. "I overstepped as a supervisor. Yeah, I slept with her, and I shouldn't have. Maybe she thought getting that close to me would help her situation. But it wouldn't have. I always had my mind set on you. I want you to take the job."

Before everything, she would've floated on clouds hearing those words from a man she once looked up to. Now, it fell flat. She wasn't ready. She liked her job the way it was. Stress was never a good thing for her.

"I appreciate the confidence you have in me, but I don't want it." She leaned forward, bracing herself for his reaction. "I honestly think you should let someone else make this decision. I stand by my words I said earlier."

"Maybe you're right."

"You know I'm right." She looked away, then forced herself to meet his eyes. "I spoke to the head of the department." She watched as his eyes widened with panic that she went above his head to his boss. "It's not okay you slept with an employee, or the way you treated me based on her accusations. I didn't tell him that you slept with her because I don't have proof." Not to mention, she couldn't tattle on him and not call herself a hypocrite in the process. She had sex in her office, which was a huge no-no. She didn't feel right outing his secret when she had her own little dirty secret to hide. She didn't regret that moment with Stitch.

"But I did tell him about the evidence logging incident, since I don't think you did yet. Rachel overstepped. Way overstepped. She tried to get me in trouble for something I didn't do, and I won't take that from anybody. For you to sit here and let her still hurts."

"I'm sorry about that."

"Me, too." She stood up, already feeling a load of stress off her shoulders. "I do wish you a great retirement. Bye, Scott."

He didn't say anything as she left his office. He had another month before he officially left. She figured his boss would hire the perfect fit for someone else to run the crime lab. Not her. She wasn't ready for that. Maybe she never would be.

She didn't want to go over his head, but when she came back to work to see Rachel still working, a smug little grin on her face, her patience snapped. She found out Scott never did a thing about the evidence room incident. So she did what she had to do. As far as she knew, Rachel was no longer employed with the St. Cloud Police Department. She didn't feel an ounce of remorse for making that happen. She was surprised Scott didn't know yet. Maybe he'd be getting his walking papers as well.

Soon, she wouldn't have to deal with Scott either, which almost made her sad, considering how much she had looked up to him at one time.

Her life felt like it was getting back on track. Less stress. Less crap to deal with. Normal everyday life stuff.

The best part of it?

She had Stitch.

HE HEARD the garage door start to open, then close shortly after.

Damn it.

He wasn't ready. Oh, well. When did his plans ever go as they should?

As soon as the door from the garage to the kitchen opened, he snagged a hand around Susan's waist and gave her a kiss that said how much he missed her.

"Hey, beautiful. How was work?" His eyes glanced at the microwave. "You're late."

She kissed him one more time, something he'd never get tired of. "A lot happened today, besides the boring part of working a crime scene of a petty theft. How was your day? What smells so good?"

"Making some chili. It's cold out today. Thought it might warm you up." He bent his head and laid tiny kisses across her neck. "Among other things that might warm you up."

She giggled as she took his assault of kisses without resistance. He held himself in check for an entire week. He couldn't hold back anymore. He needed her. Under him. Over him. Whatever way she wanted it, but he needed her.

"When will the chili be done?"

"Well, even though you're late," he cracked a sexy grin, "it still needs another hour or so."

"Works for me." She wiggled out of his arms and around the island before he could stop her.

"Where do you think you're going?"

"To change." Her eyes sparkled with delight. "Into something sexier."

"Doesn't take an idiot to see how sexy you are. Get back over here, shorty. Maybe I wanna take you right here in the kitchen."

"And maybe I bought something for you and you just have to wait."

Hmmm...well, he liked the sound of that. He honestly didn't need sexy lingerie to know she was sexy in anything.

"Wait here. We can still have that dirty sex in the kitchen like you want." She winked and started to walk away.

Worked for him. If she needed to change, he'd wait. He kind of liked the idea of taking her hard and fast in the kitchen, maybe on the island. Showing her he was here to stay. Marking his spot, in a way.

He turned to the stove to stir the chili when he heard footsteps walk back into the kitchen. "That was quick." He turned toward her. She stood near the opening of the kitchen. His brows dropped in confusion. "Or not. You didn't change."

She tossed a hand behind her shoulder. "What's with all the boxes in my hallway?"

"My shit. You know, clothes and stuff."

Her brows puckered together. "Like, moving in stuff?"

"Yeah."

"Did I miss the conversation where we decided to move in together, Stitch?" she asked with a laugh.

"No. I don't think we had it. You got a problem with me moving in, shorty?" He cocked a challenging eyebrow.

"You didn't even ask. Maybe I want to move into your house."

A chuckle slipped out. "My house isn't as nice as yours. Plus, this has a good school district. My place has a shitty one."

"School district?"

"What, are you telling me you don't want kids?"

She jerked back in surprise. "You want kids? Like, what... now?"

He couldn't hold back a sneaky grin. "Come on over here, Suzy baby, and I'll knock you up right now."

He didn't miss the flash of desire in her eyes as she laughed. "Don't tempt me."

"Oh, I'm trying my damndest to tempt you. You better either go change into your sexy shit, or I'm taking you now without waiting."

"I had a crazy day at work. I didn't expect to come home to...this."

Doubt, for the first time, started to seep in. He hated talking. He hated sharing his feelings and dealing with all that relationship stuff. He figured it was easier to make the decision and move in. Skip all that mushy stuff and do it. He didn't think she'd have a problem with it. She loved him. He loved her. What more did they need to talk about?

But maybe she wasn't as invested as he was.

Maybe he read everything wrong.

He slowly crossed the kitchen to where she stood and kept walking until he had her backed up against the wall.

"You don't want me?"

She bit her bottom lip, almost as if she were trying to drive him crazy, which he wouldn't doubt. "Of course I do."

"Good. Why do we gotta beat this topic to death? I'm moving in, we'll have kids...and yeah." He pressed lightly into her, his hard dick waiting to slide deep inside her as he boxed her in with his hands to the wall.

"We haven't even started this topic to beat it to death yet."

"What's there to talk about? I love you. I want to move in and do all that shit couples do."

Her expression as she laughed was a mixture of happiness and pain. "That sounds so romantic. Could you possibly use the word shit any more than you are?"

"Shit." He snapped his fingers as he grinned and winked. "I almost forgot the best part." He dipped his hand into his pocket and then pulled something out without her seeing it. Grabbing her hand, he slid the ring onto her finger he bought last week. Actually, the same night that asshole almost took her away from him.

"There. We'll get married, too. Can't believe I almost forgot the best part."

"Are you even going to ask me?"

"I just did."

Her eyes couldn't stop staring at the small princess cut diamond he paid an arm and a leg for, as another sweet laugh rang around the kitchen. "That was more like caveman behavior. Me man. You woman. Together. Done."

Romance and him? Not something he excelled at. Like an idiot, he practiced in the mirror how to ask her. Of course, then he skipped all that and shoved the ring on her finger, which looked mighty damn good on her.

Maybe he was doing it all wrong. Even though her eyes were twinkling with delight, she wanted him to ask. She wanted a little bit of romance.

He pressed his hands to her hips and lifted her, joining their bodies perfectly together against the wall, suddenly wishing they had no clothing between them and he could slip right inside her. He couldn't resist thrusting against her once before kissing her gently.

"Suzy baby, will you marry me? Have babies with me? Do stupid shit with me, like have dirty sex in your office?" He smirked like the devil as her eyes lit up with bliss. "Is that better?"

"It's an improvement," she said with a giggle as he attacked her neck with a bout full of playful kisses. "You know my answer was always going to be yes."

"Well, yeah. That's kinda why I put the ring on your finger, moved some of my stuff here, and..."

Her smile almost dimmed as his nerves must've been suddenly obvious.

"And?"

A tiny breath escaped as his voice lowered, "And I took my beautiful woman's advice and made an appointment with the doctor about my wrist. Even though I didn't want to. Hate it, actually."

"See, you have this couple thing down pat." She kissed him soundly on the lips, the tension that entered vanishing as if it never existed. He moaned at the loss of her lips. "You know I'll go with you to the appointment. Hold your hand and everything."

"Damn right you are. I ain't going alone." He grinned to hide the fact he was dead serious. He was nervous as hell what the doctor would say. If he couldn't tattoo ever again, he didn't know what he'd do.

"Are we engaged?"

His eyes grazed downward to her hand that rested on his arm. "Yeah, Suzy baby, we are."

"Then what are you waiting for? Love me like an engaged woman deserves."

"No need to tell me twice. But I need to take my time loving you. So a bed is needed."

He gripped her tightly as he moved away from the wall and walked quickly to her bedroom. He set her down gently, then slapped her ass playfully when she turned around to scoot farther onto the bed.

"I'm dying to see this sexiness. Go change already."

She giggled and disappeared into the master bathroom. His eyes followed her the entire way. When she walked out less than a minute later in the sexiest, delectable piece of lingerie he had ever seen, he had no idea how he came to be the luckiest man alive.

This woman.

A woman he didn't even want to take to a dumb ball over six months ago when Deena originally asked him, turned out to be his everything.

He'd have to thank Deena someday.

Because his life was finally complete.

Hell, even if he could never tattoo again, he was happy.

With Susan by his side.

EPILOGUE

Two months later

"Damn it, shorty, get your ass off that chair and put that thing down."

Susan turned slightly, her eyes lit up with laughter, her mouth curling into a devious grin, her hands holding a semi-large portrait that looked ready to topple her small stature over.

"You don't like it here. I thought it would look nice hanging over your desk."

His eyes bulged. "You are not hanging that. Now get off that chair before I spank your ass."

Her eyes glittered with delight. "Don't tempt me. You have to pick a spot."

"I don't have to do nothing. Don't make me say it again."

She had the nerve to widen her smirk.

"You. Are. Not. Hanging. That. Up."

"But you worked so hard on it. It's beautiful."

He stalked over to the desk and took the portrait from her, then grabbed her hand to guide her down off the chair.

"Yeah, I did work hard on this. But not for prying eyes. This is for my eyes only."

"I think it would help you and your teeny, tiny, overprotective streak you have with me. You don't even like it when a man dares to glance in my direction."

"No, Suzy baby, this will not help. This will only further my rage and commit murder if I see one man even think about looking at a picture of you half naked." He lifted the portrait, his eyes grazing the delicate sketch he finished a week ago. Susan was lying on their bed with only her red lace panties on. The sex after he finished...whew! He wouldn't be surprised if he knocked her up. With triplets or something.

Every time he looked at it, he knew it was the best sketch he had ever drawn. Shit. If he ever dared to tattoo it, it'd probably be the best damn tattoo of his life.

But he wasn't sharing this with another soul.

She was nuts if she thought he'd hang this up in his office for clients and his coworkers and anyone else who dared to step in here and see her naked hanging on his wall.

This would not help his protectiveness of her. Far from it. Nothing probably would. He worried about her all the time. Especially working with the police department. He thought he was doing pretty damn good. He hadn't hit anybody recently. She should give him credit for that.

A soft hand cupped his cheek, then moved to brush his hair back. "I didn't think you'd go for it."

His eyes met hers. "Then why'd you bring it here? Aren't you supposed to be working?" He set the portrait behind him on the chair and snagged an arm around her waist, pulling her closer. "What are you doing sneaking into my office?"

"Well, I wouldn't call it sneaking. I walked through the

front door and said hi to Stacey."

"Yeah, but she had me go on a crazy mission to find a dumb box of pens in the back room. Obviously, you were sneaking in here with help from her."

"I have no idea what you're talking about."

Except, the wily grin said she did. He always loved this sassy, sexy side of her. With a searing kiss, he told her exactly how much he loved her.

"I have the rest of the day off. I hear you have no more clients." Her eyes softened. "How's the hand feeling?"

She asked him that regularly. After seeing the doctor, who didn't officially diagnose him with carpal tunnel syndrome, said he needed to relax a bit on the constant strain he put on his hand and wrist. He needed to keep its strength by doing regular exercises.

So far, the dumb exercises he hated doing, but did it because Susan was like a drill sergeant, were helping. He also cut back his client list, not taking as many personal tattoos as before. People still wanted him, which put his wait list even crazier. He wasn't complaining because business was still thriving, but he felt bad the wait was ridiculous. But hell, if they wanted a tattoo, they had to wait. Because if his hand ever became so bad he had to quit, they'd be shit out of luck.

Overall, his hand felt better. If it flared back up, crazy with pain, maybe the doctor would change his mind and say surgery was necessary. Right now, he was managing. Or, more like, Susan was managing him. Nobody knew about his hand issue but her. Just the way he wanted it.

"The hand's fine."

"Don't be a baby. You better have done your exercises this morning."

He snagged a kiss before muttering, "Am I in trouble if I

didn't?"

"Well, don't think I'm pulling out the whip or anything."

That sounded like fun. He'd be up for something like that. She slapped him playfully on the shoulder after reading his expression as such.

"Come on. I haven't had lunch. Are you hungry? Can I buy you lunch?"

"As long as you put that damn portrait back in your car and make sure no one sees it."

She chuckled as she stepped out of his embrace and grabbed a large tote bag from the floor near his desk. "Don't worry. I hid it well." She rolled her eyes, reminding him of Deena. "You don't really think I want people to see me half naked, do you?"

"Then why the hell did you bring it here?"

Ignoring what he thought was a fair question, she tucked the portrait back into the tote bag.

"I'm hungry. Let's go."

She grabbed her jacket, eyed him with a motherly gaze every time he refused to wear one, then she grabbed his hand. Not even caring how sissy it might look walking out of his office and down the hallway of his shop holding her hand, he dared anyone to make a comment. Although, besides Stacey, who grinned at him with a little bit of mischief mixed in, nobody was paying attention to them. Jensen sat with a client on the couch near the window going over a sketch. Stewart and Todd, his other two artists, were applying tattoos. Stewart had a young girl sitting in his chair, probably just turned eighteen, who didn't look like she was handling the pain well. Todd had a guy who didn't so much as flinch as the needle pierced his skin, considering his arms were covered with tattoos, not an inch of skin to be seen.

"Where do you want to..." His words died as he stepped outside and lost all train of thought. Not even the cold weather penetrated his mind.

Tears started to well in the corner of his eyes. Something he never did. Susan squeezed his hand, making him divert his attention from the beautiful car in front of him to the gorgeous woman beside him.

"Suzy baby...how did...what is..."

"Do you like it? I've felt terrible since that day I totaled your car." She pulled him toward the only other thing he had loved deep in his heart before he met her. "It's the same car. Restored to its original glory."

He dropped her hand and stepped toward his baby. His original baby that he had polished and shined and waxed and took care of as if he'd die if he didn't.

His hand glided across the smooth surface of his baby, feeling revived, feeling alive. Feeling damn grateful.

"She looks just like she did. Restored completely? Original parts and...everything?"

Susan smiled wide, shaking her head enthusiastically. "I didn't do it myself. I had no clue what to do, but Dee helped me. She knew a guy, who knew a guy, who knew a guy, or something. She even made them do it as fast as they could."

He laughed, his smile as bright as the sunny blue sky. He was so damn happy to have his baby back, he couldn't even express it to her. She squealed in delight when he grabbed her around the waist, the tote falling from her hands, and he twirled her as he kissed her fiercely. His desire for her soared, wanting to take her right here and now, be damned who saw, in the back of his '69 Chevelle. No woman had ever been lucky enough to have sex in his car.

But his Suzy baby was going to get lucky. He couldn't wait to love her in the backseat of his car.

He twirled her one more time, then let her go gently to hug his car. He didn't care who saw him or what they thought. It was like floating to heaven.

"Geez, okay. Get a room already. I have no idea whether to say to get a room for you and Susan, or you and the car."

The feisty voice behind him made him stand up and turn around. He didn't hesitate to pick Deena up and twirl her, too. He even thought about giving her a quick kiss on the cheek, but he finally noticed Sauer standing to the side, who looked panicked and ready to take him to the ground.

"Sorry. I'm happy." Gently setting Deena down, he rubbed her pregnant belly before stepping away. "The little guy's okay in there. I didn't hurt her, Sauer."

Sauer stepped by his wife and tucked her into his side. "Yeah, but maybe no more picking her up and doing that."

"I don't know who you found to fix this, but you're getting the best damn baby present there is, doll."

"I better. The crib I want is expensive." She grinned deviously.

"Done. Doesn't matter the price. Matching changing table and dresser and nightstand. Hell, I'll do up the entire baby room."

Susan waved the keys in the air. "Do you want to take her for a spin?"

"Do I? Hell, yeah." He snatched the keys, gripping them tightly, afraid they would disappear if he didn't.

"Can I drive?" Deena asked eagerly.

"Sorry, doll. Nobody drives my baby. Nobody." He snagged an arm around Susan's waist and laid a sweet but deadly kiss to her lips. "Nobody drives either of my babies but me."

"Did not need to hear that." Deena rolled her eyes as she headed for the car and opened the door.

"I can crawl in the back, Dee," Susan said before she could climb in.

"Nonsense. You sit in front with Stitch. I can see he wants you to." Before anyone could argue with her, she crawled into the backseat, somewhat awkwardly, but successfully, with Sauer right behind her.

Susan grabbed her tote bag from the ground, then he waited for her to slide in the car, then closed the door. Gliding a soft hand across the hood, he took his time to savor the beauty of the outside before opening his door and slipping into the driver's seat. After closing the door gently, giving his baby the tender love and care it deserved, he smoothed a hand across the steering wheel, feeling the power beneath his fingertips.

"Is it going to be like this the entire time? You making love to the car?" Deena snickered from the backseat.

"Oh, it is like making love. You gotta treat her right, doll. Every single time you drive her."

"Are we talking about the car or Susan?"

He turned his head to glare at Deena. "Both. Now sit back and enjoy the ride."

Susan chuckled, clearly used to Deena and her crazy words. He grabbed her hand, squeezed it, then lifted it for a tender kiss.

"Thank you. I would've been happy without this car. But I'm..." He pulled her closer, snaked a hand behind her neck, and slammed his lips upon hers. He kissed her as if he'd never get the chance to kiss her again. The kiss was fast and rough. Full of his excitement and awe that she'd do this for him. It said how much he loved her and what waited for her when they were finally home and alone and he could take his sweet time to love every inch of her.

With aching patience, he slowed the kiss, making it soft

and tender, like an easy breeze on a beautiful Sunday morning. His hand still cradled her neck as he pressed his forehead to hers. "Suzy baby, I love you. Why'd you bring the portrait here when you had this perfect surprise waiting for me?"

"Honestly," she smiled with little devils in her eyes, "to mess with you. Get you fired up. All hot and bothered." She rolled her head so her face was buried in his neck, her mouth close to his ear. "Sort of like you did last week when you came into my office, turned up the heat, getting me so close to an orgasm, and then said I'd get the rest later at home." She pressed a kiss to his neck, then licked up to his ear where she bit it gently. "And we're going for a long drive around town. I promised Dee we would. I might give you flashes of the portrait as you drive."

He was hard as a rock at each word she said. He could be the devil incarnate, teasing her, building her up to torture her, so when she got home the fun was even sweeter. She was so perfect for him, she dished it right back.

Damn, but he loved this woman.

"Quit making out already and drive. I'm dying here."

He chuckled at Deena's annoyance, kissed his Suzy baby one more time, then cranked the engine.

Oh, but what a beautiful sound.

With one hand on the steering wheel and the other holding Susan's hand, he drove away from his shop.

Life didn't get any better than this.

DON'T MISS THE NEXT BOOK IN THIS EXCITING ROMANTIC
SUSPENSE SERIES!
FINDING REDEMPTION

FOR ZEKE AND ZOE'S STORY
WON'T LET YOU GO
A SLAYING LOVE NOVEL, #1

A determined detective. A woman refusing to bend. A killer who will make sure there are no second chances.

One night of passion became Zoe Sullivan's worst nightmare when Detective Zeke Chance mistook her for a prostitute. Now she wants nothing more than to forget the humiliation —and the man who caused it. But when her boss is brutally murdered, fate throws them together again as Zeke becomes the lead detective on the case.

Zeke knows he screwed up royally, and he's determined to make amends while keeping Zoe safe. But as the investigation deepens, it becomes clear that someone wants Zoe silenced permanently. With a killer closing in and their undeniable attraction reigniting, Zeke must overcome Zoe's distrust before they both become the next victims.

As danger escalates and passion burns hotter than ever, they'll discover that some mistakes are worth making twice —if they survive long enough to get their second chance.

Get ready for steamy romance, heart-pounding suspense, and a detective who'll risk everything to earn back the woman he wronged.

For Ben & Rina's Story
Doomed Love
A Slaying Love Novel, #2

A protective detective. A woman with dangerous secrets. A killer who will stop at nothing to have his way.

Detective Ben Stoyer has wanted Rina Chastain for far too long, but she keeps turning him down with sweet excuses he's tired of hearing. When the victim in his latest murder case looks exactly like her, Ben's protective instincts kick into overdrive—and this time, he won't take no for an answer.

Rina wants to give in to Ben's relentless charm, but her controlling father has destroyed every relationship she's ever tried to have. Now, with a serial killer targeting women who look like her, she's caught between the detective who's determined to protect her and the man who's determined to control her.

As the body count rises and Ben's investigation intensifies, they'll discover that some dangers come from within, and the deadliest enemy might be the one you trust most.

Get ready for pulse-pounding suspense, sizzling chemistry, and a detective who'll defy everyone—including the woman he loves—to keep her safe.

FOR SAUER & DEE'S STORY
DEADLY CRAZY
A SLAYING LOVE NOVEL, #3

A sassy woman who doesn't believe in love. A shy detective who'll die to protect her. A killer who picked the wrong target.

Dee O'Malley has learned the hard way that men don't stick around, so she's not about to risk her heart on sweet, shy Detective Sauer—even if his kisses make her believe in impossible things. When she's brutally attacked, Dee's determined to find the bastard herself, even if it drives her would-be protector crazy. After all, he's adorable when he's worried.

Detective Sauer might be tongue-tied around most women, but loud, fearless Dee O'Malley turns him into a stammering mess for all the right reasons. The moment she's hurt, his shyness vanishes and his protective instincts take over. But when the attack connects to one of his murder cases, Sauer realizes keeping Dee safe means keeping her close—and his biggest obstacle might be Dee herself.

As the threat escalates and Dee refuses to back down, they'll learn that sometimes the most dangerous thing you can do is fall in love with someone who's willing to die for you.

Get ready for sharp-tongued banter, explosive chemistry, and a shy detective who transforms into a fierce protector when the woman he loves is threatened.

FOR NEWMAN & AMELIA'S STORY
FINDING REDEMPTION
A SLAYING LOVE NOVEL, #5

A disgraced ex-detective. A woman who won't give up. A case that could save them both.

Ex-Detective Newman wants to be left alone to wallow in the wreckage of his ruined career and shattered life. When a gorgeous woman with vibrant pink hair and a stubborn streak shows up at his door, he wants nothing to do with her case—or the way she makes him feel like he might be worth saving.

Amelia Benedict doesn't take no for an answer, especially when her younger brother's life hangs in the balance. The police think he ran away, but she knows something terrible has happened. A disgraced ex-cop with nothing left to lose and everything to prove, Newman definitely isn't the right guy for the case—but he's her last hope. But as they dig deeper into her brother's disappearance, they uncover a web of danger that threatens to destroy what's left of Newman's soul and put Amelia in the crosshairs of a killer.

In a race against time to save an innocent boy, Newman must decide if redemption is worth the risk—because this time, failure doesn't just mean losing his last chance at salvation. It means losing the woman who believed in him when no one else would.

Get ready for second-chance redemption, heart-stopping suspense, & a broken hero who'll risk everything to prove he's worth loving.

For Rory & Brooke's story
OBSESSED HOPE
A SLAYING LOVE NOVEL, #6

*A detective with lethal instincts. A woman who attracts danger.
An obsession that could destroy them both.*

Detective Rory Walker's latest murder case should be simple
—kinky sex gone wrong. Until he meets his prime suspect.
Sweet, adorable Brooke Duncan with her terrifying cat and
hidden depths is everything he never knew he needed. One
look, one touch, and he's a goner. But as he digs deeper into
the case, he realizes the dead man had enemies everywhere,
and Brooke might be next on someone's list.

Brooke knows she should stay away from the intense
detective who looks at her like she's both his salvation and
his downfall. But when the investigation takes a deadly turn,
Rory becomes her only protection against a killer who's
growing more obsessed by the day. Now she must decide
whether to trust the man whose obsession matches the
killer's intensity...or face a predator alone.

As the case spirals out of control and the killer closes in,
Rory will discover that sometimes love and obsession are
separated by the thinnest of lines—and crossing it might be
the only way to keep them both alive.

*Get ready for possessive passion, heart-stopping suspense, and a
detective whose protective instincts know no boundaries when the
woman he loves is threatened.*

ABOUT THE AUTHOR

I'm a *USA Today* Bestselling Author that loves to write contemporary romance and romantic suspense novels, although I am partial to romantic suspense. I even dabble in paranormal. Honestly, I love anything that has to do with romance. As long as there's a happy ending, I'm a happy camper. And insta-love...yes, please! I love baseball (Go Twins!) and creating awesome crafts. I graduated with a Bachelor's Degree in Criminal Justice, working in that field for several years before I became a stay-at-home mom. I have a few more amazing stories in the works. If you would like to learn more about me and my books, head to my website by scanning the QR code. Thanks for reading!

Scan me

I Am Krait

VOLUME THREE
TWENTY-FOURTH CENTURY
MERCENARIES

BY
W.J. CHERF

Foxbat Publishing

DEDICATION

Dear Sweet Sue:
"Yet, another one,
just like the other ones!"
I'm on a roll.
As always, this one is for you.

CHAPTER ONE

I have been always a red haired dare-devil. I lived for the thrills, the danger, but best of all, showing off. As a youth I was invincible. I took this attitude too far at times. It got me into trouble, but I didn't care. Instead of worrying about it, I just chalked it up to my education and upbringing. Then, at the old age of eighteen, I got drafted into the United Earth Force or UEF, where I discovered what real thrills, dangers, and challenges truly meant, and the potential costs associated with them.

Being slender and tiny, I could fit into any armored vehicle or aircraft. Learning how to run them was just a matter of downloading their specs via the UEF-installed neural port behind my left ear. Then, after some hands-on training, I was good to go, and always made it a point to surprise my superiors with some unexpected, wild-ass maneuver that I had dreamed up.

When asked just what the hell I was doing, my standard response was, "Sorry, sir. I was just curious to see how, fill in the blank, would handle it. Sir, you can never know in combat, when you might need to do it."

That answer usually stunned the training instructor into silence. Usually quickly followed by some choice words about my twisted sense of reality or state of mind. But down deep, I could see in their eyes their wonder and awe that a woman had thought of it, then, did it—for the first frickin' time.

After my latest maneuver tortured the hell out of the frame of an armored sled, I got transferred to the Air & Space Command side of the UEF, as someone finally figured out that I was too much of a wild child for terrestrial vehicles.

In UEF flight school, I finally met my match. No longer was I the exception, but rather the norm. I thrived upon the extreme competition and found within myself a grounding that I had never before possessed. Then one day the major and head of the school took me aside.

"You're Candidate Katherine Kramer. Is that correct?"

"Yes, sir." I crisply replied, while wondering what this attention was all about.

"Candidate Kramer, you came to us on a recommendation that you could 'do some real damage' in the air or space arenas. Candidate, was that an accurate assessment? Be careful with your reply."

"Wwwhat?"

"I pulled your ticket, navigator, second-class. Henceforth, you are on loan from the UEF to first train in, and eventually navigate, our planet's latest interceptor prototype."

"Wwwhat!"

"You heard me right, nav. My new interceptor sorely needs a maverick test navigator to push it to the absolute limits, and just like with the UEF Army, its Air Command is not for you. I watched you repeatedly push the inertial dampers on the sim trainers to the max, that is until one actually failed. And then there is that latent telepathic element of yours. In the UEF that would be totally wasted, much less augmented. No, navigator, second-class, you need to be somewhere where you can be you.

"Now, how's that for a recruitment pitch? You in, nav?"

"Yes, sir!" I said perhaps a bit too quickly.

CHAPTER TWO

Yes, I was a young, foolish, red head of twenty years and for me Bandung City, Indonesia, was a far-away place in a story-book land that I was not quite ready for.

But first things first.

Before I became an employee of that corporation in Bandung City called GENEMEDCO, I asked for a break, and took on a wild-assed lark, a brief stint as a mercenary. The broker wanted my dad, but he pawned me off instead as a better fit. Yes, I disappeared for four months, and went A.W.O.L. from the UEF Air & Space Command, but was really on loan during that period to the above corporation. Murky, I know. But then again, at that time I was a wild child.

My first and only contract came from an unexpected source, my dad's own mercenary broker, Mr. Putnam, and not a private party. Apparently, some character named von Hunz had crossed my broker bigtime. For reasons of his own, Putnam provided me with five sets of audio surveillance units, which I now had to somehow install throughout the target's corporate offices.

That was it.

At face value, pretty vanilla. But I was not that naive to think it was, for Putnam's specific request for me to perform this task strongly hinted at the potential complexities. His generous fee also told me of the equally potential dangers involved. The greater the prize, the greater the challenge.

Contrary to common belief, mercenaries come in all sizes and shapes, with all sorts of obvious and arcane skills. In my case, for this contract, I was to rely upon my tech savvy and the fact that I was a licensed plumber and once my dad's assistant. This is why Mr. Putnam selected me from his second-class list. The fact is, I know I was the only plumber on that list, or for that matter, his first-class list as well. I won't even lower myself to imagine what he has on his third-class list. So, yes, mercenaries do come in three flavors. More about that later.

Back to the contract. So, what was I getting myself into?

When I laid these expensive items out on my workbench to make sense of their setup, I initially discovered five sets of ten, tiny, and thin audio detection wafers. These cute little do-dads were passive sound wave detectors. Each had an adhesion coating on their backside in addition to five petite prongs, which were meant to be embedded into a wall's backing. They worked with the wall, by detecting the sound waves that hit it, much like a drum skin. But what made these wafers really cool was they had adaptive camouflage. Just moments after I had placed them on my workbench, I had trouble just finding them!

Moving on, the instructions told me that every set of wafers communicated with their dedicated junction transmitters, which functioned as data repositories. All data uploads were to be preset to occur afterhours and transmitted in the form of an extremely compressed, but short ranged, data squirt. These daily data squirts were then packaged as a coherent message by the external receiver transmitter, which finally sent the message to a nearby microwave tower for its ultimate distribution. Important to all this chicanery was the data transmissions were sent via an encrypted and shielded signal.

To make all of this work, however, I first had to find a suitable location outside of the target's facility to set up the external transmitter, keeping in mind that it had to be nearby the facility and a microwave communication's tower. At first, I considered a tree. But I am again getting ahead of myself.

*   *   *

The target's corporate building was a spectacular feat of human engineering placed within the urban boundaries of Zurich, Switzerland, now known in the twenty-fourth century known as United Cantons of Switzerland, or UCS. Nick-named "the golf ball," this modern edifice was a black steel and gray transparent aluminum geodesic sphere precariously perched upon a single foundation that stood twenty-five meters in the air. To gain access to the sphere where the corporation's offices were located, the visitor had to enter via an elevator in the base of the towering concrete footing. As one might imagine, security within this unique arrangement was unprecedented. And that's just how the paranoid owner liked it; a man named Germain von Hunz. And that's why the greater the prize, the greater the challenge.

As von Hunz's city of choice had precious little in the way of development space for his corporate headquarters, coupled with the city's many zoning hurdles, GvHunz GmBh instead bought lock, stock, and barrel the grounds and lakeside docks of a sailing club. From this uncluttered coastal location, "the golf ball," was visible from the entire city and both sides of Lake Zurich and its island. This location clearly fed von Hunz's ego. Grudgingly accepted as a cultural icon by the city fathers, "the golf ball" has become a mecca for photographers, tourists, architectural students, and even had an anachronistic postage stamp issued with its image.

Unfortunately for me, the building's owner was so infatuated with it, that no trees were allowed to block its silhouette. Instead, it was surrounded by an immaculately groomed field of green grass. For all practical purposes, "the golf ball" looked ready to be teed off. But I had a possibility, actually three, for the building did have three flag poles, one each for U.N.-Geneva, the UCS, and GvHunz GmBh's own corporate flag. But looking at the brick-sized external receiver-transmitter, I needed something better. And there it was right in front of me: a nearby permanent structure, a public toilet house. I was in business at less than one hundred meters away.

CHAPTER THREE

Zurich in January is a frosty place with ice and snow as a near-daily occurrence. It would seem that the architects of "the golf ball" did not completely take that simple fact into account. In other words, the water mains and secondary piping of this very exposed, above ground structure, needed to be inspected on a regular basis during the winter season. Like clockwork, a specific plumbing service in a bright yellow truck made its rounds. The plumbers themselves always wore big smiles, would chat up soccer with the security guards, and go on their way. It was a tightly knit group, but one that I hired into, because this winter was an especially bitter one with lots of frozen pipes.

Being slim of build and flexible as a snake, my plumbing certificate and experienced resume placed me on the more challenging plumbing calls, the ones that required a certain "slither" factor. Most of my Swiss colleagues suffered from excessive front porches, all bought and paid for several times over. And rather quickly, my sense of humor, expertise, and near-acrobatic antics won over my colleagues' trust and praise. But when they declared that I was henceforth *Frau* Katie instead of *Frau* Kramer, I knew that I was on the team. In all, it took two months of absolute scut work, but the union pay was great, overtime phenomenal, and my colleagues mostly tolerable. So, I really couldn't complain.

And finally, at long last, I got my opportunity.

*   *   *

"*Frau* Katie," the job scheduler said in his always hilarious mud-thick Swiss-German, "Horst called in sick for the week. I think that his grandchildren are in town."

The ruddy-faced supervisor with a thick white moustache winked. "I'm going to put you on his schedule with Adolf and Ernst. They specifically asked for your assistance. In fact, everyone wants you on their team. Do you have any siblings? Same hours as always. Is that okay with you?"

I pretended to think about it, while my inner self was jumping up and down, and put on my very best smile. "Certainly, *Herr* Hans. I would be most honored to assist in any way."

"*Ja gut!*" Hans grunted out and thumped his fist on the counter. "I know that Adolf and Ernst will be pleased. Besides, you're far prettier than Horst any day."

I pouted, "That wasn't very professional, *Herr* Hans."

"Just kidding, *Frau* Katie." The man waved in smiling dismissal. "But you still are a pretty little thing. Report to truck number three on Monday morning."

*   *   *

A plumber's life is farmore than unplugging clogged toilets and reaming out sewer pipe. A sound understanding of metallurgy is necessary, along with the practical physics of vacuum and pressure. If not, one false move, and you're liable to get a face full of shit. But what few people realize is that plumbers, especially for commercial buildings, have access to architectural plans. After all, how else can we plug a leak quickly, if we don't know where the pipes are running, and where their cutoffs are placed? There is another thing, building codes for commercial buildings are radically different from domestic architecture.

How so?

Most walls in commercial buildings are hollow. These narrow and rarely lit gangways allow for access to all sorts of things, like plumbing, electrical, forced air heating and cooling vents, and data conduits. Working in these closed spaces is not for the claustrophobic. But for me, they were a piece of cake.

*   *   *

When Monday arrived, Zurich had been transformed into a winter wonderland buried under three centimeters of the whitest of white snow. It was magical and everyone on the street wore broad smiles to go with their rosy cheeks.

At seven sharp, I arrived with my gear, and Mr. Putnam's items, raring to go. I was genuinely happy to complete this contract, and my broker had been patient.

My colleagues for the week, Adolf and Ernst, were already loading up the number three truck with her lunch boxes and gear.

"Guten Morgen!" I greeted.

"Guten Morgen, Frau Katie!" They both piped cheerfully in unison, clearly in good moods as well, no doubt because of the snow.

Adolf then added, "The office had to call in ahead for our first stop. It's a very high security client. *Herr* Hans assured them that Horst was ill and that you were filling in for him. They, of course, asked some questions, they always do." He shrugged. "But this week, you're part of *our* team." He said slapping me on the back.

All settled in and loaded up, off we went, with Adolf driving and Ernst next to him in the passenger's seat. I sat on the jump seat behind the driver. Just where I wanted to be. I could see everything.

*   *   *

Parking our bright yellow paneled sled in an urban area like Zurich was always an issue. In the old sector, for example, the sled took up most of the pavement. Sliding up onto the curb is not much better. That tactic, which works sometimes in other sectors, blocks both the pedestrians and sled traffic. That's not good for the business. But with the GvHunz GmBh building, parking was not at all an issue, for theirs was underground.

Adolf gathered up all our I.D.s before he pulled up to the security kiosk and gate. After a peek inside at me and some knuckled headed conversation that quickly drifted between vacations needed and lost soccer matches, we were waved through. A massive security door rolled up to allow our sled access to a descending ramp that led to a large underground parking area.

Parked in a visitor's slot, we got out with our gear. The atmosphere was noticeably warmer. Ernst unnecessarily brought along the building's plans. It was more for show than anything else as these two had long ago memorized the entire layout and could probably sleep walk it. I tagged along with a bounce in my step.

At the service elevator, security again checked all our I.D.s.

The guard gave me a stern look and said with a disapproving sneer, "You're a plumber?"

Adolf said to the jerk, "Careful Manfred. If you're not polite, she'll plug your toilet."

This off-color quip first confused, then rendered the guard a laughing hyaena. Still in the fits of hilarity, he stabbed the elevator's call button, waved us on, and we were again on our way.

In the elevator, I thanked Adolf for the standing up for me with the security guard.

"*Frau* Katie." He said, "That guy is a total jackass. Always has been. Forever will be." And Ernst agreed with a grunt.

CHAPTER FOUR

The building plans revealed a circular layout stacked into four floors, each divided down the center by a hidden service gangway. The back walls of rooms of various purposes of both hemispheres formed that passageway. None of these round floor plans reached the outer steel and transparent aluminum exterior. Instead, they all ended just with what reminded me of low walled balconies. The views were spectacular.

Within each floor's long and narrow service gangway, the architects had placed the water and electrical piping, along with the thick and bundled looms of digital cables, security wiring, forced air ducting, and the like, along its ceiling. Each hemisphere had a bathroom, conference room, kitchenette, and several offices. Opposite these accommodations, management had placed either low office cubicles or utilitarian furniture arrangements, along the low outer wall balcony. This layout was mirrored on the other hemisphere, except that the elevator served only one side. Plain glistening white tile flooring covered levels one through three. However, on the executive level, the uppermost floor, which also had a central service gangway, the decoration of its hemispheres was excessively posh, bath facilities lavish with marble fixtures and even showers, and conference rooms ruggedly paneled to look like staterooms on a high-end crew ship. Flooring there was a deep, wool carpeting the color of beach sand.

Access to all hidden gangways was concealed by a service panel. The only hint that a narrow doorway existed at all was betrayed by an oddly placed circular lock plate about a meter above the flooring. While Ernst held the architectural plans at the ready, Adolf opened up the first floor's panel, turned on his flashlight, and led me into the darkness, explaining everything as he went. We walked in about ten meters and stopped.

"*Frau* Katie, this facility is very logically laid out. Directly below us is the building's central support. In it is the elevator that we just took, an emergency stairwell, and a dummy elevator shaft. In the dummy shaft, we have the ascending water mains, main electrical connection to the city's grid, and communications. To inspect them, which we will, a steel ladder in one of the walls allows us to do so. But here, right in front of us, are the two water mains. This one ascends into the water tank on the roof and that one descends into the city's sewer. All of these pipes are secondaries that branch off in either direction service the bathrooms, kitchenettes, conference rooms wet bars, and in the case of the executive level, also showers.

"Above us, is the digital cables, security wiring, electrical conduits, and of course, the HVAC venting.

"Our job, is to make sure that anything dealing with water is functioning and not leaking in any way. Understood?"

"Yes, *Herr* Adolf."

"Alright then. I am now going to squeeze by you and let you carefully inspect all the water connections. Afterwards, we will together inspect all the water connections on the other sides of these walls. For now, Adolf and I are going for a coffee."

And there I was. In the heart of the lion's den. The wolf in the hen house. All alone with Mr. Putnam's toys to install. Touching the shared walls between the aluminum framing, I quickly confirmed the gypsum wall paneling and smiled. Such wall paneling resonated sound far better than plaster and I got to work. The pipe and junction inspections took no time at all. My "extra" installations took perhaps a handful of minutes start to finish. Nonetheless, my senses were abuzz, constantly watchful as discovery was not a happy outcome. The entire experience was exhilarating.

Amazingly, Adolf and Ernst allowed me to perform the rest of the service gangway inspections on my own. Afterwards, they asked some basic questions, which I answered to their satisfaction.

Then, they had me climb down the dummy elevator shaft to visually inspect the mains and again, found nothing amiss.

Later that night, I double-checked the external receiver-transmitter atop the lavatory building, and to my great pleasure, found that it had already sent along its first parcel. I cannot stress this enough. In my line of work, the sheer thrill of completing this contract made me ecstatic. There is an electricity at that one moment, when you realize, I did it!

*　　　*　　　*

My first vid message to Mr. Putnam at the completion of the install earned me a quick answer.

"Great job. Expect a bonus!"

I was floored. I had heard that the blubbery frog of a man, usually pinched his pennies, but not this time. My already generously sized contract hadn't included a bonus clause. But who am I to complain? And that got me to wondering, why?

So, I looked more carefully into who this Germain von Hunz was and received quite an education. He was a fourth-generation corporate executive of a privately held family business. Said business owned holdings in northern Canada, southern Africa, Afghanistan, and the Ural Mountains, as a global leader in mining, processing, and terrestrial distribution. In other words, lots of slag heaps and ore to sell off. Then, GvHunz, GmBh went public.

The only downside that I could see was that the firm didn't own any low-orbital transports, but I suspected that eventually they would get with it. So, I bought some GvHunz stock with my contract bonus money   as   a   hedge.

CHAPTER FIVE

Fast forward.

After my four month "furlough" as a mercenary plumber, while on loan to GENEMEDCO, I finally showed up in Bandung. While Mr. Jonathan was none too happy about my "Australian walk about" as he put it, he still took me to intake. Maybe he had expected me to pull something. Or he needed my navigator skills. Needless to say, there remained a coolness about the man thereafter, like a jilted lover. Henceforth, I toed the line and gave him absolutely no reason to send me back to the UEF. Yes, I put myself on good behavior.

Peace made, GENEMEDCO, for its part, provided me three squares, a nice two-room quarters on its vast, green, and lush campus, and a supplemental salary in addition to my UEF pay. Yes, financially, I was now in fat city at the age of twenty, almost twenty-one. That GvHunz stock also had risen nicely.

Next, I underwent the most thorough physical examination of my life. "Reamed, steamed, and dry-cleaned," I think the old tried and true phrase goes, even if its true meaning was totally lost on me.

The next personality of note that I met, other than my physician Dr. Jazmet Singh, was this rock-solid stump of a man named Ian Gregory. He shared the burden of all of our physical training and weapons education. And by all, I mean me and forty some in-house super-soldiers.

Let me be clear. Yes, I was fit, but hardly ripped. I was more an endurance swimmer, a climber, or long-distance runner, than a power lifter. Technically, my body type was ectomorphic, i.e., lean and mean. I found my slender form to be advantageous. Sure, my freckles and pug nose could easily get me into trouble, but I could fit into tight spaces easily, like cockpits and aft spaces, which oftentimes meant I could get where others couldn't.

To this day, I will never forget that first morning physical training session. Mr. Gregory introduced me as a new second-class navigator acquisition and test pilot.

"Go easy on this one, troopers. I suspect that this red-haired lass will eventually bust all of our asses."

The entire group just stood there, with their hands on hips, each and every one wearing big, broad, toothy smiles that said, "Fresh meat." I thought they all looked like so many sharks.

Well, that first training session really gassed me,

while these super-soldiers barely broke a sweat. Frankly, it pissed me off, but also motivated me in ways that I never knew possible. As for the weapons training, that was a new world to me, as the UEF Army introduction didn't teach shit. But Mr. Gregory sure did and made it all happen, be it blind-folded tear-downs and assemblies, gun sighting, windage, and yardage.

"Kramer," he would say in this grandfatherly-like tone, "don't jerk or pull the trigger. Just caress it." And damn, if he wasn't right! And before I knew it, I was filling the black bull's eye with all of these tiny holes!

The next big step was a conversation with Dr. Singh during one of my every two-week checkup physicals that typically addressed blisters, bruises, and the like. It went something like this.

"Ms. Kramer, during your intake physical, do you remember those cheek swabs that I harvested from your mouth?"

"Why, yes. I do. Did you find something wrong?"

"Oh, my heaven's no, Ms. Kramer. Far from it. In fact, I have some very good news. After an analysis of your DNA, I can safely say that you are a perfect candidate for our "Splicer Project.""

"What's that?" I asked.

"The 'Splicer Project' is a proven, in-house effort that improves upon one's DNA make-up. In your particular case, you are a latent telepath. With just a few genetic modifications, you could develop full blown mind speaking abilities, but only after about three months of intensive training. Additionally, we can also improve upon your physical endurance, hand-eye coordination, and overall speed."

Screwing with my DNA?

Kate, is that wise?

The frown on my face prompted Dr. Singh to inquire. "Ms. Kramer. Is there something wrong?"

"Yes, and no. Being able to mind speak I suppose would be nice, but I don't immediately see its application."

"Ms. Kramer, I totally understand. But just imagine yourself in a difficult situation, needing to communicate quickly and clearly, all the while flying an interceptor during a heated engagement. Do you think that the ability of mind speak would be of some utility?"

I saw his point.

"Okay on the mind speak. But tweaking my muscles and endurance? Would I cease to be a female?"

With a broad smile, "Not at all, Ms. Kramer. In fact, your monthly menses would continue as they do now. This is not about crudely upping your testosterone. This is about augmenting your genome. Making you a better version of you.

"Ms. Kramer. I wish to assure you that your participation in the 'Splicer Project' is totally voluntary. As is, you are truly blessed with a marvelous physique, but it is a natural, unaugmented one. I note also that you are quite competitive by nature. If you train daily with super-soldiers, why would you not want to keep up with them? Perhaps, even, beat them?"

This last sentence was delivered softly, gently. And, after a moment, I appreciated what the man was trying to say.

A better red-headed me.

What a concept.

Then I surprised myself when I asked, "How long, doctor, before all of these changes take hold?"

A deep sigh from the physician.

"Usually, a splice takes two to three months to be verifiably measured. It is all dependent on how fast your body makes new cells with the spice augmentation, and discards the old. In rare cases, the splice does not take hold at all. In any event, to splice or not, no harm comes to you."

"Okay, I'll do the splice. It's high time that those super-soldiers get a run for their money!"

Dr. Singh wore a broad smile. "Funny, I thought you would see it that way."

CHAPTER SIX

Three weeks into what I thought of as my corporate dream job, I was downloaded with the specifications of GENEMEDCO's latest interceptor prototype. This was the precious baby of Mr. Jonathan's, dubbed in-house as the Praying Mantis. After first seeing this wicked machine, I totally got the name.

Now for a quick description of the interceptor and its crew, try to follow along.

Overall, the Praying Mantis is fifteen meters long by five meters wide, in other words, an isosceles triangle, filled out with many faceted planes that meet behind the forward cockpit screens and extend back to the tail. Its all-important armament hangs from not one, but four articulating arms that are mounted behind and to each side of the crew cabin. At rest, these arms fold up in half, praying mantis-like. The weaponry consists of four plasma cannons that can be individually or collectively aimed and fired from the command, tactical, and navigation seats. Each cannon has its own power supply, and in the event of a cannon malfunction, power can be redirected to the other cannons.

Got all that?

Now for its two engines, each with two separate power cells. Originally spec'd out according to the old Pleiadean scout design from the twenty and early twenty-first centuries, the Praying Mantis gets a complete engine redesign and upgrade, while still retaining the Moscovium 115 fuel. I am told that the performance envelop difference between the old Pleiadean scout configuration and the new Praying Mantis interceptor was estimated at a seven-fold improvement. In terms of raw speed, the interceptor's top end is now in the vicinity of 4.7 light. That's really quick. Needless to say, going that fast really burns through the fuel, that's why two power cells. There was also the need for redundancy due to battle damage.

Now for the people part.

This beast carries a crew of five: command, navigation, and tactical, in addition to an engineer and field medic, complete with a mini-medical unit. These last two sit aft, while the rest of us are forward. Best of all, if you squeeze your way down the central aisle past the engineer and medic, right next to the medical unit is the honey pot. This ingenious device with a sealed lid, fit your bum tight. When finished with your business, just close the lid, and press the evac button.

Instrumentation is to die for. All forward seats have multi-functional helmets with cannon command controls, viewing spectrums in standard, infrared, and ultra-violent, and 360-degree camera sighting. The control panels themselves are intuitive, clearly marked, and informative touch screens. Clearly, someone did lots of forward thinking.

After three grueling weeks of training in the simulators, I earned my nick-name after a long and prolonged engagement, where I just didn't stop attacking. Now, Krait is not to be confused with my shortened first name of Katherine, which is Kate, or some mispronunciation of it. Apparently, to someone's ears, the slurring of Kate Kramer came out as Krait. And yes, as you probably already know, a krait is an extremely poisonous snake and a member of the cobra family. And no, I don't bite, but the nick-name stuck like peanut butter on the roof of your mouth, none the less. Actually, I kind of like it. Sounded "dangerous."

That extended training simulation I could not have done without the splice. I have never before held my concentration so focused for so long. I was positively relentless. In fact, in small ways, whether during the daily PT, or just running, I could tell that my body was slowly coming online.

But the real proof were the looks that I was getting after the morning PT sessions. Looks that said, "Oh, shit. The red head is for real."

The next day after morning PT, I ran into Mr. Jonathan, or rather, he purposely ran into me.

"Hey, Krait! That was some sim you pulled off

yesterday. Any aches and pains?"

"None, Mr. Jonathan. None at all."

"Well, be advised that in the future you just might."

"Why, sir?"

"During that sim furball, you set on four separate occasions the highest inertial dampening readings we have ever recorded."

"I did? I didn't break anything? Did I?"

"No, Krait. You didn't. You just broke the record, four times, during one sim engagement." Then, he smiled. "Way to go, nav."

As the man walked away, I nearly floated.

*   *   *

While our simulators were state-of-the-art creations, nothing, and I mean absolutely nothing, compares to the real thing. My first test flight took place high above Java at the very edge of space. Once there, we were to meet up with and perform an inspection patrol around the UEFSS, or United Earth Force Space Station. We were looking for asteroid damage to the UEFSS' many hull surfaces. To do a proper job, I had my hands full, worming my way around the installation's many solar arrays and modules. That was my job. No one else. And wouldn't you know, we found some that the last crew didn't.

In all, three crews performed that inspection. Vids of our approach, inspection patterns, and departure were rigorously reviewed during that debrief. Mr. Jonathan missed little, had a lot to say, and left us all feeling a little bit shorter. Yeah, he really chewed our asses, but I rated the experience a good one.

* * *

After the flight debrief, Mr. Jonathan and Mr. Gregory met for a beer at a favored locale in the center of Bandung. It was your typical mom and pop place, tiny, two at a table seating maybe, a couple of stools at the kitchen counter, no menu, with out-of-this-world homemade food, and ice-cold beer.

"When did you first find this gem?" Gregory asked taking a sip.

"It's the first place I settled on back some thirty, thirty-five years ago. I remember that two mercs tried to kill me once after dinner, right over there, in that alley. Neither lived." Jonathan then took a long pull.

"Damn. You're not kidding, are you."

"Nope."

"Mom and Dad have retired. Their kids have taken over. And I'm practically part of the family. Now get ready for a real treat."

"Great! I'm starved." Gregory blurted out as the new ambassador to Sagittarius 43. Mr. Jonathan had stepped down from that lofty post eight months ago.

Then the food arrived. Massive portions of boiled fish, vegetables, and sticky rice, with sauces on the side from mild to wild. Random flower heads decorated the dishes in amazing ways. All were edible.

Several shovelfuls in, Mr. Jonathan casually asked, "Greg, what do you think about Krait?"

Mr. Gregory chewed his food, took a sip from his beer, and said, "I wouldn't want to fly against her. She'd eat me for lunch, spit me out, and then look for more."

Mr. Jonathan grinned. "You know she'd pinned the sims inertial dampers four times during that last training encounter."

"She did!"

"Yep. Truth be told, I wouldn't want to go against her either. All of that from a second-class nav. Jesus. I must be getting old."

"Well, Jon, you are."

"Fuck you."

Love is grand between good friends.

Halfway through lunch, Mr. Gregory made a suggestion.

"Jon, it just might be time to promote Krait to a first-class nav."

"Yeah, I've been mulling that one over. But it's too soon. It's all about timing."

After a few more chews, Jonathan added, "And you might want to consider Krait as your ambassadorial successor."

"What!?!" Mr. Gregory said.

"Yes, Mr. Ambassador. Who's currently on your short list? Think long term, you old ground pounder. She needs a grooming period, however long that might be. She even has a distinct wild side. Then recollect what impresses the Sagittarians the most. Things like courage, strength, respect, and honesty."

"But she's a…"

"A woman? Don't you remember, fathead, who

presented Nars-mob with the treaty scroll? That was an ancient and much-revered female Sagittarian. All I ask is, think about it. Oh, yeah, and she's tiny just like them."

CHAPTER SEVEN

Sagittarian Transport Commander Olen-bar sat confidently before his console. He had a load of sand and grit for the Earthers, who prized it so much. Why, he didn't know. In his mind, it was just, sand and grit. His massive transport, actually a converted Gigac assault cruiser, was running as designed and manned by a skeleton crew. Outwardly, it had the same configuration, except for the aft portion, which had been cut away leaving access its cavernous hold wide open. This new feature was sealed from the vacuum of space with three separate and non-overlapping force shields. The commander's confidence, however, wasn't misplaced, for the transport retained the assault cruiser's many energy weapon batteries in addition to ferrying six vertically stacked and launch-ready interceptors in his hold.

"Transport Commander!" the tactical technician

reported. "Something big is dead ahead. It just appeared at the edge of my tactical sensors."

"Sensors! Report!" Olen-bar barked.

Her pebbled skin blushing with colorful waves of embarrassment that tactical had sighted the object first. The sensors technician said, "Tactical is confirmed. Object ahead. It's stationary and large."

"Navigation. Immediately reduce velocity to sub-light and prepare for evasive maneuvers. Any impact would be most unwise."

CHAPTER EIGHT

This was to be her biggest endeavor—the opportunity to take such a large technological craft. The possibilities of its acquisition or sale on the open market caused her mind to flit to dreams of personal satisfaction and outright joy. Perhaps such a feat would attract an invitation from The Union. That alone could be most profitable in so many ways.

It had taken the queen of this hive many seasons to construct this space-worthy conveyance. Constructed primarily from one asteroid rich in building materials, it was now nearly hollowed out by her progeny. To fully complete it, she required further technological assistance. The approaching ship would provide it. The equation was just that simple.

*　　*　　*

The Union, which is comprised of a varied assortment of raider communities, who, without established locations, nomadically transit the galaxy's star systems. Members take advantage where opportunity showed itself. Outcasts all, some escaped their adjudicated fates, in some cases mere steps away from having their sentences brought to a final conclusion. Others, based on inclination alone, did the same, running from circumstances beyond their control. Recognition by this amorphous lot was hard earned. Membership even more difficult to attain, usually consummated by proxy or by adoption. Charles Darwin had it only partially right, "Survival of the fittest," or by the most clever and lucky.

Jarim-Pock-Ylloy counted himself among the "clever and lucky" as he was hardly the fittest, much less well-connected. But he was really nimble and good at finding things what others coveted. As a consequence, friendships were made, alliances struck, and a network of optics and aural sensors watched his dorsal. For a one-entity band, he did well, and over the cycles, became by pure accident, not only a member of this distinguish organization of misfits, but became one of its most revered and influential leaders, in addition to a story-teller and historian of sorts.

Jarim-Pock-Ylloy had a knack for listening to the most outlandish of tales and stories and gleaning from those rantings' kernels of information. Perhaps one of the strangest was about a predatory band, who thought nothing of creating colonies, and devoured everything in their path. Few survived their raids, which made the stories about them all the more alluring. No one seemed to know what they called themselves. But as far as Jarim-Pock-Ylloy was concerned, this shadowy threat, that seemed to lurk just beyond credibility, sorely needed one. So, he called them "The Curse." In his mind, such a group, even *if* they existed at all, could never be associated with The Union. For *if* the stories about them were even half true, then The Union could grant them only one thing—their complete and total destruction.

CHAPTER NINE

"Navigation. "Maneuver our course to avoid that object." Olen-bar ordered.

"Done, Commander."

"Sensors. What is it?"

"An asteroid. Surface composition, iron-nickel alloy. What troubles me it that it does not move or tumble like an ordinary celestial body. It is stationary."

Olen-bar grunted at that news.

"Navigation. Broaden our divergence. My stomach does not like this object. Report if it moves a finger-breath."

"Yes, Commander."

*　　*　　*

"Our hive's much-needed technological

assistance has detected us, has reduced its speed, and has modified its course." Stated the queen's nearby drone assistant. "This course change is a modest one. It appears they wish a near-space flyby."

"How interesting. Is their course change within the limits of our grapplers?"

"At present, no, my queen. Do You wish our hive to block its passage?"

"No. This minor coarse correction may be motivated by curiosity. If so, then, that will be their undoing. When the time is right, deploy our mining crews, and harvest what is needed."

*   *   *

While this drama began to play itself out, Commander Olen-bar thought it prudent to report back to Sagittarius 43.

Military Command.
Transport Commander Olen-bar, Transport Number Two.
Attached are scans of a stationary object, blocking trade passage.
Trajectory adjusted to avoid this object.
Appears as a sizeable asteroid.
Displays atypical behavior.
Further reports to follow.

"Sensors. Has the object moved?"

"No, Commander. It has remained stationary."

"Interesting. Firstly, how is it maintaining its status? Secondly, what are the astronomical odds that it randomly stumbled into our path? None of this is making any sense. My stomach is not happy."

CHAPTER TEN

Now well within visual observation, from the forward view screens of Transport Number Two, Commander Olen-bar did not like what he saw and what his sensors technician was telling him.

"Approximately fifty, no, nearly one hundred self-propelled objects have departed from the asteroid. They appear to be positioning themselves in line with our starboard hull, Commander!"

Olen-bar had seen enough.

"Tactical. Ready all energy weapons, target those objects, and fire when in range! Alert our interceptors and ready them for immediate deployment.

"Our curiosity will not be our downfall. That story has already been written."

*   *   *

With the Sagittarian energy weapons' batteries firing with precise and deadly accuracy, in moments the number of approaching self-propelled objects were destroyed by half, and then by half again. At this point, the transport commander launched three of his six interceptors with orders to destroy anything and everything unknown in their path, and to collect, if possible, a relatively intact example.

Meanwhile, the hive queen keened at the sudden loss of her children and vowed revenge, while she watched helplessly as the nearby behemoth cruised by with its weapons of destruction licking out at her miners. Then, three smaller ships joined in the carnage, weaving in and about wrecking everything, sometimes even twice. They too possessed such weaponry, and knew how to use them.

Within moments, the transport's image began to recede into the dark void beyond, leaving behind an asteroid and a tumbling cloud of ruined debris. The engagement had been mercifully brief.

*　　　*　　　*

"Commander." Tactical reported. "Dragon Three snagged an example and has towed it aboard. It is currently in a sealed isolation hold for safekeeping. Do you wish to examine it for yourself?"

"Absolutely! Inform the hold to treat the example as if it were a hungry Hurros!"

The mere mention of that name caused everyone on the command deck to shudder in revulsion, for a Hurros was a thing of Sagittarian nightmares, a dangerous parasite that laid its eggs within its living, paralyzed victim.

"Tell them, Tactical! In those very, hateful words!"

"Yes,   Commander!"

CHAPTER ELEVEN

First contact was always such a fragile situation. In this case, it took the form of wreckage within a sealed hold filled with the vacuum of space. The Sagittarians knew far better than most about exposing themselves to alien biologics. Again, the Hurros case came immediately to mind, its horrors far too fresh.

As the transport commander joined the load master to gaze through the port into the hold, what he saw was severe blast damage to a pod-like shape. To his amazement, he saw no metallic tears or ceramic fractures. Rather, what he did see looked organic, frightening in its simplicity.

"Does that look like an organic spacecraft?" He said to his colleague incredulously.

"Indeed, Commander." Replied the load master.

"Everything is sealed correctly?" The clearly worried transport commander almost pleaded.

"Yes, sir. When Dragon Three dragged it in, we ventilated the entire hold. We lifted it into this decon hold and sealed it to standard decon specifications. As you can see, it's quite small."

"Does it have a pilot?"

"About that subject, you had better speak with the commander of Dragon Three."

Impatient with the load master's oblique answer, the transport commander barked, "Well, where is Dragon Three's commander?"

"Here, sir."

Turning around, the transport commander now faced the stiffly standing inceptor commander. "Commander, was there a pilot in that craft?"

"No, sir. It ejected, or perhaps better said, it jumped at us and attempted to attack our Dragon."

"What!?!"

"Yes, sir. The craft's pilot, organism, whatever you want to call it, literally leapt from its damaged craft onto our hull. Once there, it attempted to burrow through our hull."

"Show me!" The shocked transport commander said.

Briskly walking over to Dragon Three's cradle, the vandalism was clear. Deep and bright scratch marks in its titanium hull were clearly in evidence. And in their center, a shallow pit had been dug, but had not broken through.

"Is that repairable?"

"Yes, Commander."

"So, tell me, how did you remove this blight from your hull?"

"We rammed against it a piece of battle debris, which dislodged the organism."

"Did you kill it?"

"Yes, sir. I believe so. It came apart in three pieces after the impact."

Now turning to the load master, the transport commander said, "Dispatch two Dragons to inspect our hull. Tell them what to look for."

"Yes, sir!"

Returning to the Dragon commander, he asked, "Now Commander, what did the organism look like?"

"Sir, you will not believe this, but it looked very much like a common sand beetle, only larger, perhaps as tall as us."

*   *   *

Military Command.
Transport Commander Olen-bar, Transport Number Two.
Engaged with an unknown, aggressive, space-capable species.
We are undamaged.
Proceeding to Earth to unload and receive cargo.
Attached are four vid-recordings of the encounter and coordinates of their stationary asteroid.
Took aboard a sample.
Held in a sealed decon hold for further examination.
Further progress reports to follow.

CHAPTER TWELVE

That lunch between Mr. Jonathan and Mr. Gregory set into motion the establishment of a revised schedule and curriculum for the future Navigator First-Class, Krait Kramer.

Her participation in the daily morning PT continued, but as her splice continued to take hold, her performance improved to the point of near parity with the other super-soldier recruits, and they had taken note. Mr. Gregory well remembered that day as well, as a former UEF splice, when he suddenly found himself not following the pack, but leading it. A week later, at the conclusion of that day's PT, the grizzled master sergeant had his troops gather around. Mr. Jonathan was there as well, and he clearly had something to say.

"People. Today is a special day. Navigator Second-Class, Krait, has just made the grade. Today, I am proud to announce that Krait has been promoted to Navigator First Class!"

Raucous cheering broke out. Krait was lifted onto sweaty shoulders and paraded about bobbing as she was handed off from group to group. Krait had made it. She was now one of them.

With her sim atmospheric and near-space training behind her, Krait suddenly, but briefly, found herself without an immediate goal to shoot for. However, Mr. Jonathan and Mr. Gregory had other ideas. After the post-PT ceremony, she received an invitation to visit the corporation's armory and the inner sanctum of both men. Krait instinctively knew that this was both an honor and a potential challenge. Not everyone was invited to make such a visit.

The GENEMEDCO campus, in truth, was a small city within Bandung, complete with its own fire department, water reclamation and purification plant, groundkeepers, educational facilities, housing facilities, underground hangers for their private fleet of eight Super Raptors, and a weaponry and armament development department. The latter was housed in a traditional above ground earthen bunker tastefully covered in luxuriant grasses and flowering bushes. Here, is where the first Super Raptor was conceived, and where its modified version, the "Frankenstein," came into being. The Praying Mantis prototype was nothing more than a natural development, and now fast-becoming a near-production version.

In the very center, among the standard weapon's storage lockers, ammunition bays, firing ranges, and machine shop, stood six highly polished, stainless-steel work benches. Stools were provided to encourage careful tinkering and contemplation. Seated around one of these work benches, bent over, sat Mr. Jonathan and Mr. Gregory, who were fingering various documents before them.

Krait, with some trepidation, entered the bunker through its wide-open doors, which were big enough to accept a full-sized, transport hauler sled. Unconsciously, they made her feel tiny, but she quickly threw back her now taunt shoulders and marched forward, greeted by the faint smells of gun oil and spent gunpowder.

"Ah, Krait, you're just in time." Mr. Gregory greeted. "Pull up a stool and make yourself comfortable."

Mr. Gregory watched carefully to see which stool she chose. Krait pulled up a stool from an adjacent work bench, looked from side to side, decided, and sat next to Mr. Gregory.

Ah, that's my Krait.

Mr. Jonathan also took note of this choice and said, "Krait. It's almost been three months since your splice. Do you feel any different?"

"Yes, sir. My endurance and physical strength are up and increasing."

"What about your sixth sense?" Jonathan pushed.

"Don't know." Krait said with a head shake.

"See that ammo box over there?" Jonathan said pointing.

"Yes, sir."

"Turn and focus on it."

Krait turned on her stool and did just that.

Meanwhile, Jonathan focused on the back of her head with a gruesome image. Krait spun back around and said, "Why did you do that!" with considerable force.

Mr. Jonathan ignored her and said to Mr. Gregory, "Schedule immediately her mind-speak training."

"Gotcha." Gregory said while writing down some notes.

But Krait wasn't finished. "Why did you project into my mind that God awful image! That was hurtful and borderline rape!"

Jonathan coolly answered. "Well now, aren't we feeling feisty. Yes, it was brutish act, but it confirmed what we needed to know. As for the charge of mental rape, may I suggest you bone up on the UEF regs. In any court of law, your charge would not hold water. And no, I will not apologize either."

With that confrontation over, a pall fell over the three. Jonathan, being naturally stubborn, wasn't going to back down. Gregory then realized that his colleague was driving Krait to side with him. The old good cop, bad cop routine.

"Okay then. It's settled. Krait, I will be adjusting your daily schedule, starting tomorrow, to include three hours of intensive mind speak training."

Mr. Gregory turned to look deeply into her forest green eyes. "Be forewarned, Krait. While this training is brutal, I can guarantee that it's well worth it. And another piece of advice, eat light before the classes.

"Dismissed."

Blinking at the suddenness of the dismissal, Krait left the armory wondering whether she had just passed some kind of arcane test.

When she was well outside ear shot, Mr. Jonathan declared, "That went about as well as could be expected. That head-strong woman needs limits to run into. The mind-speak training will provide enough of those, and then..."

"Look out." Mr. Gregory completed the thought.

CHAPTER THIRTEEN

"Military Command to Transport Commander Olen-bar, Transport Number Two. Remain in low orbit. Do not land. A special transport shuttle will meet your ship to transfer the decon container. Acknowledge."

"Understood, Military Command. We are looking forward to giving up the specimen."

Ten minutes later, following a successful dock and transfer procedure, the special transport shuttle departed the transport cruiser's hold and made its way planet-side.

"Military Command to Transport Commander Olen-bar, Transport Number Two. You may now proceed to Space Port Three. Upon landing, a scientific delegation will debrief you and the interceptor commander. Acknowledge."

"Understood, Military Command. We will be

landing shortly."

The transport commander then looked over to his navigator. "Well, you certainly won that bet. An additional debrief by a scientific delegation?"

Four days later, the investigative team from the Sagittarian Ministry of Extraterrestrial Biology and Science met at their institute to discuss what Transport Number Two had placed in their collective laps. In all, fourteen scientists attended, representing the proverbial length and breadth of the discipline. The team's lead, Dr. Juff-hobab, summarized their findings as follows.

"The wreckage retrieved during the outbound transit of Transport Number 2 to Earth does not, I repeat, does not represent an infectious threat to our biosystems. This fact alone, understandably, is cause for great relief. In point of fact, the organic remains found in the pod were chemically familiar to some of our own desert species of insectoids. While it was reported that the pilot of the retrieved pod ejected, and then attacked the Dragon Three interceptor, the fact is that another pilot, a full specimen, albeit crushed, was discovered within the pod. This find, therefore, affords us the opportunity to fully characterize this organism. On this subject, I ask Technician Gotha-mug to present his report."

"Thank you, Dr. Juff-hobab. Nest mates, imagine if you will, a dusty, brown-colored desert beetle of our size, which motivates by either its eight legs or flies with two sets of wings much like our hover crafts. The body can be wholly described as heavily chitinous and segmented into three parts, from back to front:

abdomen, thorax, and sensory bud of eyes and mouth parts.

"The abdomen contains rudimentary digestive structures, pheromone glands, and venom sacks, the contents of which are injected via a retractable stinger in the distal end. Interestingly, this individual is asexual, suggesting that it is the product of a complex society, where an individual's place is genetically assigned at birth.

"The thorax, a remarkably muscular component, contains the organism's breathing sacks and powers two sets of wings and eight legs. The development of breathing sacks suggests that their natural environment possesses a benign and perhaps even moist atmosphere. The eight legs are heavily armored with chitin and each padded footing ends in a sharp, nearly indestructible chitinous claw. The much-scarred titanium hull of Dragon Three is a testament to this claw's toughness. The rear-most of these legs possess over-developed muscles, which would make this organism a powerful jumper.

"The bulbous frontal segment includes four multi-faceted visual organs, four hooked grappling palps, and mouth parts consisting of crushing mandibular plates. The forebrain, that lies behind a massively thick frontal plate, is divided into four individual segments connected by a central nervous system. It is theorized that each segment controls one of the multi-faceted visual organs. Given the relative size and complexity of the forebrain, one cannot discount the possibility of mind-speech, which could be augmented with the use of pheromones.

"Finally, the wings are made of a specialized form of translucent chitin, which glow under ultra-violet wavelengths of light. Such signaling suggests what their natural environment might be like, one of near to total darkness."

"Thank you, Dr. Juff-hobab, for that interesting report. Next, Technician Hopp-awad, will report on the alien pod and its technology."

"Thank you, Dr. Juff-hobab, for this opportunity to share what my team has discovered. First of all, the damaged alien pod contains not one bit of technology, and is devoid of any vestige of life-support. Instead, it is a simple, oblong, and thickly layered chitinous shell that is designed to split apart in two sections, no doubt to release its two occupants. Its sole means of propulsion is an organic, turbine-like organ, located at its distal end. In sum, the pod is a purely organic construct."

The Sagittarian paused here before continuing.

"In collaboration with my colleague, Technician Gotha-mug, we have concluded that the alien pod is a birthing vessel, and not a manufactured, extra-vehicular conveyance. In other words, those who attacked our transport cruiser were freshly born pups!"

"Thank you, Technician Hopp-awad, for that most intriguing report. Our final report will be delivered by Dr. Jenn-wack."

"Thank you, Dr. Juff-hobab, for this time to share what my team found regarding the chemistry and genetic material taken from the 'birthing vessel' and organism. The genetic material extracted from the two sources proved to be the same, meaning, that everything in one is present in the other, with one exception that I will discuss momentarily.

"The organism itself outwardly represents an evolved insectoid-type. Nonetheless, its genetic material is totally different from anything heretofore studied. The genetic structure is not built in a helix formation, but rather in bud-like structures most similar to some spherical viruses. This suggests the production of dedicated sub-species types within their genome, which function in a different, but collaborative fashion.

"As for the 'birthing vessel', its genetic material is of the same structure, but with totally different virus-like budding structures. This should be seen as no surprise as the complexity of the organism is vastly different from its 'birthing vessel'. In many ways, there is an elegance to this pairing of genetic material, one destined to move about, and the other to nurture and protect.

"However, there is one last item that deserves mention—the organism's venom that is delivered via its distal stinger. It is very primitive in its makeup, and most curiously, does not share much of anything with the 'birthing vessel' nor organism's genetic structure.

"'Primitive', what do I mean by that chemical characterization? Frankly, it is the most corrosive and poisonous material that I have ever seen, whether produced in nature or manufactured. The venom is a collection of rudimentary acids and clumsy proteins that once introduced into a living organism, destroys its flesh, while simultaneously attacking the circulatory system."

When the last technician finished with his report, the fourteen sat in silence, each deep in their own thoughts.

"Thank you all for your hard work," Dr. Juff-hobab soberly concluded.

"We have much to think about and consider. Based upon the aforementioned research, it is with regret and sadness that we have encountered yet another species to avoid, and if necessary, exterminate, in order to preserve our own. This panel's results and recommendations will be shared with the rest of our scientific community and Military Command."

CHAPTER FOURTEEN

It had been a long time since I last lost my cookies. But Mr. Gregory's advice on eating light before the mind-speak training sessions had been completely spot on. I didn't know that my head could hurt so, the nausea, disequilibrium, eye strain, at times were nearly unbearable. But I stubbornly slogged on, and in the process, learning once again, more about personal discipline than mind reading. But in this assessment, I was dead wrong, for I was well on my way to compartmentalizing my mind, building mind blocks, and communicating without speech. And that was only the first couple of weeks.

By month three, my trainers blessed me as good to go. Now, without thinking about it, I could gently read another's mind, place ideas in their heads, openly converse, and totally shut down a mental incursion. The rather delicate balancing act between simultaneously conversing and blocking still needed some practice, but I was on the case.

And then it hit me. When Mr. Jonathan had placed that horrific image in my mind, he had been gentle about it. While it in no way felt that way at the time, now I know better.

*   *   *

Two days later, after morning PT, Mr. Gregory, still huffing and puffing, said to me, "Krait, step into my office." As he plopped himself down cross-legged in the grassy infield of the campus' running track.

So, as directed, I sat down, which I must say, felt delicious after that grueling "jog."

"You have been with us for the past, what, nearly three years. Is that correct?"

"Yes, sir. Give or take a couple days."

"How are you holding up?"

I cocked my head to one side, trying to figure out where he was going with this question, but dared not to reach out and prob his mind.

"I think that I have done better than average."

Mr. Gregory chuckled at that.

"Yes, Navigator, First-Class, you surely have.

"But now I have a proposition for you. In about a year, give or take, the UEF will come a calling, wanting you to either take an honorable discharge or re-up. Have you given either any thought?"

Oh, wow! I thought. No, I hadn't. I'd been so focused on the here and now, that the entire subject had slipped my mind. Suddenly, I felt embarrassed.

The frown now painted across my face caused Mr. Gregory to comment.

"Krait, I bring this up only because I have been thinking about this for you. Want to listen to some Dutch advice?" The grandfatherly Mr. Gregory said.

"Yes, very much, sir."

"First off," the man recounted using his stubby fingers, "right now, this very minute, you are flat-out overqualified for the UEF Space Force. That's a fact. Besides, that option would bore the living shit out of you.

"Secondly, an honorable discharge is just that. You honorably performed your duty to society. It is not an admittance of cowardice, failure, or an unpatriotic act. If the UEF comes back at you with, 'your time on loan to such-and-such corporation doesn't count toward your time in service,' well, that's pure bullshit. Always remember: they readily loaned you to us, and they knew precisely what they were doing at the time."

"Thirdly, as of right now, you are a much-sought after commodity. A highly trained navigator, a mind-speaker, and a splice. If you choose to become a mercenary, an honorable institution by the way, your future would open up in ways never imagined. Your personal growth would become exponential. And, let us not forget, being a mercenary is a very profitable career choice. If you are curious about this option, Mr. Jonathan would be more than willing to answer any questions that you might have, because Krait, he still is a very connected, certified, and brokered mercenary."

"Really!" I said, shocked, but now not surprised at learning that tid bit. It explained a lot.

"Yes, that's right. And guess what? Neither of us could have ever become ambassadors if we were members of the UEF. That old 'conflict of interest' thing would have shut us down in a heartbeat."

I thought about that one. He was right. The UEF military and U.N.-Geneva bureaucracy never saw eye-to-eye and seemed to be at constant war with one another.

"But, Mr. Gregory, isn't there yet another option? At my discharge, why couldn't I just sign up with GENEMEDCO?"

"Yeah, you could certainly do that. You would be a shoe-in, because Mr. Jonathan and I would totally back your application. But I would not pursue that option quite yet."

"Why? It's so obvious."

"Because Katherine Kramer, you have to give yourself the chance to grow beyond the military life, gain some life experience, broaden yourself, and see the world. If you were my granddaughter, I would kick you out of this cushy place myself. But you aren't. You're a gifted young woman who has yet to find herself. That, Krait, should be the focus of your next mission.

"Find   Krait."

CHAPTER FIFTEEN

Transport Commander Olen-bar was quite pleased with himself. The orbital transfers were performed well and on time—a first for the Earthers, who were known for their clumsiness. His holds now contained much in the way of natural resources for his planet. And that accomplishment brought a sense of pride to his stomach. Neatness, however, well, perhaps that would come with sufficient experience.

En route for home, the Sagittarian day-dreamed about his beloved mate and four pups. This idyll was broken, when the communication's tech announced. "Incoming message for Transport Commander Number Two."

"Well," he surly replied, "what do they want?"

"Encrypted message is to be read by you only, sir."

By the Great Dragon, what now? He privately

ranted.

He read the missive.

> Military Command.
> Transport Commander Olen-bar, Transport
> Cruiser Number Two.
> Proceed to the sector of the previous alien
> engagement.
> Perform reconnaissance.
> Be advised Transport Cruiser Number One's
> arrival is late by twelve orbits.
> Maintain high alert.
> Take whatever action that you deem prudent and
> necessary.

By the Great Dragon, what happened to Transport Cruiser Number One? Olen-bar worried. *Did it fall to that asteroid menace? Or did it get attacked by those Pleiadean raiders that we hear so much about? Or something else? The galaxy is a big place, so full of surprises, mostly unknown and dangerous ones.*

Because of Military Command's directive, Olen-bar's mind began to furiously churn.

"Tactical. How many crew members, including the Dragon crews, are on this vessel?"

After some quick checking, tactical announced, "I count one hundred and thirty-eight, sir, ninety-six in the Dragons alone. The remaining forty-two make up our skeleton crew."

"Thank you, Tactical. Order the six Dragon commanders to meet with me immediately at my conference table."

"Sir?"

"Just do so, Tactical."
"Yes, sir."

*   *   *

"Commanders," the transport commander began, "I believe that we will be challenged in the near future in ways most unexpected."

That got their collective attention, as if they hadn't already been plenty curious.

"In an emergency situation, how many extra crew members can each Dragon successfully carry?"

"As passengers, sir?"

"Precisely."

The six commanders furrowed their brows until one said, "Nine, sir."

"That's not good enough. How about eleven?"

More furious calculations took place.

"That can be done, Commander, but it would be most uncomfortable for the 'passengers.'"

"Better 'uncomfortable' than dead." The transport commander soberly stated.

That emphatically communicated just how dire the situation was.

Then he shared with them the message from Military Command.

"Commanders, allow me to be clear. The use of our emergency escape capsules, this deep in space, would mean a slow death for them all. However, if we use our Dragons as make-shift troop ferries, then we can *all* make it safely back to home."

One of the commanders protested. "But Transport

Commander, what about the transport itself? We cannot just abandon it to an aggressor. We must first defend it."

"Commander. Think with your stomach. Transport Cruiser Number One most likely has already been lost. I do not doubt that its crew fought to defend it to the very end. I, however, will not allow my nest mates to needlessly die for those piles of rubble in our hold. Is that clear?"

"Yes, sir."

"That's better. So, what I want each of you to do now is to gather your crews, explain to them the potential situation, and prepare your Dragons to accommodate at least eleven additional passengers.

"That is all."

Now alone at his conference table, somehow the surrounding bulkheads seemed narrower, tighter.

*   *   *

"Sensors, open our internal communications. I wish to make a global announcement to our entire crew."

"Nest mates, this is Transport Commander Olenbar. I request your keenest attention to what I have to share. I have just received a message from Military Command. I believe that it is in your best interests to listen   very   carefully."

CHAPTER SIXTEEN

The new queen was pleased with her recently acquired accommodations within the massive cargo hold of Transport Cruiser Number One. That is, once the hold had been cleared of all its cargo containers, rudely jettisoned into space. Once so prepared, the empty hold could now easily accommodate her rapidly expanding abdomen in preparation for the production of birthing pod after birthing pod. Her successful transfer from the confined space of the asteroid had been performed brilliantly by the venom compromised Sagittarian navigator, who had maneuvered and docked the transport directly to the asteroid's surface. The new queen tasked her specialists to keep this poor retch alive long enough for it to teach them what they needed to know about the transport cruiser's functions.

Frankly, the young queen clacked her mouth parts

in wonder about how few tasty morsels had occupied the cavernous craft. It seemed such a waste. Surely, there must be more secreted somewhere, and so she ordered her miners to thoroughly examine every nook and cranny of the vessel.

As for the asteroid, it remained the home of the old queen, who had grown to such proportions that she could not leave its hollowed-out interior.

CHAPTER SEVENTEEN

As Transport Cruiser Number Two came within two sectors of the previous alien engagement, Commander Olen-bar ordered navigation to idle down the engines and coast in. Meanwhile, both sensors and navigational scanners went to maximum sweep. His orders had been made clear. Anything detected was to be reported. To the crew, he had shared most of the possibilities. A rescue mission of Transport Cruiser Number One due to catastrophic engine failure. Not likely, but possible. A military mission to fend off Pleiadean raiders. Again, not likely, but possible. There were several other scenarios to consider, but he had not shared his thoughts on those. They made his stomach hurt. Further, panic was something he wanted to avoid and not foment. An orderly ship evacuation was far more preferable than a mad scramble. Every crew member had been already assigned their Dragon interceptor number in that unlikely event.

Minutes passed as the huge transport coasted into what Olen-bar thought of as the zone of danger.

Then, simultaneously, both technicians at sensors and navigation called out a distinct and familiar object at the very limits of their sensors' ranges.

"Transport Cruiser Number One detected and stationary!"

"All stop, Navigation."

"Yes, sir."

"Any evidence anywhere of an asteroid?"

"None, sir," they both answered.

"Tactical. Connect me with the commander of Dragon Number Three."

"Yes, sir."

A few moments later, "This is Dragon Three."

"Dragon Three. Remotely recon Transport Cruiser Number One at a distance of no more than five hundred double measures. Full cloak. Free all energy weapons. Confirm."

"Confirm, Commander!"

*   *   *

The Dragon Three commander had been here before. First protecting his transport cruiser, having his inceptor attacked by one of those beetle-things, and then towing back one of its pods for further investigation. His transport commander's faith in him was warming, but the task made his stomach icy cold.

"Navigation, take us in nice and slow. Pretend that we're hunting smukems."

"Yes, Commander." The navigator said with a smile, because as a pup he had been a big smukems hunter, a desert creature that required stealth, because it spooked so very easily.

"Sensors. No active scans. Just passively listen. And yes, I know we're cloaked."

"Yes, Commander."

"Tactical. I want maximum magnification on your vid-recorder. We might have to do a visual first. Be prepared to send whatever you have back to Number Two at a moment's notice."

"Yes, Commander!"

"Commander," Sensors said, "I have nothing. Just the standard galactic background hiss."

"Commander," Tactical observed, "The cruiser's hull is pock-marked with many impact-like features. Most of them have a brownish color to their center. The impacts appear to be plugged with this brownish material, instead of showing the usual shiny titanium color of the hull."

"Navigation, get us a view into the aft hold."

"Yes, Commander."

"Navigation, slip in close, but no closer than one hundred measures."

"Yes, Commander."

Once in position, the commander of Dragon Three said what everyone else in the forward command bay was thinking. "What is the name of the Great Dragon is that! Tactical! Are you recording this?"

"Yes, Commander!"

"Navigation. Slowly back off and get us back to

Number Two."

"Yes, Commander!"

"Tactical. Immediately send that recording to Number Two!"

"Yes,   Commander!"

CHAPTER EIGHTEEN

Aboard the Sagittarian Transport Cruiser Number One, the heavily compromised navigator was the only one who had detected the presence of Dragon Three's signature. His battle-oriented sensors could do that, even while cloaked. That meant its transport cruiser must also be in the vicinity, probably lurking just at the edge of sensor range. Since none of these monsters had asked him directly to report anything of note, he stubbornly hadn't, and instantly felt a bit of his mind coming back, under his own control. The sensation caused him to fractionally smile.

As he continued to pretend to be doing important functions at his console, the navigator reflected on how he could best warn off his own nest mates. Then, it occurred to him. He could fire an energy weapon in the general direction of the now fleeing Dragon interceptor. And so, he did.

That single heroic act of self-determination cost the Sagittarian navigator his life, as a nearby drone swiftly reached over and removed his head with a pincer.

CHAPTER NINETEEN

"Commander!" Tactical shouted. "The transport cruiser just fired on us!"

"At this range, we should have been vaporized. How close was it?"

"Not even close at this range. I interpret it as more of a warning shot, Commander, than a misfire."

"Interesting. Why a warning shot?"

"Navigation. Get us back to Number Two immediately!"

"Yes, Commander!"

*   *   *

Military Command.
Transport Commander Olen-bar, Transport
Cruiser Number Two.
Attached are recordings of Sagittarian Transport
Cruiser Number One.

It is no longer in Sagittarian possession.
Aft cargo recording reveals a large entity within.
Conclusion: Transport Cruiser Number One has
been compromised.
Send Dragons to destroy per sterilization statute.
Transport Cruiser Number Two on station to
monitor and track if necessary.
Send Dragons.

CHAPTER TWENTY

Sagittarian Military Command sprang into action upon receiving Transport Commander Olen-bar's message and supporting evidence. Sixteen of the planet's best interceptors roared off, their arrival plotted as only two hours away.

Meanwhile, two hours represented an eternity for the crew of Transport Cruiser Number Two. The bridge crew knew well the capabilities of their transport cruisers. And that fact didn't help their morale one bit. Waiting, repeatedly hovering over their sensors, became a torture that no one had before experienced. Each one's stomach felt like a clenched fist.

*　　*　　*

The new queen's assistant drone demanded to

know why the recently birthed scientific drone before him had killed the last Sagittarian on the transport cruiser, a navigator no less. The level of rage was such that its twin pinchers clicked spasmodically with menace.

"The little one deceived us, while we trained on the guidance of this craft. Without our direction, it fired a random energy bolt into space. I clearly sensed this as from the little one as a deliberate warning message. I was enraged at its deception and killed it on the spot." Admitted the navigator's killer.

Ignoring the killing for the moment, the new queen's assistant probed, "Do we now know how to direct this craft?"

"We believe so."

"Believe? Or know?" The agitated assistant drone demanded.

The killer of the navigator looked about to his newly birthed fellow scientists for support. None moved a leg or twitched a wing to either confirm or deny their colleague's statement.

The new queen's drone addressed the assembled and repeated its question. "Does anyone among you know how to direct this craft?"

Finally, one raised its front leg in assent.

"Ah. Good. One does. Show me."

Very tentatively, the brave new born scientist went over to the navigation panel, studied it for a moment, and then gently pressured its joy stick to the right. The maneuvering rockets of the behemoth fired briefly and the star field in the view screens subtly shifted.

"Ah. Good. Movement." The queen's drone said, then curled its body, jumped, and rammed its stinger deeply into the center segment of the navigator's murderer.

*   *   *

"Commander!" Tactical almost squeaked, "Number One has fractionally moved."

"How?"

"Someone onboard fired the port maneuvering rockets. Given that the burn was so brief, I interpret that as someone trying to navigate the transport cruiser."

"That is quite possible. Continue to watch carefully. Report any more such navigational experimentation."

"Yes, Commander."

Olen-bar then snuck a peek at the ship's chronometer. Only fourteen measures had passed since the Dragon interceptor fleet had departed from Sagittarius 43.

CHAPTER TWENTY-ONE

Approaching Mr. Jonathan for his advice was difficult for Krait. Finally, she had confirmed, he was THAT, Mr. Jonathan. The former first ambassador to Sagittarius 43. The co-author of The Agreement of Peace and Mutual Respect of 2356. The hero of the First Battle of the Dark Side. The bold negotiator of not one, but two cease-fires with Sagittarian assault fleet commanders, The Pleiadean contest champion, and the list just when on and on. Not to mention her continued feelings of guilt about her tardy arrival to GENEMEDCO. But that late-morning, she found her opportunity to ambush the solitary man walked across the green expanse of the GENEMEDCO campus.

"Mr. Jonathan, sir."

Stopping in his tracks, Jonathan turned toward the sound of the voice, and outright sensed the extreme nervousness in Krait.

"Yes, Krait. What can I do for you?"

"I would like to schedule about an hour of your time, sir. I have some questions that I would like to run by you."

Nodding, "Okay, Krait. Do you have any lunch plans for today?"

"No, sir. I'm free."

"Good. Meet me here, at this spot, in one hour. Oh, it'll be my treat." He grinned.

*   *   *

Krait felt as awkward as a kiss-less virgin on her first date. Just walking next to Mr. Jonathan seemed, well, odd, electrifying. Once off campus, she noticed the local population looking at them, covering their mouths to make a comment, and sometimes wickedly snickering. Casually brushing across their minds, she read in their thoughts the most outlandish assumptions, some even quite bawdy. One even made her giggle.

"What's up, Krait?" Mr. Jonathan asked.

"Oh, I have been eve's dropping on some peoples' minds. That's all."

"And?"

Now blushing, "Some of them have rather randy opinions about us."

The sound of Mr. Jonathan easy chuckling eased her tensions quite a bit.

Then he stopped walking.

"Ah, here we are. Krait, you probably won't believe this, but I have been eating at this family's food stall for the past thirty-seven years. Needless to say, their food is great! Let's go in and sit down."

We sat at a tiny two-stooled table against a reed-woven wall. An old paper poster of the scenic island of Ambae decorated it, while artfully covering up a hole. A server magically appeared, saw Mr. Jonathan, smiled broadly showing all his teeth, and my boss just raised two fingers, and off he went.

"What was that all about?" I asked.

"That was the owner's youngest son. I have been coming here since, yeah, I already told you. Well, I have been practically adopted into their family. I just ordered us two lunches."

"No menu?"

"Don't need one. Everything is always delicious, always fresh, always something different. Trust me, just run with it, Krait."

"Okay…"

"Now, what did you want to talk about?"

"Mr. Gregory and I had a talk. He mentioned that you are a registered and certified mercenary, and, if I had any questions, I should seek you out."

"Alright. What do you want to know? As I recall, you already tried that avenue."

"Yeah, put being a plumber is not what I want for a career."

A deep sigh.

"Well, I can see your point. The real question is: what do you have to offer that makes you so valuable? So very desirable, that someone would be willing to pay a broker his fee to enlist you, and you alone, for the needed service?

"The bottom line, Krait, is you first have to ask yourself, 'who am I,' and 'what do I have that few others have?' Then, once you figure that out, you have to find a broker to sell your very special talents. You must convince them of your worth. Once that is done, then you wait, and wait some more, for that first call to arrive."

So simply said, so impossibly hard to do. I just noisily sighed in resignation.

"Now, did I just hear Navigator First-Class, Krait, the mind-speaker, and splice, quit just like that? Or, are you planning another 'walk about?'"

The challenge was real and beatable. My pale and freckled face blushed red with anger. I hoped that my red hair would disguise my reaction. Then I realized a simple thing. I was my biggest obstacle. I was the source of my own, self-imposed limitations.

"No, Mr. Jonathan, I'm not a quitter, especially on myself."

At that moment, two ice-cold beers appeared. We clinked necks, he smiled at my cocky answer that silently said, 'prove it', as I drank deeply.

"How did you begin?" I finally asked, while unnecessarily studying the beer bottle's label.

"It was an accident. I was in the right place at the right time. I was a UEF ground-pounder and stumbled across two guys in a tight situation. I saved their asses, and they were thankful for the assist. Before I knew it, a broker contacted me, asked a whole bunch of questions, and since I was still in the UEF, I took a pass on his first offer of a contract. But I did promise to contact him once I was discharged. For me, that's how it all began."

"So, you were sort of sponsored into the trade?"

"Yes, that's a fair assessment."

"My father sponsored me. That's how I got my first contract."

Then, the food arrived.

Oh, my, God, was it good!

As I waddled back to campus with Mr. Jonathan, my stomach distended with boiled fish, vegetables, and steamed rice, I stopped and said, "Thank you, Mr. Jonathan, for that delicious lunch and for sharing your experiences. And you're right, although you never said it, I do have some soul-searching to do. Thank you for that too."

The man just smiled. "You're most welcome Navigator First-Class, Krait, mind-speaker, and splice. I enjoyed our lunch together as well. And by the way, dump that guilt you're harboring. It's corrosive."

CHAPTER TWENTY-TWO

After the fifth maneuvering rocket firing, Olen-bar now firmly believed that whoever had taken over the transport cruiser, they were now trapped within it, unable to fly it in any meaningful fashion. But the best part was this. Olen-bar was sure that the Dragon flight was near, and confirmation of that fact just then arrived.

"Transport Cruiser Number Two. The Commander of Dragon Flight Obo requests an update of the situation."

"Dragon Flight Obo, this is Transport Commander Olen-bar. Your target appears to have only maneuvering rockets for propulsion. Be aware that the occupiers of our transport cruiser have murdered its entire crew. Attack and destroy. I repeat. Attack and destroy."

"Understood, Transport Commander."

Even from afar, the sheer devastation that Dragon Flight Obo wrecked upon the transport cruiser shocked the bridge crew. Then, suddenly, the Dragons bolted away. Shortly thereafter, an explosion as bright as a small sun appeared.

"Sensors! Are your scans clear?"

"Yes, Commander. The transport cruiser is no more. Just a debris field is in evidence."

"Commander of Dragon Flight Obo. This is Transport Cruiser Commander Olen-bar."

"Yes, Commander Olen-bar."

"Sweep the vicinity for any stragglers, and if encountered, destroy them. Yours is now a decontamination, sterilization mission."

"Understood, Transport Cruiser Commander Olen-bar. Dragon Flight Obo, out."

As Transport Cruiser Number Two slowly edged its way forward toward the debris field, Olen-bar watched from the forward view screen and saw the flickering, winking in and out of lights in the distance.

Indeed, he thought, *Dragon Flight Obo was doing a thorough job of sterilizing that sector of space.*

"Sensors. I wish to make an announcement to the crew."

"Yes, Command! The channel is open."

"Crew of the Transport Cruiser Number Two. This is your commander. I wish to inform you that the alien threat has been neutralized. Our emergency preparations are no longer in effect, but never forget them, if ever needed in the future. Out."

Olen-bar sat back into his position, feeling exhausted, yet fulfilled. He had done his best to prepare his nest mates. In his mind that was all that mattered. But best of all, he now knew he would reunite once again with his own beloved nest, as he glanced over at the covered "General Destruct" button. Olen-bar had never intended to abandon his transport cruiser, nor surrender it easily.

But one item remained to nag at his mind.

Whatever happened to that asteroid?

CHAPTER TWENTY-THREE

The old queen had been canny with her plunder and politics. On the one hand, she took as her own the six Sagittarian interceptors, her excuse: to make space in the transport cruisers hold. On the other, she "generously" gave away the entire space craft to a noisome, recent queenly birth. Once rid of her presence and dedicated drone, the old queen's specialists attached the captured interceptors to her hive. With long-lived experience, they easily divined their function. Her hive now had cobbled together sufficient technology to travel where it wished, unseen, and above all, far away from this busy trade route, which had served its purpose.

As the asteroid hive disappeared into the galactic gloom, the queen would have smiled with pleasure, if her insectoid face would have allowed it. Her feelings, however, did not go unnoticed.

"My queen," her personal assistant drone remarked, "your spirits seem to have risen since our departure from the acquired technology. Am I correct?"

"Indeed, my second self. You know me well. Where should we now go on our lives' journey?"

At the open question, the drone experienced a mixed reaction of doubt, whimsy, and fear. After all, he was but one of many drones, who had quite literally "served" his queen.

Finally, he had his answer. "Somewhere practical and sensible. Someplace where a threat to the hive is minimal, but the rewards are great."

"Ah…" whispered the queen, "such wisdom from my second self. Find me that place."

CHAPTER TWENTY-FOUR

"Mr. Gregory, I have made a decision regarding my future."

"Oh, and what is that?"

"I wish to remain at GENEMEDCO until my UEF tour of duty is up. Then, once honorably discharged, I want to go home."

"And where's home, Krait?"

"Edinburgh, the former capital city of Old Scotland. That's where my family is, Mr. Gregory. That's also where the university that I want to attend is located, to help round me out."

"Ah, Krait, that's a mighty fine plan. And when you finish at the university, what then?"

"I frankly don't know. I also don't know where my studies will take me. Do you have any suggestions?"

"Why, how kind of you to ask. I do indeed. I

would suggest psychology and history."

I cocked my head to one side, "Why those?"

"Think about them for a moment. How do psychology and history blend together?"

I smiled. "That's clever, sir."

"Why thank you, Krait."

But Krait's plans to finish her time at GENEMEDCO "dead-heading it" didn't happen.

CHAPTER TWENTY-FIVE

Lieutenant Gordon "Gordi" Smithers started this day like any other one during his twelve-year stint in service to his planet. An astronomy nut since he was a kid, he considered his station at the deep space radar installation in Colorado Springs, Colorado, to be his dream job and life's work. In Gordi's mind, he had access to radars that were the best and most powerful on the globe. He used them like flashlights to illuminate the night, always looking for something new.

At ten forty-three that morning, surrounded by three empty coffee cups, Gordi's search program alerted him, while writing a bureaucratic memo. Out there in the dark void a new asteroidal signature had peeked out and made itself known.

"Well, hello there." He said to the print off of the data.

As with any new discovery, a date and name are required. So, Gordi went to what he considered "the asteroidal Bible," the definitive log amassed by The International Astronomical Union's Committee on Small Body Nomenclature. Perusing its list, he saw with some pleasure that he could not find any asteroids named "gordi." So, he named the object after himself. Now with a name and a next number generated for it, he officially logged his find GORDI 73456001.

Two weeks later, as GORDI 73456001 continued toward Earth's solar system, the lieutenant checked in on "his baby." At the time, he thought it wise to use those same, powerful radars once again. This time, however, he painted it with many kilojoules of energy, all to build a profile, an estimate of its size, density, and potential trajectory. The returning radar pulses were not what he expected, but instead would cause many a furrowed brow at the Space Command installation.

What Gordi's "paint job" revealed was a typical M-type, or "metallic" asteroid. Its roughly spherical size was about a half kilometer in diameter, making it no slouch, but certainly nowhere near the largest. But a dense M-type asteroid should not register as hollow, which GORDI 73456001 certainly was. As to its trajectory, Gordi had collected over fifteen points of reference, since he had thought to peek in on its progress. On that basis, this object was stubbornly defying the usual gravitational tugs and pulls of the surrounding neighborhood. Instead, its plot centered directly upon the orbit of Mars, and at its current velocity would arrive rather conveniently in its immediate neighborhood. A place where several of Gordi's most prized radars were positioned.

A sudden sense of guilt shot through the astronomer.

Did I somehow attract it our way with my scans?

In many respects, the object's trajectory also reminded the astronomer of another asteroid of the past, Oumuamua, first detected way back in 2017, which also appeared to defy all gravitational reason, as it beelined its way right through the Solar System. This fact helped to calm Gordi, somewhat. And one other thing. The rotation of the object was five revolutions per hour, more than enough to create an artificial gravity within its hollow core.

But the best was yet to come, for the visual radar image gleaned during the most recent "painting" of GORDI 73456001 displayed the roughly spherical object with a much-cratered and pot-marked surface, in addition to what Gordi identified as six junkyards. These "junkyards" unfortunately resembled to a very great degree crash-landed Sagittarian Dragon interceptors, all with their engines oriented outward toward space.

Lieutenant Smithers rubbed his eyes in disbelief. "Damn, if their placement doesn't look like maneuvering rockets!"

That was when the lieutenant ran his find up the chain of command. Up until now, all was fun and games, but the imagery and radar data suggested so much more. GORDI 73456001 had become just become a "too hot" topic.

CHAPTER TWENTY-SIX

It was that time of year, where, like clockwork, the next year's trade agreements with Sagittarius 43 were haggled out. This time four bidders offered their raw ore and material commodities in return for the lucrative "sand and grit" of the Sagittarian deserts. "Sand and grit?" When its composition was on average forty percent fine gold and twenty of industrial diamonds, yes, the "sand and grit" was worth bidding for.

As ambassador to Sagittarius 43, Mr. Gregory shouldered the burden of vetting and negotiating all the bids made, while revealing what the Sagittarians wanted in return for their "sand and grit." Fortunately, the formula rarely changed. Mr. Jonathan had established that during his tenure as ambassador, and for consistency, Mr. Gregory saw no reason to deviate from its central purpose of fairness balanced against a reasonable profit for both parties.

Naturally, just what "reasonable" meant to some was open to interpretation, especially once the Sagittarian gold began to hit the market. What once was considered "a steal," now had caused the value of that once precious and royal substance to become almost pedestrian. That's where logic and common sense came into play, and Mr. Gregory's final judgement was binding.

With three trade agreement offers in hand, it was time for Mr. Gregory to now make his pitch to his Sagittarian counterpart, and that was best done face-to-face, on Sagittarius 43. This time, however, he wished to plant a seed in more ways than one.

*   *   *

"Jonathan," Gregory said, "I want to take Krait with me on this next round of trade talks with Nars-mob. What's your opinion?"

"You're really keen on grooming her to be your successor, aren't you?"

"Yes, I am, but that decision is ultimately not up to me."

"Yeah. I know. It never really is. So, old man, how are you going to introduce her to Nars-mob? As your niece or granddaughter?"

"Oh, that was cruel Jonathan. But your point is well taken. How about my diplomatic assistant? She could take notes, make observations, just the way I used to do for you."

"All well and good, Gregory, but Nars-mod is no

one's fool. He'll see right through that ploy."

"I certainly hope that he does, Jonathan."

"So, that's how you're going to play it!"

"Yeppers. Just like that."

*   *   *

That very morning after PT, Mr. Gregory made an announcement.

"Troops. It's again that time of year, when I get to wrangle a trade deal with the Sagittarians. But your PT and training sessions will continue. My absence will be replaced by the elderly Mr. Jonathan, so go easy on him!"

Guffawing laughter broke out.

"Don't be surprised if he runs you all into the ground!"

More good-hearted laughter.

"That is all, dismissed."

And the troop began to disburse, some to their showers, others to their breakfast.

But Mr. Gregory called out one of their number to join him "in his office" on the grassy turf next to the running track.

"How's the day been, Krait?"

With sweat streaming down the sides of her face, which turned her red hair into a soggy looking cap, "Just fine, Mr. Gregory. What's up?"

"I have an offer for you. I need a diplomatic assistant to accompany me to Sagittarius 43. Are you interested?"

"Interested? Well, I suppose so," she said with a

grin. "But what does a diplomatic assistant do?"

"Mostly, take notes at all meetings. When not taking notes, observing, absorbing the atmospherics. Above all, making sure that I don't forget something."

"Mr. Gregory, I have never been outside of our near space, much less stepped foot on our own moon or another planet for that matter. I'd be insane to turn down this offer. But is there anything available on Sagittarian customs and mores? While you might forget something, I could potentially put my foot in my mouth and never realize it."

"No, Krait, there is no concise guide to Sagittarian culture. That book has yet to be written. But there are diplomatic documents that you can access and read, and by that I mean, you can peer between the lines. Keep in mind, you do not have to say or think a word. Your place is to observe and record."

"Well, in that case, I'm in!"

"Great."

CHAPTER TWENTY-SEVEN

Two weeks later, I was in the navigation seat of a Praying Mantis, setting my first extra-solar course plot. Mr. Gregory sat in the command seat, all business, clearing us for takeoff from Jakarta's International Space Port. Then, I heard in my headset.

"PM Two. You are authorized for takeoff." The command-and-control voice said from the tower. "Safe journey, ambassador."

With a nod from Mr. Gregory, I pulled back on the stick and ever so slowly pushed forward on the throttle slides. And there I was, in low orbit.

"Engage Navigator," Mr. Gregory smoothly said.

"Yes, sir." And I stabbed for the first time the AI auto-navigator EXECUTE button. At first, I missed it, but the star field had blurred as we leapt forward at a mind-numbing rate so quick that I was afraid to blink and potentially miss something more.

"Tactical." Mr. Gregory said. "Broad scan our general route. We really don't want to hit anything outbound. Something about 'bad form' and all that."

"Yes, sir." Tactical said with a smile.

"Navigator."

"Yes, sir."

"You're oddly quiet."

"Just taking in the experience, sir. That's all."

"Humbling, isn't it?"

"Absolutely, sir."

The AI auto-navigator computer reported, "Sub-light, extra-solar plot complete. Awaiting first light segment input."

"Damn, that was quick!" I said as I entered my first ever light speed segment into the AI computer.

"Command. Regarding velocity, what's your pleasure?" I asked.

"Three for the moment."

"Light Three selected." I confirmed.

"Engage Navigator."

This time, I thought I saw it happen. The star field became streaks of light. I felt a slight vibration from the seat of my flight suit. But that was all. No screaming motors. No flashing lights. Just, pure, raw, speed on parade.

After about ten minutes of this electric experience, my pulse finally slowed down to something that I considered normal.

"Tactical to Command. There is an unregistered debris field ahead. Recommend slowing to sub-light."

"Navigation. Slow to sub-light."

"Slowing, Command."

This required me to stop the AI auto-nav and gently slide the throttles back. And just like that the star fields returned to a crystalline focus.

"Tactical to Command, the debris field is at our ten o'clock relative."

Looking in that direction, I could finally see what tactical had warned us about.

"Nav, slow to a quarter power, and carefully guide us in. I want to take a good look around." Mr. Gregory said.

"Slowing to one quarter."

"Lots of titanium out here people. Some of it has blast damage. Now what the hell is that? Looks a whole bunch like crushed and shattered seed pods."

"Engineering. Are we recording this?"

"Yes, sir. I have been recording, ever since tactical first brought all of this to our attention."

"Good job, Engineering."

"So much titanium. Damnation! Look over there! Those are clearly hull fragments. I just wonder if our Sagittarian friends had some sort of an engagement out here. Nav, remind me about this, when we see Ambassador Nars-mob. He might know something about this."

"Yes, sir."

"I've seen enough of this carnage. Nav, gets us clear, and then input our next light segment. This time make it four."

"Yes, sir. Light Four confirmed."

CHAPTER TWENTY-EIGHT

The next thing I knew we were slowing to sub-light at the Sagittarian frontier. There, we were met by two Sagittarian Dragon interceptors, which looked suspiciously like our own Super Raptor design, but only much bigger. Our escort interrogated and confirmed who we were and then escorted us to Space Port Four, which was located smack dab in the center of a vast desert. Only later, would I find out how ignorant I was of that snap assessment.

I landed Praying Mantis Two in the precise center of octagonal pad. As I went through a quick post-flight check list, I hadn't noticed the small group of Sagittarians that had approached and who were now patiently waiting on us to emerge.

"Any time Navigator. We have a welcoming committee waiting on you."

"Oh, shit! Sorry."

My first impression of Sagittarius 43 was a blast of dry heat, quickly followed by a static, ozone-like smell. When I touched the outer skin of the Praying Mantis, I got a serious static jolt that briefly numbed my hand. As I was shaking it back into normal, I had to hurry up and join the rest of the crew, who Mr. Gregory had lined up in formation. Naturally, as the first timer, I was at the end.

Another first impression were the Sagittarians themselves. I knew what they looked like from the vids, but up close and face-to-face, I realized that they were lean of build and my size! Their finely pebbled skin appeared silky smooth to the touch and round eyes took on a golden color. As we stood there, each of us was wreathed by a Sagittarian dignitary with a garland of beautiful flowers, which, as I learned from my studies, were actually carbon-dioxide absorbing organisms. Ever curious, I moved my chin from left to right and the flowers followed my movement, while exhaling a scented oxygen back.

Following that welcoming ceremony, we were led off to a low and steeply sloped building with wide doors that opened toward our pad. During those scant minutes, I made a point to stretch my stiff runner's legs, and then realized the planet's ever so heavier gravity. I relished the cloudless light blue sky overhead, and noted the pervasive reddish golden grit that seemed to be everywhere underfoot and that stuck to everything and everyone. Again, all that static electricity. Off in the near distance, huge sand dunes of the stuff surrounded us.

Upon entering the shade of the building, the

sudden temperature change surprised me with a quick shiver. Here inside, arrayed in neat rows, were ten Dragon interceptors on display. I wanted to check them out, but our group was headed away from them toward a sloped ramp. Once again, I was being the wild child, who was forever hanging back.

Down a ramp, we gathered in a rock-cut oval chamber with the most gorgeous tiled floor that I have ever seen. Around the outer edge stump-like pillow chairs were arranged. In the room's center, a low table stood with four more of these pillow chairs around it. Fortunately, being the last of our crew, I just followed along and did what they did, heading for the back row, to sit down. Opposite our delegation, seven Sagittarians joined us, no doubt as witnesses to the transactions about to take place.

The Sagittarian, who had led us here, was clothed in a tan robe-like outfit. He stood next to the table on one side with Mr. Gregory opposite. The Sagittarian had another standing with him, also so clothed, but ever so slightly behind.

Mr. Gregory, turning around to face our side of the conference room, looked at me and thought, "Okay, Krait, come over here and back me up."

Shocked, I stumbled forward, and mimicked the Sagittarian second as best I could, standing at attention and with my hands tightly clasped behind me.

It was then I saw that the table had been set with four, tall, clear glasses of water. The Sagittarian was the first to reach for his. Mr. Gregory was second. Then the Sagittarian second, and then I got the subtle hint and took mine.

The lead Sagittarian then thought in melodious mental patterns that tingled my very being.

"My dear friend, Gregory! How good it is to once again see you. With this water, I greet you once more to my world." And then he chugged the entire glass.

Then Gregory did the same, thanking his friend for his hospitality and the glass of water. The Sagittarian second thought nothing, but drink until its glass was dry. Not being the dullest knife in the drawer, I followed suit, much to the silent amusement of Mr. Gregory. Then, we sat. By the way, that cool water was the tastiest that I have had in a long time, right down to the ever so slight minerally aftertaste.

"Krait. Get out your personal device and be prepared to take notes."

"Yes, sir."

"Ambassador Gregory of Earth, I am Ambassador Nars-mob of Sagittarius. To my left, I wish to present my assistant and ambassador-in-training, Glee-rich."

"Ambassador Nars-mob of Sagittarius 43, I am Ambassador Gregory of Earth. To my right, I wish to present my assistant, Kathleen Kramer."

With this pomp and circumstance complete, the Sagittarian ambassador got down to business.

"Greg, here is our list of desired raw and manufactured materials that we wish to trade our 'sand and grit' for." I totally caught the humor expressed by the "sand and grit" reference. And the diplomat slid across the narrow table what looked like a plastid sheet with the list written in English.

"As always, Nars-mob, it is a pleasure to discuss

the needs of our home worlds." As he glanced over the Sagittarian's wish list. "Currently, I hold three offers that cover," he stopped himself to count with his finger, "seven of your twelve trade requests. Is that sufficient, my friend?" As he now slid the list over to me to record. When he did, he gave me a quick wink.

Nars-mob just nodded his head in assent.

"As you well know, Nars-mob, Jon himself has told you that I am an honest man. I wish to remain so. Therefore, I must explain to you what is currently happening to my planet's economy. Is that agreeable?"

Again, Nars-mob nodded.

Damn, this guy's quite a poker player.

Krait, zip it! Mr. Gregory ripped at me and instantly my mind blocks went up with a crash.

Ambassador Nars-mob, however, was quite amused by the mental exchange.

"So, Greg, I am 'quite a poker player.' What does that mean?"

Mr. Gregory took in a deep and cleansing sigh.

"Nars-mob, poker is a game of chance, which is won by the individual who shows no sign of emotion, win or lose. In many ways, my assistant's indiscretion was a complement on your ability to get as much as you can of our trade goods at the best price. Does that make any sense?"

The Sagittarian produced a small smile. "Yes, Greg, it does. And for the record," as he glanced at his assistant who was taking notes, "I think that your assistant is quite a stunning choice. Her red plumage is unusually…appropriate. But her green eyes I find absolutely captivating. I had never before seen the like."

And right on que, I blushed hugely both at the attention and compliments.

"And Greg! Look! She even blushes like we Sagittarian's do! How interesting."

Then, without skipping a beat, the Sagittarian continued.

"But tell me Greg, what is happening to your world's economy?"

"In our planet's history, gold has always been a rare thing, usually collected and coveted by those who consider themselves individuals of power. Now, however, with the massive introduction of gold from your home world, that balance has been shaken. Put another way, a significant portion of your 'sand and grit' is worth less to the producers of raw ore and processed goods."

"Ah, I have heard of this phenomenon. I believe that you call it inflation. Am I correct?"

"Yes, Nars-mob. In order to trade with the three Earth producers, you will have to provide more 'sand and grit' than you did in previous trade agreements."

Then, with a careless wave of this hand, Nars-mob said. "This issue of inflation is of no consequence to my planet. It is your problem. As for payment, let us together calculate how much more 'sand and grit' will be required to satisfy the trade agreements."

I was floored by the ambassador's cavalier attitude, but then checked that my mind blocks were still up and holding firm. It took an effort, but I did it nonetheless. *After all*, I very carefully thought to myself, *what does he care about the value of his 'sand and grit'?*

In the end, it was the percentage calculation for each Earth shipment of such-and-such a materiel that took the longest time. As it was, the entire meeting only required about an hour's time. That too shocked me, when I considered, once again very carefully, how much time such a negotiation on Earth would have required.

When it appeared obvious that the trade talks had ended, I mentally nudged Mr. Gregory about the debris field we had encountered en route. He looked at me, smiled, and gave me a thumb's up.

"Nars-mob, there is a subject that I would like to discuss that may have an indirect impact upon our trade relationship. May I do so?"

"Absolutely Greg. What is it that so obviously troubles both you and your assistant?"

"While en route to this meeting, our interceptor encountered a massive debris field. Much of the destroyed and energy scorched material was of manufactured titanium, in addition to some oddly shaped, seed-like pods mixed in. Do you have any information as to what happened?"

"Thank you, Greg, for mentioning this unfortunate incident. We will discuss this in private, as it has nothing *directly* to do with our trading relationship, but everything to do with our two planets' security."

CHAPTER TWENTY-NINE

Our solar system's defensive cocoon, or network of satellites, is arrayed along the outer reaches of our solar system in a four-layered, grid-like network. They are jointly monitored by Dark Side United Earth Force Base One on the moon, and by United Earth Force Base Two on Mars Prime. These highly sensitive satellites can detect objects at a distance of five astronomical units (AU), or approximately 750,000,000 kilometers. As a consequence of each satellite's range of detection, within the four-layered network, there exists considerable detection overlap, and that was by design.

To appreciate Lieutenant Smither's accomplishment in detecting GORDI 73456001, he had done so three AU outside of the defensive network. And when last painted, the object had just crossed over the first layer of defensive satellites.

When it crossed this proverbial trip-wire, UEF took notice.

*   *   *

"My queen," her drone assistant cooed, "someone has discovered our presence."

"How do you know this, my second self?"

"Our specialists detected powerful sensors that brushed against us."

"How should we respond to such an indignity?"

"Sadly, we cannot, as we do not possess the technology needed."

The old queen stirred with annoyance, but then settled down once again, much to the relief of her second self.

"Perhaps, my queen we should turn away from the system before us. The data retrieved by our specialists from the six-space craft identified this system as, what was their term, 'trading partners', or some such."

"What is the meaning of this term?"

"A source of a valuable thing."

"If my progeny is to grow, we need more valuable things. Maintain course. And we will take what is needed."

"Yes,   my   queen."

CHAPTER THIRTY

After the official trade talks had concluded, the Sagittarian ambassador tasked his assistant to secure a data package for us. Then, the Sagittarian witnesses were dismissed, as were the rest of our crewmates. Only Nars-mob, Mr. Gregory, and I remained at the conference table.

"Greg, to be blunt, we lost a transport cruiser to an unknown alien species. My assistant is currently creating a copy of our investigation for you to have. I would strongly suggest that you share it with your military and world government. As we have discussed in the past, the galaxy is a very hostile environment, populated with aggressive and horrific species. The Hurros are but one example. Now, we have another, unnamed species to guard against. I believe, when you return to Earth, that you will find Transport Cruiser Number One never arrived. That is why we had to destroy it, as it was compromised by this unknown alien species, its entire crew murdered."

I sat there numbed by Nars-mob's silken thoughts so torn with emotion.

Then, he looked deep into my eyes. "Katherine Kramer, you do not know it now, but you have an important role to play between our planets. Never forget."

"Greg, I see your intentions clearly as well. Train this young pup well, for she will be the savior of both our planets."

The Sagittarian ambassador paused, while I physically gasped at his thoughts.

"How, you might say, do I know this with certainty. Greg, we have never spoken of The First Source, or of The Judge, or for that matter, of The Destroyer. In our culture, these are things understood and excepted as fact. Call us dreamers, call us perhaps insane, but the evidence of these entities is found throughout our history."

At that moment, the Sagittarian assistant returned with the promised data packet. I sensed that Nars-mob had much more to say, but the moment had passed.

"My dear friends, and by that I include you too Katherine Kramer, I look forward to your next visit. Travel well and safely."

CHAPTER THIRTY-ONE

"My queen, our hive has passed through a highly active field of sensors that surround us on every side."

"And?"

"And, we have not been confronted. Our presence is known. I expect that we will experience a confrontation of some kind."

"And why do you say that, my second self?"

"Because I sense that we are falling into a trap from which we cannot escape."

"Such negativity from my second self. What is your evidence?"

"Every moment of our passage is awakening ever more sensors on every side. I counsel to reverse course and journey elsewhere for our needs."

"Second self, I tire of you." And with that, the assistant drone was snatched up and devoured by his queen.

*   *   *

Lieutenant Smithers had been tasked by his superiors to monitor and report upon the progress of GORDI 73456001 as it sliced unerringly through the outer defensive network. While the object did so, it continued to ignore the gravitational laws of Sir Isaac Newton, as if it had a mind of its own, a purpose, and maybe even a destination. But Smithers was no fool. The projected track that his asteroid took ran very close to a highly predictable orbital location—the planet Mars. Gordi did not for one moment consider this an accident and so ripped off a brief alerting the brass of the asteroid's current and projected trajectories.

From his office in Colorado Springs at the base of the eastern foothills of the Rocky Mountains that was the best he could do. As far as he was concerned, Mars Prime was soon to be damaged real estate.

Why?

He didn't know. Just that he felt it in some deep, primal way. Mars, the ancient god of war, was about to be attacked.

But in the final analysis, would it be victorious?

Then, he had a thought. Smithers knew that UEF Air & Space Command must know about the asteroid, but had his doubts that they appreciated the level of the threat. So, against all protocols, he contacted some friends in the UEF at Mars Prime. The least that he could do was warn them. And while his data was considered "classified," he nonetheless sent it off to his good buddy in Falcon Flight Delta based at Mars

Prime.

While Smithers tossed and turned that night in a vain attempt at sleep, the warning program on his computer went off, which in turn sent a message to his personal device on his bedstand.

Looking at the generated message, the astronomer swore, got dressed, and promptly broke several traffic laws getting back to his post at the base. He had to watch what he knew was coming. He just knew that it wouldn't be pretty.

For whatever reason, GORDI 73456001 had finally adjusted its trajectory. Now, in Gordi's mind, there was no longer any question.

CHAPTER THIRTY-TWO

During our flight back to Earth, I had a lot to think about. Mr. Gregory apparently did too, as he was reviewing the data package that the Sagittarians had given us. The two of us discussed it in detail. Frankly, the implications gave me the chills.

Mr. Gregory's prescient suggestions about me studying psychology and history stood out in my mind with bold relief. Even the ambassador had said as much in his own way. But that pitch about being the savior of our planets, while it seemed like an overly melodramatic vid plot, nonetheless was delivered in such an honest and matter-of-fact manner that I got the creeps once again.

"Penny for your thoughts?" Mr. Gregory said, who sat next to me about three feet away.

"I'm having trouble with the ambassador's words regarding my future role."

"I don't blame you. He opened up to you in a way that I have never seen before. Face it, Krait, you're important in some way. My advice: don't fight it. Embrace it. Run with it."

"Yes, sir. I see it as yet another challenge. One that must be met."

"That's a good attitude. Hold it close."

That moment was broken by a dire message that filled Mr. Gregory's head set.

> Praying Mantis Two.
> This is UEF Air & Space Command.
> Proceed immediately to Mars Prime.
> Unknown inbound.
> Repeat.
> Proceed to Mars Prime.
> Acknowledge.

"UEF Air & Space Command, Praying Mantis Two acknowledges. Proceeding immediately to Mars Prime. Prepare to receive a Sagittarian data packet regarding the unknowns. Over."

"Navigator. Get us to Mars Prime. Maximum light."

"Yes, Commander. Max Light confirmed." Krait said as she deftly altered the interceptor's course and speed. Finished, she sat back and waited, not wanting to disturb the man's thoughts, as the star field had turned into an absolute rainbow blur, which was breath-taking.

Finally, he spoke.

"Krait, if my suspicions are correct, we are about to engage with Nars-mob's unknown aliens. The timing seems right. And if I'm right," now looking Krait straight on, "things are going to be tense, like in life and death. You ready?"

"Yes, sir. I'll just lock down and do my thing."

Again, that wry smile.

That's my Krait.

"Crew. The UEF has just put us on a battle alert status. We're going to Mars Prime. Prepare your stations and tighten down your belts. Krait will be driving this rig, and you all know what that means."

Then Mr. Gregory got another message from UEF Air & Space Command.

"PM Two. Is this document for real?"

With some exasperation, Mr. Gregory whispered to no one in particular, "No, you knuckle heads, it's a joke."

Then he responded, "Damn straight, UEF Air & Space Command. I got it from the Sagittarian ambassador himself, who told me, directly, to share it with our government and military. What other mother fricken' *bona fides* do you require? By the way, did Sagittarian Transport Cruiser Number One ever arrive Earth-side?"

"One moment, PM Two.

"No, PM Two, it never did. Why?"

"Because whatever is coming at you, commandeered it, and murdered its entire crew."

"Acknowledged, PM Two. UEF Air & Space Command,   out."

CHAPTER THIRTY-THREE

"My queen," her new second self reported, "We are now heading toward the source of the powerful electromagnetic emissions on the fourth planetary body of this system."

"Why that particular location?" She queried with interest.

"Its emissions best match the one's that we are currently passing through. Logic says, like is like. I wish us to find that rich technological source."

"Well reasoned, my second self.

"Proceed."

What is it about this new second self? The queen wondered. *His aggressive pheromones have peaked my abdomen's interest. I can feel it stimulated. My pod production is increasing. Ah, I'm feeling young again.*

*   *   *

Meanwhile, as this conversation was taking place, Mars Prime UEF Base Two was the first to scramble its two fleets of Super Raptor interceptors, thirty ships in all, and without U.N.-Geneva's blessing. In light of the current situation, the base commander had chosen to ask for forgiveness, instead of permission.

After two hours of bureaucratic blather and voiced outrage about that same Mars Prime base commander's insubordination, U.N.-Geneva finally got off their collective asses and authorized a general planetary alert, which remarkably didn't include the defense of Mars or Mars Prime! As a result, a new authorization order had to be "crafted" to rectify the previous. This was why UEF Base Four out of Brisbane, Greater Australia, received their tardy authorization to launch their two interceptor fleets, adding thirty interceptors to the defensive mix.

Then, in their infinite wisdom, U.N-Geneva, Air & Space Command held back the two interceptor fleets at Dark Side UEF Base One as a strategic reserve, as were the two fleets at UEF Base Three out of Nellis, Nevada. Apparently, the space battle doctrine of massive and overwhelming force had been ignored by the Geneva accountants and their spineless military advisors.

Still uneasy about the unknown threat, privately owned interceptors, not usually commandeered by the UEF Air & Space Command except during times of extraordinary duress, were also put into action. But since PM Two was already inbound, UEF Air &

Space Command made that call and were now glad they had. PM Two had provided them with extraordinary Sagittarian intel on the inbound threat.

Lieutenant Gordi Smithers, sitting at his console, listened in on all of this, chewed at his lip helplessly, and only wished that he had the authorization to see what PM Two had shared.

Boy oh boy! I'm glad I contacted Ricky at Mars Prime. He must have really bent a bunch of ears! And probably according to their scramble order time table, some pretty serious laws as well.

*   *   *

The old queen's hive was now well within the outer defensive satellite perimeter. Several planets of the solar system were easily detectable by eye, but one stood out from the rest, the large red one in their path.

"How do you wish to proceed, my second self?" the old queen asked.

"We do not impact the planet, but instead hover above its technological source. We release first our miners, then our specialists. We gather what is useful. Then, leave this system to a place of peace and solitude. Once there, we integrate this new technology, and we begin our search anew."

The old queen was impressed with her new second self's ambitious plans. His aggressiveness tickled her.

"I am pleased. Proceed, my second self. Make me proud."

"I shall my queen."

The interceptor engines of the asteroid's six junkyards came to life, halted its spin, and decelerated the hive for an ultra-low orbital attack upon the surface of Mars Prime.

CHAPTER THIRTY-FOUR

Blessedly, the base commander of Mars Prime UEF Base Two, Major Peter "Popcorn" Anderson, had acted upon the extraordinary back-channel intel that he received from Colorado Springs. A true maverick, Popcorn Anderson assumed central command of both his and Brisbane's interceptors, while ignoring all direction from U.N.-Geneva and the central UEF Air & Space Command also located there.

Why?

Well, other than the obvious, Popcorn Anderson was royally pissed off that his base, and for that matter, all of Mars, had not been included in U.N.-Geneva's initial planetary alert.

Those bureaucratic pricks! And then they have the gall to tell me how best to defend Mars.

Popcorn was a big believer in the application of

massive and overwhelming force. His problem, however, was that he didn't have at his fingertips the "massive and overwhelming" part. So, like every good commander, he improvised.

Ground defenses were doubled, while he enlisted the on-base UEF Third Battalion Marines to man the extra positions. His idea was to make any assault on Mars Prime a real bitch. To ensure Mars Prime's survival, he had the near-orbital blast cannon crews reinforce their installations. They had to survive in order to destroy any landings. Then, he would use his interceptors, which he would initially hold off, surgically and sparingly, with the hope in finding a weakness to leverage.

But Popcorn well knew that as soon as the shit hit the fan, his glorious plan would begin to fall apart as his various units experienced their first taste of combat. Ultimately, he knew that it would come down to a handful of seasoned master sergeants who knew their   shit.

CHAPTER THIRTY-FIVE

The first orbital flyby by the rapidly decelerating asteroid took the command-and-control staff's breath away.

"Damn, that thing's big." One was heard to say.

It only got a whole lot bigger with the second flyby of the asteroid, and many suddenly found true religion by whispering a prayer, rubbing an icon, or just covering their eyes.

By the third flyby, the asteroid slowed to a creep on Mars Prime before it actually stopped directly overhead at a distance of a half kilometer. Then, seemingly, clouds of objects began their descent upon the red planet. Gaping and momentary mesmerized, gun crews just watched.

Then, shocking them into the here and now, the voice of their base commander screamed into their communication's gear, "FIRE! FIRE! FIRE!"

The near-orbital blast cannon crews responded with furious fire. But an odd thing happened. They targeted the easy to find objects higher up in the Martian atmosphere, while overlooking those that had descended first. While wreaking havoc upon those later jumpers, and essentially clearing the sky of them, a good portion of the invaders had already landed on Martian soil.

*   *   *

Encased in thick chitinous layers and secreted on the asteroid's surface, the energy cannons stripped from the six Sagittarian interceptors responded with a fusillade of their own against the ground-based near-orbital cannon barrage unleashed upon its miners. Remotely guided from within the asteroid itself, again using stripped technology from the interceptors, drone specialists began chewing up the terrain below, while they mastered the targeting systems of their new destructive toys.

In response, several crews, seeing what was happening, began firing on the five energy cannon locations on that portion of the asteroid. To the crews' surprise, the tough iron-nickel content of the astral body made only a direct hit effective. And rather quickly, the battle devolved into a bloody punching match between opposing cannon emplacements. After four minutes, all five of the heavily bunkered energy cannons on the asteroid were knocked out. Of the sixteen ground cannon crews on the Martian surface, only seven remained operational.

And then the asteroid began to pivot on its axis, bringing to bear its seven other energy cannons. In so many ways, this fight resembled the tactics of early modern ship warfare.

Again, the hellish cannon fire erupted from both sides, but the ground cannon crews could only target where an energy weapon had discharged. The targeting now required cool patience for the enemy to reveal himself. However, the enemy already knew where the ground cannon crews were, and as a result, they initially took a beating. But what really turned the tide were the miner beetles who had successfully landed. Covering immense distances with every jumping stride, they immediately began harassing the ground cannon crews, and before anyone realized it, two ground cannon crews were overrun.

Down to five operational crews, the UEF Third Battalion Marines entered the fray. Their high energy weapons fried the bugs left and right, piling them up, to the point that individual Marines had to move off their positions to get clear shots.

Within seven minutes, the last of the asteroid energy cannons had been destroyed, but at quite a Pyrrhic price. Only one cannon crew remained operational on Mars, in large part because of a squad of UEF Marines, who flat out refused to give up.

CHAPTER THIRTY-SIX

The entrances to the underground city and UEF Base of Mars Prime consisted of triple double doors and two air locks. The doors, considered more blast doors, because of their heavy-duty construction, were hydraulically operated and accessible via three numeric key pads, one for each set of doors.

The base commander, Popcorn Anderson, stationed a rifle squad of UEF Third Battalion Marines at each of their four cardinal entrances. Their sole job was to stop anyone and anything from gaining access to the underground maze that was Mars Prime.

Two of these entrances were stormed by the miner beetles. From the inside of the South Entrance, the external vid camera chronicled the beetle's eight-legged clawing technique to gain entrance, which sounded to the scared shitless Marines like a buzzsaw.

Armed with high energy weapons, three Marines waited behind the first door. The other four in the rifle squad stood behind them in support, between the open secondary auxiliary doors. The third set of auxiliary doors were sealed in the event that the entire squad was overrun.

As the scrapping buzz rose in volume, the Marines knew that a breach was about to occur. When it did, a three-inch diameter hole appeared. Dressed in their environmental armor, the sudden depressurization didn't bother them. Then, a clawed arm reached in and thrashed about, and one Marine fired through the hole, utterly destroying the intruder. Then, more scratching and buzzing and a second hole appeared. Another Marine saw through it something that his mind couldn't quite comprehend. He fired, and like the first, another beetle was no more.

Then silence. Their sergeant checked their doors' vid camera image, and saw that four beetle intruders were now huddled together around the entrance way.

"Shit! Those critters are having a pow-wow. Smith! Jones! Fire again through those holes!"

They did, and two more 'critters' were turned into fritters. This enraged the other two, who then flung themselves once again against the blast doors to no effect. And the scratching and buzzing began anew.

But not all of Mars Prime's entrances were so lucky. At the North Entrance in particular, a mass of beetles stormed that entrance's outer blast doors. In their frenzy, and in spite of taking heavy losses, a man-sized hole was achieved, and through it, beetles began to pour in. At this point, the Marine rifle squad retreated behind the second set of blast doors.

But this bunch of beetles seemed to have a brain behind them, because once within, they began digging in the two side walls of the air lock. On both sides, they easily broke through into the maintenance corridors of the hydraulic air locks. From there, they were free to roam wherever they wanted. Meanwhile, the UEF Marines were clueless as to what just happened. Mars Prime now had a serious security breach. Worse of all, at least initially, no one knew about   it.

CHAPTER THIRTY-SEVEN

"My queen. I have just received word that our miners have gained access to their hive. When would you like to deploy our specialists?"

"Now, my second self."

Immediately, a new batch of descending invaders began to disgorge from one particular orifice in the asteroid's surface. They communicated directly to the science brood's workshops and laboratories. Unlike the newly born miners, who had descended mindlessly in their powered two bug birthing pods, the specialists represented the brain trust of the hive. Experienced and knowledgeable, they descended toward the Martian surface in twos, gripping ahold of one another before separating and deploying their wings.

A Marine from Alabama perhaps said it best. "They looked as thick as a spring mayfly swarm on a muggy evening."

Perhaps exhausted, the last remaining near-orbital blast cannon emplacement was slow to take note of this latest development. While nowhere near as numerous as the miner beetles' assault had been, the specialist beetles were far more dangerous.

Whatever.

When the lone battery finally opened up on that particular departure orifice, not only did their blast cannon seal off that port, they also toasted easily over two-thirds of the falling "mayflies." Still and all, all too many had reached the surface.

*   *   *

Secured behind their own set of blast doors and bunker, the base's command-and-control continued to function.

"Okay people. We have a reported breach at the North Entrance. Deploy two rifle squads of Marines to that sector!" Major Popcorn Anderson bellowed into his communication's stalk.

"Falcon Flight Alpha. Do you have your ears on? Over."

"Awaiting orders, Base." Came the instant reply.

"Hit the six junkyards on that damn rock, hard. Like yesterday, son."

"Engaging, base. Out."

To no one in particular, the base commander muttered, "We're going to cripple that ship of theirs. They aren't going anywhere."

"Falcon Flight Beta. Do you read?"

"Go, base."

"I want you to recon that asteroid. Buzz it like a bee and sting it wherever you think you see a target, or even think you see one. Over."

Engaging, base. Out."

*   *   *

"My queen, we have just lost all of our maneuvering engines. Further, the enemy is destroying all of our exposed surface sensors."

"I remain confident in our specialists. We have gained access to their hive. Have our specialists reported in?"

"No, my queen. Not yet."

"We have time. They are few. We have the advantage."

"Yes, my queen."

At this moment, the old queen could sense the tension, no fear, in her second self. Before she would dine on him, she chose this time, to wait. When Praying Mantis Two arrived at Mars Prime, it was literally buzzing with activity. The communications chatter alone was dizzying. As this was my first time in Martian space, I gaped a lot.

"Mr. Gregory," I said, "what's our mission?"

"The destruction of everything on that asteroid. But you're right, we probably should ask for an invitation to this party."

"Mars Prime UEF Base Two. This is PM Two from Sagittarius 43. How may we assist?"

Mr. Gregory had to make that request twice just to get through all the cross-chatter.

Then, finally, "It's about frickin' time that you got your sorry ass to this goat rodeo, PM Two! See that rock overhead?"

"Can't miss it, base."

"Do whatever you can to make their day a bad one. Out!"

"Well," I said, "that was a pretty non-specific."

"Yes, it was. And it came from a good friend of mine, who is currently stressed out to the max. Any ideas, Krait?"

"Let's go for a low altitude tour, just to see what we can see, and blast away at anything interesting. You game Command?"

"Sure am. Tactical, take the starboard blast cannons. I've got the port side. We're going hunting. Fire at will."

"Yes, Commander." Tactical replied.

"Calling all Falcon Flights. This is PM Two. We're friendlies. We want to play."

"Welcome to the party, PM Two. But you're late. We have already fried this rock's surface."

"Acknowledged. Then, we'll just make a quick tour of it. Out."

"Mr. Gregory. I have an idea. Let's go to ultra-violet and see what we can see. Remember what we discussed about them being nocturnal, UV-signaling creatures?"

"Right on, Krait. Tactical? You hear that?"

"Yes, Commander. Going to UV."

And wouldn't you know it. We found UV emissions pouring out of all sorts of cracks and crannies in the asteroid's surface.

"Blast the shit out of every UV emission." Mr. Gregory directed.

"You hear that Tactical?"

"Yes, sir."

"Alright Nav. Take us around real low and slow like."

Remarkably, it took us nearly forty-five minutes to address all those UV emissions.

"Mr. Gregory, I've got another idea."

"Let me guess, go to infra-red."

"You got it, sir."

"Hear that Tactical?"

"Yes, sir."

And once again, we found plenty of targets, some even exploded quite spectacularly. It was my first time playing the part of the angel of death.

CHAPTER THIRTY-EIGHT

The UEF Marines had their hands full cleaning out the maze that was the UEF Base and the city proper. These beetles had stingers and they liked to use them liberally, that is until they got fried by a high energy weapon. Unfortunately, the civilians took the brunt of the casualties as most were unarmed, and frankly didn't have the sense to hide and follow the base commander's orders to do so. The Marines took their lumps as well, but they dealt out a toll on the bugs that was horrific, that is, if you were a bug lover. Fortunately, the beetles jumping abilities were hampered by the many corridors and low ceilings, but they scampered around plenty fast nonetheless. And one other thing, these things stank. In fact, once the Marines noses became attuned to their distinctive smell, hunting them down dramatically quickened.

*   *   *

"My queen, I have failed you."

"How, my second self?"

"We have no engines to maneuver. Our fuel reserves have been destroyed. All access to the surface of our hive has been denied. And, I have not heard as yet from our specialists."

"That's not good news."

"My queen, I have failed you."

"No, you haven't, my second self."

Then, the hungry queen made a snack of him.

*   *   *

The fight for the control of the last near-orbit blast cannon emplacement had become epic. The specialists would swarm forward, only to be thrust back in the face of multiple high energy weapons fire. Their access to the bunker was literally hindered by the piles of scorched beetle bodies, but the UEF Marine rifle squad remained tenacious in their defense. When one of their number fell to the onslaught, an artilleryman took up his weapon and joined in. If there was ever a tale to tell of bravery, valor, and courage, "the battle of the bunker" was it. And for the record, that bunker never fell.

*   *   *

By the dawn of day two of the assault, Marine mop up details were scouring Mars Prime and its base for stragglers. By the end of day two, only a few had been found, gruesomely feasting on the dead. The question now was, "what do we do with the asteroid?"

"PM Two to Base."

"Come in PM Two."

"Need to talk to the base commander."

"One moment, PM Two."

"This is Base Commander Anderson. Who am I talking to?"

"Mr. Gregory, sir. I have a suggestion for the asteroid."

"Shit! Everyone does. What's your brilliant idea, Gregory?"

"Simple. We tow it to the sun and release it into its gravity well."

"Hot damn! What a great idea! But son, we're already on the case. If you want to join in the tug-of-war party, you're most welcome to do so."

"Thank you, Base Commander Anderson. We will take you up on that offer."

The base commander's second in command asked, "Base Commander, do you know who you were speaking with?"

"Sure do, son. Mr. Gregory and I go way back. You see, we enlisted into the UEF together right out of secondary school. He's a good man, and friend."

"Oh, I thought that Mr. Gregory was our ambassador to Sagittarius 43."

"He is. But if you met the man, you would never know it. He's not one to put on airs."

*   *   *

"My queen, I have to report that our hive is once again moving."

"Did you repair our maneuvering engines, my second self?"

"No, my queen. I did not, nor did any of our specialists."

"Then, how is it that we are moving?"

"Without any sensors or access to the surface of our hive, we cannot know."

"That is most unfortunate."

And, perhaps predictably, another assistant drone bit the dust.

CHAPTER THIRTY-NINE

Upon arrival at our hanger in Bandung, we were met by our corporate director, Dr. Marsha Burkhardt, who had succeeded into that position following the passing of Dr. Gene Crenshaw. Of medium build with thick raven-black hair, the woman, at least at this moment, looked like everyone's dream of what a grandmother should be. For me, this would be my first-time meeting with her.

Upon exiting the Praying Mantis, Mr. Gregory had us all line up at attention.

"Thank God that you all made it back safely!" She gushed. "With all the attention on Mars, I had this terrible feeling that something bad would happen. But here you are, all safe and sound, and in one piece.

"Welcome home everyone!" She proclaimed with open arms.

After many congratulatory handshakes, and

"Thank you, ma'ams," we were allowed to disburse, but not all of us.

"Mr. Gregory, Ms. Kramer, a word if you please."

As we slowly walked toward the opening of the hanger bay, Dr. Burkhardt shared some thoughts with us.

"Mr. Gregory, what in the good name of Jehovah were you doing flying over Mars? Endangering your crew. And putting into harm's way our uncertified space craft?"

But as we would soon learn, she was only warming up.

"Going on a diplomatic mission to Sagittarius 43 was one thing. Totally understandable. But then to make this young lady your navigator, an individual with zero interstellar experience, was a reckless act.

She stopped and faced us. I was flabbergasted at her rant.

"So, Mr. Gregory, what do you have to say for yourself?"

Mr. Gregory glanced at me to zip it, and I did, but I refused to step away and leave his side.

"Dr. Burkhardt, first off, our craft was commandeered by the UEF Air & Space Command to assist them in any way over Mars Prime. If you don't believe me, may I suggest you contact them directly.

"Secondly, the crew I selected are all highly trained personnel. Only Ms. Kramer and myself are not crack super-soldiers, but we are GENEMEDCO splices. So, I did not endanger anyone. I had a crew of absolute professionals.

"Thirdly, Ms. Kramer here, contrary to your opinion, is the youngest First-Class Navigator in history. It makes no difference that she is a 'young lady.' I would, right this minute, put her up against any UEF interceptor nav, and without exception, she would eat them alive for lunch.

"Fourthly, hours in service are necessary to certify any space craft. We clearly did that, in addition to putting it through the paces. All in all, the Praying Mantis performed spectacularly.

"Lastly, Ms. Kramer also went along with me to Sagittarius 43, principally to introduce her to the Sagittarian ambassador, who I might add, was so pleasantly pleased with her, that he suggested she should pursue a career in diplomacy.

"If, madam, you consider these reckless acts, then expect my resignation on your desk before nightfall." The stump of a man, with his hand on hips, concluded with a definite bark in his voice.

During this entire rebuttal, Dr. Burkhardt's lower lip extended farther and farther with each refuted point. My extremely light read of her told me volumes about how she did not approve of the corporation's militaristic programs, the Praying Mantis project, and the super-soldier program in particular. Clearly, she was a hater and not a lover of these initiatives, as had been her predecessor, the late Dr. Gene Crenshaw.

Also, during her attempted reaming, which Mr. Gregory totally short-circuited, I stood ram-rod straight, eyes forward, and at stiff attention at his side.

Royally pissed off and left with no recourse with Mr. Gregory, she now turned her rage upon me.

"Ms. Kramer. What are your credentials in the field of diplomacy?"

"I have been trained by both former Ambassador Jonathan and Ambassador Gregory. Further, I have applied to the University of Edinburgh and plan to study psychology and history."

My crisply delivered answer caused her to blink. Then I distinctly heard in her mind. *My word, this ambitious porcelain doll actually has a brain.*

At hearing those thoughts, I blushed a bright, bright red. My heart easily filled with lethal intent. Yet, I didn't move a muscle and maintained my eyes locked on the horizon. I could tell that Mr. Gregory was mightily pleased with my performance, and my restraint.

"Dr. Burkhardt. Is that all?" He simply asked.

Speechless, the corporate director just gave us a sharp chin nod of dismissal.

Chill Krait, until the enemy is out of range.

Roger   that,   Commander.

CHAPTER FORTY

Three weeks later, the entire Praying Mantis Two crew was invited to Geneva by the UEF Air & Space Command to attend an awards ceremony. Frankly, I didn't make much of the trip, but I did get to see the city, which I thoroughly enjoyed exploring all on my own, at my own pace. I especially liked the old sector, with its cobblestoned streets, quaint and sometimes brightly painted buildings. I just knew, Ambassador Nars-mob would have enjoyed all those colors.

"Krait!" I heard from behind me. It was Mr. Gregory jogging up to me. "I've been looking all over for you. There's this guy that I want you to meet. He just so happens to be involved with the intake process at the U of Edinburgh. Interested?"

"Hell yes, Commander. Where is this guy?"

"Follow me. I have him cornered in a nearby pub."

*   *   *

The person in question was sitting in the corner of a booth near the back of the pub. I judged him to be middle-aged with ghosted streaks of gray at his temples. Believe it or not, he looked like a total academic, right down to the tweed jacket with leather patches at the elbows. His silk tie was pulled away from his throat, his shirt collar unbuttoned.

"Hello," I said. "I'm Krait Kramer," extending my hand and sitting opposite on the smooth wood of the well-worn bench seat. Mr. Gregory joined me.

Taking my hand the man said, "A pleasure. My name is Dr. Peter Finch," he said with an easy smile. By the look of his half-finished pint of golden deliciousness, I figured that he had been here awhile.

"What can I do for you?" I boldly said.

"Well, I just had to meet the lass who can fly an interceptor through the eye of the needle. Is that true, or was Mr. Gregory here, just passing so much gas?"

I laughed at that one. But there was something about the good doctor's accent that sounded mighty familiar.

"No, Dr. Finch. I can assure you Mr. Gregory was pulling your leg."

A waitress arrived. No doubt waved down by my commander. "What are you drinking, Dr. Finch?" he asked.

"Boddingtons." Came the ever so slightly beery reply.

"Three, if you please." Mr. Gregory grinned.

"Right away, sir."

"Mr. Gregory also told me that you were considering attending university after your tour-of-duty expires. Is that true?"

"Yes, sir. My home town has a wonderful one that I want to attend."

"And where is this 'wonderful' university, if you don't mind saying?" He said leaning in over his now empty pint glass decorated with white foamy layers.

"It's in Edinburgh, my home town in Old Scotland."

"As in the University of Edinburgh?" He said with eyebrows raised.

"Yes, sir. I wish to study psychology and history. And thereafter, perhaps, join the foreign service."

"My word lass, you have it all plotted out, don't you?"

"Not completely, sir. But that's my general trajectory."

Now leaning back deep into his bench, with arms crossed, and eyes slitted, "Tell me what it all was like."

Confused, I said, "What was what like?"

"That flight over Mars Prime."

Then our beers arrived. Never before had I seen such a beautiful white and foaming head. After one sip, I was hooked, wiped clean my upper lip, and slipped.

"Damn. That's good."

"That's a Boddingtons for you!" Dr. Finch said eyes glimmering. "Now, about Mars Prime," he prodded, once again leaning in over his pint.

"Mars Prime. That was a little over three weeks

ago. The low-orbital space was a busy one, with our interceptors hovering about that asteroid like angry bees. The UEF boys and girls had already blasted the shit out of its surface features. But Mr. Gregory here," I glanced at him for approval to continue, and got it, "wanted to go on a tour. So, we did, real close. We went to UV and immediately found multiple targets. Mr. Gregory and Tactical made short work of them. Then, we went to IR, and found even more."

Then I looked directly and deeply into Dr. Finch's eyes. "Sir, when we were finished, we reduced that asteroid into a hunk of slag."

I didn't at first realize it, but my story had Finch mesmerized. Then, he whispered out, "How close did you actually get?"

I again glanced at Mr. Gregory and got a chin nod.

"On average, one hundred and fifty meters."

"Good God, lass. That's close."

Finally, Mr. Gregory piped up. "I told you, Dr. Finch. She's the best damn nav in all of Air & Space Command."

Clearly, Finch had made some sort of an internal calculation as he reached into his jacket and pulled out a small rectangular box. From it he took out a plastid business card.

"Ms. Krait Kramer," he said, "I want in my in-box by tomorrow latest your *curriculum vitae* and a cover letter that outlines your future career intentions."

I took the card and read it.

Dr. Peter Allan Finch, PhD FSC
Director of Admissions
University of Edinburgh
Edinburgh, Union of England
(44) (0)131 650 5737, ext. 35

pafinch@uedinburgh.edu

As I held it in my palm, I knew for certain that Mr. Gregory had arranged all of this.

"Now, Mr. Kramer, you said that your home is in Edinburgh. Where may I ask?"

Without skipping a beat, I said, "Number 4 Seton Place. On the corner."

Dr. Finch's eyes went wide, "Lass, I must have passed by that house hundreds of times on my bicycle! Does it still have those wonderful bushes?"

I nodded, feeling my eyes getting misty.

"I have a question, Dr. Finch. Is there any chance that I am eligible for financial support from the university? In mean, in the way of a tuition waver? Or perhaps something for lodging and board?"

The man made quite of show of rubbing at his smoothly shaved chin. "I suppose that something might be available. Allow me to look into that subject for you."

"Thank you, Dr. Finch. Any assistance would be greatly appreciated." I said head down and looking into my pint.

"Alright," Dr. Finch said rubbing his hands together, "in summation, home town girl, UEF veteran, Navigator First-Class, and Air & Space Command bronze medal winner for bravery and valor in the face of the enemy. Did I forget anything?"

"No, sir." I glanced at Mr. Gregory, who now shrugged feigning total innocence, "you have not."

"I will see what can be arranged."

"Thank you, sir."

Then, as if on que, his personal device began vibrating. Glancing down at it, Finch frowned, stabbed a few buttons in obvious reply, and looked up rather guiltily.

"I am very sorry, but it appears that I have totally missed an appointment and now must run off. Mr. Gregory, Ms. Kramer, it has indeed been a pleasure." And then he stacked a bunch of notes under his empty pint glass.

"That should cover us all!"

"Goodbye."

He took two steps, stopped, and whirled around pointing directly at me. "And you, Ms. Kramer, better not forget to send me your c.v. and cover letter!"

"Yes, sir!"

"Good." And the man disappeared through the crowded pub.

I just sat there, looking down at the man's business card.

"You did well, Krait." Mr. Gregory said having moved into Finch's former place opposite me.

"You arranged this meeting, didn't you?"

He just shrugged and finished his pint. Putting the glass down, he wagged two fingers at the waitress.

"Best part, Krait, you never once mentioned this morning's award ceremony and your bronze star for bravery and valor. I filled him in on that and a whole bunch more. Always remember, you're quite a find, never forget it."

Then, quite by magic, two more Boddingtons appeared before us, all deliciously foamy.

"Krait," Mr. Gregory said, "it's high time that we got to know each other better. Henceforth, I decree, that in such social situations, you address me, your Commander, as simply Greg. You read nav?"

"Yes, sir, I mean, I read loud and clear, Greg. Nice to meet you. Now, where are you from?"

"A flyspeck of a town in Greater Australia. A place called Woomera. It's about a three-hour sled drive north of Adelaide."

"Isn't that an old military testing range, a place where your territory supposedly stored crashed UFOs on the sly?"

At my reply, Mr. Gregory almost spit out his beer, rallied, but then failed as it came out his nose!

CHAPTER FORTY-ONE

On the day of my honorable discharge from the UEF Air & Space Command, I made it a point to visit with Mr. Jonathan and Mr. Gregory to thank them both for everything they had done for me. My time with them and in the employ of GENEMEDCO, I had grown so much. Now, it was high time for that next iteration in my career—university life.

But first things first. My homecoming was such a joy. Mum and Dad were thrilled to pieces that I was going to the university, and then greatly relieved that I had made other arrangements for my lodging. During my long absence of four years, they had transformed Number 4 Seton Place into a comfortable cottage perfect for two, instead of three.

I was sincerely happy for them and their peculiar ways, ways that I had long discarded. Now, I focused not on technical engineering specifications, but on me, and my interests. In truth, the UEF and GENEMEDCO had changed me. I was no longer the red headed step-child that always got into mischief, well, at least not that much. With sincere promises to visit every weekend, I departed on my new journey, and I suspected, potential transformation.

*   *   *

The University of Edinburgh was established in the year of our Lord A.D. 1583, supported by a royal charter granted by King James VIth. That made this institution the sixth oldest continuously operational university in the English-speaking regions of the planet. Those facts alone moved me. It possessed a large student body, measured in the thousands. Consequently, my tiny flat was a scarce commodity and I was blessed to have it. Best part, Dr. Peter Finch had come through on my behalf bigtime with a "full ride" that included tuition, lodging, books, and board. His only stipulation was that I regularly attended by classes and maintained a "B" grade point average.

It may be a trite observation, but as an adolescent, I had never visited the university campus, not once, and I frankly don't know why. I suspect that I was not ready for the experience. But now that I was here, I maniacally immersed myself, fully intending to prove to Dr. Finch, and anyone else for that matter, that his gamble on me was not wasted.

From the very start, it was clear to me, that I was on serious mission, while for most of the student population, that was not at all the case. Suffice it to say, I finished my double major in psychology and modern history in three and a half years, instead of the usual four to five. By that time, I had had enough of university life, its arcane and haywire politics, and above all, its student body of overly pampered pseudo-intellectuals.

Before my graduation ceremony, I contacted Mr. Gregory and said that I would like to make a visit to GENEMEDCO, just to catch up.

"Krait! It's damn good to hear from you! When are you going to be in town?"

"In three weeks' time. By then, I'll have my documentation in hand and my personal affairs all tied up."

"Great! Contact me just before you arrive!"

CHAPTER FORTY-TWO

Somehow, someway, Dr. Marsha Burkhardt found about my visit to Bandung. In fact, she met me at the space port in Jakarta. I barely had exited the passenger tunnel from the low-orbital transport and there she was. With hair now heavily streaked with gray against her former raven black, she looked a bit theatrical, a bit like an insane caricature out of an old Disney vid. To be perfectly honest, I didn't know what to make of it as I was expecting "the boys," as in Mr. Jonathan and Gregory.

"You're Katherine Kramer, aren't you?" She brusquely stated with some emotion.

"Why, yes, yes I am. Who are you?" I pretended, while gathering myself for a confrontation that I didn't want.

Totally ignoring my question, she plowed on, "I need a word with you." She forcefully demanded.

Time to play a game.

"Whatever for?" A wide-eyed and innocent me fenced.

"You know why!" She loudly proclaimed, while several people looked on, wondering, much like me, what was up with this woman.

I sighed and just looked at her.

"Alright, let's start from square one. Who are you?"

"I am Dr. Marsha Burkhardt, the corporate director of GENEMEDCO."

"Oh, now I remember you. You were the one who greeted Mr. Gregory and his crew following our return flight from Sagittarius 43. How nice to see you, again, Dr. Burkhardt. But I am confused. Why are you here?"

"To see you!"

"Whatever for?"

"Under no circumstances are you to set foot on my corporation's campus."

And with that, she stormed off through the crowd that had gathered. As I followed her impolite progress, elbowing people this way and that, I smiled.

She's   frickin'   nuts.

CHAPTER FORTY-THREE

Once I was on the train from Jakarta to Bandung, I sent a message to Mr. Gregory's personal device.

> Greg: I'm on the train from Jakarta and should arrive at the station in about two hours. A very odd thing happened at the space port. Your boss met me at the low-orbital and flat out told me not to step foot on the campus. What is going on?

Moments later, I received his reply.

> Krait. No worries. I'll meet you at the station. Welcome home!

Home. What an odd word. It caused me to ask myself, what makes a home, "home"?

"Damn, Krait! You're all grown up!" Greg said while delivering a rare hug.

"Thanks, Greg. It feels good to be back. But I'm

starved. Can we stop that Mr. Jonathan's mom and pop food stall? I could eat a horse!"

Greg just stood there grinning with his hands on hips. "Sure, Krait. Whatever you want. Let's go."

When we arrived, there were colorful balloons everywhere, the entire team of super-soldiers, about twenty-five, and, of course, a grinning Mr. Jonathan. I glanced up at Greg and he wore the same. Then, it arrived, the loudest cheer of my lifetime, quickly followed by "Welcome home, Krait!" After that, it was all a blur of congratulations, beer-chugging, and mounds of tasty morsels.

Clearly, there had been an understanding that the three of us would be left alone, as the super-soldiers eventually drifted off, and it was just us sitting at a table within a jungle of balloons. By this time, I was quite mellow and my stomach was full. Then, three more beers arrived.

"Jeez, guys, I'm a little person. Tomorrow I know that I will be paying for this bigtime."

"Yeah, PT after a welcome home party is always such a bitch," Greg sympathized as he took another pull.

"Krait, it's damn wonderful that you're back," Mr. Jonathan said. "Are you ready to reup with the corporation?"

That stopped me in my tracks.

"What do you mean? Burkhardt practically forbade me from stepping on campus. What are you talking about?"

"I see some background is necessary. Krait, Burkhardt was summarily dismissed, i.e., fired, about a year ago. As corporate director, her total and maniacal hatred of all thing's military did her in. The corporate board quickly realized that she was tearing down the fabric of GENEMEDCO and its financial independence. They could easily see that the military side of the corporation represented over one third of its annual revenue. But the schism went far deeper. This corporation is based on genetic research. The vast majority of its scientific staff support that mission. It was they who ultimately bounced that bitch out, as their jobs were on the line. As it was, we lost nearly ten precent to job jumping.

"But the board couldn't completely pull the trigger on her. So, they granted her a six-month window to go back to her research and produce something of value. When Burkhardt failed to produce, she was finally let go, about a month ago. And as a result of her long overdue departure, life and morale on campus has snapped back to its good old vibe.

"Then, by pure accident, the two of us discovered something truly sinister. During that six-month reprieve, Burkhardt had been in contact with an old enemy of ours, an Austrian named von Hunz. Apparently, both were the same peas in a pod concerning their hatred of super-soldiers and splices. Both considered them unnatural, demonic creations of man. Yes, you heard me right. These two nut cases, on religious grounds, saw us as pure evil."

During this condensed hometown update, I just sat there with my mouth open in disbelief.

"In fact," Greg continued, "all of this became

apparent shortly after you left for school. At first, no one could believe her rantings, her odd directives designed to first scuttle the Splicer Project, and to curtail all further development of the Praying Mantis. Burkhardt even attempted to sell off our private fleet of Super Raptors in a fire sale, before the corporate board brought its foot down.

"But for the 'unhuman', her words, super-soldiers, she saved her best for last. Her spider-like plans began with the closing of the entire genetic replenishment and surrogate mother programs. Again, in her words, she 'cut the head of the snake off'. When that happened, the scientific staff gave the board a rare ultimatum. And thank God, they did the right thing."

"But why did she meet me at the Jakarta space port? What was she trying to do?"

"Krait. Think about it." Mr. Jonathan said. "You were first woman to successfully integrate into the super-soldier program, even if you were only a splice. In her deranged mind, you represented the possibility of the first super-soldier, surrogate mother. The foundation of a new, demonic race. Now, I know that this sounds nuts, and it is, but that was one of her ranting arguments to the corporate board for the dissolution of the super-soldier program and all of its secondary projects, including the 'Splicer Project'."

"And there is that 'other' thing as well," Greg added. "She saw you wanted to be my successor as ambassador to Sagittarius 43. Again, in her mind, the Sagittarians had no place in her religious worldview. They were godless demons all. And now her super-soldier surrogate mother wants to be Earth's ambassador to them. That conjunction just blew her mind."

"All in all, Krait, you really missed some good times." Mr. Jonathan quipped sarcastically.

"Now, do you still want to be my assistant ambassador, oh, great and powerful surrogate mother?" Mr. Gregory asked.

"Damn straight," I blurted out.

CHAPTER FORTY-FOUR

Mr. Gregory and I sat, side-by-side, before the Security Council of U.N.-Geneva, one month later. The purpose of our requested visit was to get them to anoint me as Greg's successor. Naturally, we both knew that this would cause them some heartburn, but we wanted to get it out of the way prior our next visit to Sagittarius, given the recent round of trade talks and their resultant bids. Once again, the usual three corporations won out, because of their low-orbital capabilities, and Dark Side Mining & Manufacturing was one of them.

Again, at least for Greg, we sat before a circular table that sat fifteen representatives of the most powerful political entities on the planet. I fully expected each of them to have egos larger than the table they sat behind. By their initial surly attitudes, I wasn't far off. After all, they strongly suspected what was about to be discussed.

The security council's chair, an Asian gentleman from the Chinese Confederation of States, called the meeting to order.

"Welcome, Ambassador Gregory, to our security council once again." With a respectful head bow in his general direction. "Why did you wish us to meet with you, and your guest, today?"

"Thank you, Chairman Tzu-wong. I also wish to thank the other members of this security council, for your time and indulgence. Today, I wish to introduce to you, Ms. Kathleen Kramer. You have a copy of her *curriculum vitae* before you.

"I have had the pleasure to know, train, and go to war with Ms. Kramer. Throughout, she has proven to me and my colleague, Mr. Jonathan, repeatedly, that she has 'the right stuff'. Then, came her honorable discharge from the UEF Air & Space Command, but not before earning in battle a Bronze Star for valor and bravery, which took place while defending Mars Prime from the surprise alien asteroid attack.

"Following her career with the UEF, Ms. Kramer applied to, and was accepted by, the University of Edinburgh, where she completed her studies in psychology and modern history in only three and a half years, not an easy thing to do. Further, she did so with high honors.

"Ms. Kramer has been trained by both Mr. Jonathan and myself in the Sagittarian culture. Before the alien attack, she accompanied me to Sagittarius during our trade ratification talks. At that time, she made a positive impression upon my counterpart,

Ambassador Nars-mob, who invited her to return during our next trade agreement cycle.

"To date, the selection of our diplomatic and trade representatives to Sagittarius 43 has fallen to first, Mr. Jonathan, our first ambassador, and now to myself. In this regard, I respectfully present to this council the candidacy of Ms. Kathleen Kramer, to become my eventual successor to this diplomatic post. Why am I making this proposal now? Because the Sagittarians are a skittish bunch. It takes them time to settle in and get used to a new personality. Your approval of her now will provided that needed familiarity."

Throughout this presentation, I didn't move a muscle, stared stonily forward, and gently read the fifteen members. What I felt wasn't pretty. In fact, almost all were openly hostile to Mr. Gregory's proposed selection, and in fact, several were riled because our backgrounds were military instead of diplomatic. Once again, that schism raised its ugly head.

"Thank you, Ambassador Gregory for that impressive presentation. Does anyone from the council wish to ask a question?" The chair smoothly said as he looked around among his colleagues.

"The chair recognizes the representative from the United Community of India."

Gird yourself, Krait. Here it comes. Greg whispered into my mind.

The representative from the United Community of India, which included the territories of old Kashmir and Tibet, was dressed in the colorful folds and drapes of her Tibetan heritage. Put simply, she looked like a beautiful peacock.

"Thank you, Chairman Tzu-wong. What I want to know is why are you making this ambassadorial candidate presentation before this body, instead of the General Assembly?"

"Representative Bhasundara Zaxhi, thank you for the opportunity to answer that seminal question." Mr. Gregory said. "The first diplomatic appointment to Sagittarius 43 originated from this deliberative body, which established Mr. Jonathan first as an attaché, and then later as ambassador. My current appointment as ambassador was similarly approved by this body."

Mr. Gregory's answer caused the Tibetan to take some notes.

"The chair recognizes the representative of the United European Union.

A smallish mouse of a man, balding, and bespeckled in wire-rimmed glasses, looked over his glasses, read some notes, and then stared at me with what he thought was an intimidating bureaucratic glare.

"Thank you, Chairman Tzu-wong. Ambassador Gregory, what is your criteria for nominating Ms. Kramer to such a high diplomatic post, especially given that nowhere in her credentials can I see any evidence that has she served in any diplomatic capacity?"

"Thank you, Representative Bruckner, for that illuminating observation, and if I may, I will answer with an observation as well. While credentialed diplomats of all levels in Geneva number by the hundreds, I often wonder how many are effective at their craft."

This, naturally, caused quite a stirring among the council. But, in true Mr. Gregory fashion, he just plowed on.

"Any ambassadorial candidate, fit for assignment to Sagittarius 43, a highly sophisticated planet, society, and culture, must first be able to mind-speak, just to perform basic communication. Tell me, Herr Bruckner, how many diplomats of the U.N.-Geneva can do so today? I seriously doubt that any have even bothered to consider undergoing the rigorous three months of intellectual training necessary, much less the needed genetic splice. Also consider, sir, that to my best knowledge, no university, college, or institute provides for such training.

"Further, it is important to realize that any travel, to and from Sagittarius 43, is not a comfortable commute in a first-class sleeper berth. Far from it, and currently, only the newly certified Praying Mantis interstellar interceptor has the capacity to make that journey in four days' time. Now, sir, imagine yourself wedged into a combat-oriented seat for four days.

"Finally, any ambassador to Sagittarius 43, to be effective, must be a guileless, honest, respectful, and highly empathic individual.

"Anyone familiar with the seminal writings of the Prussian general and theorist, Carl von Clausewitz, would know that he well recognized the moral and political natures of war. And, when not at war, how the diplomacy of a nation would orchestrate its own form of warfare based on duplicity, subterfuge, and espionage. Sagittarius 43 is blissfully ignorant of von Clausewitz's legacy to our institution called diplomacy.

"In summation, all of the required experience, abilities, and personal qualities Ms. Kramer possesses for this important diplomatic assignment."

More stirring, as Mr. Gregory's list of qualities caused several to drift off into introspection.

The chair saw no more questions, and so he asked one of his own.

"Ms. Kramer, if appointed as ambassador-in-waiting, what would be your legacy?"

For this moment, I had prepared and practiced.

"Chairman Tzu-Wong, and representatives of the Security Council, I first wish to thank you for this opportunity to defend my fitness for this post.

"Up to this point, no one has considered the value of cultural exchange and outreach with the Sagittarians. To date, our relationship has been purely economic in the guise of ratified trade agreements. Without question, the benefits from this exchange have been apparent on both of our planets. But beyond those cold agreements, we ask, 'who are the Sagittarians really?' 'What do we know of their familial nests?' 'What inhabits their two polar oceans?' 'Why do they feel emotions from their stomachs?' 'Why do they value so respect and civility?' 'What can we learn about our galaxy from their point-of-view?'

"Obviously, I could go on and on, but my central point is this. The Sagittarians do not know us and neither do we know them. If serious cultural and technical exchange is ever to take place between our planets, then we need someone on Sagittarius 43, for extended periods of time.

"As a result, I propose the establishment of a cultural office at their central university. When I first asked the Sagittarians what they thought of such a thing, they readily approved of it. In short, they immediately realized what it represented—a bold initiative, a place with an open door, where anyone could enter to satisfy their curiosity. Initially, I envision that such an office be manned by only one individual. The reasons for this are both cultural and practical. The Sagittarians are admittedly a very cautious people. Their trust must be first earned. True understanding takes time. Misunderstandings will occur, and lessons will be learned.

"I hope to receive your approval to undertake such a trail-blazing effort of cultural exchange and outreach.

"Why is such an effort so important? It will be the basis for mutual trust and understanding between our species.

"I thank you for your attention and opportunity to express my vision."

The members of the security council did not expect the content of my presentation. After all, in most of their minds, I was military grunt, pure and simple.

"Ms. Kramer," the chair probed, "would you remain on Sagittarius 43 year-round?"

"No, Chairman Tzu-wong, I would not. My presence would be required here, on Earth, to conduct the annual trade negotiations. Initially, I envision quarterly visits to Sagittarius 43 to get the ball rolling. Thereafter, extended stays on-planet would remain up to the Sagittarians. I would leave it to them, whether or not, a human should be present on-planet."

The chairman looked around at his colleagues and appeared satisfied.

"Thank you, Ambassador Gregory, and, Ms. Kramer. Clearly, we have much to discuss. You are dismissed."

*   *   *

"Greg, how did you read that bunch?"

"Initially, I purposefully got them pissed off at me. That was by design. But your demeanor was perfect, and message even better. All in all, their decision will be a split vote. Beyond that, who knows?

"Let's go over to that pub we know so well. I figure after that speech of yours, you must be parched."

As it turned out, I was, and the Boddingtons tasted   great!

CHAPTER FORTY-FIVE

Upon my return to Bandung, I once again became part of the GENEMEDCO family. It's new corporate director, appointed unanimously by the corporate board, was none other than Dr. Jazmet Singh, the head of the Splicer Project and my former personal physician. As is so many times the case, Dr. Singh invited me to his new office for the intake interview, which for me, turned out to be a love fest.

"Ms. Kathleen Kramer! How wonderful to once again have you here at GENEMEDCO! How have you been?"

Always the physician with the impeccable bedside manner, "Dr. Singh my heart literally soars to be back. And if you don't mind my asking, how is your family?"

Stretching his arms out wide with a broad grin, "Krait, they are wonderful, happy, and healthy. Thank you so much for remembering.

"Now, back to business, what do you want to do, while you are still with us?"

His question hit me as extremely prescient. Then, I realized, *Krait, he's no fool. He probably knows that I'm up for confirmation as Greg's diplomatic successor.*

"I wish to assist in any way I can with the super-soldier program, the Praying Mantis project going forward, and anywhere else Mr. Jonathan allows me to play."

"Most excellent!" he said clasping his hands. "I now know that the military side of the business will do even better with you in the mix."

Then he stood, marking the end of our brief chat.

"Krait," he said with an outstretched hand and sincere eyes, "welcome back."

"Thank you, Dr. Singh, you don't know what that means to me."

*   *   *

It was time again for the annual trade talks and bids. Mr. Gregory had a list compiled of seven interested parties, and I had yet to hear from U.N.-Geneva about the Security Council's decision to approve or ditch my ambassador-in-waiting status. While I well know that the wheels of bureaucracy turn with glacial speed, still, three months seemed a bit much. So, I said, screw them. I joined Greg as his recording secretary for the upcoming trade talk proceedings. In my mind, I had to do this anyways.

Greg had already performed the task for several years with Mr. Jonathan. In practical fact, the recorder job made tremendous sense as a training tool and to ensure the processes continuity.

As before, the corporate presentations took place here in Bandung, within the white, multi-roofed, Dutch colonial-styled Gedung Sate building, surrounded by its manicure lawns, palm trees, and fountains. Inside, fragrant native woods dominated the décor with a masculine flavor, from a time far before the green movement's prohibitions on such extravagant construction.

As I took notes during the initial presentations and supporting vids, several things stood out to me. Earth-based corporations, to be competitive, had to have access to low-orbital transports that could dock in space and transfer sealed containers. Whether they were owned or leased, it didn't matter to us, but not to have them meant an instant rejection. This, Greg told me, was the first time seven concerns did have access to them. And this was good news for the Sagittarians, as good old competition was now even more a reality.

The second observation that stuck out to me was that Dark Side Mining & Manufacturing was pushing for the establishment of a specific size and style of seal container. Obviously, they were advocating their in-house container specs, but the others, seeing Dark Side's repeated bid wins, had modeled theirs on the Dark Side example. And to me, I saw this as an example of developmental capitalism at its best. Even though the Sagittarian transport cruiser's hold contained adjustable stalls for any size of container, I nonetheless smiled at the obvious copycatting.

Regarding the personalities themselves, I could not stand the bullying swagger of the Dark Side presenter. Over confident and imperious, I personally wanted to take her out at the knees, if just to knock some humility back into her. As for the rest, they all who knew who was the gorilla in the room, they all came forward with solid presentations on items that were on the Sagittarian wish list. Now, in two days' time, Greg and I had to come up with a final four, who would then make their bids to us, and that's where the real haggling would begin. In the end, they all knew there would only be three. Why three? That met the carrying capacity of one Sagittarian transport cruiser.

*   *   *

"Krait, damn this bunch is tough to choose between. If you were God, who would you go for?"

"Definitely not, Dark Side. But their location on the moon forces me to strongly consider them nonetheless."

"You didn't like their trade presenter, did you?"

"No. I did not. I found her repulsive and overly entitled."

"Krait, file those feelings away. In the end, all of this is about two things and two things only: product and price. Our personal feelings and emotions have no place here. None, whatsoever. Do you read me, nav?"

"Yes, sir. Loud and clear."

"Good. Now what items do you think will excite the Sagittarians the most?"

"Titanium, rare earths, bauxite, and chromium."

"Why?" Greg probed.

"Titanium is an essential, space-worthy material. Bauxite likewise for aluminum. But the Sagittarians pride themselves in extracting that which we miss or don't care about, but should. The rare earths, chromium, and bauxite presentations all shine in that regard."

"Okay, good choices all. But which three should we go with?"

"The best damn bang for the buck." I empathetically said.

"That's my Krait," Greg grinned. "Let's push for that."

In the end, Dark Side's titanium made the grade, but not before we hammered them on their per ton price. The other two fell to the rare earths and bauxite, both who asked for, an got, reasonable per ton prices in Sagittarian "sand and grit."

CHAPTER FORTY-SIX

"Jarim-Pock-Ylloy," the augmented humanoid, who was more tech than flesh, said. "It has come to my attention that the Sagittarians have instituted a lucrative trading relationship with a system in the outer periphery."

"Tell me more, Djad-juk." Jarim-Pock-Ylloy encouraged, as one of his segmented arms scratched at his dorsal fin, while another surreptitiously activated his recorder. To his pleasure, The Union historian noted that the other hadn't noticed.

"My group of raiders accidentally stumbled upon a heavily armed and well defended Sagittarian transport cruiser. I don't know who was surprised more, us or them. Be that as it may, we retreated from the chance encounter with light losses."

"Tell me, Djad-juk, why should your tale of woe be of interest to me?"

The near-creaking humanoid shrugged.

"Lost revenues, Jarim-Pock-Ylloy, pure and simple. Do you not protect numerous trade concerns throughout the central galaxy from unwanted predation? So, why not similar situations that reach beyond the central core?"

"Do you have the coordinates of this system in the outer periphery?"

"Yes, I do, and have even narrowed down this trading activity to two planets and a satellite within that system."

"So, you have been there?"

"Yes and no. I had to be very careful. I made all my observations from beyond their system-wide defenses." Djad-juk freely admitted.

"System-wide defenses, you say?"

"Yes. Their stationary satellites are based on a slightly above-average technology, but they are dangerous nonetheless."

"Dangerous, how so?"

"Not the defensive satellite grid. But I have witnessed myself their interceptors up close. They are very dangerous, which explains our losses at the initial engagement."

"What do you want for these coordinates?"

"Your best recommendation to The Union."

"Consider it done, Djad-juk. And I thank you for this information. And if a profitable opportunity arises, you will be appropriately enriched."

CHAPTER FORTY-SEVEN

After four days transit we arrived at the Sagittarian frontier, where right on time, two of their interceptors formed up on our Praying Mantis' flanks, interrogated our intentions, and then escorted us to their Space Port Four. And there, as always, Ambassador Nars-mob graciously greeted us.

"Krait! How good it is to see you again," The Sagittarian bubbled, while Mr. Gregory just stood there with a goofy, hang-dog look on his face.

"Oh yes, and you too, Greg!" The Sagittarian needled. "Did you think I forgot you!"

"No, Ambassador Nars-mob, how could I imagine such a situation?"

"I believe that you call such a statement "irony," am I right? Or was it 'sarcasm'?"

"Yes, you can. Either will do."

"Now, come, come, we must get out of the sun.

And, a large sand storm is about to arrive as well." As the Sagittarian got us all brisking walking toward the shelter of the open hanger, he turned to me and asked, "Krait, can you sense it?"

I looked all around and could not see it, but my ears were talking to me.

"It's the air pressure, isn't it ambassador?"

"Precisely, Krait."

On we walked until we reached the hanger and its internal descending passage, and arrived at the familiar, oval-shaped, underground conference room with its central low table. As before, four cool water glasses awaited us, as did four chair cushions placed two on a side, while the room's periphery had numerous cushions as well.

As we trooped in and milled about taking our traditional places, the Sagittarian ambassadorial assistant appeared in her tan robes that matched those of Nars-mob. Behind him filed in seven other Sagittarian witnesses to the trade proceedings. All were colorfully robed. Among them, I recognized none from my first experience. I must have let my mind blocks down as I registered this disappointed emotion.

"Krait," the ambassador thought, "our witnesses change with every meeting. It is our way of inclusion in such important matters of state."

And with that gentle admonition, we sat, welcomed one another, ritualistically drank our glasses of water, and began to discuss the four trade bids. It had become that formulaic, that cut and dried.

"So, how has the gold market been since we last

met?" Nars-mob inquired.

"Remarkably," Mr. Gregory said, "the corporations have begun to hoard their profits and have stopped dumping on the market their recently acquired bullion. Other uses for the metal have also developed. As a consequence, without the former glut, the price of gold has recovered to almost pre-Sagittarian trade levels. So, my dear ambassador, your "sand and grit" has become far more valuable. While a bitter short-term pill to swallow, these corporations are hedging their bets on the future."

"Greg, I totally fail to comprehend your planet's economics."

"Ambassador Nars-mob, that is why we are here, both to explain and protect your planet's interests." I added.

The ambassador looked at me in a way most curious. His eyes tried to read me, while his mind, no doubt out of courtesy, did not intrude. Perhaps it was because my mind blocks were totally open, my sincere and honest desire expressed.

"Thank you, Krait, for expressing that sentiment. I can assure you that my planet thanks you and Greg's role in these transactions."

And like that, eight minutes later, the deal was done, the choices made. The Sagittarians selected the titanium, rear earths, and aluminum bids without seemingly a care.

*   *   *

As what had become almost custom, after our

crews and the seven witnesses had departed, the four of us chatted in an informal and relaxed manner.

Glee-rich, Nars-mob's assistant and ambassador-in-training, felt sufficiently comfortable enough to speak for the first time. She had had her voice box modified, as had Nars-mob, and had learned English, in preparation for her future position. Surprisingly, Glee-rich had selected a deep and rich voice full of emotion and strength.

"Glee-rich," I said, "I find your voice most pleasing to my ears. Did you select it?"

She first looked to Nars-mob's approval before speaking. "Yes, I did. I wanted it to sound like Mr. Gregory's."

I glanced at Greg, who had blushed a bright red shade. The two Sagittarians saw this as well and laughed in their hiccupping tones.

Then, right out of the blue, Nars-mob shifted gears and dramatically changed the subject of conversation.

"Greg, do you remember the time that you and Mr. Jonathan defended our damaged assault cruiser from the Pleiadean raiders?"

"How could I forget, ambassador. That was some fight."

"Well, I believe that you and Krait should be informed about who they represented. There is in the galaxy a loose organization that calls itself The Union. Have you ever heard about it?"

Both of us, now stone-cold serious, shook our heads in negation.

"I thought as much. As I said, The Union is a

loose organization of raiders, pirates I believe you call them, societal outcasts, renegade Pleiadeans, and many, many others. They prey upon trade routes and exact tribute, or taxes, for safe passage. Our ability to so quickly fight them off, no doubt, has created some interest in our financial dealings. As a result, that is why our transport cruisers remain so heavily armed and protected by our own interceptors.

"The Union typically does not strike directly upon planetary economic sources. They prefer to ambush in open space, where they believe they have the advantage. But once again, our quick success at repelling them will only make them bolder. So, kindly inform your planet's government and military of The Union's existence, and, the threat that they represent."

After a brief pause in the conversation that was fast ending, Greg prodded me into speaking.

"Ambassador Nars-mob, I have a proposal for you to consider."

"Please, Krait, tell me and Glee-rich."

"I have been thinking about how Earth and Sagittarius 43 could better understand, and in time, come to respect one another. What I propose is that sometime in the future a cultural office be established at this city's university. The establishment of such an office, open to all Sagittarians curious about us, would promote who we are. It would be a place to ask questions. In turn, we would learn more about who you are. It would be a convenient place to ask questions. Initially, I would be my species' representative. To make this long-term cultural initiative work, would eventually require me to stay on Sagittarius for extended periods of time. Initially, however, I would plan on visits of only several rotations. Periodic reviews would be needed to test and assess whether this cultural outreach is effective or not. Ultimately, you and your people would be in charge of my presence or not."

"What a vision." The ambassador whispered.

"My dear Krait, this vision, however, will require considerable discussion. How long that discussion will take, I do not know, for what you propose is truly revolutionary. But for now, please understand how we Sagittarians can be, sometimes open, sometimes closed. We, generally speaking, can be very complicated. But the extraordinary opportunity that you have outlined is most intriguing."

*   *   *

On the way back home, Greg said to me, "You know, Krait. You constantly surprise me. That open-ended offer that you made to Nars-mob really shook him up. Made him think. I give your vision a fifty-fifty chance of moving on to the next step. But here's hoping."

CHAPTER FORTY-EIGHT

Jarim-Pock-Ylloy decided to grant his source what he wanted, and elevated his status to a "most favored member" of The Union. The sly influencer knew that the additional elevation to "most favored" would mollify him into silence, which it did, and at the same time ensure that the humanoid would be forever in his debt.

But that was to be just the beginning, as Jarim-Pock-Ylloy had to see for himself the truth behind the much-altered hominoid's coordinates. That day, the historian set off from his location near the Galactic Core, careful to avoid its omnipresent black hole, sped off 7.8 light toward that distant peripheral arm, and settled in.

After several weeks of very expensive travel in terms of fuel, Jarim-Pock-Ylloy arrived at a point far beyond the system's defensive grid of satellites.

Applying the gentlest of scans against one of the grid's guardians, the technology revealed proved to be a surprise.

"Above-average technology! Hardly. It possesses subtlety in design and materials. I must rethink my initial thoughts. Djad-juk had poorly estimated them."

Then a devious thought arrived.

"He had rated their interceptors as 'dangerous.' I suspect that they were much more than that. Whoever Djad-juk had chosen to join up with on that raid suggests to me the meagerness of their ships, not to mention tactics, and their crafts' stewardship."

And then fate smiled on Jarim-Pock-Ylloy, as a massive and lumbering Sagittarian transport cruiser emerged from light to begin its deceleration into the system. As it did so, the historian noted how that great mass artfully avoided the stationary satellites. Since his ship was small and shielded, he remained a silent and undetected hole in the universe's fabric.

"By all my digits and appendages! I cannot measure the value of such a star ship! As scrap or not! Much less what it might contain in transferable wealth!"

And so, a patient entity, Jarim-Pock-Ylloy waited to witness whatever he might chance to see, and in the process, confirmed that it was the third planet only, which delivered its wealth in low-orbit to the transport. Then, after another brief sojourn with its lone satellite, another orbital transfer was made. At the conclusion of these transactions, the Sagittarian transport slowly maneuvered its way through the defensive grid, and once beyond, went promptly to light.

"In review," Jarim-Pock-Ylloy spoke into his log book, "Djad-juk's information was accurate only in it coordinates. Otherwise, especially in matters concerning judgment, my new friend was prone to exaggeration. Not a surprising development. But as with all things, the core substance of his exaggeration was reliable."

Then, the historian turned off his log and said to himself, "Reliable. Now that's a concept that I have not experienced for a long time."

CHAPTER FORTY-NINE

Just as Mr. Gregory had predicted, the U.N.-Geneva's Security Council vote came down to a close, split decision. Unfortunately, I did not receive their authorization to succeed Mr. Gregory. Apparently, they had a candidate in mind, yeah, right, and had had enough of non-diplomats filling this important diplomatic post with such far-reaching economic ramifications. Never mind that Mr. Jonathan and Mr. Gregory had trail-blazed the relationship, had established an honest dialogue, and a sense of continuity with an alien planet. To this day, I shake my head at these petty and near-sighted morons.

Meanwhile they claimed to be impressed with my proposal for establishing an office of cultural outreach, but foresaw too many issues. Just how, I do not know. And then pointed out that I was not trained as a social anthropologist! Think about that *non sequitur* for a moment. Deep breath, exhale slowly. To say that I was disappointed, didn't cover it. But as future events would unfold, it would all be to the good.

*   *   *

Hidden in an asteroid belt within the galactic core, a hodge-podge of fashioned structures floated, among them, which were actually anchored to several smaller celestial objects. Originally just a discarded rocket booster cannister converted into a habitat of sorts, now it was a rambling town had been cobbled together from bits of space debris and the occasional captured transport. Within this warren that The Union called home, Jarim-Pock-Ylloy called for a meeting to discuss what he had found.

"Members," he opened, "it has come to my attention that a profitable trade route exists between the Sagittarian system and another located far out on the periphery within the spiral arm that we know as Orion. Just how profitable? Take a look at this vid I made of an arriving Sagittarian transport cruiser. Take my word, this ship was huge. What you cannot see in this recording, however, are this craft's many blast cannon ports and hidden within its cavernous hold, defensive interceptors.

"How do I know of these intimate details? A friend of mine, a good friend of mine, happened into one of these monsters and barely got out with his skin.

"So, I ask you, should we impose our will upon these Sagittarians? Should we demand tribute for their ships' safe passage?"

The question posed caused those gathered to move noisily about with uncertainty. Jarim-Pock-Ylloy didn't have to be a mind-speaker to know what the gathering were deciding. The equation was an ancient one: risk versus reward. Finally, one gestured for his attention.

"Who are the Sagittarian partners in this 'renegade' trade route? Do we know of them? How formidable are they? Are they even space-worthy?"

"Thank you, Vronk, for voicing your concerns. They are all good and valid ones. Yes, they are formidable. How do I know? From their system's defensive grid itself. Next, are they space-worthy? Indeed, they are, for I myself recorded their low-orbital transfers to the Sagittarian transport. Nothing about them appears primitive. If anything, I would rate them as almost our equals in technology."

This last caused quite a ripple in the crowd. Some good, and some bad.

"In that case," Vronk declared, "I say we deal with who we know the best—the Sagittarians. Embargoing their transports mid-way should get their attention! That is my plan. And," he added, "it is the simplest."

As Jarim-Pock-Ylloy listened to the growing enthusiasm for Vronk's iron-clad declaration, he could not help but think, *indeed, your plan is simple.*

"My dear colleagues, before we get ahead of ourselves on this new and potentially profitable venture, how many ships are you willing to send on this task?"

First, it was six, then ten, followed by twelve after more thought.

"That is nowhere sufficient, my dear colleagues." Jarim-Pock-Ylloy firmly stated. "If you even manage to corner one of these transport cruisers, which will take some ingenuity I might add, then your ships will have to deal with blast cannon batteries and at least six to ten interceptors. A previous raiding party of ours was not up to the task in hijacking a damaged transport, under tow, back to Sagittarian space. What will you do with one that is fully functional?"

More moving about, grumbling, and heated discussions broke out.

"Well, Jarim-Pock-Ylloy, why did you convene this meeting only to tell us something was not possible?"

"Jarkmarker!" The historian leveled. "You know as well as anyone our rules of profit versus risk! The greater the profit, the greater the risk! If we just capture one of those Sagittarian transport cruisers, we would double the size of The Union's habitat and enrich it as well. Think on that!"

And so, the discussion evolved from one of negotiated profit through tribute to one of open acquisition.

CHAPTER FIFTY

Jarim-Pock-Ylloy needed a convincing subterfuge. But to do so, he needed an equally convincing stage upon which to reveal it to his audience. In his mind, that which contained a modicum of truth mixed with sufficient confusion or distraction, often made the best and most believable story.

With this in mind, he visited a Pleiadean trading outpost where in the past he had made several profitable transactions. Full in the knowledge that his reputation was solid, he inquired with the outpost's management, a certain Pleiadean gray named Lutriil.

"My dear friend, Lutriil, you are looking most profitable."

The tiny gray bowed slightly to his relatively towering guest, "And you as well, Jarim-Pock-Ylloy. But why is the galaxy's most revered historian and storyteller chancing by my humble trading post? Looking for something special, perhaps? Your reputation for finding that which cannot be found is, after all, legendary."

"I am sincerely honored by those words, Lutriil. In fact, I am in the market for something special. Do you know of any relic Pleiadean freighters that might be for sale or barter?"

The gray paused in thought. His guest's inquiry, while not necessarily unusual, could have ramifications, if the transaction was ever traced back to him.

"Perhaps, dear storyteller, but this could not be a direct transaction. A third party would have to be involved, and that of course implies, a sale, and not a barter arrangement."

Jarim-Pock-Ylloy understood precisely what his little friend was really saying to him. This would be costly. But in the long run, the historian cum storyteller didn't care, for it was not his wealth, but that of The Union he was about to invest.

"I fully understand your position, Lutriil. I require an old freighter of Pleiadean origin, with engines that operate, but not that well. Just enough for sub-light will do nicely. What might you have in inventory?"

Lutriil, frankly, was surprised by his guest. He hadn't flinched his dorsal at all as to a price plus intermediary. Lutriil wondered as he unconsciously cocked his oversized head to one side, *just what is going on here? Am I being set up? Or, is my guest that desperate? No, that cannot be. It must be something else.*

Jarim-Pock-Ylloy missed none of this calculating body language, but patiently waited for a reply.

"There is indeed a possibility that might fit your needs, Jarim-Pock-Ylloy. Kindly visit hanger Number Twelve. You are free to inspect it for as long as you wish."

"Thank you, Lutriil. I knew that I could count on your good graces."

*   *   *

Upon inspection, Jarim-Pock-Ylloy seriously doubted that the true relic had had its engines fired in the past twenty cycles. But other than that, it was intact, could hold an atmosphere, and did look the part of a decrepit injured vessel. However, he would have to tow it back to The Union's asteroid stronghold, where it would be prepared for the ruse. After considerable discussion about its engines and the expense of a tow with Lutriil, the historian paid what he considered a fair amount, precisely one quarter of what the gray Pleiadean had initially wanted.

Unknown to Jarim-Pock-Ylloy, his seller Lutriil was an informer of the Pleiadean government, who was tasked to report any unusual sales of any kind. This relationship helped to protect the Pleiadean government from any unexpected surprises, while guaranteeing Lutriil's marginally legal outpost little to no official interference, much less inventory inspections.

His Pleiadean governmental contact expressed his gratitude for Lutriil's information, and in turn promised the outpost manager two full cycles of sublime non-interference. Rather quickly, the information made its way through several internal Pleiadean ministries for their review. One ministry in particular, found the content intriguing and earmarked it for further consideration.

*　　　*　　　*

Rigged up and towed into position astride the Sagittarian trade corridor, Jarim-Pock-Ylloy and his band of fourteen raider ships pulled back to their positions and readied themselves to attack. Their "Trojan Horse," the dilapidated Pleiadean freighter with registration number UXO-34985 on its dented and battered hull, hung in space. Meanwhile, from Jarim-Pock-Ylloy's ship pulsed out into the immediate sector a repeated, automated, distress beacon, which announced its failed engines and a plea for assistance.

The entire ploy the historian had seen in an old vid. He was counting on the soft-heartedness of the Sagittarians to come out of light, pull alongside, and give assistance. Once they did that, his raiders would pounce, board the transport cruiser, dump its crew, and fly off with an absolute treasure of technology, weaponry, and cargo. What possibly could go wrong?

CHAPTER FIFTY-ONE

What are the odds?

Sagittarian Commander Olen-bar of Transport Cruiser Number Two was eagerly looking forward to reuniting with his ever-growing nest of five pups and his life mate. For some reason, this roundtrip journey seemed to drag on and on.

Perhaps, he thought, *I am just getting too old for this task.*

But the rapid progression of coming events would never reflect that notion.

"Commander!" Tactical called out. "Ship dead ahead."

"Commander!" Sensors also reported. "I have a universal distress hail from that ship: engines down and request for assistance."

Olen-bar shifted into overdrive, rapidly giving orders.

"Sensors. Try to get a reply from that ship. Assure them that we wish to assist."

"Yes, Commander!"

"Navigation." Olen-bar directed.

"Bring us out of light and proceed cautiously. Do not approach nearer than five hundred measures."

"Yes, Commander!"

"Tactical. My stomach does not like this. Put all defensive batteries and the Dragon crews on high alert."

"Yes, Commander."

"Sensors. I need to speak to the crew."

"Yes, Commander." After flipping some switches. "Ready, Commander. Go ahead."

"Crew of the Transport Cruiser Number Two. Here we go again. We have encountered an unknown ship in distress. We are approaching to assist. However, remember your interceptor numbers! You know what that means. That is all."

I am indeed getting too old for such excitement.

*   *   *

Jarim-Pock-Ylloy nearly jumped for joy at seeing his sensors. The Sagittarian transport cruiser had just slowed to sub-light and was now approaching the relic ship, albeit at a very wary pace. This troubled the historian, because it signaled the transport commander's level of experience, which meant to Jarim-Pock-Ylloy the possibility of unwanted resistance, and maybe even failure. He worried that The Union's investment might be at risk.

The massive Sagittarian transport cruiser continued to slow, but showed no sign of stopping. Its distance from the freighter also indicated that it had no intention of boarding it. This too, did not bode well for the historian's plan.

*   *   *

"Sensors. Any response to our hails?"

"No, Commander."

"That's not good news."

"Sensors. Are their engines cold?"

"Yes, Commander. Cold as space."

"Tactical. Can you make out the ship's registration number on the hull?"

"Yes, Commander. It's UXO-34985. Searching… That makes it a Sagittarian hauler, very old. Records say that it was scrapped. My stomach does not like this."

"Thank you tactical. My stomach also is quite nervous."

"Tactical. Send out an interceptor to recon that hulk. Approach no closer than two hundred measures. Confirm."

"Tactical, no closer than two hundred measures, confirm."

*   *   *

The commander of Dragon Three was not at all surprised that his superior had selected him yet again to perform a dangerous recon. Because his stomach was churning so, he left the transport cruiser's bay fully cloaked. The only hint of his interceptor's departure was a brief flickering at the bay's opening as it passed through the three barrier fields.

"Navigation." The Dragon Three commander ordered. "Just like before, take us around nice and slow. No closer than two hundred measures. Remember, we're hunting smukems again."

"Yes, Commander." The navigator said with a smile that hid his nervousness.

As the cloaked interceptor slowly made its inspection of the freighter, its commander noticed that all of its sensor arrays were missing, along with several other typical appendages. Add to that, the midline of its hull was pot-marked with holes, where the emergency escape pods should have resided, but now all were empty. In his mind, the ship looked like a stripped carcass right down to the bone.

"Sensors. Is it possible to send a distress call without external arrays?"

"No, Commander."

"Alright. So, here's a question. Who is?"

"Navigation, return us to the transport cruiser. I have seen sufficient."

Half way back to the safety of their transport cruiser's hold, multiple raider ships began appearing out of light, all in positions that surrounded the slow-moving transport cruiser. Their intentions were obvious and the transport cruiser's defensive batteries immediately opened fire.

"Navigator, get us out of the way, now!"

"Yes, Commander!"

"Tactical. Once we're clear, target the nearest aggressor!"

"Yes, Commander."

Still cloaked, the commander of Dragon Three wanted to surprise these raiders from behind. And once outside of the raider's tactical envelope, Dragon Three made its presence known.

"Tactical, fire at will."

"Firing!"

Of the fourteen original raider craft, four were immediately incinerated by the transport cruiser's own blast cannon batteries. Then, to their surprise, another four disappeared into globes of exploding gases as Dragon Three began raking their rear flank. Then, almost on cue, two more cloaked Dragons left the hanger looking for targets. This time, however, Jarim-Pock-Ylloy, who had hung back in his own cloaked ship, clearly saw the flickering fields at the transport cruiser's aft cargo opening, recognized it for what it was, and made a decision.

"All raiders, go to light! Go to light!"

But that order of retreat didn't mean that the remaining eight survived. Quite the opposite. Only three did.

Suddenly, now with three angry Dragons stalking protectively around their mother ship, all had gone quiet. Only raider ship debris remained and slowly drifted astern.

"Tactical. Cease firing all blast cannon batteries."

"Yes, Commander!"

"Tactical. Have our Dragons inspect our hull for damage."

"Yes, Commander."

This is definitely my last tour, the transport cruiser commander decided then and there.

*   *   *

As for Jarim-Pock-Ylloy, he remained motionless in space, watching and observing the Sagittarian transport's defensive tactics. During the attack. he turned off the distress beacon, switched on his recorder, and began to narrate.

"Their cloaking shields are good. What foiled this ambush was the cloaked interceptor that had been deployed and no one was aware of. Their defensive blast cannon batteries are accurate and deadly. Their command leadership is wary, suspicious, and tactically creative. Conclusion: No more attacks on these well-defended Sagittarian transport cruisers."

*   *   *

While the historian was dictating into his recorder, Olen-bar was doing the same.

To Military Command.

Commander Olen-bar, Transport Cruiser Number Two.

Successfully fought off a swarm of raider space craft.

Crew unharmed.

Vessel undamaged.

Currently en route to Sagittarius.

Recommendation: expansion of cargo bay to include additional Dragons.

CHAPTER FIFTY-TWO

Like clockwork, the annual trade bids with Sagittarius 43 took place once again in Bandung, Java, at the Dutch colonial-styled Gedung Sate building, but this time, Mr. Gregory was in a foul mood.

Why?

Because U.N.-Geneva provided their own "trade negotiator" to "assist" the ambassador to Sagittarius 43 in his deliberations. The man appeared, unannounced, and without credentials, two hours before the talks were to commence.

"And just who the hell are you?" Mr. Gregory inquired.

"My name is Peter Royce Wilkinson. That is all you require."

"Oh, really. Who says?"

"The Trade Commission of U.N.-Geneva."

"Let me see some I.D., buddy"

"No. As I said before, my name is 'all that you require'."

"Why, thank you, Mr. Wilkinson. You just made my decision all the easier.

"Security! Remove this man from the premises! He has no I.D."

As two burly security guards, a.k.a. super-soldiers from Mr. Gregory's own troop, took the man by his elbows straight out the door, Wilkinson called over his shoulder, "You will sorely regret this, Mr. Gregory!"

"That's Ambassador Gregory to you!" He shouted back.

*   *   *

In the end, and only after many go-rounds, Krait's U.N.-Geneva substitute gave Mr. Gregory fits at every turn. So much so, that the former UEF Marine rapidly caught on that the true reason for his presence was not to negotiate any trade bids, but rather to gather evidence to prove the incompetency of the current ambassador. Obstructing every discussion with ridiculous and impossible objections, the annual trade bids quickly devolved into total chaos resulting in their failure. At the root, U.N.-Geneva didn't have a clue about "the Sagittarian way" of doing business, versus "the traditional negotiation of union leaders, management, their lawyers, and government" over pricing, distribution, and payment.

Frustrated, red-faced, and totally pissed off, the ambassador stood up in the middle of the talks and physically took the Trade Commission U.N.-Geneva representative by the arm and once again escorted him out of the building.

"Wilkinson, you spineless son of a worm-slug! If you so much as step once again inside this building, I will personally, and with great pleasure, escort you out yet again, and dump you into that fountain across the way. Do you read me, you moron!"

"You will regret this, Mr. Gregory."

"Unlike you, worm-slug, I am an ambassador-with-portfolio and you're not. And don't you forget it."

*   *   *

The last day of the trade talks, Wilkinson did not show up, but neither did the six corporation's representatives for that year, making this year's trade arrangements with Sagittarius 43 a total bust. I concluded that U.N.-Geneva was so hell-bent at ruining the ambassadorship to Sagittarius, that they were willing to burn down the entire house in order to kill a couple of carpet fleas.

All the trail-blazing that Mr. Jonathan and I had done, and done well, was over. Nonetheless, Dark Side Mining & Manufacturing approached me privately, wondering, hint, hint, what would happen if they attempted their own deal with the Sagittarians. While I truly hated this guy, I felt for him as well.

"Sorry, the Trade Commission of U.N.-Geneva has a lock on all extraterrestrial trade."

"Why is that? What's their beef?"

"It's all about control, pure and simple. Try to get your head around it."

CHAPTER FIFTY-THREE

"Minister, there have been repeated instances where the Sagittarians and Terrans have been involved in trade talks, negotiations, and the actual transfer of raw materials."

"Who initiated such a relationship?" The Pleiadean Minister of External Relations asked.

"From all accounts, the Terrans did. The content of The Agreement of Peace and Mutual Respect of 2356, however, suggests joint authorship by a Terran and a Sagittarian. But far more significant for me, this document was not ratified by the General Assembly of their world government, but rather by a sub-committee."

"Does that make it invalid?"

"No, Minister, it is just a curious consequence of internal Terran politics."

"I see. But these 'repeated instances' of open

trade between the Terrans and our less than friendly neighbors, where do you see a threat to our interests?"

"Primarily with their renewed military strength and capabilities. In addition to the sale of strategic resources and materials, I have in my possession the most recent plans for the Terran intra-stellar interceptor called the Super Raptor. Apparently, these intriguing designs were shared with our neighbors. What was shared in return, is unfortunately unknown."

"In summary, therefore, according to your sources, the Terrans are sharing militarily significant designs with the Sagittarians."

"Yes, Minister. I am."

"Most interesting. Have you recently communicated with your contact within The Union? The one called the historian?"

"Yes, I have. And the historian is ever interested in making a profit, both for himself and The Union."

"What, Minister, is your wish?"

"The disruption of this lucrative trade relationship between our esteemed neighbors and the Terrans. My motivation? Other than old hatreds? I do not want the Terrans gaining access to any more technology. They have already proven to be very adept at reverse engineering our own scout craft designs into low orbital transports and agile interceptors. Besides, I cannot abide by their tall stature."

CHAPTER FIFTY-FOUR

Regardless of what happened during the annual trade talks, or perhaps better said, what didn't happen, Krait and I returned to Sagittarius 43 to relay the bad news. Landing under our usual interceptor escorts at Space Port Four, there was Nars-mob and his assistant Glee-rich waiting for us.

"Greg and Krait!" Nars-mob greeted enthusiastically with arms outstretched."

Then, his arms fell to his sides. "What has happened?"

"Nothing good, Ambassador Nars-mob. I do not wish to discuss the matter on the tarmac."

"I understand, my good friend. Sadly, I too have some distressing news. Follow us."

Once we were all settled down in the underground oval conference room, our crew to one side and the seven Sagittarian witnesses on the other, and after the traditional greetings and water offerings were completed, we got down to business.

"Nars-mob, Krait and I bring you no trade offers."

With a frown on his head, Nars-mob said, "And why is that, good friend, Greg?"

"In summary, politics. My planet's government have chosen to turn their backs on the diplomatic work of Mr. Jonathan, you, and myself. Further, they have categorically denied Krait from succeeding me as ambassador. Why? Once again, politics."

Then the Sagittarian ambassador smiled and did

something quite unexpected.

"I believe that your language has a rather crude expression for times such as these. 'Fuck them,' I believe is how its expressed. Precisely what that expression means, I, frankly, do not know or care. But now I have some troubling news for you.

"Yet again, one of our transport cruisers came under attack, this time by a raider swarm. Thanks to the Great Dragon, it returned to Sagittarius undamaged, its crew unharmed. The sound recommendation of its commander strongly suggested that the cargo hold be made smaller to accommodate an additional six Dragon interceptors for defense and security. That would mean that each transport cruiser's capacity would be reduced by one third.

"In addition, Sagittarius has certain special contacts within the Pleiadean government. These contacts have told us of the Pleiadean dissatisfaction regarding our trade relationship. Further, these same special contacts have told us of the Pleiadean government's attempts at adventurism, specifically in regards to using a particular third party called The Union. We believe that these recent instances of raider attacks on our transport cruisers is a Pleiadean attempt at ruining our relationship. You see, my dear friend Greg, politics is indeed everywhere.

"Going forward, what I am about to suggest is this. Your planet's government, I believe, for whatever their reasons, has chosen to do the right thing. Intra-stellar trade has always been highly problematic. Remarkably, in this brief period of some seven cycles, our planet's resources and reserves have been completely replenished by your trade with us. For this, all of Sagittarius rejoices. We have rebuilt and refurbished all our needs.

The Sagittarian sighed and then paused.

"My dear friend, Greg. Sagittarius no longer needs Earth for its resource needs. But, my planet hungers for knowledge and intellectual exchange. We fear stagnation. In all of our discussions, those are the resources that we need the most right now from your planet."

And then the Sagittarian turned his focus directly upon me. It felt like a heat lamp's glare.

"You, Krait, represent the treasure that our planet yearns for. Honest, frank, and civilized intellectual and cultural exchange. If you are still willing to do so, my planet, as one, will rejoice at your presence among us."

Eyes large, I gulped at the invitation.

A whole frickin' planet wants me!

"Ambassador Nars-mob," I bowed my head, "Ambassador-in-waiting, Glee-rich," I again bowed in respect. "I accept your planet's most generous offer."

With that, and never before, the seven Sagittarian witnesses rose as one and enthusiastically keened loudly. The sound rang in my ears to near-deafening levels. And then like the closing of a door, it stopped.

"Krait, or should I say, Katherine Kramer, that was perhaps the highest honor that any off-worlder has ever received. Naturally, we will have to work out your accommodations, food, a schedule, and whatever else might be needful." Nars-mob concluded.

Quickly glancing at a grinning Mr. Gregory, I

said, "May I suggest initially brief periods of residency on your planet. I will have to acclimate. We, together, must also review my progress. These discussions must be honest and frank. Cultural mistakes will be made, but I wish to minimize them. Then…"

The Sagittarian ambassador raised his hand, palm toward me, a polite, but clear signal for my silence.

"Katherine, you worry too much. Please, just be Katherine."

CHAPTER FIFTY-FIVE

From that day forward, I, Katherine "Krait" Kramer became an honorary citizen of planet Sagittarius 43, free to go and do as my heart desired.

As a private citizen without diplomatic portfolio, I would eventually spend the next twenty-three years of my life planet-side, before finally returning to my home planet for good. My driving purpose was to learn, understand, laugh, cry, make mistakes, own up to them, and always contribute something to the Sagittarian knowledge base about what it means to be human.

While on Sagittarius, I wrote an authoritative vid-book on Sagittarian culture and society, which, to my surprise, made the *World Times* best-seller list, and remained there for an unheard of fourteen months.

One of my most provocative chapters concerned the very human concepts of deception, prevarication, and the outright lie. To a culture of predominantly verbal communication, these concepts are an everyday, common occurrence. They are often used as a convenience and are easy to produce and relatively easy to hide, that is, of course, if one can keep their mouth shut. But imagine living in a non-verbal culture, one where thoughts are freely shared. In such an environment, deception, prevarication, and outright falsehoods are extremely hard to conceal and to do so requires considerable effort. The slightest slip of a thought would reveal them. This observation explains the Sagittarian approach to almost everything, where respect, honesty, and civility rule. I must admit that I wrote this chapter specifically to address our own institutional brand of diplomacy, and its thoroughgoing duplicity at every turn.

Another chapter worth spending some time on is about Sagittarian body language. Again, I amassed these visual cues primarily for anyone conducting future trade talks or training for the diplomatic corps. Perhaps most infuriating, is that the Sagittarian communication system does not depend upon eye contact. Yes, their listening to your thoughts with great focus, but not your face. Sometimes, this can be very disorienting. Another hurdle is the Sagittarian expression of boredom or impatience, which is best seen when they close their eye, nose, and ear flaps. If you see that, their silence is not acceptance, far from it. Then, there is the sideways head bob or lean. This connotes acceptance or agreement of some idea or thing and is not to be confused with a stretching exercise. A raised hand with an open palm facing the speaker is a polite request for an interruption. In other words, "please shut up," I too wish to say something. To embarrass a Sagittarian, or to elicit a strong emotionally charged moment, their pebbly skin will blush in colorful waves. This is quite beautiful to behold, but do not in any way confuse or compare these color changes with that of a Terran chameleon. This is purely an emotional reaction. Speaking of their velvety smooth skin, they shed it as needed and do so much like when we have our hair cut. For example, if very dirty or smudged with oil, Sagittarians, a fastidious species, will within minutes sluff off what they no longer want. However, in an entirely different context, if a Sagittarian sheds before you, it is because, for whatever reason, they wish to cleanse themselves of your presence. Think of it as a summary dismissal and not at all a good thing. Finally, the best for last: Sagittarian's do not like being touched. Do so only in times of obvious emergency. This sense is typically reserved only for family intimacy and the closest of friends. Consequently, do not attempt to shake hands, pat someone on the back, or God forbid, hug. Such acts will be interpreted as impoliteness or outright assault.

My chapter on their religion is perhaps the shakiest in terms of absolute data. Our word "religion," itself is the problem. Earthers approach the unknowable from principally an institutional approach, in the most part dominated by teachings recorded in holy writings. The Sagittarians, in bold contrast, do not have religious institutions with hierarchies and internal bureaucracies, who in turn interpret and minister to their followers. Instead, they refer to The First Source, or The Judge, or that of The Destroyer. These concepts are universally shared and understood by them, but not by off-worlders like us, who crave definition, logic, and above all, precise, arguable dogma. Hence, the source of so many of our own conflicts. Mixed in with this loose Sagittarian belief system is an apparent "race memory," whether true or fictional, of their long-ago reptilian origins. Expressions that include an invocation to "The Great Dragon" reflect this most clearly.

Lastly, my discovery of Sagittarian humor, I found to be the most surprising jewel of their culture. If a Sagittarian makes a sound similar to hiccupping, they are not choking, but laughing—hard. Since the Sagittarian physiology lacks a voice box, unless surgically augmented, this typically reduces them to only aural hisses and grunts. The hiccupping-like noise they make is how they chuckle. As for their dry humor, expect puns galore, witty asides, and odd transpositions of thought. In short, they love being clever. Be clever back and you will have a friend for life.

Vid-book reviewers, like all humans, have anuses. The trick, of course, is not to be one. One Earth-bound reviewer praised my vid-book, *Life on Sagittarius 43*, for "its blunt, sometimes biting frankness, crystalline descriptions, and crisp analysis of what it means to be an alien in an alien's land," a clear nod to Ray Bradbury. While I didn't intend that, the comparison was certainly apt. Another remarked that it reminded her of Jane Goodall's primatological labors in the African jungles and her attempts to make sense of it all. Once again, I am honored by the parallel. A third thought that I sounded more like "a lizard apologist," than an unbiased human observer. Like I said before, we all have one.

During my many visits on Sagittarius 43, I was invited to be an honored faculty member of the city's university. This post allowed me to communicate directly with the Sagittarian youth and satisfy my desires for cultural and social outreach. It was such an honor and privilege to do so. Their sharp minds always kept me on my toes. I only hope and pray that I made some sort of a difference.

Once again permanently Earth-side, the Institute for Advanced Studies at Princeton University invited me to join their distinguished faculty with the totally improbable title, Professor of Extraterrestrial Anthropology. This position, I accepted graciously, and would come to thoroughly enjoy, although I found lecturing verbally to be cumbersome, instead of thinking about what I wanted to convey. But like all challenges, this one I beat as well. Overall, I found Princeton itself to be quaint and colorful, its woodsy landscapes very pretty, but after so long on Sagittarius, I found its climate to be too muggy for my tastes.

Ah, yet another challenge.

Finally, I wish to close with this: a vid-reporter asked upon my return, what I thought of U.N.-Geneva's decision of not granting me the Sagittarian ambassadorship? I thought about this awkwardly put question and considered several possible responses. Then, I remembered with some appreciation what Ambassador Nars-mob had to say about politics in general.

While I was ruminating on my answer, the impatient vid-reporter aggressively repeated her question about how I felt about my "failed" Sagittarian ambassadorship, once again poorly expressed. Clearly, she was digging for dirt.

So, I just looked into her vid-camera, and said, "Fuck 'em!"

ABOUT THE AUTHOR

For W.J. Cherf, this is his third foray into the realm of futuristic science fiction. *I Am Jonathan* and *I Am Gregory* kicked off this series, Twenty-Fourth Century Mercenaries. Up until now, his bailiwick has been historical science fiction, paranormal archaeology, and paranormal action-adventure literature.

Cherf is well known for his works in "historical science fiction," starting with *Bow Tie*, an award-winning, five-book. time traveling series entitled, The Manuscripts of the Richards' Trust. They are full of adventure, intrigue, wonder, and vivid description.

For a change, Cherf delved into the strange with his four-book series entitled The Adventures of Paranormal Archaeology. Beginning with *The Magician's Tomb*, here the author narrates the magical world of ancient Egypt through its remains.

Cherf's first paranormal action-adventure series, The Adventures of J.J. Stone, begins with *The First Soul,* which tells the story of a U.S. Marine who discovers his true calling in the battle between good and evil.

As to why Cherf writes in his retirement years, he says, "I always wanted to write a book without footnotes." This is an oblique reference to his treadmill "publish or perish" days as a professor of ancient history and archaeology.

Find reviews and free chapters of his works, not to mention a handy source for news in Egyptology, at www.wjcherf.com. As always, test drive a free chapter before you buy any book.

Praise for *Burying Norma Jeane*

Burying Norma Jeane is both an epic adventure novel
and a call to action. It serves as an illuminating love letter that highlights the usually overlooked intellectual,
poetic, and courageous depths of the genius responsible for creating the most recognizable celebrity icon
in the world, and it is brimming with details that will
teach even the biggest Marilyn fans things they didn't
know about her. But beyond that, it is also a carefully
constructed societal reflection, through which we can
examine the ways our media and culture have – and
have not – evolved over the past six decades. It is a brilliantly composed book with unforgettable characters
that you will want to hop in the car with, and I believe it
has the power to inspire real action. Read this and then
meet me at the cemetery! (I'm serious.)

Kona Morris,
Storyteller, comedian, and founder of *Godless Comics*

To be a woman in America means spending a lot of
our lives looking for who we are outside the male gaze,
which steals us from ourselves. To mother girls in this
culture is to try to protect them from the same. Marilyn Monroe embodies this theft, the blonde bombshell
with a big, big brain the studios didn't want us to know
about, who even in death and burial is insidiously sur-

rounded by lascivious men.

This highly satisfying mother-daughter take has the pair seeking liberation for Marilyn and themselves. It gives a more vivid portrait of her than we've previously received, and is a potent antidote to portrayals in film and literature that have focused on Marilyn-as-victim instead of highlighting her intelligence and agency. This book gives Marilyn back to herself, and to us. It's a vital addition to her legacy.

Can the mother-daughter duo rescue Marilyn from her posthumous fate? No spoilers, but I'm betting that, like me, you'll read this in one sitting to find out.

Stina French,
host of *Listen To Your Skin Reading Series*
and *Headmistress of The Sexploratorium*

Three generations of women – a mother, her tween daughter, and Marilyn Monroe – take us on a cross country journey to explore how the role of women has evolved, or more accurately, how not much has changed at all.

This is the story's take-away, and a Joseph Campbell, *Thelma and Louise*-style journey is the vehicle. But what *Burying Norma Jeane* is about is the love between a mother and daughter in the face of tragedy, and the mother's hope for a better world for a girl soon become a woman.

William E. Burleson,
author of *Ahnwee Days*

While we're young I know where I'm going
and who's going with me?
—Marilyn Monroe, from *Fragments*

For Kona, Rose, and all the adventurers,
past, present and future.

Preview

Please don't talk about me when I'm gone.

Marilyn Monroe, *Fragments*

Born Norma Jeane Mortenson, baptized Norma Jean Baker, turned into Norma Jean Dougherty when she married a few days after her sixteenth birthday to escape foster care.

Jean Adair, her first choice for a stage name before she borrowed Monroe from her mother's maiden name.

Marilyn Monroe as a studio compromise.

Naïve early star Mona Monroe posing for nude photos and signing on the dotted line to be paid.

Zelda Zonk in a brunette wig, traveling incognito, waiting at fancy hotels for her lovers in her white bathrobe.

Miss Faye Miller to throw the press off her trail as she signed herself into the psychiatric wing of New York Hospital.

Marilyn Monroe Miller (MMM) when she died, the triple MMM initialed doodles outlasting her final marriage.

I ran through all of Norma Jeane's names, thinking about the difference in the way your mouth opens in a friendly way to say "Norma" versus the way your lips close in on themselves and press together, with the

1

slightest hum when you say "Marilyn," which is similar to what your mouth does when you say "Miriam," my name, except you begin and end on that lip-touching hum, the same way your mouth shapes itself into the word "Mom." How "M" is the middle letter of the alphabet, and "Mem," the thirteenth letter of the Hebrew alphabet, representing revelation, secret, water.

I studied Marilyn, as a child, my father's knickknacks and decorative plates instructing me. I came to understand that she and Barbie were trying to tell me something.

"She's like a doll," I told my dad. "You think she's beautiful?" I asked.

"I think she's sexy," he replied, then looked embarrassed, as if the word had slipped out, which made it seem important.

I spent a lot of subsequent years holding beautiful next to sexy to understand the differences.

I thought Madonna and Marilyn were the same lady. It was the 1980s, and Madonna was working her Blond Ambition phase, and she even had a matching Marilyn beauty mark sometimes. Like Madonna, I came of age with MTV. I watched "Material Girl" as my father flinched, but no one really understood music videos yet, and they were too fascinating to turn off.

"Marilyn sure can sing!" I told my dad.

He laughed. "That's Madonna, and she can sing way better than Marilyn," he said.

I watched Madonna's dance moves, comparing "Like a Virgin" to "Gentlemen Prefer Blondes." Everything about Marilyn was softer than Madonna. I could see that now – her body, her voice, the way she moved.

My father preferred the softness. But I liked the way Madonna was hard. I liked that my dad blushed when I asked him what "Papa Don't Preach" was about.

I wanted to be hard, so I spent my teenage years in the early 1990s trying. Nirvana, Hole, grunge, even Madonna fully embraced S&M in those years. I was in good company.

It wasn't until I went to college that I remembered Marilyn. I was trying to buy my dad a birthday present in a thrift store, paging through a bin with back issues of *Life* magazine to find one that coincided with his birth month, and there she was. The Golden Dream.

The cover read December 1953, *Playboy* #1, and Marilyn waved, clothed, but inside she was laid out across the red velvet, looking as sweet and soft as a bonbon, her nipples cherried in profile. For a nude spread, chaste. Innocent compared to Madonna's newly released book *Sex*, but shocking for the 1950s.

I slipped the *Playboy* inside a *Life* magazine from the same year, and waved its *Life* side out at the cashier, slid a dollar across the counter.

I went home and inspected the photos. She looked so young and beautiful, a little lost but also completely in control of the page. I kept flipping through her spread, back and forth, examining the shadow of a nipple. I held her above my head and wondered how many people had inspected her the same way I was doing. I felt shame, but I was so aroused, I joined an international club I had never known existed, all the people touching themselves while imagining burying their faces between Marilyn's pointed breasts. Again and again, I dove into myself, rippling my body into new undulations. When I was exhausted, I rescued the crumpled magazine from underneath me, smoothing the cover, then dug into my drawer to find the pack of cigarettes I usually reserved for drunken nights. I smoked a cigarette in my bed, tucking the smoke around me.

That was the day my true obsession with Marilyn started. I needed to announce it to someone – this feeling I had about a woman who had already been dead for decades. I called my father.

"You know she never posed for those photos, never even got paid for them, right?" my dad told me when I asked if he'd ever seen the *Playboy*.

"What do you mean? I looked at the photos, Dad. She obviously posed."

"She never posed for *Playboy*. I read she was only paid $50 for some calendar pin-up before she was even a movie star. They sold it to *Playboy* without her permission."

I looked at the cover again, wondering how she felt taking those nude photos when she was so young, then having them follow her throughout her life.

Years later, when the announcement about Hugh Hefner's death popped up on my Facebook feed, I thought about that conversation with my dad, how he had mentioned the photos lightly, like gossip, while I had immediately realized that it was a story about every woman, everywhere, whose brilliance had only been used to reflect on a man, whose compensation had never been enough.

Scudda Hoo! Scudda Hay! (1947), Dangerous Years (1947), Ladies of the Chorus (1948), and Love Happy (1948)

Naked, she was always naked in the house. Six or seven or eight hours. She was naked all day long! And I'm not exaggerating!

Natasha Lytess, Marilyn's
early acting coach and lover

Before she caught our attention, Norma Jeane was raised in the movie industry, where her mother worked as a film cutter. When Gladys Baker was around, she dangled Hollywood for her Norma Jeane like a mobile, often telling her that her father was a big star, an absent mystery.

But Gladys wasn't around much. She dropped off her daughter with her first set of foster parents when she was only two weeks old. Her entire childhood, Norma Jeane only lived with her mother for a few months, long enough to bear witness to Gladys's complete mental breakdown and commitment to the state mental hospital, Norwalk, with a diagnosis of paranoid schizophrenia. From there, Norma Jeane bounced from foster home to orphanage to teen marriage, with sexual abuse as her constant companion. But throughout it all, she kept her eyes focused on stardom.

We watched her warm up by staring at our husbands' pin-up calendars during World War II, noting the way she could fill out a sweater. A teenaged bride whose husband was serving in the Merchant Marines, she supported the troops as a perky Rosie the Riveter factory worker. A full-blown modeling career by 1946 and a basic film contract with Twentieth Century Fox the same year, earning $75 a week.

In her first speaking role, in the spring of 1947, in *Scudda Hoo! Scudda Hay!* we glimpse her as an extra saying "hi" to the stars from the steps of the church, or as a waitress, Evie, with a bit part in *Dangerous Years*, as another pretty face in *Ladies of the Chorus* in 1948, where she debuts her dancing and singing talents with the uncomfortable song "Every Baby Needs a Da-Da-Daddy," featuring a chorus line of girls manipulating baby dolls into sexy dances that make us cringe, though we keep quiet about it.

Enter Natasha Lytess, the head drama coach for Columbia, a German actress twenty years older than Marilyn, respected in the industry for her strict and demanding personality. She fell in love with Marilyn's screen test and convinced the head of Columbia to hire Marilyn for a six-month contract just as her Fox contract expired. Lytess became obsessed with Marilyn before it was fashionable, and she quit her job with Columbia in 1950 to become Marilyn's personal acting teacher, moving in with her and working with her for more than twenty films. Their relationship caused problems for Marilyn's future directors because of her dependence on Lytess. We heard she preferred to hold hands with Lytess on set, leaving it to the editors to figure out ways to cut the clasped fingers out of the scenes. Lytess and Monroe were said to have lived together as husband and wife until Joe DiMaggio entered the picture years later and forced Marilyn to sever the relationship.

"I want you to help me. Some men are following me," Marilyn announces as she bursts into a hotel room in the Marx Brothers' film *Love Happy*, her final role of 1948. Groucho Marx gives his usual leer and waggles his eyebrows, responding, "Really? I can't understand why!" as he ogles Marilyn's sexy walk that became one of her trademarks.

Lytess claimed she invented the walk for Marilyn, while another acting coach said it was the result of weak ankles; a gossip columnist declared she shaved a bit off one high heel in order to up the undulation, and Marilyn's half-sister Berniece Miracle insisted it was a shared genetic weakness. We'll never know the truth, like so many myths of Marilyn. Most of us don't even know her name.

Lytess said that Marilyn hated to be called sexy, but in these early roles we can see her already resigning herself to it, taking one of the few parts available for women of our era; the simpering blonde bombshell, the role of her lifetime.

Chapter 1

"You ready to show me your designs?" Niles, the head of our firm, interrupted my contemplations with his crisp English accent, standing in the doorway watching me while he sipped a cup of tea.

I flipped through the slide show as he nodded, making affirmative sounds. We heard Karen greet the clients as I returned to the introductory slide, and they filed in, finding their seats. Letting them settle as I prepared to introduce myself, I glanced down at my notes a final time. The older white gentleman in the elegant navy-blue three-piece suit settled in the seat next to me. I smiled down a greeting at him, and he put his hand on my elbow and winked at me.

"Can you get me some coffee, hon?" he asked. "With cream, please." The rest of the men got very quiet. I crossed my arms over my chest.

Saint Emory, Catholic school for the Grand Junction elite. Mr. Wright was their patriarch. I had taken time to study their website, to know who was on the email thread, to recognize the senior member of their cohort.

I had their file in front of me, ready to discuss.

"Excuse me, Mr. Wright. I'm Miriam Renata. The head architect working on the Learning Commons redesign for Saint Emory."

I could see his face as he registered me, remembered that the year was 2017, then decided to double down on his approach.

"Nice to meet you, Miriam. It's not too late to get that coffee, though, right?" I slammed the file on the table and walked out of the conference room, heading for my office. Niles followed me out, closed the door behind him, catching up with me as I leaned against the wall outside my office door. He put his hand on my shoulder, pressing down in a way I did not like.

"Now, Miriam, there's no need to be rude," he said, his accent coming out a little more than usual with the situation and his attempt to make it light and airy.

"You think if the project manager were a man, they would ask him for coffee? Before they introduce themselves or anything? What's next, they pat me on the ass, and you tell me not to be rude about it? This is bullshit."

Niles rolled his eyes. "It's not a big deal. Please just calm down." He went to the machine and started two cups of coffee with a few touches of the buttons.

I could feel the adrenaline starting to course through me. I could feel the panic that started with a tightness in my chest and turned into a wave of nausea that I had been able to surf out before Andy had died. Now it kept crushing me. All of those years, I'd managed to stay quiet, to take deep breaths, to keep the board underneath me, and pointed towards the shore. But now I was caught in the churning.

"If you could just paint a smile on your face, let's get back to the meeting." Niles's thin lips turned up at me, and the adrenaline pulsed over me.

I was as shocked as he was when I shoved him with both hands squarely in the chest, where his arms met his trunk, so hard he lost his balance and toppled over, spilling the hot coffee down his chest.

"What the fuck?" he boomed, but I was already out the door.

* * *

I was shaking when I walked into the house. My wedding photo stared back at me from the wall, and I saw us – how young and beautiful we were – as Andy looked at me with his dark eyes through long lashes. I wanted to rage at him for being gone, but I didn't have it left in me. I broke down in the entryway of the house, sobbing in front of the photo. I found myself keening, "I just miss you. I just miss you. I just miss you." Over and over without any sense of how much time had passed.

The buzz of my phone in my pants pocket brought me back into myself, and I opened it to see a message from Nora:

[Are you OK? Thinking about you.]

I made my chest stop heaving and then sent my consciousness through my body, checking on my parts. I stretched all of my toes out from each other, thinking about the value of the tiniest pinky toe in keeping us balanced. I flexed my calves, moved my mind up to my hips, which felt so tight and uneven, through to my stomach, a mess of tangled anxiety. I tried to breathe into it, to release, but my chest hurt. It hurt all the time now and it felt like I could never catch a whole breath. I finished my inventory of my body. The bottom line was that I was fucked up, but at least I was still standing. My feet were strong, down to that little pinky. My thumbs still worked too, so I texted Nora back.

[Bad day.]

[Can I bring you and Mat dinner?]

[That would be nice.
We're home from practice about 6:30.]

[OK luv you! Enchiladas!]

I wiggled each toe as I ran the scene from work over and over in my mind until I noticed it was already almost 3:30. "Shit!" I yelled aloud as I grabbed the keys, texting Matilda as I started the car.

[Running late, OTW]

[Big surprise]

The sarcasm ran deep in my newly teenaged daughter, but, truthfully, I was late more often than I was on time, so I couldn't pretend to be offended. I turned up the volume on the radio and tried not to drive impatiently. When I pulled up to her middle school, there were no other kids milling around, just Matilda, her pale skin already turning pink in the fall sunshine and her dark curls spilling down her back as she lowered her phone and scooped up her backpack. Her legs seemed too long for her shorts, and I remembered that I had promised her some back-to-school items, but I had never gotten to it.

"Good afternoon, Mother," she said, and I tried to register her mood.

"How was your day?"

"Meh."

"Meh good? Meh bad?"

"Just meh."

"Do you have rehearsal now?"

"Yeah at 4:30."

"Getting excited for the big performance?"

"It's my first time without Dad," she said, and her face drooped for a moment. Andy had died three months ago, in the middle of summer. Massive heart attack, despite being in his early forties, his years of early morning tennis, and all the dinner salads he chose instead of hamburgers.

He was there when I woke up in the hot July morning, and we had made love quickly before we had to start the day's routine. We brushed our teeth together, decided to allow Matilda a half cup of coffee, as we each had our usual two cups. Kissed at the door. He was wearing my favorite yellow shirt, a linen button-down that I buried my face in as he held me for a quick second before he reached for the door. I could still feel the rough-soft fabric against my cheek, the pulse of his alive body underneath.

I remembered all of it because I had played the morning over and over in my head, wondering if there were a place I could pause or fast forward to a different outcome.

By the time I had gotten to the hospital, he was already deceased. I didn't see the dramatic moments with the beeping machines and the running physicians. His assistant had called me from his law firm and told me that he was having chest pains, had decided to drive himself to the hospital. By the time I got there, a nurse pulled me into a quiet room and told me they could not resuscitate.

"Puck. He would be so proud of you." I tried to smile at Matilda, but I couldn't get my lips into quite the right angle.

"Yeah," she said. "So what? He's not here. I'd rather he be disappointed in me and still be here." She turned away.

"I'm going to walk you in," I told Matilda as she grabbed her bag.

"Not necessary, but whatever."

"I just want to talk to Mrs. Deliah." She shrugged at me, stomped for the dressing room. "See you at 6:00?" I called out to her disappearing back.

"Hi Miriam," Mrs. Deliah sing-songed. She wore a deep purple dress that played off her mahogany skin and made her look like royalty. Mrs. Deliah had been Matilda's drama coach and mentor since she discovered her love of theater at seven.

Matilda had gone on to do school plays and community theater, and had just started auditioning for bigger roles. I was glad she had wanted to come back for a last production with Mrs. Deliah. Kids usually aged out of her program at twelve, and Matilda turned thirteen a couple months before Andy died.

My life was split into the BEFORE and the AFTER. Before Andy died, we had been a happy family. Before Andy died, I had avoided conflict and would have just nodded and made the coffee. Before Andy died, Matilda had been an easy kid.

We had celebrated Matilda's thirteenth birthday with a bat mitzvah. We were the kind of Jews that spent more

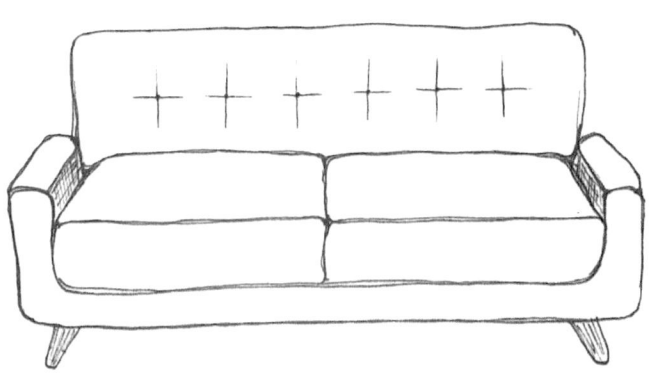

time eating latkes than reading the Torah, but we had found a laidback synagogue, and they let Matilda focus a project on Tikkun Olam and social justice. She had used her drama background to give a compelling performance. We had all applauded her and eaten amazing amounts of food. It was the last big occasion we were together. We still had a couple of months with Andy after that, but they were a blur of going our separate ways in the morning, of play practices and family dinners. I felt my eyes starting to well up and had to shove the emotions down. I could cry later, when I was alone in my shower. Mrs. Deliah laid her hand on my arm.

"You OK, Miriam?" Her face was a river of empathy, and I remembered that she had lost her husband five or six years ago.

"Every day above ground is a good day." Nothing like some death humor to lighten the situation.

Mrs. Deliah shook her head at me, then peeked to make sure none of the kids were eavesdropping as she tilted her head for me to follow her to the back of the small black box theater.

"Matilda is struggling," she told me.

"I know," I said. "She's just so angry about everything."

"I don't blame her. And I've been trying to help her find ways to channel it. You know, we might think of Puck as just being a whimsical fairy, but he's pissed off too. He's tired of doing what he's told."

"I think she just has to get through this. We both do."

"I've been trying to keep her busy. She took over a bunch of the stage crew set-up. She's got the whole lights system and music programmed with her laptop. I don't know what else to do besides try to find stuff she cares about and be here if she needs to talk."

"Same," I said. "I'm just trying to keep going through the motions for her sake."

"Have you thought about therapy?" Mrs. Deliah looked at me squarely.

"For me or her?" I tried to smile. Mrs. Deliah just kept looking at me, then pulled me into a gentle hug.

"I'm praying for you both," she said, and even though my Judaism leans toward the agnostic, I felt touched. It was nice that someone wanted to speak up on our behalf.

I could hear the kids before I saw them, roaring out from the dressing room, which I took as my cue to leave.

At home, I made myself a cup of tea and sat at the kitchen table, tried to take deep breaths and not deteriorate into tears. My eyes drifted to the Marilyn Monroe plates that I had inherited from my father a few years ago. They hung over the couch in the same place of honor I had seen Christians hang a crucifix or a painting of Jesus. Marilyn's images were the most constant female presence I could remember from my childhood. She was technically Jewish – she had converted before marrying Arthur Miller, a fact my dad shared with anyone who looked skeptically at his Marilyn collection. My father was notoriously hard to buy gifts for, but everyone knew he was a fan, so Marilyn tchotchkes dominated our small home, the only decorations besides menorahs and books. Decorative plates with her image were among my earliest memories, mugs and postcards with Marilyn Monroe winking out from the corners, ever-present, wallpapered on my consciousness.

Above the couch hung three of the plates– the scene from *Some Like It Hot* with Marilyn's skirt billowing up over the grate, one of her in the pink dress from *Gentlemen Prefer Blondes*, with a band staring up at her in admiration, and my favorite plate: from *How to Marry a Million-*

aire, showing her red-dressed reflection peering back at her from three different mirrors. Each angle showed her looking like a slightly different person. My eyes traced them, meditating on Marilyn's curves as I had done so many times before, while I played the scene at the office over in my head, feeling the impact as my hands shoved into Niles's sweatered chest.

I would tell Matilda about the work issue tomorrow when it wasn't so raw. I would tell her casually that I had decided to take a break from work for a while. I wouldn't cry, I promised myself, feeling the tears well up in my eyes. I wouldn't talk about how starting over at forty-two seemed impossible.

I rehearsed it in my head, the calm voice I would use. I checked my watch and thought about how I should probably call the office, talk to Karen about my options. What else would I do if I weren't an architect? I thought about how much of my identity was tied up in my job, how I managed to work it into every introduction within the first five minutes. Should I just beg Niles for forgiveness? What else did I have to offer? What would Andy tell me to do? Could I start over?

I looked to Marilyn on the plates, and she nodded at me in approval. "You can do it," she purred.

By now I had read all of Joyce Carol Oates, including *Blonde,* and I had watched all of the movies, and I had come to see that it wasn't the T+A, or the fake hair, or the smile that attracted people to Marilyn. It was the tragedy of her. The vulnerability. You could see it if you looked carefully, even on the plates.

There, behind the eyes.

The Asphalt Jungle (1950)

*She gave a reading that was extraordinarily good, she was
ideal. She was The Girl. However, I had no notion that she
was going to go on and be the star that she became.*

John Huston, who bookended
Marilyn's career as the director of both her first and last
major roles, from *The Asphalt
Jungle* to 1962's *The Misfits*

The moment we see the camera find Marilyn, curled up
like a cat on the couch, she comes awake in the lamp-
light of her boyfriend's gaze, illuminating the screen for
the first time beyond the bit parts where she blended into
the chorus line; in *The Asphalt Jungle*, there is no blending,
only the shine of a soon-to-be star. She is still almost girl,
though also fully woman, hints of the Norma Jeane she
was and the Marilyn Monroe she will become – not yet
platinum, no longer honey, just glowing on the screen.
The camera finds her, and Marilyn comes awake,
stretching and preening, careful with her lines but warm
and sexy.

We heard she practiced for the role, with Natasha
Lytess coaching her to lie on a couch to feel close to the
scene. When she auditioned, there was no couch available, so she insisted on laying her body on the floor.

Marilyn was worried that she didn't read as well as she wanted to on her first go, so she begged to read a second time, her self-doubt clouding the way she had already taken ownership of the role. John Huston, nominated for a best director Oscar for the film, remembers her audition and how he "immediately said yes."

The Asphalt Jungle is a black and white stylized old Hollywood jewel heist movie, which must have appealed to 24-year-old Marilyn very much. She was able to get her foot in the door, largely thanks to Johnny Hyde, Marilyn's first agent. Hyde, a Russian Jew born in the old country, was a major player in the film industry and recognized Marilyn's seductive talent enough to leave his wife and shack up with Marilyn, regularly begging her to marry him. She was thirty years younger, and he was six inches shorter. Photos show them slow-dancing, his eyes aligned with her nipples.

Though her role in *The Asphalt Jungle* as Angela Phinlay, the mistress of one of the major players, is small, Marilyn steals her scenes. Audiences were taken with Marilyn, and when the movie reached wider release, she earned a spot on the movie poster.

Censors in the 1950s wouldn't allow the word "mistress" to be spoken aloud, so she calls her lover "Uncle Lon," and he calls her "sweet kid." He has to be thirty years older than her, and in their dynamic, we can already see the mirrored power structures, the way older men like Johnny Hyde would shape her, mold her, control her, define her, throughout her life.

When she fantasizes about herself frolicking on a Cuban beach in a green bathing suit, we want to see it too. We want all her fantasies to come true. After she sobbingly recants Uncle Lon's alibi, she pleads, "What about my trip, Uncle Lon? Is it still on?"

"Don't worry, baby, you'll have plenty of trips," Uncle Lon tells her, right before he commits suicide instead of going to jail.

"You'll have plenty of trips."

Chapter 2

I was never used to being happy, so that wasn't something I ever took for granted. You see, I was brought up differently from the average American child because the average child is brought up expecting to be happy.

Marilyn Monroe, as quoted in
Life magazine interview, "Last
Talk with a Lonely Girl"

"You have to understand," Karen told me over the phone. "Niles is of the opinion that you are lucky he isn't pressing charges. I'm sorry. I know you haven't been the same since Andy. But I think this is a fair offer."

I'd known Karen for years, but I wouldn't be surprised if she was recording the conversation. This could all turn into an ugly lawsuit, and her loyalties were with the firm. The offer was to put me on leave. I would take the next three months off, with full pay and health insurance. After three months, we could meet to discuss my future with the firm. In the meantime, I needed to share information on all my projects, sign a non-disclosure agreement, and keep my mouth shut. The firm didn't like to fire people, and they certainly didn't like lawsuits, but most of all, they disliked being a source of gossip. They were trying to attract the kind of high-end clients who refused to be affiliated with rumors.

"OK," I told Karen. I could feel the panic sloshing in my stomach.

Nora took account of me, looking at me with Andy's eyes, "I don't know, Miri, you don't look great," she told me, shaking her head. "Too skinny for sure."

"Return of the flaca, right?" She and Andy had always teased me when we were in college, and I stayed skinny despite the cafeteria food and the late-night diner and fast-food runs. It wasn't until I had Matilda that the hips and curves had seemed to solidify on my body.

"Are you sleeping?" she asked.

"Not much," I admitted. "I keep waking up thinking Andy's still in bed with me for a quick sleep-second, and then I reach over and he's not there, and then I remember everything, and it wakes me up and, you know. It's hard." I don't tell her about the sweats and how often I am sobbing in the shower at 3 a.m.

"Aunt Nora!" Matilda ran downstairs and into her aunt's arms. Matilda was still small enough to receive a kiss on the top of her head, but she had to crouch down for it. Another few months, and she would probably be taller than Nora. She brushed Matilda's hair down her back and gave her the same accounting stare she had given me.

"You're too skinny, too," she said.

"Yeah, but at least I sleep. And eat," she responded, disentangling herself from Nora and sniffing around the kitchen. "I smell enchiladas."

"In the oven," Nora said "Chicken."

Matilda got down plates and put on oven mitts to pull the enchilada pan out of the oven. "Yummm," she said. "Mom hasn't cooked in days."

I glared at her, but it was true. I tried to remember the last time I cooked for us. I did fry some eggs for dinner a couple of nights ago.

"There's a salad in the fridge, too," Nora said, and watched as Matilda set it on the table and grabbed us forks. Nora pulled out a bottle of wine. "Cheap, but Italian," was how she described it as she dug around for the corkscrew. We all sat down and ate, the food warm and melting with cheese, a tingle of spice lingering on the back of my tongue after each bite. I felt at home in my body for a moment, this scene of three people eating around the table that I had repeated countless times with Andy. But once his name ricocheted through my brain, the enchiladas lost the spice and started to taste like rubber. I moved the food around my plate, hoping no one would notice, but I saw Nora looking at me with one eyebrow raised, and made myself wolf down a big bite. It got stuck in my throat, and I gulped the wine, then scooted the plate away from me, trying to ignore Nora's big eyes.

After dinner, Nora showed Matilda the cupcakes she brought and told her we'd all have one after she finished her homework. "I want to hang out with your mom for a bit," she told her, pouring us both another glass of wine.

We went onto the back porch and sat on the swing together. "Look what I brought us," she said, pulling out a fresh pack of cigarettes. We had all quit together when I got pregnant. Andy had stayed quit, but Nora and I had been sneaking cigarettes together for years, intermittently between my pregnancy and hers.

"Yes. That is exactly what I need." She smacked the pack loudly, but I shushed her, pointing to the house. She rolled her eyes at me and slid out two cigarettes. I tried not to grab one out of her hands, and, when she lit it for me, I felt my brain doing cartwheels and cheering. I totally got why people were addicted to cigarettes. It is a real shame that they are so awful for you.

My father had caught me smoking with one of the kids who lived a few buildings over from us when I was a teenager. Although I had tried cigarettes a few times before, this might have been the first time I actually smoked one. When I got back to the house, I rushed into the bathroom to scrub my hands, but my dad was waiting for me when I got out.

Like Marilyn, like Matilda, I knew what it was like to grow up with only one parent. My own mother had died in childbirth from the kind of hemorrhaging that doctors somehow still overlook. My father had raised me in a tight-knit Jewish community outside of Philadelphia, doing the best he could, shifting between sorrow and a fierce desire to keep me protected in the face of an unsafe world.

"I want to talk to you about your grandmother, your mother's mother, Myra." He told me, sitting me down to tell me how wonderful she had been, how accepting to him even though he wasn't an Orthodox Jew like my mother's family, how kind, how good at cards, and how much she liked to rub it in when she beat him at backgammon. "She died right before your mother got pregnant with you. Lung cancer." He went on to tell me how at the time no one knew that cigarettes were so bad for your health, but how once we have new knowledge, it is important to use it, how my mother spent every day she had left missing her mother, how I was robbed, growing up without my beautiful mother and my lovely grandmother. And how all of that was why I should never, ever smoke. I know some parents would just scream at you to never smoke because it's bad, but in my household, it came with a whole generational guilt trip and a side of both science and philosophy. And I didn't smoke again until college.

I met Nora and Andy at a study group; we were all in the same large Intro to Mythology class, where the teacher was renowned for his difficult midterms. Andy and Nora were cracking jokes about how Medusa should stop objectifying people and sharing all of their puns to help them remember the equivalent Roman and Greek gods. Andy was two years older, and his sister had decided to go to the same college as her big brother. Andy was a senior, and Nora was a sophomore like me, but she had made sure to sign up for a couple of classes with him. I was so charmed by how funny and kind they were to each other, something I hadn't experienced much as an only child, that when Nora offered me a cigarette before they slipped outside to smoke, I accepted, just for the chance to spend more time with them both.

"So, what's going on?" Nora asked.

"Well, I think I quit my job today," I told her, flushing when I remembered how I had lost control on Niles.

"You think you did?"

"I didn't mean to, but I think I'm done there," I told her, vaguely. "Don't say anything to Matilda. I haven't told her yet."

"Mmmm-hmmmm." She pursed her lips and studied me. "I'm worried about you, you know?" She said it in a way that was reassuring, not annoying, although it was a fine line for me lately.

"I know. I'm worried too," I told her.

"You alright for money if you quit your job?" She asked.

"Yeah, they are going to pay me for at least three more months, and there's still life insurance from Andy."

"Then maybe taking some time off isn't the worst thing in the world," she said.

"I like work," I said, and it was true. I was good at my job, and I liked spending time with that part of my brain. I liked the stress of deadlines and being too busy to think about Andy. I felt a sense of panic as I thought about waking up in the morning and not having a job to go to.

"Then why are you quitting?" she asked. I had been trying to avoid telling her the whole story, but she kept looking at me while I exhaled smoke rings, cocking that eyebrow at me until I started talking. She burst into her loud laughter when I told her about Niles, and for the first time, I could see the humor in it instead of feeling awful and guilty.

"Honestly didn't think you had it in you," she chuckled.

"Me neither," I said. "Shocked the hell out of me."

"I bet you weren't as surprised as that pretentious ass Niles!"

I remembered the shocked look on his face as he looked up at me from the floor, the spilled coffee sopping into his crisp shirt. "It was kind of worth it to see the look on Niles's face," I said. She laughed again.

"It's time for a change," she said. "And a little time off would do you good, it's been a tough year," she said.

"Yeah," I said. "Some years are killers."

"For some people, all the years are killers," she said.

I smoked, holding it into my hurting lungs longer than I should have. I exhaled, and we sat together, swinging, until I heard Matilda rustling around in the kitchen, and we went back inside. I washed my hands for a long time at the sink, hoping Matilda wouldn't mention the smell of smoke.

All About Eve (1950)

I don't think she can act, I don't think she can dance, I don't think she can walk, and I'm sure she can't talk, but there is nothing that either of us can do to keep her from becoming a star.

Joseph Mankiewicz, director
of *All About Eve*, in a memo to
Darryl F. Zanuck, then head
of Twentieth Century Fox

In Marilyn's second major role, we realize she has arrived. Even though it's a small part, it's a big film. *All About Eve* is still, even in 2017, the only movie to ever provide four Oscar nominations for four different female stars: Bette Davis, Celeste Holm, Anne Baxter, and Thelma Ritter.

The set was teeming with female talent, and it must have intimidated Marilyn, who was rumored to have spent too much time throwing up in her dressing room because of her nervousness, too many takes to get down her small comedic scenes as Claudia Caswell, introduced as a "graduate of the Copacabana school of dramatic art," a reference to her sexuality trumping her talent, a joke that would follow Marilyn throughout her career, and she is already satirizing it in her role here.

Marilyn's other big debut in the film is her famous beauty mark on her left cheek, between her nose and mouth. It became a signature look she used for the rest of her career.

Claudia Caswell shows up at Margo Channing's (Bette Davis) party, beauty mark and all, just after Margo delivers the movie's most infamous line, "Fasten your seatbelts, it's going to be a bumpy ride." Margo, an aging theater star, is subject to dramatic evenings, and we can already see her warming up for one as she starts to understand that sweet innocent ingénue Eve (Anne Baxter), whom Margo has hired as her assistant, is actually a sociopath out to steal everything she can from Margo.

In the trope of newbie vs. aging star, Marilyn was destined to never really experience the ripeness of her career, and when we compare her scant dozen years of acting to Bette Davis's sixty-plus year career, we sit in that lost potential, in wondering what she could have done with the gift of time.

Marilyn enters Margo's party, arm candy to an agent who encourages her to go make friends with a Hollywood power player.

"Why do they always look like unhappy rabbits?" Marilyn hilariously asks.

Her other big scene comes later, after she has auditioned for a role in the play in which Margo is the star. In a life-imitating-art moment, the stress of the auditions has made Caswell nauseous.

"Feeling better, my dear?" the agent asks as Marilyn stumble-glows out of the ladies' room.

"Like I just swam the English Channel," Marilyn delivers, rocking slightly and somehow looking both adorable and seasick.

Marilyn was high maintenance, even at this point in her career, and especially with Natasha Lytess on the set shaking her head at Marilyn's every move. Bette Davis had no patience for Marilyn's requests to do eleven takes so she could nail the line about the English Channel when Davis had hundreds of lines to consider. Davis and Monroe did bond over one thing, though, and that was their shared distaste for the movie's producer, Darryl F. Zanuck, Harvey Weinstein's early prototype, widely known for sexually assaulting young actresses.

In the end, the director Joseph L. Mankiewicz won an Oscar for best director, beating out John Huston for *Asphalt Jungle*, among others, and *All About Eve* scored Zanuck the Best Picture as the head of Fox, but, even with all those nominations, none of the women won a damn thing.

Chapter 3

I submitted my resignation letter on Rosh Hashanah, figuring it was a good day for starting over. I told Matilda about it as we ate apples and honey and wished for a sweet new year.

"But I thought you loved that job, Mom," she said.

"There were things I loved about it, but it was time for a change." I told her.

"What are you going to do next?" she asked.

"I don't know yet. I'm going to figure it out."

"Wait, does this mean we're broke? I mean, we don't have Dad anymore, and now you're unemployed."

I didn't like the way "unemployed" sounded, but it was true.

"We're OK for now," I told her. "I don't want you to worry about it. Dad had something called life insurance, where they pay you some money when a person dies, and that will hold us for a while."

She shrugged and dredged her apple through the honey. "If you say so," she said.

I went in the next Sunday and cleared out my office. No one else was around, and I packed my books and cried. I pulled photographs off the wall and sobbed. I had worked there for almost a decade, and I thought about how young I had been when I had first been hired, how Matilda had just been a toddler, and Andy had stayed home with her while he studied for the bar. It felt like I was packing up a whole era of my life in those boxes.

I logged onto my work computer for the last time, clearing out cookies and logging out of everything I could think of, when the headline flashed across the Yahoo homepage:

Hugh Hefner's Final Resting Place?
The Plot He Bought Next to Marilyn...

My memory flashed to that *Playboy* #1 and the way Hefner had used the images of Norma Jeane on the cusp of Marilyn Monroe to finance his whole life, the way he had profited off his pretense of empowering women to exhibit their bodies for the enjoyment of men. I felt differently about it now than I did twenty-five years ago, when *Playboy* was edgy enough to seem enticing. Now that I had a better understanding of Marilyn's plight and a teenaged daughter fielding requests for nudes every time she went on the internet.

The article described how he had purchased the plot next to Marilyn for $72,000 in 1992, claiming "Spending eternity next to Marilyn is too sweet to pass up."

I felt my stomach seize up, the nausea of it, as I realized Norma Jeane had to be buried next to this succubus for all of her days, their very bones mingling together as they deteriorate. Hef never asked her permission. She was long gone by the time he bought the plot next to her. They'd never even met, though Hefner often talked about the connection he felt to her. I tried to soothe the growing feeling of panic by surfing the web: "Athletes Must Stand for Anthem;" "Accusations Against Harvey Weinstein Heat Up;" "Trump Continues Attacks on San Juan Mayor Carmen Yulin Cruz."

Donald Trump had already been president for nearly nine months, and white women had put him in office. Trump joked openly about grabbing pussies and had pending rape cases against him, and seemed to revel in starting feuds with global leaders via Twitter. He was excellent fodder for reality TV and the most horrible person I could imagine to be sitting in the Oval Office.

I remembered the day he was elected so clearly. Matilda had gone to bed with the idea that she would be waking up to the first female president. How I had to walk to her bedroom in the morning and explain that even though Hillary had won by millions of votes, Trump would be taking office. That the country and its antiquated voting laws had somehow chosen this incompetent fool over a smart, qualified woman, and that our job was to accept it. To move on.

It had been the worst year of my life, and the incident at work just seemed like the inevitable conclusion. I spent most of my time thinking about Andy. When we met in college and he still only listened to punk rock, the way we had grown up together, me into an architect and him into a suit-wearing immigration lawyer who never lost his edge but turned into a softy when it came to his daughter.

But most of all, our last day together. I just kept playing it and replaying it. The final second before we got out of bed. Him with that smile in his yellow shirt as he slid on his blazer. I was spending more time crying in the shower than I could even calculate. Sometimes I needed multiple showers a day.

I was still here, and Matilda was still here, but we were both struggling with our rage, the unfairness of a world that would take a sweet man in his prime and let sick old perverts like Trump and Hefner live to a ripe old age.

My breathing was starting to become shallow as I thought about Trump and Hef. I stared out the window, looking out towards the mountains rising up from the desert. I loved that view. I replayed my last day in the office. How much of a difference it would have made if Niles had just said, "This is Miriam Renata, the architect in charge of your project. Please help yourself to the Keurig outside if you'd like some coffee." I could feel the waves of panic starting to knock on my chest. I picked up as many boxes as I could carry and fled.

Luckily, Matilda was at rehearsal when I got home. I went straight to the shower. Instead of obsessing about how much I missed Andy and how I was going to raise my daughter in a country full of Trump-lovers without her father, I started fixating on Marilyn. And Hef. Washing my hair and sobbing about her second husband, baseball great Joe DiMaggio, who assaulted her when they were married and sent roses to her grave every week until he died, or how Hefner built his whole career on Marilyn's perky nipple and never gave her a dime.

Weeks after Hefner was interred, #MeToo started trickling, then flooded, taking over everything. Everywhere I looked, women were calling for change, interrogating their own assaults. Though the movement had started in 2006 with a Black activist named Tarana Burke, it exploded in 2017. Different countries had their own versions: Time's Up, YoTambien, KuToo, Metoo. It was everywhere and impossible to ignore. I was quiet on social media, listening, watching, reading, thinking about my own sexual assaults even if I had never defined them that way before. I thought about that last day of work and how many days before that I had stayed quiet while men had stolen my ideas, had belittled me into being the one who made coffee despite my experience.

I thought back earlier than that, to the lack of female professors in my architecture program, to how my advisor had suggested I drop out if I wanted to focus on having a family, to the college parties I hadn't thought about in years.

I spent most of my freshman year of high school experimenting with newfound adulthood. As I developed into a teenager, my dad had been very strict about where I went and with whom. Boys were not allowed, unless it was with a group that also included girls. I didn't much try to circumvent his rules – there were never any boys I was particularly interested in spending time alone with anyway.

But college gave me the opportunity to launch off from the awkward high schooler I had been, and it didn't take long for me to realize why my father had been trying to protect me. It only took one party that went wrong – me too drunk to find my voice, the trembling bunk beds as the girl above me stuttered, then went silent, and the boy inside of me repeated, "It's OK, it's OK," like a mantra neither of us could say no to.

By the time I met Andy sophomore year, I had already stopped partying, stopped allowing myself to be vulnerable, and stopped talking to boys I didn't know.

Now, I studied my beautifully still-awkward teen daughter, struggling with the phase where she didn't think of herself as sexual, but the world was starting to look at her that way. I could see it in the motion of her long legs, how they colted out from her shorts, the men's eyes starting to follow them. How people who hadn't seen her for a while saying, *oh, Matilda is looking so grown up these days.* The way even Nora started joking about having a son: *At least I only have to worry about one dick.*

I knew it was time to start having the talks with Matilda. Since childhood, I had already empowered her to say "yes" or "no" about what other people might want to do with her body. But now I had to tell her that whatever she said or did might not matter, that no matter how smart she was, men might do things to her that were out of her control. How to defend herself with a multi-tiered layer of strategies that started with what she put on before she left the house and ended with never leaving a friend behind. Or ended with not going home with someone you didn't know. Or maybe tactics around built-in apps in your phone that would allow you to discretely notify authorities in case of an emergency.

"It never ends, does it, Mom?" she asked.

"God help us, even after you're dead you might end up like Marilyn, buried next to an old goat like Hugh Hefner for eternity." It slipped out before I even realized what I was saying.

"What does that mean?"

I pulled up the story on her phone, and she read through it. She looked up at the Marilyn plates.

"I know the plates show her looking sexy, but there was a lot more to her than that." I googled 'Marilyn and books' and showed those to Matilda as well.

"Do you think they're just posed?" my daughter

asked.

"I think it's all the photos of her not reading books that are posed," I answered. "No one wanted her to be smart. No one wanted her to read."

"It's weird," Matilda said. "Why didn't they want her to be smart?"

"It's a good question," I studied Matilda studying Marilyn.

"She was a radical," I told Matilda, pausing to explain what the word meant. "They had to tell her to stop publicly reading books about socialists and keep her mouth shut about how she liked Castro and civil rights."

"Really? I've never heard any of that about her before." She looked at the Marilyn plates more closely. "And why is Hugh Hefner buried next to her?"

"I mean, I guess it's technically a crypt? Buried isn't the right word. Interred."

"Whatever. It's fucking bullshit is what it is," she said.

It was the glow of her eyes that caught my attention more than the curse; they had caught fire.

"How can this be allowed?" she shrieked, her thirteen-year-old voice breaking.

All I could do was hold her and agree as she repeated, *it's not fair* into my chest and shoulders. I knew she was crying about more than Marilyn, more than Hef, but I just held her and let her sob.

I heard her cry herself to sleep that night, went to check on her when it got quiet. She was staring up at the ceiling, tears pathed down her cheeks, but her eyes were dry. I kissed her head, and she turned to me with so much sadness that it caught my breath, but when she woke in the morning, the fire was back.

She poured herself a cup of coffee. "I have a proposition," she told me.

"You OK?" I said, and she let me hug her, which was becoming rarer in the mornings.

"Nope. Not really."

"I'm sorry, honey. The world can be an ugly place. I wish I could hide that from you for longer."

"What I'm worried about is Marilyn," she said. "I think we should go dig her up. Or un-inter her, or whatever the right word is."

I laughed.

"I'm not kidding, Mom," Matilda glared at me. "I think we should get her away from Hugh Hefner."

"OK, I'm pretty sure that grave robbing is a felony," I told her.

"Look, the world is messed up. I already knew that, but our little talk yesterday just made me think about it more. I saw what they did to Hillary. I've been paying attention to MeToo. I know about Harvey Weinstein and Bill Cosby."

"Don't even say Bill Cosby's goddamned name," I said. I had grown up watching *The Cosby Show*, and so had she, for a whole summer, when she broke her arm and we found the reruns on Netflix. Now just the sound of *The Cosby Show* made me quiver with rage. All that time I thought it was wholesome family entertainment, he had been drugging, and raping, and lecturing other Black men about their morality. I couldn't even hear the theme song without feeling nauseous.

"So, here's the thing, I see all these women out there, facing their accusers, and I just think we should do something, too."

"Look, you know I love Norma Jeane." I deliberately used her original name, thinking about the girl-woman it evoked. With her long legs and dark, honey-colored wild curls, Matilda looked a bit like Norma Jeane. "Let's talk about something more reasonable. You do have a fall break next week, and I'm just getting started looking for a new job. What if we take a road trip to California? We can go to the beach and visit Norma Jeane's grave."

"Really?" The fire died down, replaced by the little girl glow I was relieved to see. "That sounds awesome, Mom!"

I had been thinking about something to disrupt the heaviness of fall anyway. Once winter settles in Colorado, it tends to stay awhile, even where we lived in Grand Junction, the west side of the state. We hadn't taken a beach trip this year, and suddenly putting my toes in the Pacific seemed like an idea I couldn't pass up.

"Put Junction to L.A. in your phone," I said. "How far?"

"Eleven hours and thirteen minutes."

"OK, so we'll leave Friday," I told her. "We'll spend a night somewhere along the way."

"But we can definitely go to Marily – I mean, Norma Jeane's grave, right?"

"Sure, we can."

"I'm all in," she said, and finished her coffee.

As Young as You Feel, Love Nest, Let's Make It Legal (1951)

Don't forget, darling, tomorrow you're going to be a star.

Sign hung over the casting couch of
a Hollywood producer in the 1950s

1950 was a good year for many of us. The war was over, the men were home, peace and prosperity were rising. For Marilyn, her 1950 roles in *The Asphalt Jungle* and *All About Eve* were small but well-chosen, thanks to agent Johnny Hyde's inside connections and advocacy, and they put her in the upper echelon of actors and directors, getting her the attention she deserved.

1951 was a big year for Marilyn Monroe's career, but it was a hard year, a devastating year, the year that taught her no one cared what she acted like, they only cared what she looked like, lessons we were all struggling with as we were retaught our places after the independence of the war years. It was the year of her first known suicide attempt when it became clear that even the shining star of success on the horizon wasn't enough to save her.

Hyde died in December of 1950, and his last act was to negotiate a shitty-standard contract with Twentieth Century Fox for Marilyn. The contract paid her a guaranteed weekly salary and tied her to the whims of Twentieth Century Fox. The contract was renewable for seven years, and the studio had sole decision-making over its extension. She had no choice about what she was cast in. She could be loaned out to other studios. The advantage was that she had a guaranteed income. The disadvantages were something she fought against for the rest of her career, especially when her movies started making millions and she was still being paid a weekly pittance.

It also put her in the hands of Zanuck, who was a ruthless studio head who lived for fucking and breaking young actresses. He later admitted that he hated Marilyn, and we heard rumors about his sexual assault of her for years. Hyde was no longer around to throw his body between Marilyn and the wreckage.

The 1951 films Zanuck selected for Marilyn were unexceptional, the roles as bland as possible, though Marilyn made every effort to make the most of them, there wasn't much depth to find. In *As Young as You Feel*, Marilyn plays Harriet, the big boss's secretary, and spends a great deal of time saying "Yes, Mr. McKinley" while rocking a sexy black dress suit.

Love Nest has a contrived plot about a veteran played by Jack Paar who returns to New York City to find his wife has bought a rundown apartment building in Gramercy Park. He rents a spare apartment to his old army buddy, Bobbie, who happens to be Marilyn, back from her time in the war as a WAC. The wife, understandably, is pissed that her husband never mentioned that Bobbie is a foxy babe. He responds by saying, "You wouldn't discriminate against a veteran just because of sex, would you?" Various types of mayhem ensue, the best of which is a montage that cuts back and forth between the wife's prim efficiency and Marilyn's glorious sexiness as she disrobes and showers to the tune of jazz orchestral music.

Let's Make It Legal is described in the trailer as the "hilarious story of a lady who was only slightly married and two guys who were only slightly gentlemen!" Marilyn as Joyce Mannering is the kind of sexy trouble who has no choice but to show up in a bathing suit and simper lines like, "Your father has been so divine to me even I sometimes feel like calling him Daddy." Although she works to find the humor, and she still glows on the screen with that otherworldly quality directors and critics were starting to recognize, the roles were asides, teases, possibilities of what was to come, warnings from Zanuck.

Chapter 4

I never wanted to be Marilyn – it just happened.
Marilyn's like a veil I wear over Norma Jeane.

Marilyn Monroe, as quoted
by photographer Lawrence
Schiller in *Vanity Fair*

We packed Charlotte, my white functional but not fashionable Highlander, Thursday night and loaded our last-minute supplies and cups of coffee in the darkness of Friday morning.

"Do we have everything?" I went through my mental checklist.

"As long as I have my phone and a toothbrush, I feel like I'll make it," Matilda said, tying her hair back into a pink scrunchy.

"And the good news is, we can buy a toothbrush if we need it."

"I'm always down for a new toothbrush," she said, smiling at me, and we held hands for a second, resting them on the divider between us. I started the car.

"Wait!" I thought of something and jumped out, running into the garage to rummage around on a storage shelf until I found the small tube. I slid it in my pocket with a short prayer that I never had to use it.

"Whatcha got?" Matilda asked as I slid it into the

glove compartment.

"Your dad felt like women should carry mace. A pocketknife, something. He bought me that a couple years ago."

"He told me that, too, about a knife," Matilda answered, pulling Andy's Swiss Army knife out of the top of the backpack at her feet.

"Your dad always had that on him," I said, remembering the way it looked in his hand. I could feel my throat tighten.

"I brought this, too," Matilda pulled out a compact black case.

"What is it?" I glanced down, unsure what I was seeing.

"It's a Taser," she said. "I bought it on Amazon."

"What? You bought a Taser and didn't even ask me about it?"

"I was worried you would say no," she said.

"Well, of course I would say no! Who says yes to a thirteen-year-old having a Taser?"

"Dad did. Right before."

"He did not."

"Mom, he did. I was going to talk about it with you, I was, but then, you know, I didn't. And then it seemed like it was too late because I hadn't already."

"Why do you feel like you need a Taser?" I asked her.

She laughed, and it was too bitter to be coming from the mouth of a girl. "Be for real. Have you seen the world?"

"Was there something specific that made you discuss it with your dad?" I asked.

"Just this creepy boy at school," she said.

"Wait, you've been taking this to school?"

"Dad said I should have it on me all the time, but I

should put it away and never talk about it, just to have it when I needed it."

I couldn't decide which parental response to land on. Outrage seemed a little out-of-touch, given the state of the world. I settled for curiosity.

"Have you ever used it?"

"I shot it at the tree in the front yard, just to practice."

"Never on a human, though?"

"No," she said, "never on a human."

"Good," I said.

"Yeah," she said, and put it back in the top of her backpack. I focused on backing out of the driveway.

"Can I be in charge of music?" Matilda asked.

"Of course," I said.

"I've got this whole Marilyn playlist worked out," she said. "I've been researching." She started with Ella Fitzgerald, "Stairway to the Stars."

"I didn't know you liked jazz."

"Did you know that Norma Jeane and Ella were friends?" she asked.

"I knew Norma Jeane helped her get her first major gig in L.A. by telling the club manager that she would come and sit in front with all her movie star buddies for the week that Ella was playing there," I said.

"Yeah, I was reading about that last night," Matilda said. "She and Ella were tight. They both had mentally ill mothers, they both were in awful orphanages when they were teenagers. They really bonded and hung out. Ella just wasn't into Marilyn's lifestyle with the drinking and the drugs. I guess she had enough of that in the music world. But Ella always said Marilyn was ahead of her time and didn't even know it."

"I'm glad you're doing some research about her. I think the only layer a lot of people see from her is this kind of silly sex kitten, which is a role she played very well. But she had so many more layers than that."

"She really did," Matilda said. "You know, I've always known who she was. I guess I grew up looking at those plates and just thought of her as part of the family, like your mom. Somebody I didn't really know but felt close to."

"It's funny, I felt the same way. Just that sense of her always being around, like a relative or a benevolent presence."

"I just never really thought of who she was as a person until you told me about the thing with Hugh Hefner," Matilda added. "But since then, I've been reading about her literally every night. I don't know, I've been a little obsessed."

"You're not the first person to get a little obsessed with Marilyn," I told her. She looked out the window and turned up "A Tisket, A Tasket." You could hear the way Ella had influenced Marilyn's singing, especially in this song, Ella toying with the kind of little girl breathiness that Marilyn invoked throughout her career, though Ella quickly moves to the power and the soul of the song, and it took Marilyn a lot longer to get there.

We got onto I-70, headed west. As the sun rose from the east, the horizon started to glow, catching the light of the desert rocks, showing the layers of landscape. Through the windshield, the desert in front of us became more spread out, more desolate.

"I'm going to stop for gas here soon," I told Matilda. "Any requests?"

"Something with a Starbucks?" she said.

"That might be too much to ask for in the desert," I told her.

"Something with snacks?" she asked.

"Done," I said, watching for an upcoming exit that boasted a gas station.

Pumping gas, I watched her emerge from the gas station, still in her pajama pants and thin t-shirt. She was framed in the doorway with the morning light flowing around her, and I was moved by the impending beauty of her, the potential of everything she was becoming.

"Dayum!" The reverie was interrupted by a low wolf whistle as a man in a truck with a MAGA hat pulled into the gas bay next to me. "Would you look at that?" I was confused for a minute, then followed his eyes.

"THAT is my thirteen-year-old daughter," I hissed at him.

"You're the mom?" he asked, and Matilda was beside me at that point. "You two are a fine-looking pair," he looked us slowly up and down.

"Ewwwwww! Gross," Matilda said, sliding into the car.

I thought about all the times I had let men sexualize me and remained quiet about it, how I'd been taught to embrace it, to use it to my advantage. I thought about my daughter sitting in the seat, how she deserved a world that let her develop into whatever strong, smart, quirky, brilliant woman she would be without trying to mold her into a sex object.

"What did you say to us?" I turned slowly in the man's direction.

"Whoa, sweetheart, it was a compliment. Just say thank you."

I looked him up and down, the same way he had examined me. "I'm not your sweetheart."

"Damn, honey, just smile. You looked so much prettier when you were smiling."

My brain broke and disconnected from my body, and

a flash of murderous crimson haze filled my eyesight. I pulled the gas hose out of the tank and sprayed it all over him, drenching his smarmy face and pushed out belly, his truck, and his boots.

I stretched the hose as far as I could, arcing the nozzle to douse his hat, watching it turn dark as it was saturated with gasoline. He sputtered, and when I pointed the hose towards his gaping maw, he snorted and gasped, retching and spitting it back out.

"How pretty am I now?" I yelled at him, pointing the nozzle into his eyes. He squinched them closed and made a gurgling bellow as he swung his arms around, trying to grab me.

His boot slipped on the greasy pool of gasoline, and he hit the ground, choking and squawking, mauling the air. The way he was laying there, like a turtle who couldn't flip itself back over, made me giggle, and then the haze receded, and I hung the gas hose back up and got in the driver's seat. Matilda's face was a mixture of shock and respect.

"Buckle up, dear," I said, trying to ride the wave of adrenaline as it hit me, and we pulled out of the gas station.

Don't Bother to Knock (1952)

*Marilyn seems to have had a continual craving for reassur-
ance, which I tried my damnedest to supply… Certainly she
had one overriding ambition beside which nothing else mattered. That was to be a great big international star.*

Roy Ward Baker, a British director
making his American film debut
with *Don't Bother to Knock*, went on
to direct a range of films and television, with a special focus on horror

We enter *Don't Bother to Knock* as one might stroll into a
glamorous hotel in the 1950s, which is its setting. We
open the door, and we're admiring the decor, including Anne Bancroft in her first role as a torch singer, and
then we find ourselves sucked into the casual intrigue
of break-ups, awards banquets, and elevator mishaps,
but as soon as Marilyn's Nell Forbes hits the scene, it
becomes clear that, like much of this decade, things are
very wrong once we get underneath the surface.

Forbes has been convinced by her uncle, the elevator
operator, to try her hand babysitting Bunny, an adorable
tyke whose high-society parents are partying downstairs.
From the time Nell discusses her lack of babysitting
experience in the elevator to the time we see her trying
on the absent mother's negligée and jewelry, we feel

unsettled. Not worried, exactly, because what babysitter hasn't rifled through this or that, but the clear cloud of concern settles in when Nell flirts with the man in the hotel window across the way. Jed Towers (Richard Widmark), the man Anne Bancroft just broke up with between sets in the lounge, also happens to be a pilot, which, we come to learn, is the same profession as Nell's deceased fiancé, whose death apparently drove Nell over the edge of sanity.

Once Jed shows up at her hotel room door, things go from unsettling to deeply troubling pretty quickly.

Like Norma Jeane Baker's mother, the character, Nell, was committed to a mental institution. We heard rumors that Gladys Baker was committed after trying to drown Norma Jeane in the bathtub or set fire to her in bed, and we end up waiting with bated breath for Nell to do something equally awful to poor Bunny, who escapes with merely being tied up and gagged, thanks to Jed's rescue. This role is one of Marilyn's most powerful performances, which we can fully appreciate if we understand her own history with mental illness and how she used this role to channel her mother.

While the film was largely a flop, the real issue with it seemed to be Marilyn's attempt to be taken seriously as an actress. A *Variety* review at the time states that "Monroe's role seems an odd choice, and in this she's anything but glamorous, despite her donning a negligée."

Just as Jed wants an easy romp and a little fling but has to navigate the reality of Nell's depths, so do we as viewers, as voyeurs, have to question our own relationship to Marilyn. She's there, in a negligée, looking as sexy as ever, and yet, the scars on her wrists and the razor blades in her hands don't allow any of us to simply objectify her. She defies and complicates the male gaze rippling from the interior of the film outward. Seen through a later lens, we can recognize the brilliance of her approach, but critics at the time were offended that their sex object was talking back to them.

Chapter 5

I met them all, phoniness and failure were all over them…
And you saw Hollywood with their eyes – an overcrowded
brothel, a merry-go-round with beds for horses.

Marilyn Monroe, *My Story*

It was just after the exit for Green River came and went, watching a dust devil spin off on the arroyo, that my daughter decided it was time to process the gas station scene. We had spent the last hour enjoying the playlist she had composed for the trip. She was more into pop, ballads, and show tunes than I was, but still had solidly good taste in music, favoring women of all eras with powerhouse voices. She turned the volume down, just as the first strains of "Landslide" started to play.

"So, Mom, want to talk about it?" she asked in a neutral tone.

"Well, I don't know what to say. At least it's been long enough that the police probably aren't going to pull us over." I wasn't sure what the legalities were of spraying someone in the face with gasoline, but it been on my mind a lot the last hundred miles.

"It was totally badass!"

"See, that's the problem, I don't want you to do that to someone. I'm still worried they might have my license plate number and track me down. I lost my temper and, after some reflection, I don't think that was the right thing to do."

"I bet he thinks twice before he says creepy things to the next girl," she said.

"OK, that's probably true."

"And it definitely made me feel like the next time some douchebag says something gross to me, I shouldn't just smile at him," she said.

"Well, that's also true," I said. "No girl or woman should have to put up with that shit."

"Exactly! Seems like a positive lesson to me!"

"But here's the thing: it's not OK to attack people with physical violence, no matter what. If I were a stronger person, I would have been able to have the same effect on him and you without resorting to violence."

"Be peaceful, be courteous, obey the law, respect everyone, but if someone puts his hand on you, send him to the cemetery."

"What was that?"

"I've been reading *The Autobiography of Malcolm X*," she said.

"What? Since when?"

"Well, we read *March* for school, remember? The graphic novel about the John Lewis story?"

I did remember. The third book in the series had just come out, and Matilda's Language Arts class had read them all.

"And, I mean, all the respect to John Lewis, keeping his cool like that. But I wondered how other people did it, and in class, the teacher mentioned something about how not everyone believed in peaceful resistance. And then he told us about Malcolm X. So, a couple of us started reading his autobiography."

"Wait, weren't you supposed to check in with me

before you read a new book?" Our general rule since she was eight was that before she started any new movie, or show, or book, we had a conversation about it. At what point did I let that go?

"Uhhhh, it's an autobiography!"

"So now you think that if someone lays a hand on you, you should send them to the cemetery?"

"Well, I thought it was a good quote, especially since we're headed to a cemetery."

"OK. Fair. I can appreciate it as a joke about a trip with a cemetery at the end."

"But I don't like people to touch me without my permission," she said.

"That's true. And that fool is lucky he didn't touch either of us."

"So, would you have sent him to the cemetery if he had?" she asked.

I didn't know how to answer that, so I turned the music back up. *Hamilton*'s "Helpless" was playing as we slipped through the Utah landscape, spires of desert rocks looming over us, white-capped mountains outlined in the rearview mirror.

A billboard advertising Beaver, Utah: "Not just a stop, we're your destination!" made me flashback to when I was about thirteen years old, the same age as Matilda now. I had matured a little faster than her, or maybe it was the era of the 1980s, the way parents weren't much around, so we figured out a lot of things for ourselves, including boys, cigarettes, and other pastimes I was glad Matilda had not yet discovered. Matilda was still goofy, wanting tucked in at night, wearing scrunchies, experimenting with makeup as an offshoot of her theater performances, but not much interested in boys, but at thirteen, I had already been researching my questions about sexy versus beautiful.

* * *

"One good-looking beaver," I heard the man say.

"Going to be one good-looking beaver," the other man corrected, and they cackled together. I looked up from the costume I was wearing to see the principal and my teacher looking at Kimmy Gibson. She had definitely figured out way more about sexy than I ever would, even at twelve. She was dressed up as the tooth fairy in our homegrown school play about holidays and traditions. My dad had sent me to public middle school after years of Jewish Day School, and, as one of the few Jewish kids, I was dressed up as Judas Maccabee, a warrior costume. I watched with the men as Kimmy floated around the stage, her long brown legs stretching out from the costume, her breasts requiring the full bra that I had seen the boys in our classroom snap many times, while teachers in the 1980s rolled their eyes and told us, "Boys will be boys."

"Why are you calling her a beaver? She's a fairy," I asked them.

The principal chuckled uncomfortably in a way that I was coming to realize grownups did when you caught them doing something wrong.

"Ha. Umm. No, Miriam, you didn't hear us right."

"Oh," I said, still watching Kimmy as she twirled around the stage, wishing I were the tooth fairy instead of a warrior.

* * *

Beaver, Utah, rolled past us in the rearview mirror, and Interstate 15 stretched out in front of us, the sun at high noon, the red rocked mountains parched and desolate, the road buzzing with out-of-state license plates and MAC trucks.

Niagara (1953)

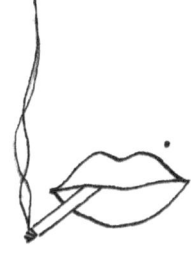 In Marilyn's first starring role, we are introduced to her naked, under the sheets, smoking a cigarette, as femme fatale Rose Loomis. Her husband, George, comes in, and she quickly puts the cigarette out, pretending to be asleep. If we're still thinking about Marilyn films as metaphors for the 1950s, this one has a surface of sexy red dresses and seductive dance scenes, but underneath is untreated mental illness, PTSD of war, and the poison of unacknowledged violence.

Niagara was the first of three Marilyn features released during 1953, each building on her star power, casting a bigger net for fans until her box office draw seemed unstoppable. Director Henry Hathaway was a good fit with Marilyn at this phase of her career. He appreciated her acting and was willing to take risks with some of the shots, including the longest walk-in cinema history, when Rose, wearing a black skirt and red sweater, takes one hundred and sixteen feet of film just to strut her inimitable stuff in a shot that defines male gaze. Hathaway enjoyed playing with jump cuts between Rose and Niagara, and the film's publicity underlines the way women's sexuality was seen as both beautiful and dangerous, calling both Marilyn and the monument a "raging torrent of emotion even nature can't control."

Between the shots of the falls roaring and gushing, the Cullers arrive and are scheduled to check into the cabin that Marilyn is stretched out in, but Marilyn isn't going anywhere, and George really isn't going anywhere, so the Cullers have to settle for an alternate cabin, though the view of the falls makes up for it.

Rose Loomis looks sexy in cute shorts and then an elegant red dress, about which Mrs. Culler notes, "You have to be planning to wear a dress like that since you're fourteen," and we all know that Marilyn was. Rose probably just wants to love neurotic war hero George Loomis, but since therapy and acknowledgement of PTSD weren't really things in the 1950s, there is a complicated murder plot that ultimately results in Rose's death.

All the rat-faced white guys look the same, while Marilyn seems to glow like the camera was made for her, from that opening nude scene, through the red dress, all the way into the running around the slick waterfalls while the Cullers try to figure out what the hell is going on, Mrs. Culler so invested in saving Rose, or saving George, or saving somebody that she doesn't even notice that her own rat-faced husband took three years to bring her on a honeymoon that is really just a glorified work trip.

But here's the part that no one talks about, which is that Marilyn could act. Even though she illuminates the

screen, there is more than that; she bares her soul with the flicker of her face and the wiggle of the hips, and at some point, we, like the Cullers, realize that her looks are the least interesting part of who she is.

Chapter 6

I had the radio on.

Marilyn, in a *Time* magazine interview, when asked if it was true that
she had nothing on when posing for
her infamous nude calendar shoot

We found the exit for Interstate 15 and said our goodbyes
to Interstate 70, so it felt like we were actually on a road
trip now, departed from our hometown road, headed
for the Nevada border. The road was hot, baking, and
air-conditioning on high was the only solution. Outside
the car was barren, Clint Eastwood overlaid on top of
Puebla, Shoshone, Paiute, kind of landscape, the setting
of a thousand delusional Westerns up against the buttes
cresting and towering into crumbling rocks as the occasional drift of tumbleweed blew across the road.

"Son of a Preacher Man" was playing, and I realized
that Matilda might be old enough to watch *Pulp Fiction.*
She had inherited my love of the soundtrack without
yet seeing the movie. I thought about the diner scene,
where John Travolta schools Uma Thurman on Marilyn Monroe versus Mamie Van Doren. All the ingrained
Marilyn references in so many cultural touchpoints, how
ever-present Marilyn seems to be, even now, almost sixty
years after her death, how her ghost still wanders around

Hollywood, and most of the rest of the country as well. Maybe even the world.

I watched a spire that looked painted in the baking sunlight, the rings of greens giving way to yellows as it reached towards the sun, when Matilda's scream pulled me back to the road.

"Mommmmmmmmmm!" she shrieked, and I looked back in time to see a massive jackrabbit charging directly into our path. Hopping isn't quite the right word; this thing lumbered, but it was too late to even swerve, or beep, or flinch before the grill of the car made contact with a soft wumph as the body gave way to the metal. I felt the impact down in my stomach as an immediate wave of nausea washed over me.

"Nooooo!" she howled, and I just kept going because what else could I do but drive? There was no chance the rabbit was alive; nothing to do on the interstate but continue our journey. I looked at Matilda, her face had gone blank. Dusty Springfield crooned about the only boy who could ever reach her, and I turned the music down and tried to take Matilda's hand.

"I'm sorry," I told her. "I didn't see it in time." She ripped her hand back from me, and I watched her face as the shadow of despair fell over it, crumpling into sobs so hard she couldn't catch her breath.

"You killed it!" she screamed at me, rage in her voice, "You should have stopped!"

"I'm so sorry, honey. It was too late," I said.

"We need to go back! We need to help it."

"We can't turn around on the interstate. There's nothing we can do," I told her. "There's no way it survived. I hit it straight on."

She sobbed uncontrollably, smashing her forehead against her window.

"Matilda, I'm sorry," I repeated as I felt the pain emanating from her. I thought about what a hard year this has been for her and how much loss she has weathered. How most days she does OK, she gets out of bed, she goes to school, she still takes math tests, and eats breakfast in the morning.

"You suck, Mom!" She howled at me. I wanted to stop and clutch her to me to hug her so hard she couldn't get any more crying out.

She smeared her arm, collecting the snot and tears into her thin forearm while she glared at me.

"You don't understand," she said.

She spent the next fifty miles just staring out the window before she finally reached over to take my hand.

"Ewwww, you have so much snot absorbed into this hand, I'm not sure I can hold it," I joked.

"Do you miss your mom and dad?" Matilda asked.

I looked at her in the passenger seat, her red smudged up face with the desert landscape whirling by. "I mean, I missed my mom my whole life, but that was different because I never even really had the chance to get to know her. So, I missed not knowing her more than anything. I missed the holes she left behind and not seeing what my dad was like before he had all those holes in him."

"Yeah, that makes sense," Matilda said.

"I do miss my dad every day," I told her. "At the weirdest times, too. Like when I read that Hef died, I wanted to call my dad and talk to him about it. And then I realized I don't even remember what his voice sounds like anymore. I can't recall it in my head on demand, anyway. Sometimes I hear it when I dream about him."

"Yeah, I keep thinking about how I never get to talk to Dad again," she said.

"I got to have my dad well into adulthood is the difference," I told her. "It's not fair that you have to live the whole rest of your life without your dad there to be part of it." Her face crumpled again, and I held her hand and let her cry until she finally closed her eyes and was quiet, enough grief released that she was exhausted and slept.

While she slept, I thought about Andy and how much he loved Matilda. What a great dad he was. How he went to every one of her theater performances, every night, every matinee. I would usually only attend one or two – it was hard for me to see the same play over and over, but he would go to every single one. When I asked him if he ever got bored, he told me that seeing the way Matilda's face would light up on the stage and the way she would say a word a little differently each time or find a new expression to give depth to a character, even if it was Captain Hook, was his favorite thing in the world. I remembered him saying, more than anything else, he just loved to see her doing something she loved.

I was surprised when I looked down to see the low-gas indicator had turned on. "Shit!"

"What is it? I'm here." Matilda sat up in the seat, rubbing the tear-glazed sleep out of her eyes.

"I don't want to alarm you, but could you maybe check and see where the closest gas station is?"

She pulled out her phone. "Should be up here in about five miles," she said.

"Whew, that's good." She pressed her forehead against the window, and I pressed the button that counted down exactly how many miles Charlotte had left.

"We've got thirteen miles left on this tank, so no problem," I told her, and she grunted in acknowledgement.

"OK, should be this exit here," she gestured towards the next exit sign, and we both saw the "Closed" sign at the same time.

"Wait, did that say, 'Closed?'" I asked as the sign moved quickly to our rearview mirror.

"It must have meant, like, the restaurant or something was closed," Matilda mumbled, pulling her phone back out and tapping buttons.

As we approached the exit, we could see the bulldozers and diggers from a half mile away, long enough to realize that the exit, the gas station, and all access to it was closed. We watched it come; we watched it go.

"This is not good," I told her. "What's the next exit?"

"Shit, Mom, it's twenty miles away."

"Oh, no. No, no, no. There's no way Charlotte is going to make it twenty miles. There's nothing closer?" I wracked my brain to think about how far it had been since the last gas station and whether I should turn around, but all I could think about was how Andy would have never let this happen, how Andy always had all the stops mapped out before a road trip even started and never let the car get below a quarter of a tank, even if we were just driving around town. I had always been more of a press-my-luck kind of lady.

"I think it's twenty miles, Mom. What should we do?"

Charlotte was already showing nine miles left before she was empty. I had occasionally gotten her down to zero, but you could tell that she was running on fumes at that point.

"OK, let me think," I said, my voice a little hysterical. It was well over a hundred degrees outside. Should I pull over somewhere that looked marginally safer, or should I push my luck and see how far I could make it?

"Try to get AAA on the phone right now," I said, giving her the details of our policy and pointing her towards the glove compartment. "They'll come and help us if we don't make it." She called them and started working through their menu to preemptively ask for help as I watched the miles tick away on Charlotte.

We hit zero, and I tried driving a slow even fifty miles per hour since I had heard that was the most gas-efficient speed, but my hands started to sweat when a giant truck blared past us, and I started looking for safe places to pull over.

A sign came up showing we had five miles to go for the next exit. "Triple A wants an address of where we are," Matilda said.

"OK, tell them to hold on a minute, and we'll give them the next mile marker," I said, hoping for a long downhill to carry us the last four miles. Three miles now. Charlotte had already blanked out the zero miles left, replacing it with two dashes.

Two miles to go.

"What do you want me to tell roadside assistance?"

"Maybe we're going to make it," I whispered, not wanting to say it aloud, even as Charlotte starting drifting down the exit ramp, the gas station in sight. "Maybe we're going to make it," I said a little louder, as we breezed through the stop sign and into the gas station. "Tell them we're going to make it!" I pulled up to the pump, patting Charlotte lovingly.

The gas station even had a Dairy Queen, which felt like the most serendipitous of all possibilities. I sent Matilda in for mint Oreo Blizzards as I filled up the thirsty car. After scrubbing the windshield and silently thanking Charlotte for her perseverance, I knelt to check the grill, to see if there was any remaining Jack Rabbit fur, when I realized that the critter had taken its own revenge.

The bumper was crushed in, the bolts undone, inches

off the ground.

"What the actual fuck?" I yelled, just as Matilda emerged, delighted, with Blizzards in hand. The prim lady in a dress at the next pump glared at me.

"What's going on, Mom?" Matilda rushed over to inspect the damage with me. "Wait, the rabbit did that?"

"I guess? I had no idea a rabbit could do that kind of damage."

"It was a big ass rabbit," Matilda muttered, and it made me laugh. A fly circled the ice cream, trying to land on the protruding spoon. "What do we do now?" Matilda asked.

"Let's eat our ice cream and celebrate not running out of gas," I told her, and we pulled the car up to park in front of the store and sat on the curb, taking a moment to savor the overly sweet ice cream.

"Sometimes you have to celebrate the little victories," I told Matilda.

"Yeah," she said.

"Is this still your favorite flavor?"

"I don't think I even know what my favorite flavor is," she said. "I bet I haven't even tasted it yet."

"You've got a lot of flavors ahead of you, that's true," I told her as we slurped up the fake mint bottom.

Fortified with the cold sugar, I went back into the store and bought a range of zip ties and cargo straps. Luckily, it was a big truck stop kind of gas station, so I had a few options.

I laid down on the scorching payment, looking up into Charlotte's grill, and Matilda helped me feed the ropes and straps through until we had everything tied back together enough to limp through the rest of our trip.

"I guess I'll call the insurance company when we get

to the hotel," I told her as we piled back into Charlotte.

"At least we didn't run out of gas," she replied, and it made me giggle.

"Your face when we hit that bunny, though!"

"I'll never hear Dusty Springfield the same way again," she laughed. "Right before you hit the bunny, I was looking at her face on my playlist and thinking how she looks like a secret sociopath. Now I'll always think of her as a hidden bunny-killing monster."

"Better her than me, I guess." I backed the car up, and we were back on the road with a full tank of gas.

"OK, Mom, but from now on, we don't go more than half a tank before we have our plan for the next gas stop, OK?"

"Deal," I told her. And we shook on it.

Gentlemen Prefer Blondes / How to Marry a Millionaire (1953)

I found Marilyn Monroe alert, enthusiastic, and especially hungry for knowledge, for being better… she wanted so much to be so perfect… she never felt she was ready to face the camera… but the moment she arrived in front of the camera, there was this romance, this love affair between her and the lens.

Jean Negulesco, director of *How to Marry a Millionaire*, the first film fully shot in Cinemascope and in stereo

When we look at the arc of Marilyn's career, 1953 was the year she made it. Between the serious acting of *Niagara* and the musical and comedic skills she showed in *Gentlemen Prefer Blondes* and *How to Marry a Millionaire*, it was becoming clear that Marilyn was in full bloom as an actress of tremendous talent and range. So what if, because of her contracts, she was still only making $500 a week while her movies were making millions? And if Jane Russell was paid $200,000 for a film that Marilyn was only paid a few thousand dollars for, all the more reason for the studio to love her.

Gentlemen Prefer Blondes, adapted from the Anita Loos novel and the 1949 stage play, showcases Marilyn's Lorelei Lee in full Technicolor, sumptuous costuming, and good company. She and Jane Russell got along famously. Perhaps no scene in the movie is as hilarious as the one where Dorothy (Jane Russell) spoofs Marilyn in a courtroom farce where she pretends to be Lorelei Lee, perfectly imitating Marilyn's intimate whisper-voice.

Other highlights of the film include Jane Russell's subversive "Isn't There Anyone Here for Love?" which turns the male gaze upside down by using a chorus line of hunky male Olympic athletes in the most homoerotic tribute to male athleticism this side of the *Top Gun* volleyball scene. And of course, the big showstopper, the truly iconic "Diamonds are a Girl's Best Friend," showcases all of Marilyn's singing, dancing, breathy sexuality in a pink satin gown and big sparkly diamonds and has been paid tribute for six decades now, from Madonna to Beyoncé.

But maybe no scene is as simply Marilyn as when her fiancé Gus accompanies her on board the boat and she tests out the bed by bouncing on it, leaving us to understand that as far-ranging as Marilyn's talents may have been, nobody, no body, bounces on a bed the way Marilyn does.

How to Marry a Millionaire was the last movie of Marilyn's big year, and it cemented her place as a star in Fox's highest-grossing picture of the year. It co-stars Lauren Bacall and Betty Grable as a trio of young ladies trying to set themselves up to meet gentlemen who are "holding" rather than just falling in love with the same old "gas pump jockeys." Their scam is renting a very elegant, furnished New York City apartment, even though they regularly have to sell all the furniture to make ends meet.

Gossip columnists were poised to make the worst of the set, hoping the stars would rip each other to pieces, but Lauren Bacall and Betty Grable were fast friends, and, according to Bacall, they made a pact to treat Marilyn with as much kindness as possible. Grable, heading out to pasture as she neared forty, famously assured, "Honey, I've had mine. Go get yours." And even though Bacall expressed some frustration with Marilyn's constant delays and insecurities, she recalls working through them with patience, trying her best to be supportive. The main drama seems to have come from Natasha Lytess, who was still ever-present and rumored to constantly erode any confidence Marilyn had while filming a scene and undermine everyone else on the set as well, including the director, Jean Negulesco.

The film itself had additional challenges and rewards – Negulesco took advantage of the tools of Cinemascope and stereo sound, beginning the film with a full orchestra performance and peppering it with amazing shots of New York City that had never been experienced in widescreen before. While the film itself is a fairly simple comedy, Negulesco elevated not just the performances and camaraderie of his stars, but the visual and audio aspects to turn in a film that was more than the sum of its parts.

Though Marilyn had started the film with bottom billing as the least known of the trio of stars, by the time it was released she was the biggest movie star of them all, and publicity of the film gave her top billing. By June of 1953, we admired her joining Jane Russell to add her handprints to the Hollywood Walk of Fame. We could see that she had made it; to those of us looking in, it seemed all her dreams of success and stardom were being realized.

The film premiered in Los Angeles in November 1953, and inside the Fox Wilshire Theatre, Marilyn joined Lauren Bacall and Bacall's husband, Humphrey Bogart, in photographs that have become the epitome of old Hollywood's elegance. The night meant a lot to Marilyn. Speaking to reporters outside, Marilyn glittered, 'This is just about the happiest night of my life. It's like when I was a little girl and pretended wonderful things were happening to me. Now they are."

Chapter 7

I'm not interested in money. I just want to be wonderful.

Marilyn Monroe, in an interview with Pete Martin in 1956

"OK," I said, glancing at my phone, "we should start thinking about where we want to stay, and then you can book us a room before we get tired."

"I think we should just keep driving 'til we hit L.A.," she said.

"It's too far," I told her. "My eyes start to give out after about seven hours of driving these days. I've got another hour or two, max. Especially after the bunny incident."

"Wimp."

"It will be easier when you're old enough to drive," I told her.

"What are you trying to say?" she asked, waggling her eyebrows at me.

"No. That is not what I'm trying to say."

"If your eyes need a little break, is all I'm saying."

I remembered the first time my aunt let me drive. It was on a little road around her farm. She pulled the car over and got out. Told me to slide over. The exhilaration of it flooded back to me. The power of hands on a steering wheel, feet straining to reach the pedals. I was probably younger than Matilda.

I slowed the car, pulling off an easy exit for reentry. Matilda gaped at me.

"I was just kidding, Mom."

"Come on, my eyes could use a break." A MAC truck buzzed past on the highway, but other than that, it was deserted. "And we've already had our car wreck for the day. Statistically speaking, we're unlikely to have another one." I got out and walked around to the passenger side door, and she looked at me skeptically before sliding into the driver's seat.

"Let's get going before somebody notices us," I said, remembering that I might be a person of interest.

She clasped the wheel, looked over at me with her mouth agape. It made me laugh. I liked the feeling of shocking her a little and letting her know what we were both capable of. We had both been wallowing so far down in our grief, but it also felt like an opportunity to reset. To let go of the weight of grief and find its wings.

I showed her how to adjust the mirrors, a quick crash course in turn signals, and played ten quick rounds of "put your foot on the gas / put your foot on the brake," and she drove, merging back onto the wide-open interstate.

"This is the best thing ever!"

"You're doing great, honey. Just keep it slow and between the lines."

I snapped her photo, her scared-beautiful face against the towering red canyon walls. I turned up the music. I car-danced to Missy Eliot while Matilda whooped. Then we saw the police car.

"Mom, is that a cop behind us?" Matilda spotted it first.

"Yup, it sure is," I said, turning down the music and

keeping my voice calm. "You're fine, honey, just keep your speed steady, no don't slow down too much. Keep it steady and between the lines. Don't slow down."

She sped up a little suddenly, and I peeked into the side-view mirror. The police had his turn signal on and was pulling alongside us.

"Just keep looking straight ahead," I told her. "Don't look over at them. Keep your speed up. Keep it between the lines."

I didn't tell her how much my hands were sweating.

"You're doing great!"

The police accelerated, pulled ahead of us. Matilda kept driving, not slowing down too much, keeping it between the lines, and we kept quiet, willing the police to keep driving, to ignore us, to be unseen.

"Just pull off at that exit, OK? Stop at the stop sign and put it in park, and we'll swap places, OK?"

She finally looked at me, her eyes as wide as I'd ever seen them. "Whoa, Mom. That was... AWESOME!" she crowed as she put the car into park, and I pulled open my door.

"It seems like it might be time for a hotel room," I told her as I adjusted the mirrors, surreptitiously wiping my sweaty palms on my pants.

"How about Las Vegas?" she asked.

I snorted.

"Really, it's the only big town between here and L.A.," she said.

"We do NOT need a big city," I said.

"But why not?" she asked, and because I couldn't think of a single good reason why not, I conceded. It felt good to say yes to her. Since the last time I talked to Andy, since the suddenness of that day jolted me into under-standing how quickly we can move into Afters when we were Befores without even knowing it, ever since then, I felt like I had been holding my breath, tensing my body against the world, saying "no" to everything before it was even spoken.

"OK, Las Vegas it is," I told her. "Just nowhere with clowns. You know how I feel about clowns."

"Circus, Circus is out, got it," she said. "But obviously we need a pool."

We ended up at the Bellagio because I guess, Matilda is classy like that. We took a walk down the strip, marveling at all the beautiful lonely people, the women strutting around in fur coats despite the eighty-degree heat, the men in either fancy suits or t-shirts and cargo shorts.

"Dinner's on me," Matilda told me as we retreated to the air conditioning of our room.

"Ha. Good one."

"No, really. I have my babysitting money saved up, and as a gesture of my growing independence and desire to be a good daughter, I'd like to take you to dinner for a change."

And who could argue with that? We dressed up in our nicest dresses, which for me just meant the same presentable black dress I had been wearing for ten years, but for Matilda meant a fancy red dress we had bought for the eighth-grade dance. She had grown a little since the dance, so her legs looked even longer than usual. She requested to do my makeup and whipped out her large caboodle of theatrical-level makeup. I had no idea that she had this range of eye shadow at her disposal, as she was pretty modest about it when she wasn't on stage. She sat me in a chair in front of the bathroom mirror and caught my chin in her hand as she examined my face.

"What do you want?" she asked.

"Well, you know better than I do."

"So, you're giving me complete control? And you won't complain at all about what I do?"

"Yes," I told her. "Whatever you want."

"Just remember you said that!" she responded gleefully.

As she leaned in close enough for me to smell her sweet cotton candy mixed sour-teen aroma while she added swoops and wings to my eyes, I tried not to cringe. I was not much into makeup myself, and I couldn't even remember the last time I had even bothered since leaving work.

"I'm a little worried about the way you keep laughing to yourself," I said.

"Well, I did mess the right eye up pretty bad, but I think I fixed it," she said, giggling. "Ta-da!" She spun the chair around so I could see myself in the hotel mirror over the dresser.

"Better than I could do!" I leaned into the dresser to see myself more closely. The eyes were big, and Las Vegas fabulous.

"Which is not saying much," she said. "Seriously, Mom, sunscreen and Chapstick do not count as makeup."

"They count as being heavily made up, if you ask me," I said.

She leaned into the mirror and put the finishing touches on her own face, making the lipstick redder, the eye shadow a touch more dramatic.

"Let me pee, and I'm ready," she responded. She pulled the door closed after her, but it didn't really click, and I ducked back in to see if my purse was on the bathroom counter. Matilda had her dress hitched up around her waist, checking out her ass in the bathroom mirror. I didn't mean to burst in on her; I didn't intend to catch her in this private act of self-examination, but when my eyes saw the reflection in the mirror, the thong gliding up her butt, all of my carefully cultivated sentiments about my daughter being responsible for her own clothing and growing sexuality went out the window.

"What the hell is that?" I squeaked.

"A thong, duh." She straightened her dress back out.

"Where did you get it?"

"At the mall, probably."

"Take it off! You are way too young for that! Take it off, now."

She glared at me. "Are you serious?"

My voice had gotten high and my breath quick, and I wasn't sure where this was even coming from. I couldn't really understand why I was having a fight or flight panic attack about my daughter's underwear. I had done so much work in the last year of reminding myself to back off, to encourage her to develop her own sense of style and control over her body and looks, letting her dye her hair, and experiment with makeup and crop tops. Trying to let go of the internalized responses I could hear from my own father as he attempted to shame me out of my sexuality. Remembering how I smuggled my lipstick and daisy dukes in my backpack, how my best friend would bring me her sexiest halter top, so even though I left the house in a father-approved outfit, I didn't arrive anywhere looking like that. The only real effect was that I was always terrified my dad would find out, so I kept my out-of-the-house interactions a complete secret from him, which only created more danger for me.

I had promised myself after Andy died that I wouldn't be that kind of mom. I would be the kind of mom who my daughter would want to confide in. Would let me see her true self without having to put on so many disguises and barricades. So why was I freaking out about a pair of underwear? It's not like anyone else was going to see them anytime soon, except now I wondered if that hope was naïve. Of course, it was naïve. Define soon, I thought to myself. I took a deep breath.

"I'm sorry. I just… I had no idea you were wearing that kind of underwear."

"Not a big deal, Mom, just forget about it."

"I was not emotionally prepared for that."

"I'm trying them out," she said.

"I mean, they're not very comfortable, right? It's like having a permanent wedgie, I always felt."

"Mom, no offense, but you are literally the queen of granny-panties, so it's not something I'm really seeking your advice about, you know?"

"That's fair, I guess." I tugged at my sensible cotton undies and wondered how long it had actually been since I had on a thong or anything that even faintly resembled a pair of sexy underwear. Even before Andy had died, I had pretty much given up in that department. After about thirty, it just seemed like life was too short to be in uncomfortable underwear. I closed the door behind me and gave her the time she needed while I collected myself, repeating the Kahlil Gibran meditation on parenting that has helped get me through this last year: "You may give them your love but not your thoughts, for they have their own thoughts."

When she emerged, she looked like a lovely young lady who was perfectly capable of picking out her own underwear.

"You look too beautiful to be going to dinner with your mother," I told her.

"Just the right amount of beauty for that," she said, and we linked arms on our way to the elevator. The hallway was immaculately decorated, like everything about the Bellagio. Plush carpets, extravagant chandeliers, artwork with European pretensions. There was something about the unapologetic artificiality of Vegas in general and the Bellagio in particular that I enjoyed.

The steakhouse was a lush red velvet that matched Matilda's dress, and the waiter put us at a very visible table next to a small fountain. As I looked at the cocktail menu, Matilda fished out some coins that were not American, and I didn't say a word about it because I was so relieved there was still a little girl in there somewhere.

The waiter returned with my wine and her Shirley Temple. I ordered a New York Strip, and the waiter turned to her, his pen poised.

"For the young lady?" he asked.

"The ribs, please," she said.

"Very good." He strutted away, and she snuck a sip of my wine, which I had been letting her do lately.

"Ribs were always Daddy's favorite."

"Yeah," she sighed, and her face got the faraway look.

"Did you know that Eve was supposed to be made from Adam's rib?" I asked her, just to change the subject.

"Yeah, but did you know before Eve there was Lilith? And that she was made from the same clay as Adam, so she was supposed to be his equal? But he didn't like that because Adam was a big baby, so he made Lilith leave and then cried about it until God made him a more subservient partner?"

"For a while, I thought if I had a daughter, I might name her Lilith. Did I ever tell you that?"

"Really? Why? I thought after Adam's stupid ass got her kicked out of paradise, Lilith turned into a demon who kills children or something?"

"Well, when I was in college, they used to have this Lilith Fair thing that was all female musicians, and I got really interested in Lilith. I always thought she was a much more interesting figure of feminine energy than Eve."

"Get back to the part where you thought about naming your daughter Lilith."

"Well, there was this Lilith Fair for a couple of years. I went to see it with some of my girlfriends from high school as kind of a last hurrah. I saw so many good musicians play there, like Sarah McLachlan, and Liz Phair, and Missy Elliott, and Erykah Badu. And it was kind of like paradise, women outnumbered men by radical numbers. It was the first time I ever truly felt safe in a big crowd like that. We could all wear whatever we wanted and do all the drugs we wanted without having to worry about what might happen to us."

"All the drugs, eh?" she said, raising an eyebrow at me.

"Sorry, I was drifting there. Don't do drugs! My point was that it was the first time in my life that I actually felt safe as a woman, and I didn't realize how unsafe I usually felt until I was there."

"So, it was all about how great Lilith was?"

"The idea was that Eve was boring and Lilith was where it was at. And the more I learned about her, the more I thought that was true. That society wants us to be like Eve, this kind of meek victim, but that Lilith was powerful and strong, and all the ways that she was punished for that. I went into college with that fresh on my mind, and it really changed my perspective. And I promised myself if I had a daughter, I would want her to be more like Lilith than like Eve."

"How'd I get stuck with the name Matilda, then?"

"Oh, that was your dad's idea," I said, not wanting to get into my love/hate relationship with Roald Dahl.

"Humph. You met Dad, and all that girl power just dried up, huh?" she said, and before I could start listing my denials, the waiter set the food in front of us. Matilda picked up one of the thick ribs and sucked the meat off of it in one motion, tossing the bone back on her plate.

River of No Return (1954)

She had no talent as an actress… but she was a born star.

Otto Preminger, director who started
his Hollywood career on Zanuck's
shitlist and saw making *River of No
Return* and working with Marilyn
Monroe as just another punishment

We heard that *River of No Return* wasn't Marilyn's favorite. She called it a "Z cowboy movie in which the acting finishes third to the scenery and Cinemascope," but it is not without its charms, including the epic denim jeans from her personal collection that were eventually auctioned off to Tommy Hilfiger for more than $40,000.

She starts the movie with about five costume changes in five minutes while she's still a showgirl in the gold camp, but after she heads downriver with her scumbag fiancé, those jeans get ample screen time, clinging to her as she gets wetter and wetter, womaning the oars while white men dressed up as Indians and white men dressed up as cowboys track her and Matt Calder (Robert Mitchum) and his son down the river. The cinematography is exceptional, especially for this era. The nineteenth-century setting of the Salmon River in Idaho's gold rush invoked by the lovely scenery of shooting in Banff and Jasper, BC. It's the closest Marilyn ever got to being an action star, and you can see hints of Meryl Streep's inspiration for *The River Wild* as Marilyn grabs the oars and charges down the river.

The set was a bit of a mess. The director, Otto Preminger, like Marilyn, had been forced into the movie because of contractual obligations. Neither was happy with Zanuck, who had made those choices, nor were they happy with each other. Preminger's overbearing approach set off constant feuds with both Monroe and Lytess, who he had thrown off-set at one point. Mitchum was arrested for marijuana possession and kept calling the movie "The Film of No Return," joking that it would be lucky to make a dime. Actors were encouraged to do their own stunts, and Marilyn injured her ankle, which was a perfect opportunity for beau Joe DiMaggio to come charging up to Banff with his cavalry of sports-medicine doctors.

Ultimately, the movie and DiMaggio's attention and marriage proposal perfectly set the stage for another kind of showdown between Marilyn and Zanuck over the movie he chose for her next: *The Girl in Pink Tights*. Marilyn requested to read the script in advance, pointing to her dissatisfaction with *River of No Return*, and Zanuck reminded her that she has no right to turn down the roles he selected for her – that her contractual obligation for several more years was to do as she was told. We cheered as Marilyn refused to follow his orders, and then Twentieth Century Fox suspended her.

She responded by marrying Joe DiMaggio on January 14, 1954. When DiMaggio and Monroe started dating, she was a minor starlet, but by the end of 1953, she was one of the most famous movie stars in the world. He wasn't much into having a working wife; he was more into having a wife with movie star good looks and an appetite for homemaking. Marilyn was willing to play that role for a while, but, like many of us, she wanted more. And the world wanted more from her.

River of No Return, much like her marriage to DiMaggio, served more as a steppingstone than as a cornerstone. While Marilyn, with her hair long and wild, grabbing the oars in those jeans against the gorgeous backdrop of the Rockies, shows a different side of her than many of her carefully coiffed images, the rest of the movie is pretty easily forgotten. "The longer you last, the less you care," Marilyn whispers as a giant wave knocks some hypothermia into her, and that seems to be the theme of this era of her career. Gone was the sense of a meek newcomer, clinging to whatever crumbs she was offered, eager to please. Here to stay was our new Marilyn, bold, unapologetic, taking control of the oars.

Chapter 8

People had a habit of looking at me as if I were some kind of mirror instead of a person. They didn't see me, they saw their own lewd thoughts, then they white-masked themselves by calling me the lewd one.

Marilyn Monroe, *My Story*

"You have to at least go to the casino before we leave," Matilda said as we sipped the room service coffee. We had decided to splurge on breakfast. I couldn't remember the last time anyone had brought me coffee in bed, but it was a lovely feeling. Andy used to put Baileys in my coffee and bring it to me on lazy mornings.

"I can't take you down there, they'll kick us out in a second."

"I looked it up, it says I can walk through, as long as I don't stop."

"How am I going to gamble without stopping?"

"Can't you just slip a quarter in the slot machine on the way by? Just, like, some symbolic gambling, you know? Since we're in Vegas and all."

"OK, that's fair. Let's pack first, and then we'll do a quick walk through on our way to the car."

"Deal."

We hadn't done too much unpacking, other than Matilda's makeup kit, which she professionally organized after carefully spending some time with her face. It was still strange to me how little girl she was sometimes, with tangled, unbrushed hair, but also how womanly other times, devoting hours to studying glamorous makeup applications on YouTube. I wanted her to feel empowered to present the image of herself to the world that made her feel comfortable, and if that included fake eyelashes and red lipstick, who was I to complain? I knew there were lots of ways to be a woman and that there wasn't anything more valuable about my own minimalist approach. I did go through a makeup stage when I was younger, heavy on the black eyeliner, but it was always to make myself look more dangerous, more edgy, I never had any particular investment in looking pretty that I can remember.

We gathered our bags and cut through the casino on the way out. I slipped a quarter in a digital poker machine and played through a hand, surprised when the virtual dealer gave me three queens on the first hand, and even more surprised when a straight flush on the second hand raised my winnings to $250.

"Holy shit, Mom! Look at you!"

"Let me cash out while I'm ahead. That pays for most of the room and breakfast!" I whooped. I had never gambled much before, but I could see where the buzz came from. Just like that, I had broken even in Vegas!

The window to cash in my receipt was a little hard to find, but I was determined not to get distracted by all the flashing lights, bells, and whistles. But when the gentleman behind the glass asked me if I wanted cash or chips, the strangest voice squeaked out, "Chips!" Matilda had visited the restroom while I was collecting the money so as to not raise any eyebrows, and when she came back out, I showed her the five $50 chips I had collected.

"It sort of seemed like a shame to stop already," I told her.

"Mommmmm! That's how they get you. You win a little, and then you get hooked. And next thing you know, you're selling our car for your next turn at the roulette wheel."

"Roulette sounds about right." I always thought that seemed like the best kind of old-fashioned gambling, the ball clanking through the wheel, the physicality of betting that it would land on a particular number or color. We spotted a table and hovered a little closer. Two gentlemen were spreading huge stacks of chips around the table, covering a spread of numbers. I didn't realize what a variety of betting options there were – you could bet the number, or just red versus black, or even or odd, or a range of numbers, and it looked fun, the way they pitched a chip here, a couple of chips there.

We were feeling emboldened by our success with video poker, but Matilda still hovered behind me, acting like she was admiring the art, while I scooted up to the table.

"What should I put it on?" I whispered to her.

"What about your age?" Matilda asked.

"Forty-two? I don't even think it goes up that high." I turned to the dealer, except I guess he wasn't really a dealer, the spinner? The operator? "Thirty-six is as high as it goes?"

"Yes, ma'am," he answered, "thirty-six is the end."

"Marilyn was thirty-six when she died," Matilda whispered to me.

I put one chip on thirty-six, and one on the thirteen for Matilda, and one on the black, and one on the even and the odd.

"You're canceling yourself out there," one of the men pointed out, gesturing towards the even/odd split.

"No more bets! No more bets," the operator said, waving his hand over the table in a terminal motion before giving the wheel a hard spin.

"I figure at least I'll win something," I told the man, who sighed a little at my lack of savvy.

It was like *The Price is Right*, with Matilda and I hooting every time the ball got close to thirty-six or thirteen, but it kept spinning for a surprising amount of time, finally slowing, clattering smoothly right into the thirty-sixth slot.

"Holy shit!" Matilda cheered as the operator eyed her suspiciously, and she clapped a hand over her mouth. He started stacking up chips on top of the thirty-six. "How much did you win?" She asked me out of the corner of her mouth.

"Thirty-five to one," the gambler to my right said.

"$1,750 on a fifty-dollar bet," his friend added.

She pulled me away from the table for a second. "OK, Mom, now this seems kinda unbelievable, but we learned in math class that every time you spin the wheel, you get a whole new set of odds, you know? So, it seems counterintuitive, like if you got thirty-six once, you should bet anything BUT thirty-six the next time, when actually, every time you spin the wheel, the odds start over, so it's just as likely that you'll get thirty-six this time as last time."

The real gamblers overheard and snorted, one rolling his eyes at the other, as they continued to distribute their chips. I left a stack of five chips on both thirty-six and thirteen, and squeezed Matilda's hand for luck.

"OK, we'll test your theory, but this is for real the last time, OK?"

"No more bets, no more bets," the operator repeated, expressionless, at our chips. The ball clattered through the wheel, and I squeezed Matilda's hand the whole time as the ball fell a second time into the thirty-sixth slot.

"Impossible!" the gambling man shouted.

"It's ridiculous!" his companion agreed.

The operator counted out a huge stack of chips, using different colors from before, and Matilda and I were giggling like crazy as we gathered them, trying not to drop any.

As we walked away, I saw one of the men placing a large stack on thirty-six.

The Seven Year Itch (1955)

The Seven Year Itch begins with a blandly offensive scene about the "Indians" who used to occupy New York City and how the men focused on "hunting" (hunting is emphasized several times) while the women and children gathered, but there is no acknowledgement that Manhattan occupies Lenape land. Apparently, in 1955 New York City, all of us respectable women-folk were sent with the children to Maine for the summer while our big, strong men stayed behind. In our absence, everyone from the janitor to the bossman hunts the unmarried female prey who don't have a protector to shield them from the heat of the city / loins of the men.

Tom Ewell plays Richard Sherman, a reprise of his bumbling husband role from the Broadway play; he won the Best Actor Oscar for the film version. Marilyn plays "The Girl," and no, she's never given a name since her main character traits are to serve as a blank slate for Ewell's fantasies.

The Girl's claim to fame is an honorable mention for an "artistic photo" that has her splayed out on a beach among the sand and the driftwood, and we note the coy nod to the 1949 "Golden Dream" photos of Marilyn that had recently been published in *Playboy*'s debut issue.

An opening scene shows Sherman slashing necklines with a marker on the cover of *Little Women*, and the slashing continues onto the frame of his secretary. Cut to a scene with a battleax waitress in a vegetarian restaurant who refuses Sherman's tip but offers to put it into their nudist camp fund and then waxes poetic about the joys of nudity and how all the world's ills are caused by clothing.

And finally, we cut to Marilyn's silhouette in the doorway of Sherman's apartment building as she frantically rings the buzzer. He lets her in, and she tells him she'll be living upstairs for the summer. We hear the audible crick in Sherman's neck as he cranes to watch her mount the stairs in her polka-dot halter dress.

The next scene has The Girl peering out from behind the patio plants with no clothes on, right after she nearly takes Sherman out with a plummeting tomato plant.

And of course there is one of the most iconic film scenes of all time, the white dress subway grate scene. It's important that we recognize the way Heat is a character in this movie, the same way it's a character in Spike Lee's *Do the Right Thing*, set in the same month, just fifty years before and one borough over. One of Sherman's main seduction techniques is his air conditioning, and The Girl blithely tells him, "When it's hot like this, you know what I do? I keep my undies in the icebox," which apparently was a line that Marilyn added to the script based on her own practices and something we believe showcases her genius. The Girl is standing over that subway grate because the slight breeze caused by the subway feels like heaven. But much of the tension in the movie is caused by the heat of the city, and, let's face it, the enticements of air conditioning on a hot day have caused many of us to make regrettable choices.

Because the subway grate scene hastened the end of Marilyn's marriage to DiMaggio, she spent a great deal of time in New York City, where she moved to rejuvenate and recover after she wrapped up filming on *The Seven Year Itch*. Living with Milton Greene, her soon-to-be partner in Marilyn Monroe Productions, she studied at Lee Strasburg's prestigious acting school, befriended the Rat Pack, and embraced New York intellectualism.

The movie exists in a sort of fantasy space where we are never entirely clear about what are Sherman's fantasies and what are realities. He fantasizes about trying to explain to his wife all the women who throw themselves at him, including a nurse who has to be removed from kissing him by an entire medical team. Presenting it as fantasy also thwarts an era that didn't permit actual adultery to take place on film.

Billy Wilder, the director, would go on to direct Marilyn in *Some Like it Hot*, often thought of as her best movie, but for Wilder the five-year gap made a huge difference. Marilyn aged from a fresh, young newlywed up-and-coming actress with whom he "never had a bad day" to the drug-abusing train wreck who could barely make it to the set. And by the time another seven years had passed since the making of *The Seven Year Itch*, Marilyn would be gone.

Chapter 9

Hollywood is a place where they'll pay you a thousand dollars for a kiss and fifty cents for your soul. I know, because I turned down the first offer often enough and held out for the fifty cents.

Marilyn Monroe, *My Story*

I had Matilda wait in the lobby while I collected the rest of the money. When they gave me the choice of cash or check, I couldn't help but take it in cash, but I immediately started to feel paranoid as I grabbed Matilda's arm and walked towards the parking garage. I slipped the manila envelope into the glove compartment and locked the doors as we inspected the bumper and tightened the straps holding it together.

"It's probably not going to fall off in the middle of Nevada," Matilda said, in the high-pitched voice she used when she was lying.

"I keep thinking of this book I used to read you when you were a kid, where the character assumes something is bad luck, but then it ends up being good luck in the end."

"I remember that book. Sometimes he says, 'What good luck!' And it ends up being bad luck, too."

"That's right. It's hard to tell sometimes, right?"

We patted Charlotte's hood and got back in the car, hoping for continued good luck.

As we pulled out of the garage, Matilda pulled the manila envelope out and paged through the bills, whistling. "Holy shit, Mom, I've never seen this much cash before."

"It's over ten grand!" I couldn't help gloating a little.

"What should we do with it?" she asked as I pulled out of the parking garage.

"Well, I guess we better book the nicest hotel in L.A., right?"

"On it," she whipped out her phone and started describing all the different hotels where Marilyn had ever stayed, and in what part of her career, and what their current state was.

The Charlie Hotel, where she lived in a two-bedroom cottage in the 1940s after she left her first husband and was getting her start modeling.

The Avalon Hotel, known as Beverly Carlton Hotel in Marilyn's days, when it was more of a residential apartment building that housed others in the industry like Mae West and Lucille Ball. She lived there in 1948, when she first met Johnny Hyde, who became her agent with the William Morris Agency.

The Beverly Hills Hotel, nicknamed the Pink Palace, where she lived in 1952 and on and off until 1960, was her sanctuary. She stayed there with her second husband, Joe DiMaggio, after they married in 1954 and waited for their home to be finished, and she returned with Arthur Miller in 1960 to stay in Bungalow 20, though rumor had it that she spent a lot of time in Bungalow 21 with Yves Montand, her co-star in the movie she was filming at the time, *Let's Make Love.*

"Didn't she ever just, you know, live in a house?" I asked.

"I don't think she liked houses much," Matilda said.

"She only ever owned one house."

"Seems symbolic, that she never really could find a place she felt at home."

"She died in that house," Matilda told me. "It was the house she bought when she was thirty-five so she only got a year there."

I felt my neck tingle when I thought about putting money into the neat little thirty-six box on the roulette table, the last number on the wheel, and all the numbers beyond thirty-six that Marilyn never got to experience.

"Now that house is owned by a Marilyn lookalike who swears it's haunted by Marilyn's ghost. In fact, apparently seeing Marilyn's ghost is, like, a thing you do in L.A."

"I guess that's what we're going there for, right?"

"Well, I think we should stay here. At the Hollywood Roosevelt Hotel," Matilda announced. "They say it was her favorite of all the hotels. You can even rent the suite she liked best – the one where the maids say sometimes her face shows up in the mirror."

"That sounds perfect. And it is close to the cemetery?"

"Yeah, just a few miles away. And it's real close to the Chinese Theater. You know, where the stars put their handprints."

"I have heard of that, but I've never been there. I guess I've never had the desire to spend much time in L.A."

"She and Jane Russell put their prints there after *Gentlemen Prefer Blondes.* Guess Marilyn said that if the prints were supposed to represent their screen image, Jane should just dip her tits in it and Marilyn should sit on it and leave an ass print."

"Ha. She was so funny. That was one of the things I

think went underappreciated in her time. Some of the quotes from her are hilarious. Smart-funny."

"This suite is seriously like a thousand dollars a night, though. You sure I should book it?" Matilda asked.

"There couldn't be a better way to spend our earnings. I feel like Marilyn would have wanted it this way."

"Done."

We high-fived, and I noted how, all of a sudden, her fingers were almost as long as mine.

We were fully in the desert, gone from the outskirts of the Vegas mirage. The road had gotten surprisingly pretty and desolate, with red-rock mountains cresting into the blue sky, spires forming like turrets in castles. The sun baked, but we put the windows down to let the hot air blow around us like a hair dryer. I could feel the moisture exiting every cell of my body, my face and throat parching. Matilda started a new playlist of the most Marilyn songs yet: Elton John's "Candle in the Wind" and Pharrell's "Marilyn Monroe," and every other song that either blatantly or subtly referenced Marilyn or Norma Jeane.

We drove through the Mojave Desert and let the legend of Norma Jeane spill over us. It's funny how many people have so many different interpretations of her. The sexbomb. The damaged little girl. The drug addict. The breathy lounge singer. The little wife. The accomplished actress. The hilarious comedian. The well-read intellectual. The mentally ill daughter of a mentally ill mother. The diplomat. How was she able to encompass all those symbols? Somehow, even while dying at thirty-six, her career barely lasting more than a decade, the mythology of Marilyn has survived and continues, even while it fragments into new shards.

I thought of how many people have written about

her, from Norman Mailer to Gloria Steinem to Truman Capote to Joyce Carol Oates. Maybe only Warhol got it right – all of those overlapping and almost satirical images, commercialized and glamorous yet somehow so tender. Of all the actresses from her era, she seemed like the one who has best survived into twenty-first-century consciousness. Nobody Matilda's age really remembers Jane Russell, or Bette Davis, or even the powerful directors who treated Marilyn like a pawn. Gen Z barely recognizes the names John Huston, or Laurence Olivier, or Billy Wilder, but everyone still knows Marilyn. All the imitators who still don the iconic white dress and find a way to make it flutter.

As we rolled across the desert, the exits grew farther apart, the landscape more rugged and empty. Matilda's playlist became more obscure in its references, and I wondered how many times Marilyn must have done this exact same drive, starting with when she came to Vegas at twenty to get a divorce from her first husband. She was still Norma Jeane then, but we are in Marilyn's territory now.

"Let's stop at this diner," Matilda piped up.

"That's fine, how far?"

"Hour or so, I'll tell you when to exit," she said. "It's called Peggy Sue's."

We got off at Ghost Town Road, and she directed us to the diner. It seemed to hold a wide array of charms, including, but not limited to, a murky green turtle pond, a giant plastic dinosaur exhibition, and a five and dime, as well as a traditional diner with a jukebox and tons of Hollywood memorabilia.

The diner was moderately busy, but a hostess with big hair and even bigger lips escorted us to our booth.

"Y'all want something to drink?" she asked, her long

fake lashes dipping down to us.

"Milkshake sounds great," I said.

"Chocolate malt?" Matilda added.

"You got it!" the hostess cheered us on.

After we ordered a giant club sandwich to share, my favorite diner classic, Matilda and I took a brief tour of the place, appreciating all of the knick-knacks and carefully dusted mannequins.

Matilda dug around in my purse until she found enough change to play the jukebox, starting with "Learnin' the Blues" by Frank Sinatra. We found a life-size mannequin of Marilyn, her undies hanging out as that white dress blew around her waist, the ceramic pleats tucking into each other.

"You know that dress probably ended her marriage to Joe DiMaggio, right?" Matilda asked me.

"He always seemed like such a gawky buck-toothed jock, I never got what she saw in him."

"Seems like he wanted her to be something she wasn't, and when he learned who she was, he didn't want her anymore. They didn't even make it a year."

"Well, I guess showing your underwear to the whole world kind of blew that cover. Get it – blew!" I gestured toward the bare leg as Matilda glared at me.

"Just can't resist your mom jokes, can you?"

I shrugged. "At least I am not showing the whole world my undies, I guess?"

Matilda huffed at me. "You know she had on two pairs of underwear, right? And the scene was shot at 1 a.m. to try to keep the crowds down? And they did fourteen takes, and every time her skirt went up, the crowd hooted and screamed, and they eventually had to refilm the whole scene in L.A. on a closed set? And in the middle of it all, Joe DiMaggio calls her an exhibitionist and storms off the set. Then, after all that, rumor is that he assaulted her in their hotel room. She filed for divorce three weeks later."

I looked at the statue a little differently. The blushing, playful smile looked different now, like a mask.

"And check this out, Mom: they think that scene, that one moment of her life, has been imitated more than maybe any other moment of any other scene of any other life in the history of the world. Like it's been redone in everything from rice in Japan to a thirty-four thousand-pound statue in New Jersey."

"To this cheap replica right here," I said, and reached for the diner's version, taking Marilyn's cold plastic hand in mine.

I stroked the replica of the petite, chubby girl's fingers while "I Wanna Be Loved by You" came on the jukebox.

Bus Stop (1956)

Seen through our daughters' eyes, *Bus Stop* is a movie
that doesn't age well, even from an era that built rape
culture. We recognize it's going to be bad early on when
Bo (Don Murray) compares landing a wife to breaking a
horse, saying "a horse doesn't want to be broken either,
see? But it doesn't matter what the horse wants." And
it is bad, with lots of cringey moments between Bo, the
Montana virgin cowboy whose original approach to the
relationship is literally lassoing and abducting Cherie,
the Phoenix angel-showgirl, in an attempt to force her
to marry him. The cast enables Bo as the film rotates
between madcap domestic abuse humor and the drama
of Cherie's poverty-stricken Ozark past.

The backstory is important. She's no longer just The
Blonde or The Girl who shows up fully formed as part of
a male fantasy. In *Bus Stop*, she represents herself with a
line on the map, showing where she has been and where

she is going, which happens to be to L.A., her tongue-in-cheek dream, the direction she is headed to be discovered and to "get a little respect."

And there is a moment in there where Cherie finally earns Bo's respect and gets what she wants, which is, after all, not just respect, but permission, control, and compensation. These were the same qualities that Monroe was working towards in 1955 and 1956, when she showed herself to be a savvy businesswoman who fought studio head Darryl Zanuck and Twentieth Century Fox and won, establishing her own production company, Marilyn Monroe Productions, and making a major contribution to a shift in the Hollywood landscape.

Monroe leveraged her success in *The Seven Year Itch* into a complete renegotiation of how Hollywood conducted itself, both with her and with other stars. It took a year-long sit-down strike in which she lived in New York and essentially refused to make films unless she was given not only a raise but story, director, and cinematographer approval. She declined to allow herself to be cast in mediocre, nameless roles that only capitalized on her looks without allowing her to explore her depth as an actress.

It's important that we pause a moment and understand the landmark nature of this approach. The *Los Angeles Mirror News* called it, at the time, "one of the greatest single triumphs ever won by an actress." It changed the face of how stars were treated in Hollywood and continues to have repercussions today.

We have to remember all of this in the context of *Bus Stop*. Monroe had just triumphed over the biggest movie studio in the world, gotten them to acquiesce to every single one of her demands and laid down a contract that still has implications for artists sixty years later.

She started her own production company, and she chose *Bus Stop* to be the vehicle for all of that. She had unprecedented control, and she used it on everything from the shots to the costumes. She even won a Golden Globe for her performance, though the Academy Awards continued to snub her while awarding her male co-star.

So, while the moment when Bo comes to her, hat in hand, to apologize and recognize her personhood might seem too brief to us, especially compared to the previous hour spent throwing her over his shoulder like a cowboy-caveman, let's linger in the way Monroe managed to triumph, both in the role and in life. She would no longer be the studio's plaything, and she was announcing herself as a serious actress and businesswoman, refusing to allow the press to keep treating her like a sexy baby.

Yet, she remained herself. In an interview to publicize the film, she wore a dark suit, which one reporter hinted was to suggest a "new Marilyn," but Marilyn just laughed, catching the reporter's eye and replying, "Well, I'm the same person. It's just a new suit."

Chapter 10

I only wear Chanel No. 5.

Marilyn's response, as quoted in *Life*
magazine, when asked what she
wore to bed

Matilda directed me through the streets of L.A. with ease, and I remembered the days before Google Maps and how confusing it was the last time I came to L.A., more than fifteen years ago, where a wrong turn could cascade into a series of catastrophic events.

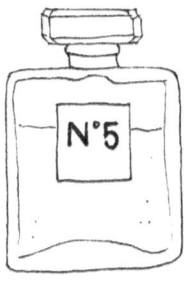

Matilda's phone took us to a side entrance, and I parked in what appeared to be a parking spot. As we got out, a white woman with grizzled gray hair nudged her shopping cart into our back tire and peered into our car. "It's a mess in there," she screamed at us, wagging her finger in our faces. "You don't deserve nice things." A bellman walked over and talked quietly with her while we tried to decide if we should check in or stay to monitor the car.

"Sorry about that." The bellman came and spoke to us as the woman took her cart and headed down the street. "She's having a hard day. We recommend parking

in our lot so we can keep a better eye on your vehicle."
I assured him we would move when we got checked in,
and Matilda and I walked towards the lobby of the Hollywood Roosevelt Hotel.

"L.A. is weird, man," Matilda whispered as we
looked at the opulence in front of us, with the woman's
voice and clattering shopping cart still lingering in our
ears. Across the way, in front of *Ripley's Believe It or Not*,
several bodies were bundled against the late fall afternoon sunshine, but as we entered the hotel, the lobby
was old-school Hollywood Grand, with two-story fres-
coed ceilings and a massive chandelier. A giant fireplace
centered the room with inviting nooks and crannies. I
was expecting pretension and hard fake L.A. corners,
but I immediately saw why Marilyn loved this space – it
felt like the best L.A. had to offer, a luxurious coziness
that softened and soothed.

"Are you checking in? Let me help you." A uniformed
bellhop steered us through the maze between the extravagant lobby and the more tucked-away front desk. Even
though I was wearing cargo shorts and Matilda had
chocolate dribbled down her shirt, no one seemed to
think twice about it. The lobby was filled with a range of
people – beautiful women in glamorous dresses preparing for afternoon receptions, business casual folks shaking hands after wrapping up lunch meetings, and kids in
bathing suits demanding room keys.

There was a multiplicity of Marilyn obvious in the
lobby, from the Warhols that hung over the couch to
abstract sculptures that silhouetted her naked form.

"May I help you?" I expected the receptionist to take
measure of us and find us lacking, but his tone was warm
and friendly.

"We're checking in," I said.

"The Marilyn Suite!" Matilda cheered.

"Oh, are you fans?"

"Yes," Matilda told him. "I know she lived here for two years."

"Oh, yes, the suite is more than just named after her, it was one of her favorite places to stay," the receptionist grinned at Matilda, and his response managed to sound both rehearsed and genuine.

"When she lived here, she actually lived in one of the bungalows, right?" Matilda was phrasing it as a question, but she was also subtly letting him know that she wasn't just another casual tourist.

"Yes, but when she came back, and she always came back, she liked to stay in the upstairs suite," he told us. "But it has been remodeled from how it was when she originally stayed there. It's been added to and mostly redecorated. It's more like an homage to her than the actual suite she stayed in."

"They say she met Arthur Miller here." Matilda said, looking around the lobby as if she expected Miller to show up to confirm or deny.

"You'd be hard-pressed to find a hotel with more Hollywood history than this one. Did you know The Roosevelt hosted the first Oscars way back in 1929? I can walk you up to your room and show you a couple things if you want."

"That would be great!" Matilda said, and he nodded at the other front desk worker to cover for him. We waved off the bellhop since our backpacks seemed too grubby to ask anyone else to carry them.

"I'm Russell," he told us as we walked out yet another exit from the lobby I hadn't noticed. The property felt designed for outwitting paparazzi and hiding from wives and lovers.

He pointed out the Tropicana Pool as we walked by it, surrounded by trees and chaise longues.

"Wow, that is a nice oasis," I said. The pool was gigantic, and painted blue squiggles lined the bottom, giving the water extra movement making it seem to dance.

"It was hand painted by David Hockney in the 1980s. It's actually the only pool in the whole world with a Hockney mural that isn't at a private residence," he informed us. "They think Marilyn stayed in that bungalow. Number 219," he gestured to the far side of the pool. I could picture her here, lying by the pool with her giant sunglasses and her overly intellectual book.

"We're up these stairs," he led us to an overlook, and the pool looked even more magical from this angle, the Hockney painting acting like an impressionist artwork that captured the essence of water, the play, the flickers. He gestured to the plaque outside the door that read "The Marilyn Suite" as he opened the door for us.

When we entered the room, for a second, I smelled a sweet burst of perfume. The air seemed heavy and full. The walls were pristine white brick, with a gorgeous photo of Marilyn over the white leather couch.

"So, most of the furniture is a replica of what was here in the 1950s," Russell told us. "The things that are original are the radio, the intercom, the fixtures, the countertops." He gestured at each. I ran my hand over the vintage countertops, admiring the mirrors and the furniture.

"Here it is," Matilda said, kicking off her shoes and flopping down on the white leather couch. I noticed Russell staring at her and cleared my throat. He snapped back to attention and gestured towards the outdoors.

"Out here, we have the balcony," he said.

I opened the door to the balcony that overlooked the pool.

"The diving board isn't there anymore," Matilda said, coming out the door beside me on the deck. "The one where she filmed her first professional magazine shoot." She flashed me her phone with a photo of Marilyn grinning from the diving board, her legs dangled over the edge and toes pointed.

"That's true," Russell chimed in. "The diving board was removed for liability reasons. Is there anything else I can help you ladies with before I go?" he asked as I dug into the still-unbelievable wad of cash in my purse, fishing out a twenty.

"Ever see anything like a ghost?" Matilda asked him. "Like, I heard that people have seen her face in the mirror and stuff."

"People say that she appears in the mirror on the stairs in between the lobby and the second floor," Russell told us. "I guess that mirror has been in different parts of the hotel for a long time. They say if you want to see ghosts, you should take a lot of photos of that mirror."

Matilda nodded, looking thoughtful, as Russell showed himself out.

"Do you believe in ghosts?" I asked Matilda.

"Don't know," she said. "Guess I've never seen anything that made me think there were ghosts, but that doesn't mean nobody else has. How about you?"

"When your dad died, I was sure he would come back in some way. Show me a sign. I thought I'd feel his presence. But I haven't. Not since the second I said goodbye to him the morning he had the heart attack. All I've felt is his absence."

"Yeah," Matilda said, staring out at the pool as it seemed to squiggle in the sunlight.

"I do want to get in that pool, though." I told her, and she squealed and raced for her bathing suit. I loved it when I still got glimpses of her as a child, although when she emerged from the bathroom, the bikini she was wearing was all woman.

"Where in god's name did that come from?" I asked, cringing at the judgey ring to my voice as I took in the white-string bikini, remembering the thong incident and my promise to do better.

"Oh, it used to be Sienna's," she told me. Her curves were starting to emerge – the tuck of a hip there, the fold of a breast here. I took a deep breath, thinking about the right thing for a mom to say when presented with the undeniable maturing of her daughter.

"It's a lot of skin," I bumbled. That was probably not the right response, but I managed to make it sound neutral.

She twirled, admiring herself in the multi-paned mirror that covered one wall. "Yeah, isn't it?"

I put on my black one-piece, trying to pretend it was old Hollywood class instead of the only bathing suit I owned. Matilda eyed me critically.

"Might be about time for a new bathing suit, Mom," she said, raising one eyebrow at me.

"Leave me alone. It's comfortable."

I found my old t-shirt dress for a coverup while Matilda opened one of the closets and found a white bathrobe.

"Do you think it was Marilyn's?" she asked.

"I doubt it. Marilyn's robes probably sold for millions of dollars on eBay to old perverts."

"Yeah, but I'm going to pretend," she said. "I read it was the one article of clothing she always brought on every trip."

We chose two large lounge chairs and sunscreened each other's backs. I eyed the people arranged glamorously around the pool, all looking like potential movie stars. A couple of luminously pale girls in bikinis that made Matilda's look chaste wore giant hats and sunglasses and drank cocktails. Two men in fedoras with deep olive skin fed each other grapes and giggled.

"So, about tomorrow?"

"Yeah, our trip to the Corridor of Memories?"

"The Corridor? I thought it was called the Westwood Cemetery or something generic like that."

"All of the crypts have names. The area where Marilyn is buried is called 'The Corridor of Memories'. She's right around the corner from Truman Capote, which is cool because they were besties. Hefner's beside her. Above her is some creep named Richard Poncher. He told his wife that he would haunt her if she didn't bury him face down so he could leer at Marilyn for all eternity."

"Sounds like you've done your research."

"Oh, Mom, you have no idea," Matilda chuckled.

"So we'll go in the morning, before it's too hot?"

"Yes, we will," and before I could ask any more questions, Matilda stood up and dove in the pool from the spot where the diving board used to be, her body sandwiched between the ripples of the water and Hockney squiggles, alternately making her look like a miniature, then a giant, the water creating a funhouse mirror of bodies. The saltwater pool was warmer than the air, and we swam laps until we were exhausted.

We dried off and lay by the pool, watching the late fall sunlight disappear behind the buildings.

"I'm going to take a shower," Matilda said.

"I'll meet you up there in a couple of minutes, OK?" I figured since there was only one shower in the room, I should let her get a head start. I put my dress back on and explored the hotel, finding Marilyn smoking a cigarette in a red and black dress, smoldering out from a gold and glass frame with a man's face in the corner. Next to it was an enclave with library books, which looked as if they could be spun to open a secret tunnel if one knew the right book. I studied them, trying to figure which one was out of place, and wiggled a few, but the wall of books did not give. I wandered into the Library Bar and figured I had time for a cocktail.

It was the kind of place Andy would have liked: lots of low lighting and solid furniture. Despite his love of punk music and a big doobie, he also enjoyed a suit and a Martini now and then. I missed him so much. Missed how our bodies would find each other in the night, how he could turn anything into a joke, how if he were here, he would hold my hand with one of his warm, broad hands while we held our drinks with the other. But if he were still alive, we probably wouldn't even be in California, right? Not in this hotel or this restaurant. I thought of all the ways his absence affected every part of my day. I couldn't let myself get too maudlin. If I sank into the grief, I would never pull out of it.

"Can I settle up?" I asked the bartender.

"Sure," he said. "You OK?" And just his noticing of my mood, the gentleness of his tone, it made me want to break down sobbing. He smiled at me, his white teeth against his tan skin, reminding me of Andy.

"Yeah," I told him. "But you make a mean champagne cocktail."

"Marilyn's favorite," he returned. I almost told him all about our trip, how we were staying in the Marilyn Suite. I thought about flirting a little and inviting him upstairs. These were things I could do, theoretically. If I didn't have a thirteen-year-old daughter showering off from the pool. If I weren't wearing the same worn-out cover-up that I'd had for fifteen years. If the idea of another man looking at my body didn't fill me with revulsion. I slid some cash into the bill holder and headed for the stairs.

When I let myself into the room, I called out Matilda's name but didn't get an answer. I found her sitting at the little alcove by the bathroom, staring into the mirror. The smell of perfume was heavy in the air.

"You, OK?" I asked, looking over her shoulder into the mirror, where I saw a little sliver of white cloth that must have been one of the towels. I looked more closely, and there was only Matilda's face, half made-up, her eyes big with fake lashes and expertly lined, while the lips were still natural.

"Yeah," she said, "but do you smell it?"

"Phew, yeah, maybe chill a little on the perfume," I told her.

"Mom, that's the thing, I haven't sprayed any."

"Hair stuff, then," I said. "It's just kind of a lot."

"It's not me," she said, and I noticed how pale her face had gotten. The fluttering white cloth had returned to the corner of my vision, but when I looked directly into the mirror, it was gone. The smell of perfume faded.

I opened the door and stepped out onto the balcony in time to see the lights come on and sparkle up the pool area. Matilda joined me, overlooking the pool, and we watched for a few minutes as the evening settled around us. Did Marilyn stand on this balcony, peering over the grounds, watching the comings and goings of other stars?

"Want to find that big mirror on the second floor that guy told us about?"

"Let's take a stroll."

We walked down around the pool and back through

the lobby, already getting used to the strange pathways of the hotel. Wayfinding is interesting to me: how a building or its grounds can direct and influence the pathways people take through any space. I thought about how the design of the Roosevelt made it easy for people to navigate around one another in private ways. The pool area had maybe a dozen little bungalows hiding in the lush vegetation around it. I imagined that each one probably had a different secret entryway. I wondered if Marilyn chose her suite for JFK to visit her without being noticed.

We mounted the grand center stairs leading up from the lobby and spotted the impressive mirror at the top. It had to be eight or ten feet with the ornate wooden frame. The mirror glass had a silvery, ancient sheen to it.

"I love a good mirror," Matilda said, admiring her reflection's wide-legged pants and crop top.

"Let's snap some photos," I suggested.

"Wait, you're asking me to take selfies?"

"I know, what a day, right?"

"Yes!" she said.

"You have all the good angles," I told her as she positioned me professionally, slanting the phone over our heads.

She snapped some of the two of us, then begged me to take a few by myself.

"Five is my limit," I told her. "And only because I want to snap one with Marilyn lurking in the mirror."

"OK, OK, just pretend you're looking in the mirror. What do you see? Ponder it." I laughed at her movie director's stance.

Then she made me take a thousand photos of her as she looked up and looked down, stared into the mirror, looked away and looked back at me. She didn't smile, and I didn't tell her to.

The Prince and the Showgirl (1957)

I didn't make the best of Marilyn.

Sir Laurence Olivier, famed British stage actor turned director.
The Prince and the Showgirl was his
first non-Shakespearean film

We were thrilled for Marilyn's new era of positivity
following her year of joy in New York City, in a role
deliberately sought out and chosen for her through the
production company she built, Marilyn Monroe Productions, in a newly negotiated contract with Twentieth Century Fox. We also appreciated the way her new
husband, famed playwright Arthur Miller, looked at her,
like he doted on Norma Jeane and also wanted to help
Marilyn get the respect she deserves.

And *The Prince and the Showgirl* seems like a respectable
film, starring, produced, and directed by famed British
Shakespearian devotee Laurence Olivier, who plays the
regent of Carpathia, an imaginary Balkan kingdom, His
Grand Ducal Highness. And yes, the formality of Grand
Ducal Highness is something that the film leans on for
laughs with Marilyn, in her usual role as a showgirl,
making Grand Ducal sound both ridiculous and endearing and sometimes ridiculously endearing.

Can we just talk about Olivier for a moment? He

couldn't come off as more pompous on-screen; it's the humor of his character to see his dour European pretension bumping up against Marilyn's brash American showgirl. His character refers to Marilyn's Elsie Marina as having "the mind of a backward child, the muscles of a boxer, and an approach to life of such stomach-turning sentimentality," a description that underlines the tension between all of Europe and America at this historical, post-World War II juncture. Europe appreciated American muscle but still struggled with some of the other American qualities, which is an underlying theme of the movie. But the humorous tension on screen turned into toxicity off screen.

Olivier's punishing, condescending approach sent Marilyn into a spiral of insecurity leading to insomnia, then to abuse of Seconal and other sleeping medications prescribed by the movie studio doctors, the downers leading to uppers, and the waves of drug abuse contributing to more insecurity and increasing lateness on set, with Marilyn leaving the other very serious, very British, very theater-oriented actors sometimes waiting for four-plus hours in full costume on the set before she showed up and did her usual dozens of takes to perfect a single line.

But here's the thing: we are so fucking bored whenever Marilyn is off-screen that we can feel ourselves doing an internal cheer when she reappears after his Grand Ducal repeatedly tries to send her away and she is, yet again, retrieved. There is a moment when she is standing in front of a window wearing a white dress while the sunlight spills into her hair that we could lose ourselves in, but Olivier couldn't lose himself.

In every interview he has done about Marilyn, Olivier uses the word "little" repeatedly: "She was a very curious little person" and "her little mind wasn't built for acting." In his recollections, she was always the "little child" who needed his big, strong Shakespearian guidance, and he found any deferrals from those roles to be humiliating. Like so many men, what he feared most was being laughed at so he made sure, instead, that Marilyn was the subject of humiliation while he remained the ruler.

Meanwhile, Miller, brought as a protector, as her knight in shining armor, didn't particularly like this on-set, drugged-out version of Marilyn he was meant to be shielding. He found he preferred Olivier's intellectualism and also started undermining Marilyn in all kinds of unexpected ways. The final blow came when he left his journal open in close proximity to Marilyn's script. What exactly he wrote in the journal has never been revealed, but it effectively ended all of Marilyn's love, trust, and devotion to him. From that moment on, while she continued to play the part of adoring wife for another couple of years, she saw Miller as another enemy, another man who used her. The combined cruelty of Miller and Olivier wielded what should have been a triumphant film against her, gaslighting her into a tower from which she never climbed down.

Chapter 11

It might be a kind of relief to be finished. You have to start all over again.

Marilyn Monroe, in a 1962
interview with *Life* magazine,
shortly before her death

After our photo session with the haunted mirror, we decided to venture out beyond the curated boundaries of the hotel. The air was warm, and there was a moment, as the night started to descend, when I almost loved L.A. The hotel was between Hollywood Boulevard and Sunset Boulevard, at the center of Hollywood, the base of Runyon Canyon, and the Hollywood Hills. The streets were paved with stars, and Matilda and I followed them for a couple of blocks, elbowing each other when we saw Jim Henson's or Dolly Parton's name engraved in bronze.

As we walked, the street ahead of us was closed off, with security guards directing us to go around. We crossed to the corner and watched the limousines release thin young white women in glamorous dresses onto a red carpet, where they posed, and paused, and posed some more.

"I think I saw a Kardashian," Matilda grinned at me, and even though I didn't care about the Kardashians, it was easy to get caught up in the quest to see stars.

"Ooooh, which one?" I peered towards the women on the carpet.

"Like you know the difference," Matilda scoffed.

"Well, there's the tall one, right? And Kim – everyone knows Kim. And the babies."

"The babies are all grown up now, and they aren't really Kardashians." Arguing about Kardashians while watching the paparazzi snap photos in the new evening seemed like the perfect L.A. outing, and for a second, I felt joy radiating from me, between Matilda and me – that lightness when sometimes you just forget all of the heavy things that weigh you down and remember that joy is what really matters.

I leaned into it for a moment, the smile on Matilda's face, seeing her, a young theater geek wondering if this was her own future, imagining herself in one of the dresses, trying not to upstage a Kardashian. We paused in that joy, pressing against the barrier, caught up in the privilege, and beauty, and youth of a Hollywood moment.

Then we turned and headed towards the Chinese Theatre to find Marilyn's iconic handprints. I paused for a moment to tie my shoelace, and Matilda got a few steps ahead of me. As I stood to catch up with her, I noticed a white man with dreadlocks making a beeline for her from one of the sleazy stores on Hollywood Boulevard. I quickened my pace to overhear him trying to slip her a business card.

"You're underage, aren't you? That's good, that's fine," he was saying, his hand outstretched with the card in it. Matilda looked bewildered, not reaching for the card, not pulling away.

"You know, I can get you things," the man was telling her. "What do you like? Weed? Acid? Molly? I can get you things, do you want to come in with me? We can talk."

By this point, I was standing beside her, and her face had crumpled from joy into a scowl. At first, the man's eyes traveled up my body. "Oh, this is your friend. Hey hon." When he got to my face, he stopped.

"Actually, I'm her mother. And yes, she is underage. I'll take that card." I snatched it from his hand while he started stuttering.

"I – I just want y'all to have a good time out here in Hollywood," he said, backing up.

I snorted at him. "Yeah, right, a good time. Listen, can you write your mother's phone number on the back here? I want to give her a call and let her know what her son's up to." I pushed the card back at him. "Just write her name and number down right there, so we can have a little chat."

"You crazy," he said, still backing away with a little grin. I followed him, getting my face so close to his that I could see his pink picked-over scabbed face and thin eyebrows, and smell the weed heavy on his breath.

"You'll find out how crazy I am if you keep talking to underage girls out here," I told him. "You hear me, mister? Don't make me come back. Next time a girl looks underage, you shut the fuck up and don't say a word to her. You hear me?" Suddenly, I was the person raving on the street corner. The man had disappeared back into the crowd, me still yelling, "You hear me? You hear me?" until Matilda grabbed my arm and pulled me down the street. Suddenly, I could see all of the dog shit, the grime, and the man hunched over a bucket with flames hopping up to his spoon.

I thought about being on the beach in San Diego with Nora in college. We had decided to walk in the waves for as long as we could. We weren't wearing bathing suits, and the water was splashing up around our t-shirts. The day was warm, and it felt lovely to be hot in the sun with our feet in the water and the waves splashing around us. We giggled and leaned into each other when the bigger waves came. And then there was a man there, right in front of us, with his dick in his hand, showing it to us like he had a pretty shell we might be interested in gathering. I thought about all the collective moments of joy and revelation that have been interrupted by a man demanding attention.

"What was that about?" Matilda asked as I grabbed her hand, keeping close while we waited to cross the street.

"I'm sorry, honey. I lost it a little bit."

"Are you kidding, Mom? You don't have to be sorry. I just don't understand why that guy was talking to me."

The walk icon glowed and chirped, and I held her hand the whole way across the street to Grauman's Chinese Theatre, through the forecourt area with the stylized Exotic Revival architecture, to visit the back courtyard, filled with almost a hundred years of handprints and footprints of the stars. I expected it to be packed with people, but there was one other couple lingering and three women snapping photos in the last of the light. Matilda pointed out Mel Brooks' 11-fingered handprint, and I nudged her at Will Smith's "Change the World" note. Eventually, we found Marilyn's high heels and handprints next to Jane Russell's, with the *Gentlemen Prefer Blondes* heading connecting them. Matilda handed me her phone as she knelt down to place her hands in the handprints.

By the time we had snapped a few photos, we were the only ones left in the courtyard. I kept expecting someone to tell us it was time to leave, but it was still early by L.A. standards.

"I can see why she loved L.A.," Matilda told me. "It's the weirdest place I've ever been."

"And this isn't even L.A.," I said, "just one little corner of Hollywood."

We found a taco truck on the way to the hotel and brought a feast of tacos back to our room, then got into our pajamas and made popcorn, snuggling on the couch to watch *Bus Stop*, a Marilyn movie I had never seen. We mostly mocked its out-of-date chauvinism and felt sorry for poor Marilyn, who keeps getting lassoed by the male lead. Then we sat out on the balcony, uninvited guests to the night pool party at the Tropicana, and made up stories about the different people partying below us.

"See, this one is like the dude in *Bus Stop*, he just got here today and has no idea," Matilda said, nodding to a shaggy pale man in a too-long bathing suit.

"And that one is a rock star who comes to stay at The Roosevelt after every big concert." I nodded at a rotund Black man with his shirt unbuttoned, and a cocktail resting on his large belly while he lounged on the pool chair.

When our eyes finally started to droop, we packed it in, though I wasn't sure that the pool party would be stopping anytime soon. Matilda stretched out on the couch with her laptop, humming and twirling her finger around her hair the way she did when she was focused on something.

"Want first dibs on the bathroom?" I asked her.

"No. Thank you," she said in the robot voice she adopted when she was being sucked in by a device.

I took my time. The lighting was soft and rosy and felt like being in a gentle bath, even though the sink was the only water I had running.

When I emerged, Matilda had a look that my dad called the cat-canary look.

"What are you looking so pleased about?" I asked her as I snuggled into the ridiculously sexy sunken bed surrounded by white cushioned walls. Matilda stretched out on the couch, flexing herself in what I recognized as an exercise Deliah had taught her troop – first stretching each finger, then the hands, then the arms, then repeating the action through her toes, feet, and legs – the feline glint intensified by the stretches.

"I like how the photos came out," she said.

A vintage-looking gilded mirror over the bed reflected me back to myself.

"I hear her voice in my head," Matilda said. "It's strange."

"What's she saying?"

"Wait! I haven't put my lipstick on yet!"

"Isn't that a line from the movie? It just got stuck in your head. Echolalia"

"What's echolalia?" Matilda asked.

"It's the psychiatric term for what happens when people get something stuck in their heads."

"Huh. Echolalia. Now that's stuck in my head." She clicked off the light, but I laid there in the dark for a while, thinking about the movie and how stupid Bo keeps calling Marilyn's character Cherry when she's real clear about her name being Cherie.

It was the darkest part of the night when I heard strains of *that old black magic has me in its spell* in Marilyn's throaty whisper. *That old black magic that you weave so well.* It's the song she sings at The Blue Dragon Club in *Bus Stop*, her Ozark accent purposefully turning it into a joke.

I heard it so clearly that I got up and checked the living room to make sure we didn't leave the TV on. I headed for the balcony to see if someone was playing it in the pool area, but no one was there.

Some Like It Hot (1959)

I miss her. It was like going to the dentist to make a picture with her. It was hell at the time, but after it was over, it was wonderful.

Billy Wilder, after Marilyn's death

When we remember Marilyn at her best, for many, it is for her performance in *Some Like It Hot*. It's hard for us not to picture Sugar Kane as Marilyn's most fully realized alter ego. *Some Like It Hot* was Marilyn's great triumph. After a layoff of nearly two years, spent in relative seclusion trying to save her marriage to Arthur Miller, struggling with a tubal pregnancy that had to be terminated in 1957, diving deeper and deeper into the oblivion that drugs offered, she returned to Hollywood to make her most financially and critically successful movie, which is still appointed to many lists as one of the great comedies of all time, including number one on the American Film Institute's one hundred best comedy list released in the year 2000. Among her other talents, this movie more than any other lets us applaud Marilyn's resilience.

On set, though, we hear it was a shitshow. Director Billy Wilder, who had directed Marilyn in *The Seven Year Itch*, remarked when the film was finished that he could "look at my wife again without wanting to hit her because she was a woman." Aside from the hilarity of domestic violence jokes, he also recognized that Marilyn was luminous on screen and called her one of the great comediennes of all time, but her lateness to set and occasional need to reshoot even basic lines thirty or forty times created ugly tension between her and Wilder as well as her co-stars, particularly Tony Curtis, who famously commented that "Kissing her is like kissing Hitler."

The movie itself, set in 1929, is basically one long-running sexual harassment joke in which two male musicians (Tony Curtis and Jack Lemmon) witness a mob-based hit similar to the St. Valentine's Day Massacre in Chicago and, in order to flee, dress like women to take a gig with an all-girl band in Florida. Sugar Kane first makes her appearance as they are all about to hop on the train to Florida, and her movements are followed with a throaty wah-wah-wah horn line and Curtis's line that she looks like "jello on springs." Throughout the film, both men-now-ladies have to field the many unwanted advances of other men, from financial manager Bienstock's quick grope of their asses when they tumble into the train to the attentions of aging millionaire Osgood Fielding, III, who feels up Lemmon in the elevator before later revealing himself as a more serious suitor, to the creepy bell-boy who periodically pops up to remind Curtis of his availability ("Never mind leaving your door open, I've got a passkey") to Curtis's third persona, a wealthy if impotent heir to the Shell Oil Corporation whom Sugar must initiate into the ways of sexuality.

And yet, the film's approach to gender roles somehow holds up better than we might have expected when we watch it today. While "why would a man marry a man?" might give twenty-first-century viewers a moment of awkward pause, by the end of the movie, Lemmon finds himself listing all the things that would prevent him from marrying Osgood ("I smoke, I can't have children...") before finally ripping off his wig and saying, "I'm a man!" to which Osgood responds lightly, "Well, no one's perfect." There is some play and inquiry into gender roles in this movie that is unique in this era. Binaries are broken down as Lemmon's mantra, "I'm a girl, I'm a girl..." has to be shifted into "I'm a boy, I'm a boy..." and by the end, the layers of what it means to be either a boy or a girl have evolved, even if it's all in the name of farce.

Ultimately, though, while the on-screen chemistry between the actors defines it, Marilyn steals the show. We can't help falling into the glamor of scenes like the glittery naked dress she wears on the yacht with her alleged millionaire. The way the dress dips almost to her behind, the way her breasts seem destined to fall out at any moment, the way she plays her extreme sexuality like another running gag. It feels like much of the decade was spent on warm-up roles that helped her prepare for her final comedic masterpiece.

Marilyn's miscarriage and crumbling marriage as the film went into its final production sent her down an even greater spiral of depression and drug use that included overdoses and hospitalizations and a growing sense that she wouldn't last through her thirties, but the directors, studios, even her husband, seemed more interested in squeezing her out and using her up than helping her rebuild. While she would go on to complete two more movies – the studio-forced musical *Let's Make Love* and the Arthur Miller-forced *The Misfits* – she never recovered her equilibrium.

Chapter 12

The cemetery had green lawns and old trees. Some of the oldest plaques marked gravesites in the ground, but most of them were crypts with plaques stacked on top of one another in marbled tombs, each area labeled with names like "Sanctuary of Tranquility." We wandered, looking for the Corridor of Memories, pointing out the names of old Hollywood stars and writers. We found the Gabors' grave, Ray Bradbury's grave, and Zanuck's grave, which I noticed Matilda spit on from the corner of my eye.

I thought about all the bones in the ground here and the beautiful green-leaved trees they were fertilizing. It was the only kind of afterlife I could really believe in – the idea that maybe our essence went on to fertilize plants, and those plants fed animals, and we became part of everything even if we had to say goodbye to our egos to do it. Andy had been cremated, and his ashes sat in an urn on a shelf in my closet. I was glad he wasn't anchored down in a cemetery. I knew I would have to set him free eventually, but I hadn't been ready yet. Whatever was left of him in this world, I wanted it close to me.

While we walked, Matilda filled me in on more details of Norma Jeane's childhood. She was taken back out of the orphanage by her mother's best friend, Grace Goddard, who then hatched a plot to marry Marilyn off at fifteen to avoid Doc Goddard's sexual assaults and prevent her from being sent back to live in the orphanage. The marriage, which took place a few days after her sixteenth birthday, forced Marilyn to drop out of high school.

"I read one interview where she talks about how her husband would call her in from playing with the neighborhood kids," Matilda told me. "And that made me cry."

"Poor Norma Jeane," I said. "I think so many people just saw the Marilyn version without realizing everything it took to get there."

We found the Corridor of Memories, her friend Truman Capote's nameplate just around the corner from hers.

"Did you ever read any Truman Capote?" I asked Matilda. "There was a time when he was one of my favorite writers. *Breakfast at Tiffany's?*"

"I want to read that! Did you know that he wanted Marilyn to star in the movie of it?" It sounded familiar, but I couldn't picture anyone else besides Audrey Hepburn in it. I tried to envision Marilyn as Holly Golightly, and for a second her face flashed into a scene, petting a cat and looking golden and disheveled, the way only she could.

"She would have made a perfect Holly Golightly, goddamn it," I said, and I felt my eyes cloud over as Matilda placed her hand across the pink marble of Marilyn's nameplate.

Even her presence in the crypt seemed to shine, covered with lipsticked kisses and large-enough bouquets of flowers that covered and blocked out Hugh Hefner's plaque next to her. The bench in front of her space read, "In remembrance of Marilyn Monroe from all of her fans." Hef had tried to match his pink marble to the same shade as Marilyn's, but his was just a little grayer and more lackluster.

"Did you know DiMaggio sent her a dozen roses every week for the rest of his life?" Matilda asked me. "They weren't even married a year, but I don't think he ever got over her."

"It doesn't seem like any of us ever really got over her," I said, thinking about how she had died long before I was even born, but still, here I was, pining away for her.

Matilda had a fancy red lipstick that she pulled out of her backpack, applied lavishly, and kissed the front of the crypt. She handed it to me and offered to take a photo of me kissing the plaque. But when I looked up from applying the lipstick, she had some other container that looked like a giant compact in her hand.

She snapped my photo but seemed more invested in slathering the contents of the compact into the cement underneath the headstone. A toxic smell like nail polish remover hit my nose as she doused the crypt with it.

"What is that?" I asked.

"Extreme anti-adhesive," she whispered. "Let's pose for another selfie," she said loudly as an elderly couple shuffled by, and she snapped my photo. The heavy, toxic odor hung in the air as she pulled out something else that looked like a spray paint can with a thin straw that she inserted into the cement. She held down the nozzle, drenching the remaining area until everything turned into ooze, including the cement.

"What are you doing?" I asked, alarmed.

She unrolled a large leather tote bag from her pack and extracted a crowbar, which she used to snap the marble plaque off the tomb.

A thin layer of sheet metal protected the inner sanctum.

"Mom, keep an eye out!" she hissed to me.

"What?! Matilda, no. We can't do this. What are you thinking?"

"Mom. You knew what we were doing."

"It is not right."

"You think it's right to leave her here with Hugh Heffner's creepy old corpse rotting beside her? And Poncher's crotch in her face? With Zanuck down the way, prowling around? I'm telling you, I'm doing this with or without you, so you better get on board. Keep an eye out!" She hissed at me, then broke into a sudden smile as two white men wandered down the path towards us.

"Yes! I do want to post this on Snapchat! This one's going straight to Insta! OK, ten more! Oh, who am I kidding?" She giggled aggressively and made her body big enough to block the space. Her disguise as a teenage loudmouth seemed to encourage the couple to move on.

"They'll be back, let's go," she whispered to me, and she pulled out a bundle of screwdrivers that I recognized from Andy's toolbox. I stood in front of her, blocking the view from her to the path. My heart stirred with hysteria that felt like joy. Joysteria. I giggled to myself, then remembered what she was actually doing.

I looked back as she removed the thin veil of metal, revealing the crypt inside. A wave of death smells hit us, and I choked, nausea welling up from my stomach.

"No coffin," she whispered under her breath. "We can do this."

She reached her hands, her arms, and almost her whole chest all the way inside and pulled out what looked like a disheveled green dress, a shroud around remains. I shivered.

I stood there, stuttering, while Matilda extracted the green shroud from the crypt. It was silky and glamorous, and for a moment, it was shaped like a body. She gently hugged the form to her chest and whispered, "It's OK, we've got you now. We're going to help you be at peace," before she lugged the bundle into the leather duffle, which she handed to me.

"Hold her a second," she said, as she quickly screwed the sheet metal back in place.

My mouth gaped, and I didn't know what to do. I didn't know whether to embrace the bag or throw it down and run away, but the weight of the duffle in my arms felt heavy at first, then became light.

Matilda had packed up everything else as she worked and now pulled out what looked like a large sunscreen container and applied something cement-like with a blush brush before she popped the marble plaque back into place.

"Should buy us some time," she said, winking at me. She started walking quickly but casually back towards the gate, the large leather tote bumping up beside her. I hurried to catch up with her, trying to find the right thing to say.

"Matilda, we can't do this. I'm sure they have cameras, we'll get caught."

"I hacked into their system before we left the hotel and put the cameras on a loop of what it looked like before we got here. If no one is rushing out to stop us right now, we're fine. Just walk."

I looked around. The park was quiet. A family huddled around a grave several hundred yards from us but didn't even seem aware of our presence. The elderly couple had disappeared over the knoll somewhere. The two white men's voices echoed, but I couldn't see them.

"It just doesn't seem right," I repeated.

Her face got a little red as she turned to face me. "And what, Norma Jeane having to spend all eternity here with the perverts who profited off her and took advantage of her, who used her up and let her die at thirty-six, having to spend all of eternity with their disgusting corpses still trying to suck the nutrients out of her soul, that seems right to you?"

"I mean, no," I stuttered.

"Just walk, Mother," she hissed, and I realized how fully she was a person apart from me, a person with her own agency, her own capabilities, and her own agenda. I shut up and walked behind her to the car.

The Misfits (1961)

You're the saddest girl I ever met.

Arthur Miller to Marilyn, years
before they were married, as quoted
in *The Guardian*, then recycled as
a line to Roslyn in *The Misfits*

We want to love it. We want Marilyn to have her happy ending with the perfect role that actually shows her range, a loving valentine, crafted just for her by her devoted playwright national treasure of a Pulitzer Prize-winning husband, shot with her childhood hero surrogate Daddy figure, Clark Gable. The director, John Huston, Marilyn respected and had formally approved, still having fond memories from her *Asphalt Jungle* days. We want it to be the fairy tale that proves we are in a new decade of growth and women's rights, that we can have it all: the babies, the industry admiration, the business savvy, the awards, the accolades, the family, and the fame. We want that for Marilyn at this stage in her career and life, she has earned it. She deserves it.

Instead, this movie just makes us tired and sad. Huston, having worked with her at both ends of her career, saw Marilyn's rise and disintegration in real time, and it seems undeniable that this movie finished her. Shot in the broiling Nevada desert, actors suffered from heat stroke and dehydration on set. Though Miller had written the role specifically for Marilyn, by the time the movie was being shot, their marriage was essentially over. Marilyn had a complete mental breakdown on the set, having to be hospitalized for several weeks, which shut down the whole production. When she was on set, she was later and even more drugged out than ever. It was the last movie for both Marilyn and Clark Gable; he died twelve days after the filming wrapped up, and she made it a little over a year.

The condescending writing and plot seem designed by Arthur Miller to mock and even torture Marilyn. Our daughters would say it is all big dick energy, with the two cowboys, Gay (Clark Gable) and Perce (Montgomery Clift), and their pilot friend Guido (Eli Wallach) pestering her on the day of her divorce to immediately choose one of them to be her new man. Arthur Miller goes heavy on the symbolism connected to the capture and slaughter of wild mustangs in the desert, which continues *Bus Stop's* lineage of showing Marilyn as an animal to be lassoed and broken. Roslyn (Marilyn) is equally worshipped and derided by the three men, though the head cowboy, Gay, played by Clark Gable, is the clear frontrunner as well as being the head horse-torturer.

In these days before CGI and American Humane Society oversight, the decision was made to put a soft-hearted animal lover on a set where the only way to create these images was through the actual abuse of wild horses. The horses were ill to start with, and the way they were treated on set didn't improve their health. Neither was it improved when they were mutilated by the low-flying airplane used to round them up, which occurred in an on-set accident during filming.

* * *

Juxtaposed against the cruelty and animal abuse, the most replayed scene of the movie is a lighthearted moment in a bar where they take bets on how many consecutive times Roslyn can smack a paddle ball. Hilarity ensues, with lots of shots of Marilyn's ass and breasts wiggling and jiggling. Of course, Huston is just giving the people what they want, as is Marilyn, though she has little control over the way the male gaze reduces her to her parts that occurs throughout the film. She is never a woman riding a horse through the desert; she is an ass, waggling into the camera's focus.

Or we see her portrayed as a nagging, crazed voice, set on destroying the hopes and dreams of the men who only want to capture wild mustangs and have them slaughtered for dog food. Roslyn objects, first calmly and then more insistently, in a heartbreaking scene of a foal circling his bound mother. Roslyn finally starts screaming hysterically, and only then do we see her whole body, tiny and powerless against the massive Western landscape weighted against her. It's hard not to hear Arthur Miller's voice coming through Guido's mouth when he says, "She's crazy, they're all crazy. You try not to believe it because you need them. She's crazy – you struggle, you build, you try, you turn yourself inside out for them, but it's never enough. They put the spurs to you. I know, I got the marks."

The film has been referred to as an "anti-western," in that rather than glorifying the cowboy days, it is focused on the death of the Wild West, and perhaps similarly, it could be called an "anti-romance." While, in the end, Roslyn and Gay ride off into the sunset together, none of us are cheering about it. Even though Gay does finally release the horses after Roslyn's begging and pleading, the way he makes her grovel for it doesn't bode well for any of us. Even while Marilyn snuggles into Gable's chest, we are filled with a deep sense of foreboding.

Rather than a valentine, it feels like her husband wrote this role as a final humiliation of the woman he couldn't quite break. At least Arthur Miller got his happy ending – he met his next wife on the set and married her shortly thereafter, turned his experiences with Marilyn into a play and a movie called *After the Fall*, and lived to the ripe old age of eighty-nine, but the spurs he put to Marilyn never really came out. "We're all dying, aren't we? Every minute." is one of the first statements we hear from Roslyn, and it's impossible not to see the ways this film represents everything that Marilyn was tired of fighting.

Chapter 13

I was full of a strange feeling, as if I were two people. One of them was Norma Jeane from the orphanage, who belonged to nobody, the other was someone whose name I didn't know. But I knew where she belonged, she belonged to the ocean, and the sky, and the whole world.

Marilyn Monroe, *My Story*

Matilda placed her stuff in the trunk as I started up the car. She plunked in the seat beside me and looked at me, then burst into laughter as I started to drive away.

"Woohoo!" she yelled as we turned the corner.

I crossed and uncrossed my fingers three times. "Just hold your woohooing 'til we're on the other side of this!" I hissed at her. "Where in god's name are we even going?"

"Well, that is the question." She looked at me seriously. "I've spent a lot of time over the last week trying to figure out where Marilyn – well, Norma Jeane, really – was the happiest."

"And whatever you discovered, you better start pointing me in the direction because I'm not going to just drive around in circles with a corpse in my car," I told her.

"OK, we're going to head south, towards Long Beach," she directed. "We'll take the 405 towards the 710."

"I don't know what any of those numbers mean!" I shrieked as someone blared their horn at me because I couldn't make up my mind which lane I belonged in. She slowed down and gave me impeccable directions, navigating me through the maze of L.A. roads onto stop-and-go highways where my hands sweated on the steering wheel, and I scanned my rearview mirror until we exited at Long Beach and followed the road around into a parking garage.

"Where the fuck are we going?" I hissed as I turned off the car.

"Catalina Island," Matilda said. "Take everything." I grabbed our bags as she lugged the tote bag, and we stumbled into the building to buy tickets for the ferry. I stood in front of the ticket agent, bewildered, while Matilda negotiated our fares and elbowed me in the side. "Credit card, Mom."

"Oh, yes," I giggled, hoping the ticket agent wasn't looking at us suspiciously.

"They're loading the ferry now," the ticket agent told us. "Good timing! Just head to the end of the dock there. It will be departing in fifteen minutes."

Matilda slipped on her backpack and lugged the leather tote bag, and I followed her over the ramp aboard *The Catalina Express*, a massive catamaran already packed with people.

"Drop your luggage here," a uniformed man said to us as we boarded. Matilda clutched the duffle bag close to her and looked at me with an alarmed expression, making me remember that I was somehow the adult here.

"We'll just keep it with us," I told the man, and he shrugged.

"Suit yourselves."

We lugged it up the stairs to an open deck looking out over the ocean. A few dozen seats were already filled, so we stood against the rail, looking out at the water.

"How far is it to Catalina?" I asked Matilda.

"I think twenty-five miles or so," she said. "It will take us about an hour."

We heard a siren in the distance, blaring, seeming to get nearer, and I hugged her close to me. We stood against the rail as we felt the boat come alive when the engines turned on. I watched the loading dock, waiting for a posse of policemen to pull in, bullhorns blazing to stop the boat from launching, while Matilda kept her eyes focused on the gray blue water. She placed the duffle bag on a bench under the railing as the boat started to move away from the dock.

"What's this?" a uniformed man gestured at the bag, and I felt my body clench as Matilda started to stutter.

"That? I mean, that's our bag." I managed to get out, placing a hand on it, feeling the cold sweat on the back of my neck.

"Please keep the luggage off the seats," he said, look-ing down at us as Matilda hastily placed it on the deck.

His walkie-talkie buzzed as he strolled away from us, and my stomach clenched, watching his face as he listened intently. I caught Matilda's eye and raised one eyebrow. She winked at me, looking as carefree and innocent as a child could.

"Listen," I said so softly she had to put her face right next to mine. "If something happens, you hand the bag to me and call Aunt Nora." Nora would be on the next plane to L.A. if we needed her, although I wasn't look-ing forward to explaining what we'd done. "That doesn't even make any sense, Mom," Matilda whispered. "It's obviously better if you play innocent and find me a good lawyer. I mean, I'm a juvenile and all, right?"

"This is not a conversation I ever imagined us having."
I giggled a little, a sudden feeling of levity boosting me,
even as an additional siren caught the chorus.

"I feel like it's going to be OK," Matilda said.

"You know what? Me too," I told her, and I put my
hand on the railing, and she clasped hers on top of mine.

We were silent for a moment, counting our blessings.

"Why Catalina Island?" I asked once I had grown
accustomed to the movement of boats on water. "I know
she lived there when she was with her first husband, but
I don't understand why you think this is the place she
would want to be?"

"I've thought about it a lot," Matilda said.

"So I gathered."

"And I really want her to be in the place where she
was the happiest, where no man had control over her,
where she wasn't being foisted from foster home to
orphanage, where she had the most hope, and I think
Catalina Island might be the answer."

"But wasn't she married off to husband *numero uno*
when she lived here? Since she promptly divorced him
the second she had a chance, it doesn't seem very likely
that this is where she was happiest," I said.

"No, you're not seeing it the same way I am," Matilda
answered. "When she was here, was when she had everything in front of her. She was trying to put the hardest
parts of her childhood behind her, and Jim joined the
Merchant Marines and was busy with training every day
and about to get shipped off to the war. It was the first
time she was ever alone, without anyone telling her what
to do. And she knew she had her whole life ahead of
her."

"I do love the photographs from that timeframe, right

in between being Norma Jeane and being Marilyn," I said. "She looks so young, and, it's true, she looks beautiful and happy."

"Right? I thought about Yosemite, too, because she took that road trip with André de Dienes, this big-deal photographer who helped to discover her. She ditched her husband to go on that road trip and take all these photos of rock climbing and frolicking in the desert. I thought maybe that was when she was happiest because it was all happening. But then I read that Dienes was a crazy creep who got obsessed with her and tied her up in his car, and so already by then, it was too much."

"Ewwwwwwwww," I said. "It seemed like men just lost all sense when she entered the picture – get it, picture?"

"OK, stay with me now," Matilda said. We were moving past the industrial containers of Long Beach, and the mist from the water rose up in front of us. "So, when she was on Catalina, was when she made up her mind. She started doing weightlifting with an Olympic coach. She wanted to get strong. She found a space on the beach, or maybe on a hill looking down on the beach, and she sat there. She looked at the Pacific Ocean, and she made up her mind to leave Jim Dougherty and to become Marilyn Monroe. She chose to remake herself and she didn't tell anyone, and who knows if she even wrote it down or whispered it to herself or what, but she did, she looked out at the ocean and made up her mind."

I could see it, just the way Matilda was describing it. Norma Jeane was gazing out towards Hollywood from across the water, deciding that Jim Dougherty was too small for her that even Norma Jeane was too small for her. I pictured her waking up alone at the beach one afternoon after a nice long swim and saying it to herself, in that throaty voice that she adapted as a pathway through stuttering, *Next thing you know, you'll be a movie star*, and how she must have leaned into that. How she must have allowed it to blow through her curly hair, still too dark to be called blonde.

"I see it. I do," I told Matilda. The sky was a beautiful shade of blue, and it was hard to tell where water ended and sky began.

"Just seems like once she was Marilyn, things got hard and complicated for her in a bunch of other ways," Matilda said. "Everyone just wanted her to be a dumb, sexy baby, and she had to fight so hard for everything, and she wanted so badly to be perfect, and to be loved, and all of it. And the way all the producers, and directors, and actors just fed on her like a bunch of wolves. Like, they just turned her into this drugged-out zombie shell to meet their own needs. She seemed really miserable in lots of ways during the last ten years of her life."

"You really have done your research," I said. "I'm impressed."

"Once I started learning more about her, I literally couldn't stop," Matilda said. "I think I never really understood anything about the twentieth century until I read about her. It always seemed like so long ago, like the Middle Ages. A whole millennium before I was born. But that she lived through the middle of it, and the way she connected the film industry to theater to art to music to politics to civil rights. It just made me care about all of that."

"I've definitely never heard you talk about the twentieth century before, at least not in any different context than the nineteenth century or the fifteenth century," I said.

We could see the outline of the island starting to

emerge – a giant elegant, red-roofed building on its corner.

"What do you think that is?" I asked Matilda.

"Not sure," she answered. "I didn't get much past this point in my plans." The details of the island started to emerge, cheerful-colored houses dotting the hillside with greenish-brown hills layered above it as we pulled into the dock.

Matilda hoisted the tote over her shoulder, staggering a little from the weight. I steadied her, and then the boat rocked a little, making me stumble, and she leaned her weight against me, giving me a ballast. "Let's go bury Norma Jeane," Matilda whispered in my ear.

We lugged everything off the boat into the small town of Avalon and found ourselves blinking in the sunshine, peering over the rail into the clearest aquamarine water, where giant orange fish made the ocean look like a coy pond.

"Now what?" I asked.

"I don't know," she said. "Like I said, this was kind of as far as I got."

The disembarking tourists drifted in different directions, to the art deco hotels and the fish and chip stands. We looked around us, waiting for the next step to hit us as the light started to take on a golden hue.

I looked up and saw a stand advertising golf cart rentals across the road.

"Golf carts?" I kind of giggled, it seemed so silly. "Why golf carts?" I looked around, realizing how few cars there were. A few parked on the streets leading up to the harbor, but I actually didn't see a single person driving a car. Instead, there were a dozen golf carts of various levels of swankiness meandering the streets.

"Yes, golf cart! Let's rent one," Matilda interjected.

"Of course, a golf cart!"

We crossed the street and negotiated a sunset golf cart rental. The bearded man behind the counter gave us a quick tour of the island via the map he handed us. "And make sure to watch out for Catalina foxes crossing the road," he warned us.

"Catalina foxes? Like movie stars?" I said, picturing done-up extras scooting across the roads. It had been a long day.

"No, they're a special breed of fox," he told us, "only found on this island." He pointed to a photograph hanging on the wall with the most adorable tiny catlike fox, their ears extra big, and their tail, more gray than red, was long and fluffy.

"No freakin' way," Matilda said. "They live here? That is easily the cutest creature I've ever seen. It looks like some kind of Pokemon."

"Keep an eye out for them, they like sunsets. Can I help you with your bag?" He tried to grab the duffle bag to throw it in the back of the golf cart.

"I've got it," Matilda said, scooting away from him just as his fingers wrapped around the strap.

He gave us a quick lesson on brakes, gas, reverse, lights, and turn signals, and we were off, exhilarated considering we could only reach max speeds of fifteen miles an hour.

"Oh my god, we're doing this!" Matilda screamed, putting her hands in the air as the sunlight kissed her head. At this point, there was no chance anyone was going to stop us before we set Marilyn free.

"Hell yes!" I released the last four hours of fear as we chugged around the curves leading out of town. We could see the water glinting down from the small cliffs below the road, and a pull-off appeared to our right, marked with an elaborate blue bike rack in the shape of a fish.

I hit the brakes as a small creature strolled across the road, pausing to look at me with big, intelligent eyes.

"It's one of the foxes! Look at her cute tail!" Matilda squealed, the sound causing the fox to speed up her traipse across the road, jumping for the hillside sloping up from the parking lot, her fluffy gray tail the last thing to disappear.

"That was a sign as sure as I've ever seen one," I said.

"I thought you didn't believe in signs, ghosts, or divine intervention," she said.

"I don't, except sometimes I might. Still, are you sure we shouldn't find something a little more remote?" I asked.

"No, here," Matilda said, "can't you feel it? She was happy here."

No golf carts were parked in the pull-off, and we were far enough out of town that it seemed unlikely anyone would stroll to the beach. Avalon faced east, towards the coast of L.A., so the sun was setting on the other side of the island, but the layers of blue and purple, yellow, and pink were starting to form on the horizon line above the water. A sign marking a rickety set of stairs identified the spot as "Lover's Cove."

"Here. This is the spot," Matilda said. We maneuvered down the stairs, me going first and helping to navigate the weight of the bag.

Instead of sand, the beach was covered with large rocks. Not even pebbles, but stones worn smooth by the water, not yet broken to sand. We set the bag down just past the line where the water lapped at the rocks and sat on either side of her, looking out at the water.

"This is where I want to think of her," Matilda said.

"Away from all the men who wanted to use her, away from the whole industry, but close to it, sitting here with her dog, a blanket over the stones, fantasizing about what was going to come next for her. Oh! And I forgot this. She came here with her mom, too, did I tell you that?"

"No, you're just trying to make me feel like I'm part of the narrative," I teased.

"I'm serious. There's this whole famous letter that she wrote to her sister, Berniece, in 1943. Listen." She pulled the letter up on her phone and read it to me:

> My mother brought me here for the summer when I was about seven years old. I remember going to The Casino to dance with her, of course. I didn't dance, but she let me sit on the side and watch her, and I remember it was way after my bedtime too. But anyway, what I'm getting at is that at Christmas time, the Maritime Service held a big dance at the same Casino and Jimmie and I went. It was the funniest feeling to be dancing on that same floor ten years later – I mean being old enough and everything. Oh it's hard to explain the feeling I had...

I could see The Casino, the large building we had observed from the boat, jutting out down the coastline. I thought about it: the way time moves and warps, that sense of *déjà vu* that surrounds us, how years can feel circular and loop back around like a rubber band, the way minutes expand and snap back on themselves. How we connect to our younger and older selves in every moment, in strands and threads.

"Are you ready, Mom?" Matilda asked me, solemnly

holding up the duffle bag.

"I don't know," I said. "What happens next?"

"This is the part I haven't figured out."

"Do you think we should say a few words? Or sing her a song?"

I thought about Andy's funeral and how numb I had felt. Other people had done things, spoken, sung, cried, hugged, but all I could do was watch, feeling like I was hung on the wall. I thought about Andy and resolved that when we got back, I would get Matilda to help me take his ashes to the top of our favorite mountain and let them go into the wind. It was time he was released.

But right now, it was Norma Jeane's time, and I focused on the moment. Her plaque could stay there on the crypt and people could come and kiss it and pay their respects, but her earthly remains needed to be freed, Matilda was right. I looked at her, silhouetted against the sky, her strong chin and shoulders, her chest open and radiating power and righteousness.

Matilda squinted towards the road. "I don't know what we should do, but I guess we should do it kind of fast before anyone else shows up," she said. A half-moon was glowing through the clouds, starting to stand out against the twilight sky. "How about this?" She held up her phone and recited:

"Life – I am of both of your directions, but strong as a cobweb in the wind – I exist more with the cold, glistening frost. But my beaded rays have the colors I've seen in paintings – ah life they have cheated you."

"That's beautiful! What is it from?"

"It's one of Norma Jeane's poems," she said.

"It's perfect." We walked together in the water, and I carried one end of the bag while Matilda carried the other. I stumbled over the stones, but Matilda was graceful as we entered the water. Let it lap our ankles.

"It's fucking freezing," I said, my legs starting to tingle.

"Do it for Norma Jeane!" Matilda cheered me on, and we sank down to our thighs, the cold waking me up. It was a wonderful thing to be alive in the frigid water. As Matilda unzipped the bag, gentle waves rocked us to our chests, and I started to hum "Diamonds are a Girl's Best Friend," but slowly, so slowly it felt like a dirge.

Matilda tipped the bag, dumping its contents, the green shroud swirling in the moving water, concealing, sheltering, and finally releasing whatever remnants of Norma Jeane were left as it floated out to sea. When I looked over, tears were running down Matilda's face and dripping off her chin, falling into the ocean.

"Now you can be free," I heard her say in a small voice, and when I looked again, she became a small girl, and her face broke into sobs. I remembered myself as a young mother, holding a sobbing toddler. I thought about how badly Norma Jeane had wanted to have children. The rumors of being coerced by the studio into illegal, botched abortions that destroyed her chances. The deep undercurrent of fear of turning into her own mother, or her uncle, or her grandfather, all of whom struggled with consuming mental health issues.

I felt so lucky to have Matilda, so grateful to see the ways she was turning into her own strong, self-sufficient, brave, resourceful woman. But it stabbed at me also, the dread for her to come into this world and understand that sometimes it didn't matter how smart or capable you were, the world wanted to eat women like that, just as it had devoured Marilyn. That the world runs on all the brilliant women it has devoured. I reached for her hand and entwined my fingers with hers, pulling her to me, the water embracing us both. "You're right," I told her. "Thank you for doing this. It is the right thing." She turned her watery smile toward me.

"Yes," she said. We held our clasped fingers above the water and then both dove in, our heads submerged, as the sand and silt and pieces of Norma Jeane floated around us.

Credits

Something's Got to Give (1962–unfinished)

We're worried about Marilyn. Things aren't going well. There was the incident after *The Misfits* where Clark Gable dropped dead and the wife blamed Marilyn, and she had another breakdown and was institutionalized against her will, and Joe DiMaggio had to save her because no one else would.

Still, Marilyn decided to do *Something's Got to Give*, about a woman who has been lost at sea for five years and returns to find that her children don't remember her, and her husband (Dean Martin) is about to remarry. In the weeks before filming began, Marilyn had gallbladder surgery, lost twenty pounds, and was generally struggling with her health. Henry Weinstein, the producer of the film, talks about finding her the day after she did her screen test for the movie, in a barbiturate overdose in her home. He recalls his shock at phoning the studio, sure they would need to postpone the shooting, only to be told that they expected Marilyn to stay on schedule. Both her psychiatrist and her lawyer advised the studio that she was too ill to complete a movie, but the studio was more concerned about the money they were losing while filming Elizabeth Taylor's epic *Cleopatra* and saw a cutesy Marilyn farce as a way to recoup some of their losses.

The last film Marilyn worked on contains infamous

footage of the first nude scene ever shot by a major star in a Hollywood film. Marilyn invited the press to the set and lost her flesh-colored bikini for a four-hour, photographed skinny-dipping session.

The movie itself, shot over an agonizing eight weeks, is not complete. Marilyn missed as many days of shooting as she attended due to cascading illness, both mental and physical. The scenes that have been captured disappeared in the wake of Marilyn's death, and we did not see them resurface again until 1982. The set was plagued with what had become fairly typical for a Marilyn picture: delays, illness, tension, and drug use. The footage that was shot, however, undermines the studio's account of an incompetent actress wasting everyone's time. Marilyn's scenes have a settled-in sexiness that speaks to her potential as a mature actress.

We also enjoyed seeing Marilyn's first movie playing a mother, and the scenes between her and the children on the set, the youngest being about the age Marilyn's child would have been if not for the miscarriage she suffered at the end of *Some Like It Hot*, are particularly magical, adding a maternal layer to Marilyn's acting toolbox. Her last day on the set, on any set, was her thirty-sixth birthday on June 1st, 1962. They had a subdued party for her, and she missed the next week of work due to sinusitis, at which point the studio fired her and sued her for breach of contract.

Exacerbating the sense of frustration with her work ethic was her "impromptu" trip to Madison Square Garden to serenade probable lover and president, John F. Kennedy, for his birthday, although subsequent documentation shows that the studio knew of and approved the trip in advance and then punished Marilyn for taking it once it was over and filming fell further behind.

Marilyn had handpicked her close friend Dean Martin as her co-star and he was a force of support, both on set while they were filming and after she was fired, when he refused to work with her replacement. Eventually, the studio saw the error of their ways and rehired Marilyn, offering her five times her original salary. She was meant to resume filming the month after she was found dead in her home.

In the end, as so many times before, Monroe proved the victor. But in the real end, none of it mattered – not the victory, not the lost footage of the nude swim that showed Marilyn at her most playful, beautiful, and free. Not the conspiracy theories or the subsequent Marilyn revival. In the end, there was only her lifeless hand, clasping a telephone, and all the people who did not answer.

Credits: Reverse

You could put it all in reverse. How you collected yourselves and sat on the beach together until well after dark, how you swerved the golf cart down the dark roads and returned so late that the manager of the rental stand harumphed at you while you both giggled, and you missed the last boat back so you had to find an on-island hotel to stay in for the night.

How neither of you slept but told stories and jokes and little things you remembered from your childhood and snippets of lines from different plays, how you finally dozed an hour or two with "Else the Puck a liar call," reverberating in your ears.

Ferried back to shore, quietly watching Catalina recede in the distance, then you drove across the desolate landscape without stopping except for gas and to tighten up the bumper, for coffee and bugles and In-N-Out Burgers, double animal-style, how you kept driving, playing I Spy and the alphabet game, and collecting license plates, and taking long hours of silence to stare out the window. You didn't bring up Norma Jeane once, and when you got home, you were so exhausted and wired that you took a scalding shower that burned your chest, pink and flushed for days.

How the next weekend you and Matilda released Andy's ashes on the last day that still felt like fall, hiking up to an overlook he loved, a few golden aspen leaves clinging to the trees as you and Matilda played "Don't Worry About Me" by the Ramones.

And then you waited for months to hear something on the news, to see your images somewhere, for the knock on the door. But none of it came.

You could talk about the ways it spun out in the rest of your lives. How you told each other every secret so you didn't tell anyone this one. You started your own firm so you never had to have a man towering over you in that particular way male bosses have of holding themselves over a woman. The way that #MeToo splintered, giants toppling in all directions, yet how everything somehow remained fundamentally the same. How Trump left office to face rape charges but still ran for president again. You don't want it to sound like you actually fixed anything. You still talked to the Marilyn plates on the wall, but you never heard her talk back.

You felt differently when you looked at her now, though. You didn't feel the sense of pity and dread you used to feel when your eyes connected. Instead, you could see more of the joy that emanated from her, the way she glowed, a reminder that life was for the living. She was always more than a cautionary tale, a sex symbol, the quintessential blonde. She was a whole crypt of ghosts who won't stay buried.

You've told your secret now. Whisper it to your sisters when they're feeling low. The next time Marilyn's silhouette shows up on your horizon, drink a toast to her. The next time you swim, do a lap for her. Throw your bathing suit on the deck and let yourself be a body full of life.

When you're crawling around trying to figure out how to get from here to there, how to avoid the pills on the nightstand. When you feel the wisp of time like a spider web brushing your cheek, think of all the selves you've been and still have to be before we dissolve back into water.

Resources

Please note: there are countless books, articles, interviews, photographs of Marilyn Monroe in the world, and I've only included the works that most influenced me. I would wager more has been recorded about Marilyn than any human in history, at least before the age of social media.

I explored these works in a haphazard way, starting with reading *Blonde* on a Covid writing retreat years before it was a movie. I watched the films in a random order, looking up interviews with directors and to complement the snarky reviews I wrote as I went. My teenage daughter watched many of the best ones late at night with me. Only then did I discover that Marilyn herself was a writer and had recorded her own experience in ways the world mostly ignored during her lifetime and largely continues to overlook in favor of men's biographies about her, though her own writing is the original source of many of the Marilyn quotes that are scattered around us. If nothing else, if you are inspired to learn more about Marilyn by this book, read her memoir and collection of poetry and journal entries to hear from her directly about her experiences. She is a shockingly good writer, and you'll find her poetry compared to Emily Dickinson in *The Paris Review* article cited below. I also highly recommend watching *Don't Bother to Knock* if you only envision her in showgirl romantic roles.

As I moved along the writing process, I did a deep dive in some of the many, many books written about her, amazed to find the range of writers and photographers who had engaged with her. Throughout the process, I regularly paged through the books I inherited from my father, mostly photographs of Marilyn, and, of course, discovered countless random minutiae and articles on the internet. This list is an attempt to leave breadcrumbs for much of my research and process. It is in no way intended to be a comprehensive list of everything that exists. I've omitted most of my casual online research since it is impossible to replicate and easy enough to do your own. Some works may be left out accidentally, and others are omitted on purpose. Arthur Miller, Norman Mailer, Laurence Olivier, Andrew Dominik, and especially Hugh Hefner can all go fuck themselves.

Movies referenced, in chronological order from when they were filmed

- *Dangerous Years*, directed by Arthur Pierson (1947).
- *Scudda Hoo! Scudda Hay!* directed by Hugh Herbert (1948).
- *Ladies of the Chorus*, directed by Phil Karlson (1948).
- *Love Happy*, directed by David Miller (1949).
- *The Asphalt Jungle*, directed by John Huston (1950).
- *All About Eve*, directed by Joseph L. Mankiewicz (1950).
- *As Young as You Feel*, directed by Harmon Jones (1951).
- *Love Nest*, directed by Joseph Newman (1951)
- *Let's Make It Legal*, directed by Richard Sale (1951)
- *Don't Bother to Knock*, directed by Roy Ward Baker (1952).

- *Monkey Business*, directed by Howard Hawks (1952).
- *Niagara,* directed by Henry Hathaway (1953).
- *Gentlemen Prefer Blondes,* directed by Howard Hawks (1953).
- *How to Marry a Millionaire*, directed by Jean Negulesco (1953).
- *River of No Return,* directed by Otto Preminger (1954).
- *There's No Business Like Show Business,* directed by Walter Lang (1954).
- *The Seven Year Itch,* directed by Billy Wilder (1955)
- *Bus Stop*, directed by Joshua Logan (1956).
- *The Prince and the Showgirl*, directed by Laurence Olivier (1957).
- *Some Like It Hot,* directed by Billy Wilder (1959)
- *Let's Make Love,* directed by George Cukor (1960).
- *The Misfits,* directed by John Huston (1961).
- *Something's Got to Give*, directed by George Cukor (1962, unfinished).

Articles

- David N. Young, "She Came as Norma Jeane; She left to Become Marilyn," *The Catalina Islander* (June 18, 2021).
- Elisa Gonzalez, "Marilyn the Poet," *The Paris Review (*June 28, 2022).
- Grady Johnson, "The Story Behind Marilyn Monroe," *Coronet* magazine (October 1952).
- Jamie Kahn, "Inside the friendship of Ella Fitzgerald and Marilyn Monroe," *Far Out* (April 2022).

- Karina Eileraas, "Hello, Norma Jeane," originally published in *Ms.* magazine in August 1972. (Republished online 8/3/2012).
- Lawrence Schiller, "A Splash of Marilyn," *Vanity Fair* (June 2012). Reflecting on his 1962 *Paris Match* assignment to photograph Marilyn on the set of *Something's Got to Give*. Photographs used in *Life* magazine*'s* last look at Marilyn after her death a few months later.
- Lois W. Banner, "The Creature from the Black Lagoon: Marilyn Monroe and Whiteness," *Cinema Journal*, (Summer 2008).
- Louis Sahagun, "Exhibit shows little-known life of Marilyn Monroe on Catalina Island," *Los Angeles Times* (April 25, 2011).
- "The Monroe Doctrine" (writer unknown) *Life* magazine (April 7, 1952).
- Richard Meryman, "Last Talk with a Lonely Girl: Marilyn Monroe," first published in *Life* magazine, (August 17, 1962) and all of the *Life* magazine articles and coverspreads between.
- Peter Feuerherd, "The Many Meanings of Marilyn Monroe," JStor Daily (August 5, 2017).

Books

- Alan "Whitey" Snyder, *The Life & Curious Death of Marilyn Monroe* (1974).
- Steve Christ, et al., *Andre De Dienes: Marilyn* (2004).
- Berniece Miracle and Mona Miracle, *My Sister Marilyn: A Memoir of Marilyn Monroe* (2012).
- Charles Casillo, *Marilyn Monroe, The Private Life of a Public Icon* (2020).

- Elizabeth Windor, *Marilyn in Manhattan: Her Year of Joy* (2017).
- Gloria Steinem with photos by George Barris, *Marilyn* (1988).
- George Barris, *Marilyn: Her Life in Her Own Words.* [Especially The Last Photo Shoot] (2009).
- J. Randy Taraborrelli, *The Secret Life of Marilyn Monroe* (2010).
- Joyce Carol Oates, *Blonde* (2000).
- Marlys Harris, *The Zanucks of Hollywood: The Dark Legacy of an American Dynasty* (1989).
- Marilyn Monroe with Ben Hecht, *My Story,* (originally written in 1950s, first published in 1972).
- Marilyn Monroe, *Fragments: Poems, Intimate Notes, Letters* (written throughout her life, published in 2012).
- Ralph L Roberts, *Mimosa: Memories of Marilyn & the Making of "The Misfits"* (2021).
- Susan Doll, *Marilyn: Her Life and Legend* (1990).

YouTube Clips

- "Director John Huston Interviewed About Marilyn Monroe And The Asphalt Jungle," posted 2013.
- "Director Of Bus Stop, Joshua Logan, interview About Marilyn Monroe," posted 2014.
- "Movie Directors - Jean Negulesco and George Cukor Interviewed About Marilyn Monroe in August 1962," posted 2014.
- "Sir Laurence Olivier talks about Marilyn Monroe!" posted 2019.
- "Jack Lemmon and Billy Wilder Talks Marilyn

Monroe," posted 2022.
- "John Huston on Working With Marilyn Monroe for 'The Misfits' | The Dick Cavett Show," posted 2022.
- "Marilyn Monroe – 'Something's Got To Give, 1990 documentary,'" posted 2022.
- "Marilyn Monroe And The Making Of "The Misfits" – Documentary," posted 2017."Very Rare Interview With Drama Coach Natasha Lytess About Marilyn Monroe in July 1962," posted 2013.

On Location

There are countless locations where Marilyn lived, visited, acted, danced, sang, and glimmered. But there are three I visited in the writing of this book that I think every Marilyn fan should spend some time with. I invite you to share other Marilyn art and destinations at my Instagram @WheresNormaJeane:
- Catalina Island, especially The Casino, 1 Casino Way, Avalon, CA 90704.
- The Hollywood Roosevelt: 7000 Hollywood Blvd, Los Angeles, CA 90028.
- Marilyn Monroe's grave at Pierce Brothers Westwood Village Memorial Park & Mortuary 1218 Glendon Ave, Los Angeles, CA 90024.